The Blackwarren Heists, Part 2
Settle the Score

by Vaughn R. Demont

Published by Blackwarren Books at Smashwords

Cover art by Ivy Beth Gladstone

This book is available in print at most online retailers.

Table of Contents

1

...what? Why ya lookin' at me like that? I told ya this ain't that kinda story, buddy. But I ain't ever said the story's over...

"Have I mentioned I fuckin' hate vents?" My voice is at a whisper, 'cause echoes ain't what I need right now. It's cold too, no one ever mentions that, because vents move fuckin' air and when it's in the eighties outside ('cause City weather ain't never made a lick of fuckin' sense), the central air's gonna be on, and that air is blowin' right on my ass. My balls are crawlin' up my throat right now, buddy, that's how fuckin' cold it is.

"Then ya shouldna said 'it'll be simple, I'll just go through the vents!' Hold on a sec." The voice is in my ear, earbuds linked to my phone. I ain't talkin' to you, buddy, but my fuckin' cousin Vincenzo who can't do his own fuckin' work. "A'right, wait a couple seconds more. Little more. Okay, go, ya got nine seconds."

So, I army crawl forward as fast as I can while tryin' to not make too much noise. I see the sensors on the walls of the vent, since alarms are in fuckin' vents, now. I'm draggin' myself because there ain't enough room to crawl faster. This is takin' fuckin' forever, buddy.

"Okay, yer clear for the next fifteen feet, Nick. Another fifty to go." I sigh, loudly. "Hey, no bitchin'. Be professional."

I pull the right sleeve of my hoodie up, revealing the dark steel vambrace clasped around my forearm, three rubies along the length. I close my eyes.

"Okay, don't neither of us wanna go this slow. Diner switches to the lunch menu in thirty minutes and I want my fuckin' French toast." I hear the soft turnin' of wheels and gears within it, the soft snap as the middle pops up with a hole in the front. I clench my fist, flexin' my forearm, and hear the pfft and soft whir of a line unspoolin'. I tug back a little, test the tension. Good.

"When's the next flicker?" I ask, keepin' my voice hushed.

"Almost set up, I gotta time it for when the guard ain't lookin', Nick." Cenzo sounds like he's pissed at me, but he's the reason I'm in a fuckin' vent right now. Had to listen to a recitation of all our mutual relatives 'fore I agreed. Shit ya do for family, Shadow take me.

"Hit 'em all, I can speed this up. Just need fifteen seconds."

"Yer pushin' yer luck with ten-"

"Just fuckin' do it, Cous'." I roll my eyes, and I'm grateful he can't see it since he practically sees everythin' else.

I mute the headset.

"Shadow shroud me from the light
Body quiet, steps are light
Let my will remain unshaken
Let the Shadow's blood awaken"

"Fine. Yer fuckin' funeral." A couple more seconds. "Go."

I clench my fist again and hold it like that as I'm pulled forward. I can see the vents in perfect detail, the sensors dim, and I keep myself narrow to avoid contacting them. I'm counting the seconds in my head. Eight. Nine.

"Nick, he's looking at the panel."

Fourteen. Release.

"Clear." I can't hear myself breathe, but that's what that charm does. I feel cold, not because of the airflow, though. The Shadow is a dark, cold place, no light, no heat. It's usually used by... assassins. I'm not one of those, don't worry. Besides, the Shadow and I have been cool since I was four, so it's not like I'm gettin' pulled to the fuckin' dark side, okay? Thieves live in Shadow, too.

Assassins are murderin' assholes. Thieves? We're dashin' romantic charmin' rogue types. So, we're better than that. I'm a thief, okay? I'm a thief. Not a murderer. Thief.

Ah, fuck yer "methinks he doth protest" bullshit. I know. I'm workin' through some shit, 'kay buddy?

"Okay, Nick, ya should be over the correct grate. Ya gotta charm it, vent's locked. Ain't Knocker shit, so ya should be clear."

In case ya ain't got no fuckin' idea what we're talkin' about, I'll give ya the quick and dirty since I ain't got a lotta time.

Knockers. Rivals to us Goblins. They make steampunk kinda shit or want ya to think it's somethin' cool. Their locks are strong against Goblin charms to crack locks and break machines. Since there ain't any in the grate, I can pop 'em with a simple charm.

Ah fuck, I lost ya already. Ever quicker and dirtier, now. I'm a Goblin, I got green skin, big fuckin' toenails and ears and a nose and sapphire blue eyes. I'm one of the Fae, but ain't one of the pretty ones, the Sidhe. I'm on the lowest social strata, so bein' a burglar is one of the few options I got. That enough to get by on fer now? Great. Back to it.

"Shadow open, lift the gate
Sentries bumble, blind to Fate
Treasures lit and mine to see
Open locks and ways to me"

Another flow of cold over me as the charm is worked. Several clicks under me on the grate, which swings open, the room below me filled with inky darkness. A gently glowin' golden grid is visible on both walls below, visible only to me. Nifty trick, yeah?

I drop down to the floor, rollin' on impact to soften the sound of the landin'. It's pretty cold in here, but I can handle it for what I'm doin'. "A'right, I'm in. Where to?"

"Box nine-two-seven. Think ya got two minutes before… Fuck, the camera's busted. Screen's black."

"Yeah, that's me." I turn around slowly, 'cause when I look around too quick the glowing lines blur together. "Easier than loopin' it, right?"

"Cute ya think we still do that, Cousin." He sighs, grumblin'. "Ya better not trip any of the lasers."

"Shadow eats 'em long as the charm's up. Ya want me to explain it, or get the item, Cenzo?" I think I see two-ninety-seven, buddy, and yeah, I'm thinkin' about the French toast and bacon in my near-future.

He sighs, resigned. "…get it."

The box is in front of me, both locks side by side. I know what yer thinkin': "A'right, smart guy. How ya gonna pick two locks at once, huh?"

Here's how. I raise my vambrace-clad arm in front of the locks and take a breath. "Okay, yer time to shine. Try not to break my brain, a'right?"

The raised bar lifts slightly, does a one eighty, and then, well, there's a reason its name is Shadow's Edge. Lame, yeah, I know. I can feel the icy tendrils of night creepin' out from that hole in the vambrace, splittin' in two, and wormin' into the locks in the box.

Then? Then everythin' goes black vision-wise, and my mind is split between those fuckin' locks. And I'll tell ya, *that fuckin' hurts.* I can hear my breathin', it's gettin' faster, my body panickin' from fear and cold and yeah, my mind bein' split between the innards of a couple locks. Ain't like a Knocker lock, human-built shit here, but that don't make it any easier.

I gotta think of the darkness that slipped into the locks as my fingers, find the pins and ridges and everythin', concentrate on matchin' both locks without slippin' in my concentration. It's tough as hell, pal, so I got a little trick to keep myself from goin' insane.

"Nick?" Cenzo sounds a mile away. "Why the fuck ya singin'? I told ya, I ain't gonna put on yer fuckin' playlist!"

I can hear lyrics in the lock, shiftin' the focus, lettin' my "fingers" go by touch and instinct. Fuck, this hurts. Little longer. Just make it through the bridge to the chorus. Little longer.

"…lights. We're in a city of wonder…" Turn my hands… Now!

Click-click!

Aw, fuck.

I yank the box out and open the lid, grabbin' the thing that's in there and stuffin' it in my bag before-

"Fuckin' Shadow, Nick, ya just barf?"

"Don't… don't worry. I got the item out first."

"Aw fer fuck's sake, in the deposit box?!"

I push the box back in, close the door, and catch my breath, which smells fuckin' nasty right now, pal, so I ain't goin' into detail on exactly what I left in that box.

Rice. Mostly rice. It's all I got to eat, current-

What was that?

"Cenzo? Why's the fuckin' vault openin'?" Oh yeah, buddy, I'm kinda sorta iffy maybe robbin' a bank in the most insigificant way right now. Don't tell or I'll name ya as my accessory. Just kiddin'. Or not. Depends on who's comin' through that heavy as fuck vault door.

"Aw, shit." Pro-tip. If ya ever plan to rob a bank, the second to last thing ya ever want to hear from the man in the chair is "aw shit."

The *last* thing ya wanna hear is "I'm bangin' yer sister/mom/brother", if ya were curious.

"Need more than that, Cous'." I'm movin' toward the door to put my back flush to the wall, 'cause the charm keepin' this room inky black is gonna wear off soon, and I don't see me gettin' back up through the ceilin' in time.

"I'm locked out, Nick. I'm fuckin' locked out. I ain't got security. Shit." I hear some frenzied typin' comin' through the earpiece. "Fuck, it's all turned off! I ain't got cameras or the alarms. Only thing I can see is the vault door and it's already openin'."

I chuckle softly. "Cen? Did you by chance double-book this job?"

Door's slowly startin' to open.

"No! What kinda idiot ya take me for?"

"So, we took the cameras, the alarms, and I just doused the whole fuckin' bank in darkness… while another fuckin' crew is robbin' the Shadow-damned bank." I bump the back of my head against the wall as the door opens fully.

"Fuck. Me."

2

Y'know what, buddy? I'm gonna try really fuckin' hard not to blame ya for this happenin'. I ain't sayin' yer bad luck or anythin', maybe it's me. I ain't ever had a fuckin' clean-as-clockwork job since I came back to the City.

The charm drops as the light from outside the vault leaks in. I keep in the corner as someone comes in dressed in loose clothin', cargo pants, boots, black hooded jacket, all probably picked up from a surplus store. It's a human, and from the build I'd guess a him, and he's wearin' a full face mask that I see when he starts walkin' to the drawers. Not the uh... bales of money.

"Which one is it?" He got a headset too, looks like. A pause. "Then shut 'em up! We gotta be out of here in five!"

Them. Hostages. Thank fuck he's wearing a full mask. Means they don't want anyone seein' their faces, so they probably ain't killed no one yet. Innocent fuckin' humans who were just workin' a shit job or standin' in line. Fuck. Fuck. Fuck. Fuck.

I move quick-quiet behind him, checkin' outside the vault to see if anyone's coverin' him. All clear for now.

"Nine two seven. Got it." Are ya fuckin' kiddin' me, pal? They're here for the shit I just stole? If he opens that box, yeah, he'll be grossed by the puke in there, but then this gets fuckin' complicated too fast. If ya broke into a bank, took a bunch of hostages, and what yer lookin' for ain't there, what would ya do with the hostages if ya were intendin' to get out in five minutes?

"Huh. It's already open? Might be somethin' goin' on. Gonna check."

Shit, shit, shit! I hop on his back, foldin' my elbow around his neck, applyin' pressure on his carotid while my free hand covers his mouth. "Shhh. That's it, buddy, night-night time."

My second cousin taught me to do that, for the rare occasion ya need zero body count. His words, not mine. For me, every occasion calls for zero body count. Once he's down, I search him, find a phone, active, on a call, number visible, looks like a conference, so that's how they're all talkin'. I text the number to Cenzo.

tra+loc others, tell me ovr blu to

"Got it, Nick. Gimme a sec. Mind tellin' why ya ain't gettin' the fuck out through the vents? Ya got the item. Time to go."

"Hostages," I whisper. Findin' zipties on the would-be robber, and I get his wrists and ankles, then take off his hoodie and cram a sleeve in his mouth to gag him. Still breathin'. "How many on the call?"

"Lookin' like four. Fuck. Dammit, Nick, ya don't need to be there for this. Just go." I know that sounds cold as fuck, but it's not too surprisin' considerin' Vincenzo and I are Goblins, and human lives ain't really a priority for us. Well… For him, at least. I have humans to thank fer French toast and the entirety of my streamin' playlists, and manga and all the books piled 'round my apartment.

"I go, and humans die, and I did nothin'? Guard would be on my ass, and ya know the Lightnin' Rod would be pissed." The Ra'keth, the Sorcerer King, the human we're all fuckin' scared of. Kill humans, and ya get his attention, and ya don't want his attention.

"A'right. A'right. Fine. Gimme a sec, I'll get better pinpoints."

"Thanks, Cenzo." I pull the tied-up robber out of sight from the door. Okay. Gotta do this. "Who's closest?"

Gettin' the location is easy enough, just a matter of telling me the layout of the bank, hallways, all that shit. A lot of words, mostly, and I don't think yer interested in widths and heights and depths and shit. I listen to it so ya don't have to, buddy. Also, so ya don't have to hear me and Cenzo bickerin' 'cause that would take up too much fuckin' time.

Sneakin' ain't too hard, just about payin' attention, movin' quick when ya gotta, and takin' a minute when ya need to be patient. Steppin' light, bein' aware of how the weight of yer gear is distributed 'round yer body and how ya need to adjust yer gait and rhythm. It's like a dance, really, and that's where I got some experience.

The next robber's ahead of me. He's taller than the last one, so I gotta plan out my attack. We're in the hallway that'll lead out to the lobby, and I can hear a couple people echoin' out in the lobby.

"Please! Just let us go!"

"Shut up! Stay there and shut the fuck up!"

Oh, fuck. Okay, gotta take this guy. He's dressed like the one in the vault, 'cept he's got a familiar shape stuffed in the back of his pants.

A gun.

Yeah, I'm a Goblin, kind of a mythical creature, but a bullet will take me out easy as anythin' else. If I try to choke him out, it'd have to be perfect or I'd risk the lives of who knows how many people out there.

Okay, buddy, you know what I need right now.

The center rail on my vambrace lifts and spins again, a small sight popping up near my hand. I can't risk him makin' noise. He's getting' closer to the way out. Shit, I gotta go.

"T! Where the Hell's P?! Check him in the vault!"

Oh fuck. I run diagonally toward the wall.

"Yeah, sure. Just a minute."

I jump, my feet catch just long enough to push off. I land on his back, my hand on his mouth as my fist clenches, pushin' into his neck. A soft pfft comes out, a dart piercin' his skin. He struggles, but both my hands are over his mouth as he falls to his knees. "That's it, fucker. Take a nap."

Zipties are quick. I peek around the corner into the lobby.

I count nine hostages, three of them in bank uniforms. Two other men dressed like the rest. Both holding guns, one a pistol, the other a shotgun. Hostages are split into two groups, one bad guy coverin' each. They're on the far side of the room under the lights, and I can't slip across without bein' seen, obviously.

I gotta breathe. I can't dart 'em from this distance. Eventually they'll notice that two of their buddies ain't on the call anymore. I didn't have time to hide those two, and even if I did, it ain't like a video game where they'll just forget they had two other people on the team.

This has gotta be fast. I need 'em confused, but not in a way that they'll just start shootin' and hit somebody. It worked in the vault, but that was a small room with a bunch of drawers and a couple bales of cash with obvious dye-packs. The lobby is much larger, ceilin' is higher.

Fuck. This is gonna suck.

I reach a finger back into my mouth, behind the caps that make my smile look nice and human, and find one of the pointy, sharp, dagger teeth. Some pressure breaks the skin, and I taste blood, but it's enough on my fingertip to draw some Sigil, the language of magic, onto my forehead.

"Father Redcap, lend your sight
In the bloody dark of night
Father, let the darkness flood
Let them fear my icy blood
Shadow, leave them cold and blind
Shadow, let my blade stay kind
Anchor violence, hold my breath
Shadow, lead me not to death."

There's screamin' as the lobby is suddenly a cold, black void. This'll only last as long as I can hold my breath. No one can see anythin'.

No one but me. I've done this but once, and I don't become some ghoulish monster or somethin', but durin' this, they will see me as I drew in blood. And I don't mean they'll see me. I mean they'll see me.

I'm a Goblin. Mentioned that. People like humans don't see me as a Goblin, though. They see a short guy with a big nose and indiscriminate ancestry (my family's a blend of Sicilian and Black Irish), and probably think I just stole a wallet or I'm gonna jack their car, or hold up a store, or beat the shit outta 'em to take their money.

But right now? They'll see a green-skinned thing with wide ears like Dumbo, a pointy nose, black fingernails lookin' like trimmed down claws, and inhumanly blue eyes. Well, normally. For this, they're literally burnin' hard blue faerie fire, and I'm comin' outta the darkness, outta the depths of Hell and nightmare, and jumpin' right at ya.

Scared the shit outta me first time I did it, buddy.

Does pretty much the same for those first five people. I gotta move faster. Lungs are startin' to ache. I run up the guy with the shotgun, dart him in the neck, and ride him back and down to the floor. The hostages are obviously fuckin' terrified, but I gotta keep movin'.

Fuck, I am doin' too much on two lungfuls of air. Gettin' a little lightheaded as I run toward the last one. Buddy, he got a pistol, I know what to do.

SHUNK

A shield snaps out from the vambrace. I hear the gunshot, and then I feel like a fuckin' sledgehammer punched it. I jump at the final bad guy, hearin' him scream as my eyes burn in a conflagration. The shield slams into his chest, knockin' him onto his back. The impact knocks the gun from his hand, and I collapse the shield as I dive for the gun. I dart him in the neck, he goes down, and I inhale loudly.

I'm pantin' as the lobby is well-lit again, the hostages are still terrified, and I'm holdin' a fuckin' gun. Great.

I eject the clip, pull the slide, pop out the bullet in the pipe, cast it aside, and then toss the gun away. The people ziptied on the floor freak out as I approach. "Weird how the lights went out, huh? Y'all okay?"

"Don't hurt us!" One of 'em says, still scared. I roll my eyes and pull a short knife from my kit.

"Show me yer ties so I can cut 'em? Y'know, free ya?" 'Course, they're shrinkin' away. They'd rather stay tied up then let someone like me cut the bindin'. Then again, they saw me as somethin' outta nightmares, they don't want a monster's help. I ain't expectin' gratitude, pal, but…

Fuck it. I toss my knife toward one of them, lettin' it skid 'cross the floor. They can do it themselves.

"Cous'?" I say, walkin' toward the door as I pull up my hood. "I'm headin' out. Trip the alarms."

"Done. Ya got maybe two minutes until the closest pig is on site. Anything needs cleanin' up?"

I'll admit I smile as I reach the door, warmth returnin' to my body.

"Nope. Zero body count."

3

The K Street Diner is at the intersection of 69th and K streets in Beckettsville. If ya need remindin', pal, it's the borough of the Unified City that's the north central part of it. Was working class, now it's middle class, gentrifying itself into upper middle. The diner's one of the few places that's held it off, probably because the owner also owns the buildin'.

The fact that the owner's a dragon don't hurt either.

The diner's one ya'd probably see in a sitcom or some shit. Lunch counter, booths, pass-through from the kitchen, two waitresses handling the counter and tables. Now that I've become close to a regular over the last few months, you'd think I'd be greeted with my name, asked if I want my usual, maybe workin' on getting' a sandwich named after me or something.

Instead, I get glares, or shudders of revulsion.

I'm a Goblin, I got the green skin, big ears, big fuckin' toenails I trim down with a belt-sander, weird colored irises in my eyes. A monster, a half-assed one hit die monster from cliché fantasy that's used as a stand-in for Italians and Jews. I ain't even gonna go into how we come across in most anime. But that ain't how I look to humans.

Most of ya see me as whatever POC you personally think is only near you to steal your shit, mug you, kill you, or sell you drugs.

Other mythics, though? Well, they see me and think I'm only there to steal their shit, mug 'em, kill 'em, or sell 'em drugs.

But ya get used to it. Note I said, "used to it", not "okay with it", 'cause there's a difference, and I don't want to make a scene that'll put the putsch on my French toast. All I gotta do now is convince the gatekeeper, Sharon, to let me order it.

I take a seat at the counter, smile without showin' teeth, don't make full eye contact when she comes over to me. "Too late to order the French toast and bacon?"

I've sweet-talked my way into getting it at 10:35am, since they stop at 10:30 and...

"It's past eleven. Breakfast is over." Her voice is stern, a mother's voice.

Don't get me wrong, she's perfectly nice and welcomin' to other people, this is just how humans are 'round me. Granted, since she's been workin' for a dragon for the last decade or somethin', it's surprisin' she ain't gone crazy yet.

"Uh, could I get coffee and a Reuben with fries?" I chuckle nervously, but she's never kicked me out no matter how uncomfortable she's been around me. Her and her sister, and-

"I'll take him, Sharon." Harder voice, and I turn on the stool and thank fuckin' Shadow it's Hannah.

Hannah's a werelion, like, she can turn into a lioness if she wants, but more important, since she's left of human, she can see me how I am, and doesn't automatically assume I'm a criminal. She leads me to a booth.

"I heard the order, I can talk to Dave and get the French toast, if you want it." She's a little impatient, though, so I've learned to answer quickly with her.

"Whatever's fastest, had a late morning and I need to get goin' 'fore noon." I glance at the clock over the counter, I'm not in a rush. I'm not! I just want to be outta here so I can take the goods to the drop point and be done with it and wait for my fee. "He, uh, come in yet?"

A measured sigh. "No."

"You think I should go?" I avoid eye contact; don't want to let slip how I'd feel about the answer either way it goes. "I don't wanna..."

"Then why come back?" Hannah's not one for small talk.

"I dunno, exposure therapy? I like the food here, y'know? Don't like giving up slices of my life to avoid awkward conversations." I manage a weak smile. "Don't mean I wanna have 'em, though. How's it goin' with you?"

She takes a deep breath. "Fine. I'm practicing. So many rules and tones and double meanings, and the males are upset when females are direct and honest and unimpressed."

"Didn't work out with that guy, huh?" I wince at the growl she makes in response. "Sorry, sorry. Just noticed ya ain't been in a good mood lately."

"He wanted… what is word you used? Dumb male, and too many capable females fighting over him when they should hunt as a pride and leave the dumb male on his own?"

I'll admit I laugh. "A harem anime. Yeah, I could see not wanting a guy like that. His loss, ya know?"

Hannah shrugs and heads to the kitchen, and I hear her relay the order to the dragon workin' the grill, so apparently, I'm getting the sandwich. It'll work. It won't take an hour to eat and then I can go. Ya might be wonderin' why I'm so antsy to leave early, and if I am, why I'm even eatin' here? I ain't proud of it, buddy, okay? So, let's not linger on it and-

"Mornin' Officer!" I hear Sharon, and I already know who came in.

"Morning, Sharon! Could I get my usual?"

I sag in my booth seat. I guess we're gonna linger on it.

What just came through the door is someone you could call my ex, if someone's your ex after you were only together for maybe a day. As you can guess from the "Officer" bit, he's a cop. Sorta. He's a cop for us mythics, also known as one of the Queen's Guard, or just the Guard, who are almost entirely made up of Sidhe and Trolls. He's the exception as he's a Phouka, the trickster kith of the Fae, the storytellers, the poets, the bards, and the romantic, charmin' rogues that can seduce you with a wink and a smile, and hold you warmly, protect you, make you feel safe and-

Yeah, uh, I'm speakin' from personal experience. His voice has gotten a touch more Irish, which is not helpin' a certain issue I'm dealing with now.

"Had a call, but it was taken care of before I got there, so I figured I'd get an early lunch before I head back." Please don't see me. Please don't see- "Nick?"

Fuck.

This is your own damned fault, Nick. Don't turn around. Don't do it.

He's just over six feet tall, "Black Irish" in complexion, short coal black hair, dark brown eyes you could lose yourself in, strong but carin' arms. While he was wearin' a patrol uniform the last time I saw him longer than half a minute, now he's wearing jeans, a leather jacket, button-down with the top two buttons loose, his badge on a chain 'round his neck.

"North Trust Bank. That you?" Constable Thomas Canmore has seated himself across from me. It's said quickly, almost impatiently.

Well, *humans* see a badge, us mythics see the crest of the Queen's Guard, which means he can speak with the Queen's authority, which means ya can't lie to him. Unless yer a Goblin who *ain't* all googly-eyed like he usually gets me.

"No, I ain't a bank. I am a Goblin, Krupke."

"You know what I mean, Nick. And don't call me that." We were both on the verge of sayin' the Three Words to each other before he decided to use me as bait to catch a hitman. Didn't go well.

As pissed as I still am about it, 'least I'm honest, so I ain't gonna lie to him. At least, not *again*.

"Y'mean, did I knock out the robbers and free the hostages? Yeah. That was me. Didn't kill anyone. We done?" I'm lookin' at the table, not at him. My fries are put down in front of me, and I nudge 'em to the middle of the table without thinkin'. Fuck, Blackwarren, stop actin' like yer in fuckin' middle school.

His hand takes one of the fries. "So, you were the 'green monster that they barely escaped with their lives from?' What exactly did you do, Nick?"

"I darted two, choked out two. That's it. The rest is just humans seein' somethin' their minds can't handle." I take a fry for myself. "Ya here for me?"

"I'm here for *lunch*, Nick. I haven't tracked you since…"

Since that day. Goblins have a distinctive scent. (We don't stink or reek, for fuck's sake!) Before, he could track me across the City with one sniff of his nose. I've been layin' the deodorant enough to smell like a beach fulla horny douchebags all summer as a result. I didn't know that he'd stopped. Guess this means he's gettin' over me. I should be happy about it.

I'm not, by the way, but I should be.

"Yeah." I take a breath. "Yeah."

"Nick? Are you ever going to forgive me?"

Now I look up at him, a little incredulous. "Are ya ever gonna apologize? Do ya know what was taken from me that day, Thom? I'm a damned *Redcap* now, the last thing I ever wanted to do. I told ya again and again that I don't kill people and I took a person's life. For. You." I sniff softly. Don't fuckin' cry. Do *not* fuckin' cry for him. "Thom, I…"

He's holdin' my hand. I pull it away.

"Ya hurt me, Thom. I fuckin' cried for almost a week after that day. You don't get it, I never… I never felt like that with anyone other than you." I rest my chin on the table, my head feelin' heavy.

"Like… what?" He takes a breath. "Nick? Do… did you love me?"

I look up to him, my eyes brimmin'. Fuck me. Shadow take me, I fuckin' nod my head.

"Why did you lie, then?" His brows furrow. "How could you lie? We're both Fae, right? We always have to tell the truth. I was convinced that you hated me."

"Thom, I'm a Goblin-"

"Do *not* start up with this shit again, Nick. Your being a Goblin doesn't change the way I feel about-"

I hold up my hand to stop him. "Thom, yer never gonna let me just talk, are ya? I'm tryin' to tell ya that Goblins can *lie*. Why ya think Fae hate us so much? We don't gotta bother with the labyrinths of petty honesties and all that crap, we'll just bullshi-" I catch Sharon's glare. "Tell ya what ya wanna hear, or whatever. We're closer to human than all the other Fae. I'm probably closer to human than *you*, come to think of it."

Yeah, I know, he looks more human than any of the Fae, but if Thom and I were in a car accident and needed blood transfusions to live, all I gotta worry about is that the ambulance got some type O. Thom? He's the son of the First Phouka, so he would need him for blood. Even his brother wouldn't have the right type. I think. He don't talk about him much.

"Don't believe me? Cut yer finger, check the color. I'd bleed red, I'd lay down a few bucks ya bleed silver like the rest of the mythics, 'cept the Sidhe, *literal* bluebloods, and the Twin Bloods who bleed purple." I am stopping every sentence to have another fry, ya know, I ain't ate yet.

"But… why would you lie?" He's a bit off, I can tell.

"Why does anyone lie?" Another fry. "Don't think we don't come in handy fer the nobles. Somebody on the payroll who can lie, and ya can maintain your air of absolute honesty 'cause ya believed it? Imagine what ya can get away with, Thom, seriously. Why else ya think the Left Hand's a Goblin? What better way to keep up that plausible deniability?"

"No." He looks hurt. "Why did you lie and say you didn't love me, when I know you do?"

"Do *you*, Thom? Or was that just somethin' ya said that day?"

"Nick… It doesn't matter if I do. The Queen has bidden me to seek a husband or wife among the peerage." The Phouk looks away. "At least she's entertaining the possibility of marrying a man, but…"

"Shadow take me…" I rub my face with my hands. "Yer gettin' married and ya wanna know if I still love you? Did… Did ya just want to twist the knife, or what? Did you *have* to tell me that? No, ya didn't. So why?"

"I don't know, okay? I'm not familiar with stuff like this. My relationships before this were casual, or the one relationship I had before you ended because I 'awakened'. Then I meet a Goblin who treats me like everyone else, who's good, and honest, has a sense of justice. You risked your life to save mine, to save those people in the bank. If anything, I don't feel worthy of you, Nick."

"What, so if I was a noble, you'd get down on one knee?" I gotta chuckle at that, the idea of a Goblin elevated to the peerage is practically a hilarious idea and-

"Yes." He don't hesitate. "In a heartbeat." Thom chews his lip. "To propose marriage. To you. So, you don't think I'd get down on one knee to tie a shoelace or something."

This, of course, is when Hannah shows up with my sandwich. She places mine and Thom's on the table, and I look up at her.

"Can I get a to-go box? I ain't hungry no more." She nods and leaves, and the Phouk's still lookin' at me. "Why ya wanna talk about somethin' that ain't gonna happen, Thom? Ya still love me and wanna marry me, huh? Ya really think that makes up for everythin'? That I'll just flutter my eyes and fall into yer arms? Shadow, Thom, ya ain't even ready for a relationship like that."

"I *was* engaged before I awakened, you know."

"And ya also just said ya ain't been in anythin' else that was serious 'sides that. You 'n me? We don't count. We had an interrogation and a night of protective custody where the two of us could've made a fortune if we streamed it online."

"It was enough for you to tell me you loved me after you thought I was asleep." I chew my lip at that. "Yeah. I heard you. That's when I knew, okay? How are we supposed to be serious if we don't even try, Nick?"

"What's my middle name? My favorite color? My favorite book? Favorite song? You ever been to *my* place? Otherwise, we're

just a couple fun buddies." I'd say 'fuck buddies' but Sharon would ban me for life.

"Arsenne. Lighter gray or white. You tell people it's *Beloved*, but you read through *Fruits Basket* every year. Anything by Rihanna, because you can't make that choice responsibly. You've never asked me over."

"H-how do you know all that?" Seriously, buddy. Holy *shit*.

The Phouk gives me an indulgent look. "I'm a detective, Nick. And you'd be amazed how loose-lipped Goblins get when it's only a dog in earshot." He smiles. "Nicholas Arsenne. Your name just glides off the tongue, you know?"

This is why Phouka are dangerous, buddy. They can do *this*. Ya end up makin' bad decisions, y'know? They slip in with their sweet nothin' and smooth talkin' and then-

"Ya wanna walk me home?" Then ya do somethin' stupid like *that*. Fer fuck's sake, Blackwarren, ya got loot to drop off and yer askin' a *Guard* to walk ya home instead of takin' it to the dead drop! Tell yer heart and yer dick to shut up and let the brain take the wheel and handle this sensibly and responsibly and-

When the fuck did I get home?

My apartment, by the way, is not that great of a place. 4th floor walkup in East Benedict, so, y'know, an industrial slum. The Benedict was nice, I guess, a few decades ago, but all the jobs left when The City got its own version of the Rust Belt. City got richer, more expensive, so the Benedict became where the working class would call home.

Or for people who ain't got the credit rating to get a lease anywhere else in the City. My buildin' is owned by a landlord somewhere down south, so ya can guess how the maintenance is here. The stairs are creaky, trash strewn here and there. The Phouk's steps are heavier, louder than mine as we climb upwards to the fourth floor.

My apartment is... habitable. Sorta. Studio, bathroom partitioned off, bed's just a mattress on the floor, stacks of books everywhere, no TV, a sink, a teakettle to boil water to make it potable, and a tiny apple tree that's kept me alive some weeks as it never seems to run out of ripe fruit to pick so long as I don't eat too much. My dishes consist of two mugs, one bowl, one plate, a spoon, a fork, and a butter knife. What? Just 'cause I'm a thief don't mean I'm a rich one.

"Jesus, Nick." Here we go. Thom's in my apartment, now, for the first time. "Are you sure you're okay?"

"I've lived here a few years, Richie Rich. If I wasn't okay, I wouldn't still be here." I roll my eyes. The Phouk is fuckin' loaded, okay? Rich family, fat trust fund, a duplex on Shoreside right down the street from The Queen. He calls his A-1 home theater his "TV room", and has three full bathrooms on the same floor, and floor-to-ceilin' ocean views. I ain't bitter, no, why ya askin'?

Of course, he's huggin' me now, and I do feel patronized, yeah, but he's so fuckin' *good* at it, ya know? The man could hug you once and you'll be convinced that everythin' is gonna be okay. Warm, safe, protected. "You don't have to live like this, Nick."

"I'm not movin' in with ya, Thom." No, I ain't exited the hug. Ya don't get to judge me, okay buddy? I've had a time of it lately, and not just 'cause of him. "That's movin' way faster than either of us are ready for."

"I… do know of a place that just opened up, rent would be cheap."

"Ugh. Really, Thom? Ya want me to move into one of yer properties?" 'Cause rich people always got properties.

"No? More it was a crime scene that just got the all-clear to go back on the market." He lets me go, rubbin' my shoulders, lookin' in my eyes with a soft smile and a sincerity that would twist a knife in yer fuckin' heart. "Better than this place, at least."

"This why ya wanted to come over, Thom? To judge my place and magically have a better one to move into?" I roll my eyes, but his face isn't givin' any hints as he shakes his head, and he ain't never had a poker face. "So, why'd you wanna walk me home?"

"You asked." He steps closer, takin' me in his arms again. "And I've missed you, Nicholas Arsenne." The last bit is whispered, carryin' on his warm breath into my ears, which twitch softly. Fuck. I know what he wants.

"I missed you too, Constable." I'm just as disgusted with myself as you are, buddy. I can't believe I just said tha-

The Phouk's lips are on mine, his tongue slidin' along my own, heads movin', mouths hungry, needful, heat risin' in my body when he presses me to his chest. I didn't know how much I needed, wanted this. Usually, I don't lose myself into gettin' all hot and bothered. Gotta be a real connection, which is why I still don't get why Thom gets me this way. I'm pretty sure I love him, probably, maybe, kinda, but I got no real idea why, or at least, an idea that I'd buy.

When the kiss breaks, both our eyes are dreamy, almost drunk lookin', his fingers strokin' along my face. "Nick?"

"Yeah?" I'm catchin' my breath, rational thought eroding away from me.

"May I nibble your ears?" A caress, a pinch at the tips, and all the fuckin' blood in my brain just took a cruise south of the fuckin' border. Our ears are, uh… sensitive. Like…

Like I wanna *fuck* this Phouk 'til we're both *howlin'*. I'll worry about the other shit later.

My eyes go wide, intense, and I'm grippin' his shoulders to make him look right at me. "On the mattress. Take my fuckin' clothes off. And ya better get naked too, Constable, because if yer gonna work my ears ya know what's gonna happen."

Means I'm gonna be on fuckin' top is what's gonna fuckin' happen. Sorry, buddy. I usually skip this part, 'cause it ain't supposed to be that kinda story, but there's a reason I read a lotta romance novels. Usually that sorta sex don't happen in real life, but if ya ever get the chance to get with a Phouka in the sack?

Fuckin'. Do. It.

We only been together like this twice before, but each time was a marathon, not a sprint. Thom's an attentive, givin' kind of guy, wants who he's with to feel as good as he can make them, because that makes him feel good, so I'm the lucky guy right now. The idea of "he's supposed to get married to some nobleman or noblewoman" is the furthest thing from both our minds right now. He knows every part of my body, a quick study with a good memory, and fuckin' Hell, buddy, what he does to my ears.

Touchin' our ears is a way of sayin' "let's fuck", because Thom has before, and already has, gotten me off just playin' with 'em. I'm a short fuse with a quick reload, he's an hour-long job. I've learned enough about him to know the places on his body to push him closer to the edge. I also know how to pull him back. And I kinda relish that I can prolong it for him.

Granted, I ain't never held him this long. He certainly didn't start jabberin' in Gaelic before. Fuck, I didn't even know he could speak it. He's repeatin' himself, that's one thing, and I'll admit it's pretty hot, so hot I forgot to hold him back.

"Tha mi a 'gealltainn mi fhìn dhut, a ghràidh, buinidh mi dhuit gu bràth." He's heavin' breath, gettin' whatever those words are outta his body which clenches around mine. *"Tha mi a 'gealltainn mi fhìn dhut, a ghràidh, buinidh mi dhuit gu bràth."* I… I can't last any longer. I let free the metaphorical reins, my own body giving its heat and life and essence of everythin' that's me.

The Phouka practically howls in response, *"Tha mi a 'gealltainn mi fhìn dhut, a ghràidh, buinidh mi dhuit gu bràth!"*

His body is shiny with sweat, the smattering of body hair matted, his breathing closer to canine panting. *"Tha gaol agam ort, Nicholas Arsenne."*

"…huh? Only part of that of that I understood was my name, Thom."

I'm on my back, and he's kissin' me, eyes bright, happy. "What? I was talking normally. What are you talking about?"

"That wasn't English *or* Sigil, Thom. Not even bad Engli-" Back to kissin'. I know how this can turn out. We'll be here screwin' for the next few hours, at which point I'll be so blissed out from Phouka sex I'll giddily move into his place and run off to Atlantic City to get married ASAFP.

I push him back, even if my body is eager to go again and again. "Thom, okay. I'll look at this place yer tellin' me about. Plus, I gotta run an errand, and I think we ruined my mattress."

The Phouk nods, calmly, oddly not wanting to push me to fuck again, like he did the other two times. "I'll text you the address. Still the same number?"

I nod, warily. "Yeah?" I mean, I'm happy that he's calmed himself down a bit, and that'll make disentangling a bit easier. Wasn't expectin' him to calm down this fast.

"Okay. I'll head back to my place. No offense, but your shower doesn't look safe, hygienically as it were." He leans down to help me up and kisses me softly. "As amazing as you smell right now, you should probably take a shower yourself or anyone in three blocks will know what you and I did."

So yeah, I sniff myself and I smell... sweat. Then again, I ain't a Phouk, or a satyr, or dragon, or Dwarf, or Troll, or... Yeah, I should take a shower.

Thom gives me a lingerin' look before he leaves, and damn it, my heart skips a beat. Shadow take me, I might still love that fuckin' Dog.

Yeah, buddy, I better make that a *cold* shower.

4

Ya'd think it'd be fuckin' stupid to take a shower and then make yer way down into a sewer.

Buddy? You'd be right.

But when ya indulge in the pleasures of "sex with the ex" for over an hour when ya were supposed to deliver stolen property to a dead drop, uh… 'bout an hour ago… Well, ya miss yer contact and exit the shower to about forty texts and eight very angry voicemails from yer cousin who's already talkin' about how he's got yer credit score up and he'll tank it to under a hundred if "ya don't get yer fuckin' lazy green ass over here right now!"

My cousin, Cenzo, short for Vincenzo Giansiracusa, is a Gremlin, one of the Goblin clans, and they live in the sewers. Ain't nobody wanna live in the sewers unless they gotta, but in the Gremlins' case, there's a method to the madness. Sewers are by and large pipes and tunnels and water runoff and abandoned stations the UTA let die.

Also? Sewers got trunk lines, power lines, water lines, and all those abandoned stations, which are viable for sustainable habitation given adequate repurposin' and retrofittin' of available resources and technology.

What? I got a vocabulary and education; I just prefer talkin' like this.

Still, I gotta run through the fuckin' sewers to get where I'm goin', so my Timbs are gonna be fuckin' filthy by the time I get there. Ah fuck, I think I just stepped on a fuckin' diaper. Shadow take me, it fuckin' *reeks* down here!

I got one bar on my phone given I'm underground, but I try a call to Cenzo anyway. I'm not sayin' I'm lost down here, but…

"Where the fuck's the package, Nick?" I hear a lot of mutterin' in the background, so he ain't alone. His voice gets a little muffled.

"Shut the fuck up! I'm on the fuckin' phone with the Luddite Redcap!"

Fuck you, too, Cenzo.

"I'm in the fuckin' sewer ya *baciagaloop*, so where the fuck am I goin'?" Word I picked up from Mom, she's a Tinker, and from the Sicilian branch of the family. She called me that when she was in a good mood. I'm won't share what she called me when she *wasn't*.

"Where ya at, then?"

"If I knew that I wouldn't be callin' ya, I'd be there!" It's a straight shot ahead for now, so I walk forward, the loot in my knapsack with the rest of my tools. I sigh, gritting my teeth. "Gimme directions, will ya? I came in by the access at 81st and C like last time."

"Just go back to the beginnin', I'll fuckin' lead ya from there. Should take this out yer fuckin' cut, y'know."

"We agreed. Fifteen percent of the value recovered, 'cause you said some prick stole this off ya. And by the way, I ain't no idiot. I know what an Action Comics #1 rated at 9.8 could run at an auction, so ya ain't payin' me the two grand ya offered."

Before I tell ya this next part, buddy, I want ya to know how important it is to pay attention while yer on the phone, especially if yer walkin' in the sewers and yer only light is from yer phone and a charm ya worked to boost yer night vision. Ya need to pay attention where yer steppin' is what I'm sayin', and I always do that, ya understand?

"Try it, Nicky. I can get the Left Hand on the horn and let him know yer fuckin' that Dog again." The Left Hand of the Queen, her personal assassin, Captain of the Queen's Guard, and my second cousin twice removed. "By the way, never leave yer phone on when yer cousins are Gremlins."

What next fills my ear is a recording of me cryin' out that I'm going to climax and tellin' the Constable to pinch the tips of my ears so I'll shoot clear 'cross the room.

I'm tellin' ya this, buddy, because it's important ya understand I was distracted, and misstepped, and I step on that fuckin' diaper again (which has no traction, obviously), slip, and fall hard on my back, hearin' a *crunch* as the loot is compressed between my back, and my quality steel tools.

And a hammer.

"What was that?" My face goes stone. "Nicky, what the fuck was that?"

"How 'bout ya tell me why yer recordin' me havin' sex, ya fuckin' perv?!" I pick up my knapsack, and peek inside with the ambient light from my phone (careful to *not* point the cameras at it, now). I suck in air through my teeth, wincin', tryin' to not react out loud, but...

"Nick, ya ain't changin' the subject, damn it!"

"Can't hear ya, Cous'! Goin' through a tunnel!" Tap end. Stuff phone in pocket. Give eyes a few seconds to adjust.

Lights in the tunnel switch on, suddenly, and my phone vibrates. A text from Cenzo.

follow fckin lights u got 10m b4 email LH vid

Well, shit.

At least the light will let me check the loot-

No.

No. No. No. No. No.

So, uh, old comic books are kinda kept in vacuum-sealed plastic cases to ensure that nothin' gets damaged. It's rated 9.8, meanin' someone read it, like, once, and immediately put it in somethin' hermetically sealed. It's a fuckin' unicorn, is what I'm sayin'. Or, uh, it was. Because the case is broke open, and the comic is bent.

It's lookin' as busted as the car on the cover, is what I'm sayin'. One of these went at auction for *eight million dollars*. I just wrecked *eight million dollars* because I slipped on a fuckin' *diaper*.

I am so *fucked*.

Shadow take me, even the thick case lock at the top has popped open. Normally I could call on Mama Tinker to do me a solid and fix the case, but it's just simple plastic, and restorin' an eighty- or ninety-year-old comic ain't in her wheelhouse. Besides, I finally paid off all the favors she did for me and-

And...

Hold on a minute, buddy. I just saw somethin' that I need to have a chat with my cousin about. Mind if we zip forward a little? Thanks, buddy, glad we're gettin' along again.

Y'know, the best conversations start by kickin' open a door, don't ya think?

"My dear sweet Cousin Vincenzo! How long since we talked? It's been far too long!" Pull the fuckin' blade back into the vambrace, I ain't here to kill anyone. That's better.

Said cousin is like any other Goblin, just thinner, a little shorter, scalier skin, bigger eyes, sharper claws, if he weren't trimmin' 'em to play keyboard cowboy. He's wearin' cargo pants for the pockets, and a T-shirt clearly for a human child. "Ya got the loot, Nicky? And ya really flashin' steel in our burrow? I can fuck your life with eight keystrokes, Redcap."

He was kinda dickish when I was a Whitecap, too.

"I got it." It set down my knapsack and pull out the broken case. "Fifteen percent of the value recovered, right?"

His eyes are wide. "...the *fuck* did you do to it?! You know how much that fuckin' thing's worth?"

The comic is pulled from the case, I hold it by the cover page, and let it fall open. "Don't a comic need to have somethin' on the pages for it to be worth that much?"

He grits needle teeth. "Fuck, ya got me, okay? It's a fake book and I didn't want ya to know-"

"Oh, so it's *all* fake, huh?"

Cenzo meets my eyes. I'm impressed by how much he's committed to this. "Complete bullshit, yeah."

"So ya don't mind..." I hold the case by the thicker case lock, the 9.8 visible, the plastic dark. "If I snap this in half, then?"

His eyes go wide, but he stays still. One of my other, more distant cousins, does mutter, "Aw, shit." Cenzo then curses under his breath.

I sigh, and pop the case lock open, where hidden within is a smaller black box with a USB port. "Cousin, ya don't lie to, or screw over family. I had my own suspicions, seein' as the number of people who were holdin' hostages at the bank. They had the vault, they had control, they had time, they could've loaded up more than eight million dollars and got out fast. Split that four ways, it would've been a decent payday a couple decades ago. Nowadays? Two million won't even get ya a two-bedroom co-op in Beckettsville. So, it would have to be more."

Cenzo sags. "Nick, ya ain't getting' fifteen percent of that."

"What's on it, Cenzo?" I hold up the drive in my hands. "'Cause to me, all this is right now is a forty dollar flash drive ya bought on the internet, and I can break it and just get ya a new one."

"Don't!" He takes a breath. "Yer a real fucker, ya know that?"

"I did a job. I brought ya the item. I would like to be paid for my services. Ya tried to put one over on me. Pay my fee, and all's forgiven. Ya don't? *I* will be the one who gives Cousin Damon a call and let him know yer fuckin' over family." I sigh. "C'mon, Cenzo. We were friends growin' up, right? I don't want shit to get sour 'tween us, okay?"

"It's Thundercoin." I perk a brow, he rolls his eyes. "Crypto. Fuck, who's the *baciagaloop* now? Blues made it and mined it, humans got in on it, we fucked around with demand." By Blues, he means blue dragons, buddy. They're even more into tech than Gremlins and Knockers combined. "We thought we'd pump and dump it, but fuckin' humans will hold onto that shit until they die, so a bunch of 'em started buyin' it."

"So, it's worth more now, I take it?"

"Yeah, we did a scheme where we siphoned a bunch of coin, funneled it onto a drive to take it out of circulation to drive up the scarcity. We were gonna dump it to crash the market, and then some fucker stole the drive to keep the price up. Now we can go through with it, but I doubt it'll kill the coin or the market. Lay down money a fuckin' Coyote did it."

"So, uh, my fee?" I toss the drive to him, and he visibly exhales in relief once his hands are on it.

"Gonna take a bit, Nick. We ain't got *cash* here and you ain't got a bank account we can transfer into. I'll make sure ya get paid, a'right? Just ain't gonna happen right now." He smirks. "So, yer movin' outta the shitbox, huh?"

I'd ask how he knew that, but if he was recording me and Thom *in flagrante delicto*, it ain't too much of a stretch to assume he heard Thom bringin' up that place he knew about. "Ya already saw the text, didn't ya…"

"I mean, at least it's *West* Benedict, border of Beckett, if ya don't mind a fuck-around apartment." It's exactly what it sounds like, buddy.

"Less I know, the better, Cenzo. Love how all of ya's are decidin' where I'm gonna live without consultin' me."

"Well, that firetrap ya live in?"

I nod, warily. "Yeah?"

"That's been condemned for two months? Ya ain't even wondered why ya ain't had to pay rent?"

Shit. "Who got it condemned?" Thom, I swear to the fuckin' Machinist if you got my building axed to get me to move into a place you own, I swear I'm gonna-

"Board of Health, who the fuck else? Ya didn't smell the eight raccoon latrines that were found in the basement? The black mold that was in all the walls? I only had to read the fuckin' report and I almost puked. Fuck, Cous', didn't ya fence a bunch of shit from the Riverwood job?"

"Cenzo, ya know how deep in hock I was 'fore that happened? I had enough to pay my back rent and utilities. Rest had to go to the royal coffers 'cause it was originally noble property."

"Ya actually let 'em take the loot? The fuck's wrong with you?"

"Cenzo? I was still bein' looked at for three murders at the time, I'm lucky I got to keep what I did." I exhale with a grumble. "My buildin' is really condemned?" He nods back at me. "Fuck me, now what? I ain't got the cash or credit history to get a lease outside the slums."

"If ya don't mind givin' us half an hour and a few points off yer take we can handle that, Cous'." Cenzo's smirkin', 'cause of course he fuckin' is.

Don't get me wrong, buddy, it ain't like I liked that place, but it was mine, and I wasn't expectin' the sudden change. Makes sense Cenzo would be the one to do the final push to get me out the door. Gremlins don't hate nothin' more than stagnation. Ah, fuck it.

"Throw in a movin' service fer all my shit and ya got a deal."

5

Takes about a week, all told, which I'll skip for the sake of yer interest, buddy. I will say that Cenzo and the rest of my Gremlin cousins are good at their jobs. My credit score? Over seven hundred. My employment history? Four years of paystubs and taxes filed listing me as an "asset recovery specialist." ID? Motorcycle license registered to Nicholas Arsenne of San Francisco, California, recently moved to the Unified City, with a P.O. box in Beckettsville. Two credit cards with decent limits and a light balance. Oh yeah, and a fuckin' *locksmith's certification* with the City *and* the state.

And they did all that shit in forty-five minutes.

Gremlins, buddy, they get shit done. And the Knockers still think they're better at this shit than Goblins. Adorable.

Granted, the fuckers still registered my ID with the middle name "Berettorosso."

Redcap. A Goblin who's taken a life and got a taste for it. That's how they're seen, and it's generally accurate. I killed someone in self-defense (it was me or him), but a life taken's a life taken, and once yer cap's dipped in blood, that blood ain't ever comin' out. Bein' a Blackwarren means I'm sorta genetically predisposed to murder and assassination, even if Pa was a sports photographer before he dipped his cap under financial duress. Also, bein' a Blackwarren in the assassin's profession is the equivalent of bein' a thoroughbred.

But I can't complain too much because it's how I got Shadow's Edge, the mystic blade of the Goblins, one of five magical weapons in the City. One's held by the Sidhe, Rain Cutter, which is so sharp it can cleave a raindrop in twain without splatterin' it. The Kitsune have a katana that can kill even the eldest demons in one strike; they keep the name secret. The Adamant Heart was broken in two in a duel, but word has it that the Dwarves are workin' to reforge it, and the Claw of Shoshare is lost, and we should all be grateful for that.

The last is a staff, simply called Sigil, and it's held by the current Ra'keth, the Sorcerer King, the Lightning Rod.

So it's in rare company, buddy, is what I'm sayin'.

Even if it's a clockwork vambrace on my arm instead of a blade that occasionally drains a pint of blood off me to do whatever the fuck it's doin' with it. Better me than some innocent person, y'know?

But now, buddy, looks like we're home, the new home, at least. I ain't got any decent furniture, mostly the found stuff that was in my last place and a lot of boxes of books, a couple duffels with my tools for "asset recovery", and another one for my clothes since I ain't got too many. The neighborhood ain't too great, but a damned sight better than where I was before. The landlord thinks I'm either a spy or a future serial killer, since he's human, but at least when I asked him about whether I had to boil the tap water he was insulted instead of tellin' me where to buy purification tablets.

So, I can take my first hot bath in… Y'know, if I try to complete that sentence it's just gonna fuckin' make me sad. It's not like it's a bubble bath or any of that shit. Not that I think it's too hoity-toity, more that I didn't pick any of it up. The hot water will be more than enough, and my muscles relax once I'm almost submerged, my size allowing me to stretch my legs instead of huggin' my knees like most people would. Bathroom is lit okay, no shower curtain 'cause I ain't picked one up yet, floor is plain white with occasional black tiles, toilet, sink, wall mirror.

Not like I can do anythin' other than look around since I didn't bring in a book, or even my phone to play music or a podcast or somethin'. I do think about Thom a little, but not in *that* way, buddy. I gotta go over the fact that he'd marry me if he got the go-ahead to.

Don't get me wrong, it feels kinda nice, as a Goblin, to hear someone say the three words, and say "If ya'd have me, I'd welcome ya into my life." Ain't like I never thought about it, just didn't see it with someone like him because ya don't see a Goblin with anyone other than a Goblin. Much less Phouka royalty, if they even got somethin' like that.

A Prince out a fuckin' fairy tale wants to hold me close and...

Ah, fuck. I'm startin' to think about him, y'know, that way. How his hands feel on my body, lips on mine, teeth on my ears... Fuck, I ain't gonna last long if I keep on this track.

I close my eyes, tight, imagine my hand as his, pinch my eartip...

"Thom... Thom, I'm..."

KNOCK KNOCK KNOCK KNOCK KNOCK!

"Aw, fer *fuck's* sake." Who the fuck is bangin' on my door? I'm paid up on rent and I don't know nobody here. There's some splashin' as I get outta the tub and wrap a towel around my waist. I'd get dressed, buddy, but a towel's all I need to tell somebody to fuck the Hell off.

Another bunch of knocks at the door, but I get there in time before it starts up again. "A'right! A'right! Fuck, be patient, would ya?"

So, I open the door to a coupla white people, I shit ya not. Man and woman, both near six feet, I'd guess husband and wife. They're dressed upper-middle class so fuck if I know why they're here. "What?"

Both of 'em sputter a few seconds since I'm guessin' I ain't what they were expectin' to open the door. Fuck knows what they see when they look at me.

"Y'see, what ya do is move yer lips and tongue and use yer words, pal. Can I help ya?" 'Cause despite bein' a thief, Mom made sure I had basic fuckin' manners down.

"Th-this is 4C, yes?" The woman, and she sounds like I'm about to slice her soon as look at her. Ya get used to it.

"Uh huh. Like it says on the door. Whatcha want?" Her husband is still, well, still, and lookin' ready to bolt if I make a sudden movement.

Sucks that my "white voice" only works on the phone.

"H-how long have you lived here?" Still tense, but she's powerin' through. Must be important.

"'Bout a week, ma'am. Mind tellin' me why yer askin'?"

She closes her eyes. "Was there anything here when you moved in?" Now she's tremblin'. Ain't scared, though. Huh.

"Hey, uh, how 'bout ya gimme a minute to put some clothes on. I didn't find anythin', but maybe ya know somethin' I don't. I'll put on some tea and we can talk, yeah?" I back out of the doorway, leaving it open. "Sorry I ain't got a lotta chairs. Oh, help yerself to an apple from the tree if yer hungry."

I fully expect to find them gone or still in the doorway when I come back out in my regular clothes (t-shirt, zip-up hoodie, jeans, Timbs, yer familiar, buddy). Instead, they're both sittin' on the foldin' chairs, lookin' around the main room/foyer/kitchenette. I really gotta get better furniture since now I'm entertainin', 'parently. I take my cue and fill up the tea kettle, gett'ng' it goin' on my actual workin' stove.

"All I got is green tea, hope that's okay." I take an apple off the tree and get a big bite, still sweet and fresh as ever. "So, mind tellin' me what's goin' on?"

"This was our daughter's apartment." She's a little calmer. Psychopathic murderers don't invite ya in for green tea. Or maybe they do. Was never into readin' that shit, seemed exploitative of mental health issues, ya know what I'm sayin'?

"Bridget." Husband found his voice, looks like. They're both human, obviously, so I'm guessin' this Bridget was too.

"And... she run off or somethin'?"

Wife starts cryin'. Husband does too. Fuckin' Hell. It ain't ugly cryin', but it's pretty fuckin' close.

"I say somethin' wrong?" I take another bite of the apple, 'cause my manners ain't *that* proper.

"She was murdered," the husband manages to get out, almost glarin' at me. Why would he be so pissy at me? Ain't like I knew the girl was murdered, how the fuck would I know? Why assume I'd… know…

Oh, fer fuck's sake.

"She was killed in this apartment, wasn't she…"

Thom? Cenzo? You two miserable fuckbags coulda told me I was movin' into a fuckin' *murder house.*

"Hey, uh… If yer lookin' fer somethin', the cops would probably have it. You uh, did call the cops, right?"

Another glare, but c'mon, I come from a world where casual murder is rarely acknowledged let alone investigated. Hell, I solved a triple murder, and the guilty party only lost his fuckin' title.

"Yes. The man who…" Wife's taken over, and she's holdin' up, holdin' back more tears.

"The man who did it." I get up. Tea kettle's whistlin', because before I was a Redcap, I was Tinker clan, and I tinkered my fuckin' teapot to boil faster.

"Take the time ya need." I only have two cups, but I drop in the tea bags and pour in the water, settin' 'em in front of 'em on the banged-up card table I've had for three years.

"He was convicted, he's in prison. He hasn't told us where it is, he said he doesn't even know what we're talking about." She steeps the bag, more for something to do with her hands.

"So… what is 'it'? Hard to tell ya if it's here or not."

"Sheet music." The father takes a breath. "Bridget finished her fellowship at the conservatory, and she's writing a symphony for the… She… was writing a symphony for the philharmonic."

"We want to give it to the conservatory at Allora University. She loved her time there. She was going to write scores for films, the symphony was going to be her 'Here I Am' to the music world." A smile breaks through her mother's sadness, the memory of hopes, dreams, and a future.

I tilt my head. "Her… what?"

"Her way of telling them all 'here I am!' That's what she always called it. Like she and music had always been searching for each other…"

"I get it." I nod, finishing my apple because I take big bites. "Haven't seen any sheet music, sorry. Ya think someone took it?"

"This was our last hope." They're both on the verge of breakin' down again.

"Hey uh…" Fuck, I mean, I can't just leave 'em like this, buddy. I invited 'em in! They're my guests and shit! "Maybe I can help ya?"

The wife sniffles, fetchin' a tissue from her purse. "How? Who are you?"

"Nick Arsenne. Head of Blackwarren Asset Retrieval." They both look at me like I spoke to 'em in Sicilian Italian. I didn't, by the way. "I track down stolen or lost items for retrieval to original owners. Was originally out in California, but came out here to the Argent City, and if ya want, ya can hire me to track it down for ya and any other of her possessions that were taken."

And now the suspicion. They come lookin' fer stuff in their murdered daughter's apartment and suddenly there's a sketchy guy sayin' he can find it for 'em? "How do we know you're telling the truth?"

"You can talk to another client of mine. Thomas Canmore, of the Allora Canmores, he'll vouch for me. I done work fer him and he was very satisfied. He lives down on Shoreside, you can call his buildin' and ask fer him, just say yer callin' for Nicholas Arsenne. If ya'd like, I can start work *gratis* and update you at your pleasure, ya only gotta pay me if I find it and return it to ya intact."

What? I'm a decent guy. And takin' care of unfinished business in, again, a *murder house*, will likely make livin' here easier. I've walked the Shadow, buddy, ghosts ain't a stretch for my particular paradigm.

"No, we don't know you. You could be lying. How do we even know you aren't connected to that man who killed our daughter?!"

The father stands up, glarin' down at me. I don't take it personal. Grief finds anger easily, and anger finds prejudice and bigotry, and, like I keep sayin', I'm a Goblin.

He storms out pretty soon after that. I don't get up to stop him. It ain't my place, and he'd probably try to take a swing at me and then it'd get way too complicated. Bridget's mother gets up as well, and walks silently to the door, which her husband left open.

Her hand rests on the door frame as she stops, not turning around. "Can you really find it, Mr. Arsenne?"

Mr. Arsenne.

I ain't never been called "Mister" anything, much less by a human. To her, I'm a rat-faced lookin' fucker with a criminal skull shape. Somethin' deep inside of her is tellin' her to run, to pull back in disgust, 'cause in me she sees the worst of humanity. Ugliness, raggedy morality, tainted soul and greedy heart. Beady eyes that reflect every flaw, everythin' she despises, 'specially about herself.

And still, she asks me to help her. She calls me by my name, not defeated, but clinging to that last gossamer thread of hope she got left in her. She treats *me* with what respect she can muster for me, carried on a mother's love for her daughter, a need to grant her some measure of peace.

I mean, fuck, buddy… What else can I say to that?

"Yes, ma'am. Ya got my word. I'll take the case."

6

I'm sure before all of this is over, buddy, I'm gonna regret havin' said any of that. At least I ain't bein' asked to solve a triple murder that shakes the foundations of polite Fae society. Instead, I'm now tangentially connected to the murder of a human woman. If I hadn't been told the killer was already in jail and found guilty, I wouldna touched it, buddy. It's not that I ain't that much of an asshole or anythin', it's that when a Fae is connected to the death of a human, ya got the Lightning Rod to worry about.

The Lightning Rod, the Sorcerer King of the Argent City, bearer of Sigil, and from what I hear, currently sharin' a bed with a Dwarf. Eh, good on 'em both, but I'd rather not have the guy who ended the world with a blizzard and almost killed the Fates herselves (which us Goblins are fuckin' sore about) thinkin' I murdered a human. I ain't heard about him killin' anybody, save the Recluse and the Frozen River, the Sorcerer Kings before him. Hell, the River's reign didn't last a night before the Lightning Rod usurped him. This is a guy who can rewrite reality if the whim catches him, and he don't want any mythics killin' humans.

So, we don't kill fuckin' humans, obviously.

Fuck, I heard a rumor someone once tried to give him shit and all that was left of 'em was a fuckin' *shoe* that had the consistency of gray Jell-o.

Ya can guess I'm gonna be plenty careful with this one, y'know? What I gotta do now is start from scratch, but at least since I only got a stolen symphony to worry about, I'll start by doin' what Bridget's parents wanted to do:

Search the apartment.

The obvious ones are first. I check cupboards, defrost the freezer to see if anything was buried under ice, closets, the couch that was left behind. All that turns up is a few nickels and pennies. So, her parents woulda left disappointed, is what I'm sayin'.

Then, I go into the less common hiding spots. Doorknobs, outlets, anything that's hollow and things that aren't expected to be, behind drawers, heating grates, the ceiling fan, behind the thermostat, anything that can be unscrewed or pried and reset with ease includin' doorjambs and wainscotting.

Nothin', but I found some decent spots to hide shit.

So now I gotta get a little extra-legal. Well, by that I mean I gotta call Cenzo.

y u call

Of course, he fuckin' texts instead of pickin' up the damned phone.

pick up need talk

I toss in a couple choice emoji before I send, and then dial again.

"Ya know what the fuckin' eggplant means, don't ya Nicky?" He's laughin', but I don't give a fuck.

"Yeah, means ya fuckin' pick up the phone to rub it in. Need to ask ya about the place you and the Dog put me up in. Y'know, woulda been nice to know it's a *murder house*, Cenzo."

"How the fuck else ya gonna find a place that ain't been snapped up? Yer lucky it's still the Benedict. If that place was in Beckett or Grunstadt it would been taken 'fore her body was cold."

"And Allora or Destry whoever took it would probably be the one who killed her."

"That surprisin', Nick? *Really?*"

"Nah, but ya gotta admit that sheds some light on why they see what they see when they look at us."

"Nick, I ain't in the mood for metaphysical bullshit, I'm fuckin' workin', kay?" I can tell he's about to hang up.

"I need to know about the girl that was killed, Cenzo. Guy who did it was found guilty, in jail, and her parents hired me to find somethin' of hers. I figure the guy who did it might know somethin', can ya help me out?" I just wanted to take a fuckin' bath, fuck me.

"Ya coulda just fuckin' texted me that, Nick."

"Ya'd leave me on read for two hours 'fore we got even halfway into the fuckin' conversation ya *baciagaloop*. Now, how 'bout ya do me a solid so I can do the job ya say I'm doin' on my taxes." I sigh. "Ya can take a half-point off my cut."

"Full point." So at least I know he can do *somethin'*. Granted, I ain't happy about havin' to spend my money 'fore I get it.

"Cous', I know half a point of however much my cut is could likely buy me a godsdamned car. A fuckin' human got murdered and ya know what helpin' the parents will do if the Lightnin' Rod comes askin' any of us questions. Ya know we can't lie to *him*."

"Ugh, fine. Yer own fuckin' fault fer gettin' involved, Nick. Couldna just been happy with an apartment and a whitened-up identity, ya gotta go diggin', don't ya?" He half-chuckles. "But no, ya gotta offer help without a thought to people who treat us like we're a talkin' fungus growin' on a pile of dogshit."

"Yeah, yeah, yeah, put it on yer fuckin' Tumblr. Ya gonna gimme shit fer havin' a soul or help me out, huh? Whatcha got on the murder? The killer? Shit I can't find on Google." 'Cause I learned if ya ain't specific 'bout that, that's all yer payin' for.

"*Tumblr*? Fuck, Nick, ya ain't still on MySpace, are ya? I'll call ya back in thirty, Nick, 'less yer in a hurry." Meanin' I will get what he pulled off Google.

"Take yer time, Cous'. By end of business, yeah?" I hear a grumble on the line. Now he *has* to put in some effort or I can tell the family he fucked me over despite me givin' him plenty of time in good faith.

"Fine. End of business. Half a point. Leave my name outta this, 'less ya end up a big damned hero, yeah?"

"Got it." I sigh. "Thanks, Cous'. Love ya."

A grumbled response. "Love ya too, ya fuckin' *mamaluke*. Take care of you."

"Take care of you." Then he hangs up.

What? We're still fuckin' family.

I bring up my notes app and write in "Expense – 3rd party IT specialist", 'cause even though I do want to help this family and bring peace to a murdered woman, I also ain't a charity. I'm doin' this *gratis* until delivery of an intact item, not fuckin' *pro bono*. I've read books with supernatural detectives, and I noticed that not a one of 'em leaves a bill for services rendered. Save the city from a crazed necromancer raisin' zombies and skeletal demons, yes, absolutely, but have the fuckin' sense to collect yer goddamned hazard pay, y'know what I'm sayin'? I can walk the Shadow and curse machines and cloak myself and all that shit, but ain't none of that payin' my rent or groceries.

So, I plan to charge fifteen percent of the value recovered, or a per-diem plus expenses, whichever's higher. I do wanna help people, yes, but I ain't gonna devalue my skills, either. "Bein' a hero is its own reward" looks great on a coffee mug, but only works in practice if yer loaded.

While I'm waitin', I figure a trip up to Kirkland County Men's Prison is gonna be in order just in case I gotta talk to the guy, which'll probably be the case. At least this ain't gonna be like my other visits there, back when Pa was alive. It's usually an hour drive to get up there, longer if ya take the bus, and it's a max facility, no white-collar boys' club - unless they really fucked over the people who pull the strings there, and by that I mean the Sidhe.

Cruelty is their stock 'n trade, after all, and a place where you can have someone slit or put in solitary or wrapped up in iron chain with nothin' but a few phone calls is always handy to have a few fingers in.

Usually if the Queen wants someone dead for crimes against the kingdom, that's where they end up, no matter their title, and then if they happen fall on a shiv, ain't nobody saw nothin' and ya can say ya never intended for such a thing to happen. Her Majesty, after all, ain't in the business of bloody vendettas against hopeful usurpers.

Not when she got a Blackwarren there to pull the snicker-snack.

'Cause nobles always, *always* wanna see a head.

And Cousin Damon's pretty good at that. Fuck, I seen him do it, and promptly puked on his boots after.

Regardless, since I ain't goin' up there for a slit, 'cause I don't fuckin' do that, I still gotta work out a route, and a way I can get there and back without needin' an app or takin' the bus.

Yeah, yeah, buddy, I know, I'm killin' time.

Fuck it, I'll read.

Selection usually depends on my mood, but 'cause most of my shit's still in boxes, I gotta go with whatever I can dig out first, could be anythin', really.

Stop lookin' at me like that, a'right? Yeah, I sorta fudged my way into pickin' a romance novel. I like the reasonable assumption I'm getting' an HEA. (Happily Ever After, but if ya don't know that ya ain't never been on social media when someone talks shit about the genre. Ain't no one with half a fuckin' brain in their head dumb enough to fuck with Romancelandia.)

So, I'm readin' one where a too-cool-to-care vampire public defender runs afoul of a case that sets her against a prim-and-proper tough-as-nails ADA. They know each other way too well from the barbs they're firin' off. She hates her, she hates her back, fine line between, complication that the PD is a vampire, ADA's gotta wrestle with whether to use a forced confession, tension bubbles over, complication of ethics, physical danger, and the heart wants what it wants. Passes the fuck out of the Bechdel thirty times over, subtle subtext of fighting ableism, crucibles of female friendship, and then an HEA.

Yeah, the sex scenes are pretty good, too, at least, I think. Romances are easy to find and cheap as fuck at used book places, so ya grab what ya can grab when ya got some extra bucks to spare. I could read it in the tub, but that of course would be when Cenzo calls me back.

Instead, he calls at two minutes before five, literal end of business, so I ain't expectin' too much.

"Nicky, I uh…" I know that tone, it's the one he uses when he just dinged yer car or ain't got any cash to put up for the pizza he just ate four fuckin' slices of.

"Fuck, Cen, don't tell me ya fuckin' forgot." If I'm going to put a per diem on the invoice I gotta show I did *somethin'* other than make one phone call and read a book. "If ya ain't got nothin' ya can't have anything off my cut."

"Nick, would ya let me talk? Fuck, I'm tryin' to tell ya."

"With two minutes to close? Well, one now. Sure."

"Fuck you, Nick. I'm tryin' to tell ya I did what diggin' I could, and I'd just call yer clients and tell 'em it's a lost fuckin' cause and don't charge 'em nothin'."

"Shadow take me, Cen, just tell me what's goin' on, yeah?" I think this is what a stress headache feels like, buddy.

"I'm sayin'… Look, guy who went down for killin' yer girl, Bridget O'Hare? They got him dead to fuckin' rights, kay?" I start to interrupt. "No, I ain't found nothin' about the item. Just… drop this one, Nick. It don't feel right."

"Cousin, I got caught up in a triple murder, I think Lady Fate has given me enough 'don't feel right' for the year. Just gimme what ya got, yeah?" I'm sittin' up on my bed, the cheap sheets I picked up still not yet on it. "Lemme know what I'm walkin' into. What, it was some fucked up Cronenberg kinda shit?" I should learn, buddy, that ya don't fuckin' chuckle after sayin' shit like that.

'Cause Cenzo don't say a fuckin' word.

"Cen, tell me the poor woman wasn't the subject of shit that would make *giallo* flicks look *tame*?"

"Nick, I can't hardly find her *anywhere*. And it ain't like someone made her up, she got *scrubbed*. As far as human intel goes, she don't exist. Fuck, I can't even find her on social media, how can anybody do that nowadays 'less its ordered by a shrink… She ain't Keth now, is she?" A sorcerer, humans who can work magic, and when ya awaken as one, ain't nobody who knows ya, heard of ya, nothin' in the system. 'Cept…

"Nah, her parents remember her, otherwise they wouldn't be lookin' for her symphony. Why the fuck would somebody scrub her?" I take a breath, 'cause there could be lots of reasons.

I doubt she's a federal witness, because Cenzo could find that out, and he probably poked around a little. No social media, and it ain't like she didn't have anything if she was tryin' to get noticed for her work. So, to figure why she ain't got it, ya gotta ask yerself why she would.

I mean, c'mon buddy, it's right there in the name. *Social* media. Friends, family, pets, interests, hobbies, jobs, separate accounts for all of those, accounts just for close friends where ya can be yerself, the horny accounts for all the porn stuff ya follow... "Yer tellin' me they scrubbed *all* of it?"

"Far as I can tell, Cous'. I can't find hardly anythin'. All I got is a memorial post from her parents. I guess she was a nice girl. I wish I had more, it's fuckin' weird there ain't anything I can find." The Gremlin sounds exasperated, probably more for the fact he couldn't deliver than about the girl.

"How about the hard copy stuff?"

"...the what?"

I roll my eyes. "Written record? Typewritten? On actual paper or tape?"

"Ya tellin' me people still do that?"

"Fer fuck's sake, Cen! Ya didn't even look into the hard copy? Fuck, don't scare me like that, yeah? Can ya at least look up the killer's name? Where he was arrested? Where in Kirkland he's bein' held? And figure out a way for me to get a ride up there?" I'm rubbin' my temples, buddy, this is... This is whatcha get when ya call yer cousin a Luddite, Cenzo, fuck.

"I got Dieter Kirschbaum, incarcerated last Friday, he's assigned to uh..." I hear some tapping on keys. "D-block looks like. I can swing ya a ride-share if ya don't mind it bein' one way, but it's gotta be now 'fore the rollin' codes change."

I take a long breath. "Do it. And see if my ride can stop for burgers on the way."

"Whatcha gonna do, Nick? Not like ya can get in to see him, it's past visitin' hours." Cen sounds nervous, weird. "Ya ain't gonna do nothin' up there, right? Ya know who runs the place."

The Sidhe. I mentioned that. "I took the job, Cen, I made a promise. People gotta know us Goblins can be counted on fer *somethin'*, y'know?" I half-chortle. "But 'course then I'll probably get referred to as one of the fuckin' 'good ones'."

"Don't get me started, Cous'. Why ya think we never leave the fuckin' sewer?" I hear him pause, and we both know we could end up on rants for the next two hours. Cooler heads and all that shit. "I got some bad news, too."

"Fuckin' Shadow, Cen, *now* what?"

"I been checkin' into the UCPD's network while we been talkin'. Nothin' jumpin' out, yer right about the paperwork. Bad news is that I got Cousin Tina to fish around with some phone calls, phreak 'n spoof some three-letters to dig a little."

"Why's that bad news? Valentina's always been solid, she got that collection agency off my ass."

"It ain't Tina that's bad news, Nick, fuck. The records fer yer guy? And the reports and court papers and shit? She found 'em."

"Again, Cenzo, the fuck's the problem? Sounds like I should be callin' *Valentina* from now on."

"I'll tell ya when stop fuckin' interruptin' me, Nick! The shit's all gathered up and it's on the move."

I grit my teeth, gettin' ready to head out the door. "Fuck, so what, I'm hittin' a records storage? I can do that, ain't so much security on one of them buildings."

"No, Nick. It's goin' upstate. Like… locked up behind a lot of human security. And nowhere near the prison. Ya gotta tell me where to send yer ride. Prison? Or chase down the truck?"

The fuckin' things I do so some middle-aged white lady don't think I'm an asshole.

"Make sure it's a fast car, I'm gettin' on that truck."

7

I already regret this.

"There really wasn't anyone else who could gimme a fuckin' ride, Cen?"

In case yer curious, buddy, I'm standin' on a fuckin' street corner where a sex worker across the street is givin' me the stink-eye 'cause 'parently this is her spot.

"We live in the fuckin' sewers, Nick, ya really think any of us got a car?" 'Least he can hear my aggravation. "'Sides, ain't my fault yer fuckin' him."

"First, fuck you. Second, ya sent a fuckin' *cop* to pick me up. And third? Fuck you again." I call across the street. "I won't rat, but the one pickin' me up's a cop who got a bad case of white guilt, so ya might wanna make yerself scarce for a couple minutes."

I ain't got no clue how she took it, I'm too pissed that my ex turned sorta-ex turned I-don't-know-what-the-fuck's-goin'-on is gonna be pickin' me up to technically hijack a state vehicle. A member of the fuckin' *Guard*, at that.

Seriously, fuck me.

And, 'course Cen hung up on me. Well, fuck him, too.

That bein' said, said Guard has a beautiful BMW tourin' bike that I wouldn't mind bein' sat on even if I'm ridin' bitch. Trust me, buddy, she rides like a dream, and if I actually get paid for this gig then I'll look into buyin' one with a ridin' jacket, tailored, 'course, fer my five-foot frame.

But life don't work out like that, y'see, 'cause 'stead of that masterpiece of German engineerin' with a "come hither" engine rev, a black Jaguar pulls up instead. Funny, I don't remember him havin' one of these, but then again, if yer rich enough to refer to yerself as "comfortable" (I fuckin' hate that term) ya probably got a warehouse or some shit filled with exotics. Gets my Tinker blood rushin', no lie, the thought of all those engines and playin' with 'em, but my Redcap side drags me back on task.

When the window rolls down, it's Thom, as expected, he's smilin', my heart melts a little, and the *shunk* of the door unlockin' fills my ears. I get in, buckle up 'cause I ain't stupid. "Ya know where we're goin'?" I don't make eye contact, buddy, that way lies madness. And torn clothes.

"I was only told you needed a ride somewhere." I can feel him lookin' at me. "So where to? What's this all about?"

"Get on the 5R headin' north, and step on it. I'm on the clock. I'll get my cousin to drop a pin to make it easier." I take a breath. Really hard not to look at him. In case ya didn't know, like a lot of people, I'm a fuckin' sucker for a Celtic accent, and he sounds a little more Celtic every time I see him.

So, I'm covering a, uh, growin' issue, is what I'm sayin'.

Car's in motion, at least, and it's comfy as fuck. Smooth ride, too. Five liter V-8 engine, that thrum and cycle and shiftin', like a fuckin' lullaby for a Tinker like my Mom, and by extension, me.

"Are you going to tell me what this is all about, Nick?"

"I'm on a job. Asset retrieval. Client wants some papers returned that probably got lost in the shuffle, so I need to get to 'em before they go into storage and the access window closes." I stretch, nice thing about bein' so short is that any seat's got fuckin' good legroom.

"Nick, are you stealing something? I thought you were doing better." Disappointment in that tone.

"Thom? This is seriously my job. Asset retrieval. Client loses something, or something was stolen, and I get it back for 'em. It's a real, legal job. Even set up a business that's all filed up and everything." I finally do look at him. "So maybe cut the judginess, huh? Fuck, isn't this what you suggested I should be doin'? Or was that bullshit 'cause ya were usin' me to catch a murderer at the time?"

He sighs, himself. "I thought we were doing better, Nick. I thought we were okay. What's going on?"

"Thom, I almost died, dipped my cap, and it was only *three months ago*. Ya can't expect me to recover from trauma that fast, I ain't some social media executive." Off his look. "Y'know… The book where… I mean, it… Fuck, am I the only one who reads?"

"But I thought we could work through it together, there's clearly a lot you want to say to me, and it looks like it's going to be a drive, so go ahead. What do you want to say?"

"Thom, it ain't that I need to get stuff off my chest. Ya hurt me, okay? That takes time. 'Sides, again, what do ya care about it, yer gettin' married to some noblewoman, or nobleman. There some weird Phouka condition that ya can't get married if ya ain't resolved shit with your ex?"

We're finally moving onto the highway now. My phone gets a notification from Cen, and Thom's car punches it right into the GPS. This ain't goin' the way I expected, but I'm seein' the way I push aside wantin' to fuck him by bein' pissed at him. I ain't the type to fall for that tired cliché of two people screamin' at each other and then suddenly suckin' face and ready to bang it out right then and there. Pretty sure people don't actually do that.

"I love you, so I don't see why there's so many obstacles between you and me. I screwed up, I put you in danger, and I will always regret that, but will you ever find your way to forgiving me?" Fuck, he sounds like a kicked puppy, and I got a soul, Shadow take me.

"Eventually, Thom, yeah. Eventually. We ain't there, not yet. Can't just skip everythin' that needs to be worked through." I'm leanin' against the window, watchin' the world passin' by through the window. I get a flash of memory, of my doin' the same thing in July, when Cousin Damon gave me a ride home after the whole thing with the Redcap, when I found out that Thom was one of the Guard, and he'd been usin' me to catch the bad guy.

I ain't gotta remind ya, buddy, it sucked.

"So…" I know that tone too, means he wants to change the subject, and I agree. This ain't the shit I signed up for tonight. "The job, what's it about?"

"Parents came to me, distraught. Their daughter was murdered, and somethin' important to her was missin', so I offered my services. That's why we're chasin' down a box truck."

"Sounds like a good cause, Nick, but why go to you?"

"'Cause I live in the place were she was murdered, Thom. The apartment that 'just opened up'? *Murder house*. Thanks fer that, by the way."

"No, no, I mean, why not go to the Guard about it? If someone was killed and something was taken, there are a lot of avenues they could've taken in the Fae Court, even if they're not noble-"

"They're fuckin' human, Thom. The girl was human. The Guard, 'cept you, probably, wouldn't give a shit. As long as it weren't no Goblin, even Damon wouldn't get involved save wantin' names if Fae *were* connected." I close my eyes, "And 'fore ya ask, I ain't gonna deal with a pissed off ghost with unfinished business in my apartment, so I figure it'll clear some shit up for her. They caught the murderer, he's in jail, I'm just checkin' through the paperwork."

Granted, there's a lot more I'm lookin' into, seein' how hinky the whole thing's comin' off. I really should just leave it at findin' the sheet music and get the fuck out, but I got the same itch in my brain like I had when I was sleuthin' my way across the City over the summer. Somethin' ain't right, I gotta find out what really happened, get at the truth, and not just 'cause I read too many mysteries to not see this got a lot more angle than it seems. If those books taught me one thing, it's that nothin' is ever tied up with a pretty red bow.

"So, why'd ya even agree to help on this? Ain't as simple as Cen askin' ya 'cause you'd do it if I were involved, right? Please tell me that ain't the case, Thom, I'll lose all respect fer ya."

"That, or your clients called me checking your reference."

Okay, now I look at him. "So ya knew the whole fuckin' time and let me blunder through all that? Ya knew it was a human and ya still ask why I didn't go to the Guard?" Ah, fuck. "Ya *asked*. Fuck that petty honesty bullshit, seriously. I almost feel bad fer ya that ya can't lie. Too much convoluted fuckery just to have a Shadow-damned conversation."

Hold on, there's somethin' there I gotta tug at. Indulge me a bit, buddy, yeah?

"Okay, what ya told me at the diner, knowin' my middle name and favorite color and what I read and all that? How the fuck'd ya find all that out?"

"I told you that Goblins are rather loose-lipped when they think only a dog is listening." He says it so matter-of-factly.

"Yeah, I think that was true for some of it like my middle name, and it weren't the first time someone's given me a fuckin' dossier on myself. But there was shit that I don't talk about with people, like how I read the same manga every year." I sigh, shaking my head. "That bit…"

"What?" That look of a confused puppy. Everything he said wasn't wrong, it was all correct. Still…

"Thom, ya took a lot of the mystery about me out. There was stuff I didn't wanna share, or would rather decide when the other person knows. Ya just know that I read *Fruits Basket* every year, but ya even know why?"

Because the love interest is an outsider in his own family, doesn't quite fit in society, and pushes away anyone who tries to reach out and connect.

"Do ya know why I say *Beloved* is my favorite book, which it is?"

I'll be honest, buddy, I first picked it 'cause it won the Nobel Prize, but I fell in love with Morrison's prose. It's like yer brain takin' a warm bath at the end of a long, tough day. Complete and utter trust in the author telling the story, and that's a fuckin' rare treasure to find.

"I don't gotta read a book every year for it to be my favorite. That was… personal shit, Thom." And he wanted to impress me instead with a gesture.

The Phouk blinks a few times. "But, it shows how I know you, how there are so many things about you to love. I thought that was romantic. We know each other so well. I've told you about my life, what I've gone through, and how my life is brighter because you're in it. What did I do wrong? Have I hurt you? I'm sorry, I apologize."

"Thom…" My head's restin' against the window again. "Ya robbed yerself, okay? I-"

Ya ever want to just climb out a movin' car jump onto a box truck to get outta awkward conversations?

Nobody? Just me? Okay.

"Nick, what the hell are you doing?!" That's what ya expect to hear when ya roll down the passenger side window of a Jag that's doin' eighty-five on a two-lane highway, unbuckle yer seatbelt, and hold onto the roof of the car while ya start makin' yer way out.

"Hold it steady! I only got one fuckin' shot at this!"

"I'm not going to let you jump out of the car!"

Now, buddy, the Dog's not bein' an asshole when he starts rollin' up that fuckin' window. I am doin' something pretty crazy and gettin' back into the car is the saner idea.

But buddy? I got the Edge.

We ain't a hundred percent, yet, but if it wanna earn some goodie points, I need it to make this work. I gotta get in that truck, so I gotta shoot the hook into it, and it needs to reel me in *quick* so I don't get dragged along at speeds that'll scrape my skin off.

"Nick! Don't! You're going to kill yourself!" Again, he's probably right, and I am doin' this for an unknown amount and to satisfy my fuckin' conscience and misguided sense of justice and virtue. What can I say? Some of us Goblins are more human than the rest of us. Well, that ain't true, we can all be like this, but it would involve us doin' stupid shit like *this*. Ain't nothin' else to do but wuss out or take the shot.

Ah, fuck it.
Let's fire away, buddy.

8

Fuck, fuck, fuck, fuck, fuck!

Good news? I'm on the back of the truck, the hook is set, I'm still alive.

Bad news? Fuckin' doors are locked and my lockpick is what's keepin' me from flyin' off this truck at seventy miles an hour. Shadow take me, this might not've been the best idea.

Thom's got his Jag close enough to be danergous, and for me to hop over and get back inside. He looks like he's havin' a panic attack behind the wheel, and who the fuck could blame him after what I just did. But I can think about damage control, later, buddy. I gotta get inside this truck.

First, need to see what I'm workin' with. That involves lettin' out a little slack so I can sink along the rollup door down to the latch.

Human lock, thank fuck.

"Shadow shroud me from the light
My steps a whisper in the night
This one the sentries do not see
What ways are closed open to me"
Click.

Carefully, I lift the latch, rollin' the door up slow, the charm keepin' it quiet. There's enough of a gap in a few seconds, and Thom's got a white-knuckle grip on the steerin' wheel when I get my legs under, slidin' on my belly, right arm still raised, keeping on that hook.

Okay, buddy, hard part's over.

The hook compresses and reels in quick to the vambrace, the gap still open enough. I figure I can get what I need and slip out, and if I'm lucky enough get me back in Thom's Jag with nobody the wiser. I take out my phone, keep a firm grip with my left hand, shake it a couple times to turn on the flashlight, and...

There's a lot of fuckin' boxes and crates in here. And ain't one of 'em stamped with anythin' for the UCPD or one of the borough offices. There should be some of that, otherwise I went through all that action-movie bullshit to bust into a cargo truck I don't even gotta be in. There's a subtle scent of sandalwood, sage, some mint, I think. It don't smell like a truck fulla junk, is what I'm sayin'.

Most of these containers are big, too big for the simple stuff I'm lookin' for. I'm on the hunt for somethin' like a file crate, documents, shit like that. It ain't a warehouse, so it ain't like I gotta ransack the place, there's only so many boxes. I can narrow 'em down to two, but while I'm lookin' around, I start gettin' a bad feelin', buddy.

All of these containers are marked with fuckin' heraldry.

Nobles own this shit.

So why use a fuckin' City cargo truck to move it?

Well, if I wanted to rob a truck, I'd go after a bonded truck, somethin' that can slide easy through customs 'cause the decent loot is usually international. Failin' that, something where the driver and co-driver's doors got them little murder holes, 'cause then it needs armed security. This truck ain't neither of those, so I wouldn't look at it twice. If uh, I wanted to rob a truck, that is. What I'm doin' now don't count.

But that's why, probably. This thing was written up and in the fuckin' system as movin' documents up the Capital. But that don't mean that's what's really in here. As long as ya got *one* box of documents ya ain't really lyin', y'see? And that's where ya slip under the honesty bar, buddy.

So ya could, in theory, say yer movin' official documents, toss in a bunch of noble shit, and move it without anyone the wiser. Why'd anyone wanna move "noble shit"? 'Cause of people like me who'd steal it, duh. Fuck, try to keep up, buddy.

Priorities, though. This truck is movin' and eventually they gotta notice a Jag sittin' behind 'em. So, like I was sayin', the three containers. Two got the same house's emblem, a flute crossed with a sword against a red backdrop. Other's a green lion and bear above crossed axes.

I read a graphic novel once about how tools are the subtlest traps, and considerin' I left my regular picks at home 'cause I've gotten in the habit of plungin' my brain into a lock, I can see where it's a good lesson. Also, 'cause I tend to puke if I gotta shove my mind in a lock even if it's just a human one.

And fuck me, this one's porcelain. Fancy lookin' bolt lock, subtle Sigil that's easy enough to read as "fuck off, Greenskin", 'cause I'm hardly the only Goblin who steals from nobles. Heavy seal against charms, the kind that'll kill ya if ya try to pop the lock the Goblin way.

Fuckin' Knockers.

Considerin' the pleasin' scents, anybody would notice if I barfed on the floor, even if I only get pictures of the docs, and sorry buddy, but ya take it outta me, and I'd rather not risk my work gettin' fucked by nausea.

Still, all this means I'm onto somethin', at least. Fae are makin' sure ain't nobody checkin' their shit, yes, but ya ain't gonna be too surprised by how many nobles got fingers in City institutions. I can't bitch *too* much, they're the reason the UTA is free to residents, but my fuckin' bus pass ain't gettin'... me...

Fuck, Blackwarren, yer slippin'. Human problem, Fae solution. And vice fuckin' versa.

Ya see, people think they can jimmy a lock with a credit card based on pretty dated TV shows and movies. That shit don't work in real life, not really. Not fer a door. A box that, without all the Sigil and heraldry, is just a fuckin' box? Well, then, it's just about touch, buddy.

I gotta close my eyes, block shit out, work the problem. The card slips in, 'cause it ain't like it's hermetically sealed or anythin', that's what the charms are for. Ya'd think they'd prep against low tech, but Knockers are vain, and I gotta be honest, so're my Mom's family. Goblin charms against Knocker ingenuity. What I'm doin' would be considered cheap as fuck, somethin' a *human* would do.

"Shoulda put yer own bolt n' spring in ya haughty fuck..."

Keep pressure on the bolt… Pull the lid slow…

And that, buddy, is how ya bust a fuckin' Knocker lock.

Why the fuck's the truck slowin' down?

Alright, gotta pull the rip cord on this. I don't see much in there, a thick file, a few metal jars. Better just grab the file, it's time to… Aw fuck, we're stoppin'. I look through the gap and we're on the side of the highway. I can see Thom still in his car, and he's mouthin' somethin'. Looks like…

Hide.

Shit.

I pull the door down, lookin' for somewhere. Anywhere. Need a gap or tall stack of boxes I can hide behind or somethin'. Fuck, fuck, fuck. Maybe behind the bigger boxes. There's a plastic tub with no lock on it, looks pretty opaque, so that'll work. Hopefully it ain't too full up-

Empty? Fuck it, I ain't gonna ask. I climb in, into a box like a fuckin' coffin flush against the truck's cargo door, close the lid. I am so, so, so fucked. This was such a dumb fuckin' idea, buddy. What the fuck was I thinkin'?!

"Guardsman! We did not request formal escort." That's outside, muffled through the box, and the truck, but, y'know, big ears and everythin'. Ain't hard to tell it's a noble's servant, who's probably carryin' his master's authority, 'cause ya don't usually talk to one of the Guard like that. Then again, Sidhe are all Karens to the fuckin' Nth degree.

"Can I see your formal heraldry, sir? And your clearance to travel through three different baronies that aren't branded on your vehicle?" A couple of seconds pass. "And it's *Constable*."

Haven't seen him in action like this before, even if it's a traffic stop.

"On whose behalf have you detained us?" It come off a lot angrier than it sounded, trust me.

"Under the bylaws set by Captain Damon Blackwarren, enacted by Queen Alana the Seventh-"

"May her warmth bless us all," we all say, though I say it real quiet 'cause I ain't a fuckin' idiot.

"I may detain you for up to twenty-four hours if you prove uncooperative. Are you planning to be uncooperative, sir?"

Okay, I see what he's doin'. He's distractin' 'em so I can slip out and get back in his car. Good fuckin' plan, now I just have to get out of the box and make my way to the gate to get out and-

"Run along home, Dog, this is not your affair."

Fuck, it ain't even directed at me and I can feel the weight of his authority pressin' on my chest like a bear takin' a nap. I'm havin' trouble breathin', fuck.

"I... You..." I can hear the strain in his voice, he's fightin' it hard, but bein' Fae means ya can't say no to someone high up the ladder, and this voice is on par with one of the Princes. I mean, I know the Crown Prince has been raisin' stress at Court, which I only 'cause it's so major in our world, but what the fuck's the Crown Prince got to do with a dead human pianist?

Still, I wanna believe Thom can stand strong. He's son of the First Phouka, that's gotta count fer somethin'.

"Y-yes, sir," comes next, like he just got punched in the gut.

Aw, fuck.

I hear a car door close. Then an engine. Fuck.

"Check the package, make sure the Dog didn't slip anything in." Same voice, same heavy tone.

"Yes, my lord." Gruff voice. Driver, I'm guessin', but I take the time to keep still. Ya know what I gotta do, buddy, this gets bad if I get found. Probably a Troll.

I hear the bar in the middle of the vambrace raise, spin, the sight popping up, the light pain of it drawin' blood to form the darts that'll knock a guy out. I spent 'em all at the bank, so need to "reload". Just need one, at least.

The sound of the door bein' slid upward, heavy steps. Yep, Troll. I hear him liftin' boxes, crates, openin' things. Not mine yet, thank Shadow.

"A parcel's been opened, sir!" There's concern. "Heraldry for-"

"Is it *mine*?"

"No sir!"

"Then close it and continue your search! Make certain the Dog didn't sully my goods, servant!"

"Of course, sir." I do catch a sigh there. Trolls can be mean, yeah, but it don't mean they like bein' under a noble's thumb like anyone else. The searchin' sounds are faster now, he's in a hurry. Closer to the back, though, so where I am ain't what he's lookin' for.

"Sir! I believe I've found it. Would you confirm that nothing is missing, my lord? You would know better than I." He is right fuckin' next to me, buddy. I hold my breath.

A moment passes, and I hear steps, lighter, probably the Sidhe. "Yes, everything appears to be in order. The Dog will only have to be disciplined for delaying me, it seems. Come along. I must keep my appointment."

"Of course, sir."

Thank fuck, I might actually get outta this. Sometimes the Shadow's got yer back, y'know?

There's a hard *thunk* as something is put down. Above me. I hear the slide of the door being closed, latches being closed and locked. "Damned Phouk. A proper lock will do for now."

Sounds of heavy steps heading toward the driver's side of the truck. Then a loud engine. I push upward and...

Fuck, that's heavy, and I literally ain't in a position to get the leverage I need. Not to mention by a "proper lock" I know he means one made by a Knocker. And the lock's outside.

And me trapped in a container that only got so much air, with a weight atop it, and a Sidhe Prince and his Troll bodyguard drivin' Shadow knows where, and my backup was ordered to drive back to the City.

Seriously, buddy.

Fuck. Me.

9

Okay, so let's review the options, buddy, 'cause I ain't got no one else to bounce ideas off. Always start with takin' stock of what ya got.

I got you, buddy, duh. Also got my wallet and phone, clothes, the file I lifted from the box that weren't noticed by the Troll, left my hat at home. I usually do, you know why, buddy, 'cause of the blood. Ya think I'd just get rid of it, but a Redcap don't get rid of his, well, red cap. It's the sign ya've dipped, taken a life, that yer to be taken seriously. Also, bein' a Blackwarren means I gotta fuckin' wear it when the family (my Pa's family, mind ya) meets up, which is rare, but when they do, ya wear the cap ya dipped, which, thanks to our bloodline, means it'll be as fresh and red as the day it got dragged through the blood of the one you murdered.

Even if it was self-defense, buddy.

A'right. Work the problem, Blackwarren. Ya got this. Ya got somethin' that can bring ya through. Ya got a fuckin' smartphone.

I unlock it, and it's awkward and hurts my arm and neck to see it, but if there's one thing anyone under thirty's learned, it's how to text with one hand. I got a couple bars, thank Shadow, and I know why who to text.

911

Damon 911

911!!!

Takes a bit, but I finally get a response.

where r u

dunno ask thom

y

thom left

wut

I grumble.

in truck trapped in box Troll + noble

No response, but the phone starts buzzin'. I swipe up and keep hushed.

"Nicky, what the fuck is goin' on?! He fuckin' *left ya* there?!"

"Keep it down, Damon? He was ordered to. Think they're with the Prince."

I hear an aggravated sigh. "Fuck, Nicky, what did ya get yerself into?"

"Get me outta here and I tell ya everythin'."

"Nicky, I ain't got no clue where ya are. It ain't like there's some mystical connection 'tween Goblins. Where *were* ya? Remember a mile marker, anythin' like that?"

"Thom might, but ya gotta wait for him to finish his single-minded drive back to the City. Noble authority really fucks ya up, don't it?" Yeah, I ain't mad at him. I mean, I'm a little peeved, yeah, because I was about to tell him that this thing between us ain't gonna work.

Don't look at me like that, buddy. Be fuckin' realistic. The Queen's told him to get married, I had a crush, and Thom and I fucked a lot. That's the fuckin' extent of our connection. Shit don't work like that, y'know, like two people meet and they're ready to defy the odds and fate and make it through on that *amor vincit omnia* bullshit. Yeah, it's romantic as fuck and why I read all the romance novels I do, but ya can't expect that in reality.

And now it's only gonna be more awkward.

"You in danger?" Heavier there. "If they're workin' for the Crown Prince, Nicky, I..." I can feel the pain in his voice.

"Ya can't do nothin', can ya?"

"He's my Lady's son, Nicky. I can't raise a fuckin' finger against him. Can't even cut in line ahead of him for the fuckin' men's room." Bein' the Left Hand of the Queen gives ya a lot of power, but I'm sure his chest's a fuckin' tapestry of oaths and bindin' seals. I still don't get why anyone'd do that to themselves.

"If I get loose, and get clear, then can I call ya?"

A sigh, don't know if it's relieved, or acceptin'. "Yeah. I'll have someone on standby to go, but that's the best I can do Nicky."

"I understand, Damon. Take care of you."

"Take care of you, Nicky."

Call ends after that. Ya might think, "Nick, just have him trace yer phone!" Trust me, if there's Knocker shit on this truck and it's movin' on the business of the Prince, it got wards to make sure it can't get located unless yer literally followin' it with yer own two eyes. Cenzo only found it 'cause it drove by traffic cams.

Another test of the weight on the bin I'm in. No luck. Okay, simple stuff is out.

Charms? I can hide and stay quiet. That don't help me in the situation unless they open the bin, and even then, it don't hold up well under direct attention. Curse the machine I'm in? I'll cause an accident, possibly die, and set off fuck knows how many Knocker alarms. I don't wanna die, so that's out.

Walkin' Shadow? I either gotta have a gate set up somewhere or see where I'm tryin' to Walk to. Latter's out, and the former I ain't done either 'cause it's a fuckin' involved process that requires bloodwritin' and let's face it, buddy, vambrace is the one takin' most of that.

Speakin', er, thinkin' of that, buddy, a grapplin' hook got me in here, but it ain't gonna get me out. The bin ain't locked, so I don't need the lockpick. The darts are loaded, but I ain't got nothin' to shoot yet. I mean, there's the shield, but that ain't gonna…

Wait.

Wait, wait, wait, wait, wait.

Okay, I gotta get on my side, make room, make sure I'm facin' away from the truck's wall. It's a little noisy, and I ain't gonna lie, painful. I press the vambrace against the side of the bin, scrunch myself as much as I can. Okay…

Gimme a shield.

SHUNK

I don't feel a rush of air, the bin wasn't sealed or anythin', but I still feel the cooler air comin' in. I worm the fingers from my left hand into the gap, and my muscles and bones are lettin' me know that a body shouldn't be tryin' to lift weight in this position. But I don't gotta get it open, buddy.

I just gotta widen the gap enough to see through.

"Shadow take me
Shadow shroud me
Shadow guide me
Shadow guard me"

Best way I can describe Walking the Shadow is this: y'know them crazy fucks who strip naked and jump in the ocean in the dead of winter? Imagine they didn't get the benefit of goin' numb. Now add in that all of that through an intense fuck-yer-mother kinda cold, ya drop out of the darkness and gotta land without knockin' anythin' over or makin' noise.

So, add landin' in a center split onto that and you'll get an idea of the silent fuckin' agony I'm goin' through. It's a good thing Redcaps got strong jaws, otherwise I'd be clenchin' my teeth so hard I'd snap every bone in my face.

Slow breathin', clear yer head, pain is an illusion, fear's the mind-killer and all that bullshit. Run through the lyrics of one of the many songs where a car's a metaphor for sex. Still stuck in the truck, but at least I can find a better place to hide.

Also? *Fuck* this guy, I'm stealin' some of his shit.

I get to my feet, my muscles crampin' bad seein' as I went from fetal position to makin' my legs a continuous straight line. Usually, I at least have time to stretch first.

Okay, so the nice shit was in the back, 'parently. I shake my phone again, get the light on, and step light to the rear. Truck's still movin', but I don't know how long, so I gotta move fast. I know I'm gettin' greedy, buddy, but this is my middle finger to the fuckin' establishment, kay? I'll grab a little bauble and work out how to move it later.

It ain't hard to pick the crate, it's the one with the royal crest on it, and I know this means I'm stealin' from the royal family and if I get caught my family's in trouble. But I'd like to add that I'm pissed off and annoyed and that mindset don't exactly make fer the smartest decisions, buddy. I mean, look at where I am right now. This was s'posed to be a simple in-and-out, photo some papers, and slip away easy as breathin'. 'Stead I'm stuck in a royal goods transfer, and if my Mom taught me anythin'?

Always hit the best loot in transfer.

First? A charm to awaken Brother Gremlin's vision and then-

Holy *fuck*, that's a lot of seals and Sigil.

There's a few, and all of 'em look temptin', trust me, but I gotta go with what feels right. The thick heavy cube with what looks like nine locks and multiple curses that was on top of me? I'll bet some nice shit's in there, but it'd probably take like, an hour to crack, and I ain't got that time to gamble with Fate. The tall one? Plenty too, but the shape suggests armor, and that ain't the type for an easy grab.

Smaller, rectangular one, not too thick, about three feet wide, eighteen inches long, 'bout a foot deep. There's a dense lookin' lock, but that's it. It's top-tier Knocker shit, no lie, but buddy? I am ready to push my luck and take a crack at it.

It don't matter how many times I've done this, it fucks with my head when I go into a lock. First the darkness, then the forms come out into view. A simple one I did once was just a wooden model of the lock's innards with the key phrase carved deep inside. This… is different.

This ain't wood, it's steel, movin' and turnin' and twistin' and spinnin' and cuttin' the air. Shreddin' saws, spikes jabbin', reflections dancin' and confusin', and this is for just *one* fuckin' lock. I wish I could say I'm smart enough to pull back out, buddy, I really do. But this is high-end Knocker masterwork, and my Tinker blood's *boilin'*.

'Cause this fuckin' lock reminds me of my mother's mother's work. Fuckin' Knockers can't even come up with an original fuckin' idea. Granted, it's a lot *prettier* than the locks my *nonna* built, shinier, and the "fuck you" of all the false leads and pins and failsafes ain't as subtle as we do it (not that we *couldn't* do it, mind ya), but if they really lifted one of my family's designs, well, there's an easy way to tell.

I grew up a Tinker, it's where I got my love not just for technology, but *human* technology. Million ways to build the same fuckin' thing, with the same number of problems, and the same number of similarities.

I'm goin' somewhere with this, don't worry.

I mighta told ya that my Pa's family is a mix of Briton, Scottish, Cornish, and some Saxon. My Mom's? Sicilian. *Nonna* was the first of the Volpes to come over and learn how shitty Americans were, and still kinda are, to Sicilians and Italians. She weren't the first one to take up the "work twice as hard and wait twice as long to get half as far" shit, but she threw herself into factory work, garage work, junkyards, anythin' to put food on the table and put shit together and just invent, chase that all-too-human urge to create. Yeah, I know, makes ya wanna sing the national fuckin' anthem.

So where'm I goin' with this? She wanted to build American technology, American machines, American contraptions, all goin' 'cordin' to American philosophies of engineerin'. When she built a lock, the fuckin' thing was like a vault, but it was still American technology, and there's one definitive quirk of the tech built here in the good ol' U.S.A.

I run my fingers along the case, just above the lock, and give the spot a hard whack with my fist.

The lock pops with a small *fzzt!*

I fuckin' love ya, humanity, don't ever fuckin' change.

Openin' the box, though…

Buddy, I think I just stepped in somethin' I shouldn't be a part of. Like, when ya read a book where the adventurer or tomb raider or somethin' delves into an area the locals told him to stay the fuck away from? Kind that has a heavy stone door with countless lines of etchin' tellin' ya to fuck right off 'less ya want yer whole family to be cursed and bring catastrophe upon yer people?

That's what I'm gettin' off the contents of this box.

This is a royal treasure. From the royal armory.

Two lengths of metal. Ain't steel, ain't iron, ain't Faesteel (steel made without iron). I don't know what it is, but I see Sigil or somethin' like it. A lot of it. The dialect ain't modern, it's old. Like, not from this world or the one before it and probably not the one before it, meaning this thing is that old. Every part of my brain is tellin' me to slam this box shut, find a place to hide, and convince myself that I didn't see *nothin'*.

My body's got other ideas, though. My right hand's already on them, fingers curling around the metal, pulling them free.

Once my hand's retrieved them, they slip free, snap together into a five-foot length, curling, literally bowing, a soft light pulling the top and bottom together. A longbow, at least for someone my size. Recurve or shortbow for someone taller, like a Sidhe, like the Royal Family which is chock full of deadeye archers. I do know one thing, buddy.

This thing has to come apart so it can go back in its fuckin' box.

Obviously, it don't fit all together, and no amount of tuggin' and pullin' and tryin' to snap it apart works. Uh... Maybe Sigil will work?

"Come apart?" Nothin' "Uh, *disassemble?"* Fuck. *"Return to your case."*

Shit, shit, shit. Okay, despite the filigree and etchin' and scenes of natural beauty, this might be a military bow? What would a haughty blueblood royal tell a military bow...

"Stand at ease?" Nope. What else do they say... Wait! *"You are dismissed."*

There we go! Already comin' apart and uh... Coming apart and then it's s'posed to go in the box. Any minute. No, not laying against my hand.

Why is the vambrace sendin' out the lockpick tendrils? Don't do that. That ain't a fuckin' lock, just keep yer eldritch mitts off the damned-

Darkness. Cold. So fuckin' cold.

It is sleeping fitfully. It may awaken.

That wasn't me. Who is that? I try to answer but ain't no words comin' out.

Be at ease. It still follows the thread.

The fuck they talkin' 'bout? Sounds like a younger woman and a slightly older one.

I fear it will wake her. An even older woman. *But my children will slit the thread.*

Wait, *slit*?! I'm gonna get slit?! This is bullshit! No. Nope. No way. I'm not gonna die. I got shit to do and 'bout fifty books in my to-be-read pile. That's a reason to keep livin' all on its own. I don't wanna die. And for what, 'cause my magic sword vambrace multi-tool thing had to grope an ancient bow?

"It's mine." I didn't say that. I mean... I *did*. But I didn't say it, say it.

"This is mine." My throat hurts.

I don't know who the fuck I'm talkin' to.

"The Aeolian Shear is MINE." The what?

"Aw fuck, I'm gonna..."

So, I snap outta this soon enough to barf in the case where the Shear used to be and why the fuck am I callin' my bow that? No, it's not my- 'Course I call it that, that's what I named the fuckin' thing. 'Kay, this is etting' a little concernin'. I look down at it, chuckling.

"Fuck, I ain't got no fuckin' clue what's... goin'..."

Okay, so the uh, vambrace is gone, and I'm holdin' a collapsed bow with gears and clockwork and three sapphires above the grip. "Uh, buddy? Are ya in there?" I smile nervously. "Ya do know I ain't got no fuckin' clue how to use a bow, right?"

I mean, I don't got nothin' to worry about, he knows how the Shear works and he'll help me out and *where the fuck did that thought come from?*

Okay, I'm... confused and a little freaked out. This is the price ya pay fer gettin' greedy, Blackwarren, yer brain gets fucked and ya get convinced that yer soul is bonded to a magic bow from the World of Nightmare's Birth-

The *what*?

Wait... What the fuck?

Aw, shit. Of fuckin' *course* the fuckin' truck is slowin' the fuck down, now!

Buddy, I just wanted to lift some paperwork. That's it. This is why ya stick to the fuckin' plan. I'll figure it out later, I gotta hide.

It bears repeatin', buddy.

Fuck. Me.

10

Okay, okay. First, put the case for the bow back 'cause I don't think I could put the Shear down if I tried. Simple enough, let's pray they don't open it 'cause I don't want a repeat of what happened at the bank. Next, I need a way to hide the bow, or at least make it so I can hide with it without everyone seein' it's majestic clockwork opus of Goblin engineerin' and-

Fer fuck's sake, Blackwarren, just hide the damned thing!

SHUNK-SHUNK-SHUNK-SHUNK!

So, uh, now my whole fuckin' arm's covered in armor and I got a shoulder plate and somethin' 'round my neck! Fingers can move, elbow bends… Can circle my arm, the thing on my neck is snug, not tight. So, yeah, great. They'll find a Goblin with royal treasure and important documents stuffed in his hoodie sleeve.

No, Blackwarren, don't start doin' that. This is a problem. Work the problem. I check my phone, it's after sunset, and now that the truck's stopped, I can hear rain. No idea where the fuck I am, but if it's dark and rainy, I might have a chance. Just gotta kill the lights and hide in the dark places.

"Shadow, shroud me from the light

Silence, Shadow, is my right

Know me, Shadow, hear my call

Shadow catch me when I fall"

It's cold, but I can feel the darkness more concentrated around me, like a weighted blanket, comfortin', but makin' ya aware of its weight every second. Though my breathin' is silent, I hold it anyway as the door leading out of the truck slides open.

"Sir, the light went out inside." The Troll is standin' there, unsure of the truck's complete contents, probably. But c'mon, ya checked, and then started the truck up and locked it all nice and Knocker special, didn't ya? Ain't no one able to break in while the truck's, movin', and ya scared off the Phouk, right?

"Then use my phone! Why else would I carry such a uselessly human trinket?" The Sidhe enters view, and fuck, yeah, that's the Crown Prince.

More formally, Prince Hadryn II, eldest (still living) son of Queen Alana VII (may Her warmth bless us all), crowned heir to the throne of the Kingdom of Rainbows. (Seriously, when we showed up in America, there was a rainbow. Sidhe ain't always original, y'know?) Touch over six feet, cut, lithe, athletic build, impeccably dressed in a three-piece suit in the royal colors of red, orange, and fire yellow that he makes look like finery. Long flowin' ebon hair, pale skin, dark eyes like coal, thin chinstrap beard and goatee. I ain't gonna lie, he can fuckin' get it, okay?

Still a fuckin' asshole, though.

But if that Troll uses his flashlight and sees an impenetrable wall of Shadow, then…

"Brother Gremlin, hear my plea
Carry words 'cross Shadow's Sea
Bring your curse across the span
Break the vain machine of man"

Hopin' the shroud muffled that enough, but if there's a complex bit of technology a Gremlin curse was made fer, it's a fuckin' smartphone.

Fzzzt! Pop! Crack!

That is the sound of a phone shortin' out, overheatin', and the rapid change in temperature breakin' the screen. Have fun at the Apple store, ya prick.

First, the Troll curses, and then starts apologizin' fer usin' "such coarse, undignified language." I mean, shit, I use coarser language than that just takin' a piss fer fuck's sake. But while the Troll's frantically runnin' to get the first aid kit outta the cab, and His Highness is wincing from a phone almost blowin' up in his hand, I move quick quiet outta the truck, into the air, and break for hidin' spot behind a car so I can figure out where the fuck I am.

Parkin' lot, asphalt, brutally bright lights, high fence behind me. Okay, startin' to get an idea. The light inside of the truck's cargo bay flickers back on, revealin' everythin' is where they left it. Well, 'cept for the royal bow that I'm 'parently wearin' now. The Troll returns quick, and the first aid is, uh, an apple.

Lemme give ya the quick 'n dirty, buddy. Fae are made from dreams, and that means they can subsist on 'em. Y'know the old warnin' to never eat any of the Fae's food or drink? Imagine that apple is the perfect apple, right amount of sweetness, crunch, taste, everythin', not like the apples on my little tree. Those are real apples. *That* apple isn't real, it was taken likely from a seminary student's dreams about the Garden of Eden. Fae, 'specially Sidhe, can eat dreamfood, and it heals 'em up fast. On the same page? Great, 'cause I think I know where I am.

The signage, the brick, the distant lights, fenced in areas, lack of a lotta windows. I know it, I been here before.

When I was visitin' Pa.

I'm at Kirkville County Prison, where Bridget's killer is servin' a life sentence.

11

Now, I could be askin' the simple question of why the actual fuck the Crown Prince of the Fae is at the loading dock of a fuckin' prison, but I just stole what's likely a legendary magical bow from him and he's gonna notice when he opens the case and finds Goblin vomit instead of one of the rarest of the rare. I mean, fuck, buddy, it's not like I was lookin' to pick up another magical weapon!

So, instead, while they're unloadin' the, uh, empty bin I was inside, I can beat fuckin' feet and find a way to the road or in front. Only thing I can say is that whatever's happenin', it probably ain't anything good if Prince Hadryn's involved.

I should probably explain, huh? While Queen Alana (may her warmth bless us all) is more… tolerant of Fae who ain't Sidhe, and even elevated one of us Goblin's to her royal guard (it just means they're her hit squad, buddy, but at least they get some recognition for it, so, uh, yay progress?), there are three Princes who have different views.

Prince Boreas, her kid with the last King of the Winter Court (who she put down in an attempted usurpation), has the position of blendin' in with the fuckin' wallpaper so he don't end up like his dad. Prince Richard Firemane, better known to us commoners as Dick Stone of the *Ass Commando* series of gay porn, is the more progressive, pushin' for Twin Blood rights and relaxin' kith restrictions (like, say, a Brownie could be a Knight and a Troll could be a butler for a noble house, fer instance). Obviously, polite Sidhe society hates his fuckin' guts.

And then there's Prince Hadryn, the son who's supposed to eventually become King, but the Queen has deigned to not step down despite her reign lastin' four decades longer than expected. He's the type who'll read uppity snootyfuck "studies" that only got the barest shreds of evidence to make ya think, "I mean, I guess?" Y'know, like a wellness and weight loss program. And he amplifies 'em by givin' 'em a platform like he got a syndicated talk show to spoon-feed it to gullible idiots. Oh, and he mostly uses it to justify pretty racist beliefs. Pretty sure he's got a signed copy of *The Bell Curve* somewhere.

So, what I'm gettin' at is critical thinkin' is a vital fuckin' skill so stay the fuck in school, kids. Thanks fer attendin' my Shadow-damned G.O.B. Talk.

Anyway, he's a fuckin' prick. That's all ya need to know, buddy.

Gives me time to slip away, trudge over to the main entrance of the prison, text Damon *"@Kirkland visitor entr"* and put my hood up 'cause I mighta mentioned that it's fuckin' rainin' and the doors to the visitor section are locked up.

Phone starts buzzin', I swipe up.

"Ya safe, Nicky?" Damon is grumblin'.

"Yeah, I'm clear." I take a breath, "You okay?"

"Nicky, I got so much shit to handle now. 'Parently someone tried to jack the Crown Prince so I got 'bout a hundred fires this shit just started, I ain't got a lot I could do fer ya." I hear him sigh. "Whatcha need, anyway?"

Oh. Fuck. Word travels pretty fuckin' fast, I only got away a few minutes ago. "Uh, he okay?"

"Yeah, but he's bitchin' about how someone tried to assassinate him 'cause his phone bricked and overheated, so I got that on my plate. Whatcha need, Nick?" His voice is heavy, stressed.

"Uh… a ride home from Kirkland? Maybe some intel on the killer, Dieter Kirschbaum? I'm guessin' he was Fae since yer freakin' out this much?"

"Nicky, I just told ya I gotta handle a hundred things right now. What'd I tell ya my job is, huh?"

I sigh, defeated. "…twenty-four—seven."

"Twenty-four motherfuckin' seven, Nicky. And ya want me to drop everythin' and pick ya up over an hour away?" If I tell him the Crown Prince is here, I'll have to explain how I know that, and then it's family loyalty against fuck knows how many oaths he's tied up in. I hear some cursin' that I ain't gonna translate fer the sake of both of us. "Wait there. I'll make a call and get someone out to ya. Don't call the Phouk, I got him busy with shit work. He's still payin' off that fuckin' stunt he pulled."

When Thom lured a murderin' Redcap, who slit five people, with a confession I recorded. Also, with me as the cherry on top of the lure. Obviously, I lived through it, but if yer wonderin' why I ain't hoppin' into his arms, buddy, despite the world-shakin' sex, there's a reminder fer ya.

"Well, who are ya sendin' out, then?" Nothin'. "Cous'?"

I look down at my phone. "Fucker hung up on me."

Oh, and 'cause the day's been shit so far, of fuckin' course it starts fuckin' rainin' harder, and in the fall that just makes it cold enough to pull my fuckin' balls into my goddamn throat. Hood's up, and I can't exactly wait inside the prison, so I start the walk back to the main entrance of the complex where the buses usually pick up and drop off. If omethin', it'll kill time, and I can't expect my ride to know which block I was at when I called. Gives me time to think, regardless, y'know?

So, since I'm makin' lots of bad decisions, I call Thom.

What? I gotta make sure he's not dead or drivin' to Canada or omethin' under compulsion.

"Nick! You're alive!" I've never heard anyone so happy. "Are you okay?"

"Yeah, I'm fine." I edit a *lot* out, 'cause I ain't got no clue how to explain half the shit that just went down. "Hey, ya still got connects with law enforcement, right? Could ya look up Dieter Kirschbaum? He's the one who killed my client's daughter-"

"I know, your clients told me. I'd come get you but even trying to walk to the elevator hurts." First time he got commanded that hard, I'm guessin'. "I did find out about your guy, though."

"Hit me." Fresh info, thank fuck. I can always hitch to a motel and visit tomorrow to get some truth outta the guy.

"He's dead. I found out when I got back. One of the guards let me know he was attacked before he was put in his cell for the night. No witnesses, no video, no testimony from guards." I can hear that aggravation, and yeah, it's shitty, but ya don't really find justice in a jailhouse, and ain't nobody gonna rat unless they wanna end up the same. Still.

"Fuck. Don't suppose he had sheet music in his personal effects?"

"Nick, a man was murdered!" His shock is almost adorable.

"Thom, a murderer who killed a pretty young white girl got shivved, ain't nobody gonna go down fer that. What fuckin' sucks is the information that died with him." I rub my face with my right hand, rain splatterin' the armor. "Thom, this is part of my life, and will probably keep bein' part of it, just so ya know."

"Nick… How can you want a life like this?" Fuck. There it is.

"Thom, you… You don't really know me, do ya?" I sigh. "This life ain't some kinda *choice* I made, it's who I *am*. And if ya can't see that, or more important, like me for it, then maybe we ain't…"

Fuck, Blackwarren, rip the fuckin' bandage off.

"Maybe this ain't gonna work for us."

I hang up. Turn off the phone. Everythin' is happenin' too fast, too much. I know I shoulda heard him out, made a clean break, let him say his piece, and that makes me kind of a shitty person. I mean, he stepped up for me, I get that, but he's still thinkin' this is omething' I have to do before I step outta the life and forge omething' new with him. I shouldn't have to defend what I wanna do with my life, right, buddy?

I'm actually glad ya don't talk back. Same with the new "guy" on the rest of my arm. Okay. I can check the file when it ain't rainin' and wait fer the ride Damon sent.

So, in the meantime, let's take a look at the pieces, such as they are. I got the center of it, Bridget O'Hare, because she's the focus, not the fuck who killed her. Next, I got, well, the fuck who killed her. Probably a Fae but I want confirmation which I can get from askin' Cenzo or just pokin' around to see if this guy acted alone, and then it's just about motive, or if he was actin' on someone's behalf. Either makes this harder, but "harder" ain't a factor. Can't exactly beg out for 'something' like this. After all, I gave my word to her mom. And I ain't worried about what Father Redcap would do if I fail, I'm worried about what my mom would do to me if she knew I blew off a grievin' mother.

I ain't familiar with nobility, at least the hundreds of names for noble houses and bloodlines and offshoots and shit, so I got no clue if Kirschbaum was a blueblood or a servant, but that can be answered by simply findin' out which kith the killer was. If he was someone's cutthroat, I'm surprised they didn't just hire a Redcap, but then again, it was slittin' a human. Damon's made sure we don't do that no more.

Plus, the whole kingdom knows ya don't kill a human, even if the Cobalt Order still does it when they find out someone had a Twin Blood (or "tainted dream", as the Cobalts call 'em) and they kill the kid and the parent, or both parents. They're bigoted fuckers, so I wouldn't put it past 'em.

Was Bridget pregnant? I'm thinkin' no, seems like somethin' her parents would notice as I got the vibe that she was at least close with her mom. And if yer killin' a human mother of a Twin Blood, why make off with a symphony of all things?

That's what my head keeps catchin' on. A symphony can be beautiful, life-definin', precious… To her. Why kill her? Sheet music would be a fucked-up motive, it was probably an afterthought to grab it. Maybe some of the killer's blood splashed on it and could be used to identify? That would be feasible, but feasible ain't shit 'til ya got evidence. If Thom taught me anythin' over the summer, it's that ya gotta look at every angle like a prosecutor droolin' for a guilty verdict (and a couple of 'em do, I hear). And without evidence yer just blowin' smoke out yer ass.

I gotta find out what the motive for takin' the sheet music was, either literal, or a thumb drive, so I got an idea how to find it. As far as the law, human law anyway, is concerned, Bridget O'Hare was murdered by Dieter Kirschbaum, who was murdered today by an unknown assailant in Kirkland Men's Prison. Ain't no reason to go further, case closed.

But not for me. I gotta push forward. For her.

As soon as I get into some dry clothes 'cause *fuck* I'm drenched.

Also, it sucks to stand out in the rain when it's cold because a shitty part about bein' a Goblin (yeah, yeah, yeah, like there weren't already enough), is that we're not just human enough to swap blood and organs, we're close enough that we can catch colds and the flu, too. And trust me, buddy, with a nose like mine, I go through a box of tissues like a teenager whose parents are gone for the weekend and has his brother's OnlyFans login. Reason I'm sayin' this is I know I'm gonna get sick if I'm out here too much longer.

I see the headlights before the car, and since I seen a lot of headlights over the last hour, I don't think too much of it, thinkin' someone's gettin' picked up for whatever. I recognize the shape the closer it gets, the spoiler in the back, circular headlights. Even without Tinker blood I can tell it's a Porsche out of the late 80s or early 90s: a 911, probably a 964 Speedster. Saw a lot of 'em out in California.

This one's black, ridin' low, and it pulls right up to the curb, passenger window rollin' down. Behind the wheel, I see a Goblin, and the red cap upon his head. "You Nick Blackwarren?" Weird accent, but it's muddled, mix of Grunstadt and somethin' else I can't place, British? It ain't rough, either, this guy wouldn't even have to try hard to do a white voice.

"Who's askin'?"

He gets out of the car, a knife in his hand as he narrows his eyes. "I've been looking for you." He raises the blade.

"Wait, wait, wait!"

The knife flies right at me. I ain't got time to react. I'm so fuckin' sorry, buddy, this might be it.

12

It's bullshit, by the way, when they say yer life flashes 'fore
your eyes. Yer thinkin' "oh *fuck!*" as fast as yer brain can spark
those neurons and issue a DEFCON 1 to yer adrenal glands. All that
don't matter, 'course, 'cause the fuckin' blade was a few feet away
from me when I finally saw it.

Lucky fer me, yer brain and yer body are on different
wavelengths sometimes, like with yer reflexes. While yer brain is
panickin' and tryin' to come up with somethin' poignant as a
thought to die on, yer body takes over. Good thing, too, because the
shield thunks out of my vambrace as I duck down behind it, but I
ain't sure if all this happened in time.

What I can tell ya, buddy, is you and me are ain't goin' out
'cause of stupidity. So, I can lean on that if this is my final breath
and thought. I ain't thinkin' 'bout Thom, though, which I should
probably ruminate and shit about, but yer brain can only go so fast in
a second, know what I'm sayin'?

I heard the wet impact of the blade, the gaspin', impact of knees
on flagstone and the pourin' rain. Damon, you better avenge my
green ass or I'll haunt ya every second 'til...

'Til...

Okay, buddy, I know shock is a thing. I know ya can get shot or
stabbed and ya don't really feel it because yer brain ain't gonna let
that kinda pain get in the way of more important shit, but...

Shouldn't it still, y'know, hurt?

When I hear an impact behind me, somethin' bigger splashin'
down, I'm about to turn to check, but...

I see some red in the puddles I'm crouched in.

And hear a knock on the shield I'm still hidin' behind.

"Didn't graze you, did I?"

When I look up from behind the shield, the Redcap is there,
black cargo pants, black leather jacket, black shirt, eyes like a
northern ocean. It ain't a traditional long cap, more a dyed red knit

cap, a few bars and rings on his ears. His expression is one of genuine concern, I think.

"What fuckin' late 90s action movie did *you* claw yer way out of, fuck." I start to look behind me, and his hand pushes my face back toward the front. It's firm, but gentle enough that it don't feel forced. "What're ya doin'?"

He takes his hand back, raises both. "Don't want you vomiting on my boots, that's all."

"What're ya talkin'…" Dead guy. Dead guy. Knife stickin' outta his face dead guy. Body's still twitchin', blood and rain poolin' in his mouth dead guy. One eye still open, the other with a *fuckin' knife still stuck in it* dead guy.

It uh… Fresh Goblin puke on his neck dead guy.

Seriously, fuck, where does it all come from?

"Who the…" I cough a few times, spit, open my mouth and let rain get in to gargle and spit some more. "Fuck is this? No. No. Who the fuck are *you?*"

"Get in the car. I have to call for pickup on… that. Better if we're nowhere near here, understand?" Is there a little dirty British in his voice? "Unless you have more to empty your stomach of," he says, and is he fuckin' *smirkin'*? "Then please do so before you get into my car."

"Ya fuckin' serious?"

"I don't joke about my Anna."

"The fuck is Anna?"

"My car." He pulls the knife out of the man's head. "This on the other hand, is Thelma-"

Yeah, I ain't got nothin' left in the tank now.

"How exactly you are a Redcap I'll never understand. Get in the car, turn on the radio." He takes out his phone and shoos me off to his car. "Oh, and don't touch my levels, please and thank you."

What a dick. He shows up, kills a guy, smirks at me, and tells me to get in his car. He ain't even family, the bastard, where the fuck does he get off? On the other hand, buddy, it is fuckin' pourin', and if he's still a fuckbag, I can wire that car in eight seconds and leave his ass here.

First, it's modded, 'cause of course it is, and I ain't talkin' him bein' a bougie asshole, I mean it's modded for a guy his height (about two inches taller than me at 5'2") to drive it and not get pulled over. Adds credibility to it bein' his car at least. Also modded with heated seats, which sure as fuck were not standard on a Speedster, but it's fuckin' October so I ain't gonna bitch about havin' a warm ass.

But I'm still in the car of a Redcap that just killed someone easy as breathin', and if the last Redcap I was this close to in proximity is any indication, I gotta be ready for anythin'. I could still die tonight.

He gets in shortly after, the blade snaps out of the vambrace, and it's soon against his throat. No struggle, he stays still, cool customer.

"I could drive like this, but then you wouldn't be wearing your seat belt."

"Will ya shut up? Who the fuck are ya, huh?"

He don't answer. I press the edge against the skin of his neck. Don't let this go farther, please. "Tell me, and don't get cute, Ocean Eyes!"

"Ocean eyes? They are a darker shade of blue, but it's a curious moniker to mantle me with. Whyever were you paying attention to such a detail that you'd already determined a hue?"

"Tell me yer fuckin' name!"

"And don't get 'cute'? I mean, look at the two of us, I don't think 'cute' will even be in reach for either side of the conversation. Probably more you than I."

"I got a blade to yer throat and yer callin' me *cute*?"

"No, I'm saying that if one of us were to be considered cute, you would be the far more likely suspect."

"Shut the fuck up!" I grit my teeth. "Tell me your fucking name."

No response, just looking at me out of the corner of his eyes.

"Dammit! Say somethin'!"

The Redcap sighs. "You told me to shut the fuck up. Now you want me to tell you my name. Which is it?"

"Tell me yer godsdamned name, fucker. My cap's dipped too, so ya know I can drag the edge and slit ya right here all over yer upholstery."

"Are you like this with everyone who saves your life?"

Yeah, after tonight I'm fuckin' done, buddy.

"Answer. The. Fuckin'. Question."

"You were expecting someone to drive you home? You called Captain Blackwarren? I am the one he sent."

"Tell me your fuckin' name, asshole."

I feel pressure, sharp pressure against my abdomen. "*That* has been there since you pressed a blade to my throat. Might we dispense with, as you'd likely put it, 'the bullshit'? Sheathe your blade, I'll do the same, and we can get you home before the police likely arrive." His eyes meet mine. "Please."

I sigh, and lean back into my seat, the blade slippin' back into the vambrace, and I look over to see... His finger. No knife.

"You were just *pokin'* me?"

He winks in response, and puts the wipers on a high speed, shifts into gear, and off we go. His attention is primarily on the road, which makes sense given the weather, but... "Ya ever gonna tell me yer name? Ya already know mine, at least."

"Yes, you are Nicholas Arsenne Blackwarren."

"Fuck, why ya gotta be so withholdin' about everythin'? I'm just askin' yer name, fuck. Ya can't answer one question?"

He chuckles softly at that.

"What's so funny, smart guy?"

"Nothing, you just sound like my ex-husband."

"Ya were married. You. Guessin' it didn't last too long. What... two months before he couldn't take yer shit?"

"Three." He shoots me a faux-glare. "And it was a cover. We parted ways after the job was done. It was… good when it was good. Did convince me that I'm not the marrying kind, at least."

"Well, look at me, dodgin' another bullet."

"It was a knife in both cases, but I see what you're getting at. And you? Any wedded bliss you want to boast about?" Finally gettin' to the damned highway. "I have heard rumor about-"

"The Phouka, yeah."

I can at least get a better look at him. Bigger ears, his skin looks a little… scaly? Wait…

"You a Gremlin?" I peer at him more intently. Nose is shorter, ears stiffer, eyes brighter, tufted beard. "Why you wearin' a dipped cap if yer-" He holds up a hand to stop me.

"Rhys. You can call me Rhys. Do you prefer Nick?"

Touchy subject.

"Yeah. Ya gonna tell me who the fuck ya killed, Rhys?"

He chuckles again. "You are certainly trying to sell playing dumb, aren't you?" That fuckin' smirk again. "I compliment you on your commitment, at least. You mannerisms, speech patterns, the hobo clothes…."

My response is a finger. Guess which one?

A slow peer at me. "You're telling me a *Blackwarren assassin* working in this City dresses like he's hanging out in a convenience store parking lot?"

"Better than lookin' like an old Goth who's waiting to read his poems on the nature of angst. Ya do know there's more than one color that clothes come in." I look out the window. "I'd ask ya to put on some music to fill the time but I don't know if I can listen to 'Bela Lugosi's Dead' that many times in one sitting."

"Please, send your playlists to my car, I'm aching to hear the groundbreaking prose of an old white man writing for an eighteen-year-old girl about *love and relationships*."

"Wow. Look at me. I managed to find the *one* snootyfuck bougie *Blade* wannabe in the fuckin' tri-state area. Tight black leather all over, you fuckin' fashionista icon, you."

"Whereas you choose clothes made for *children* that only serve to stretch and hug every inch of your body. Well, aren't we a *hipster*."

"You really piss me off, ya know that?"

"Yes, you are an *oasis* of serenity."

"*Oasis*. Yeah." I lean toward him. "You listen to them when no one's lookin', dontcha?" He takes a grumbling breath, mostly through his nose. I'll take that as a point for me.

"Regardless, enough stalling. You know who the man I save you form was, the charade has gone on long enough."

"No. I don't."

"You went to Kirkland for him, and you didn't recognize him?"

"Well, it was dark, and rainy, and… Oh yeah, *yer knife was in his fuckin' face*. So, I couldn't really pick him outta a lineup, yeah?" I roll my eyes, what the fuck's he talkin' about? Who I went to Kirkland for-

"Oh, fuck me. Was that Dieter Kirschbaum? Couldn't be, though, he was slit in his… Well, he was slit so it couldn't have been him."

"I believe there's a term called 'back-door parole'? On paper he's dead, but he walks out the front door or is carried out the back by a coroner who's been paid for his services? Clearly, his master exerted influence to have him freed from bondage and from the possibility of answering incriminating questions."

"Fuck! I was just gonna ask him about some sheet music he mighta stolen, and they killed him to prevent that? Shadow take me, what the fuck have I gotten myself into. Can I have one normal fuckin' job?" I ain't sayin' that to him, more to Mother, Father, Brother, and I guess you too, buddy.

"Or, instead, you simply managed to visit on the same day of his scheduled 'parole'." Am I a bad guy that I expected him to pronounce it 'sheduled'? I ain't, right? "Simply a twist or two of fate. One can never be certain of how an encounter will go-"

"Okay, ya can stop, 'kay?" I rub my face. "Any reason yer talkin' like a white guy in a Langston Hughes play? I ain't never heard a Goblin' talkin' as high falutin' as you."

He pulls off the highway, parks on the shoulder, full on glare now.

"Perhaps it's because I've been places other than the slums of the Argent City shoveling offal into my mouth three times a day. *T'es chiant, plouc!*"

"Y'know, insultin' someone in a language they don't know don't make ya a posh fuck, it makes ya an asshole. No." I get in his face. "It makes ya a *poseur.*"

"…what did you say?"

I smirk. "I see ya with yer Blade wannabe getup, tryin' to be all mysterious and shit, showin' off all yer five-dollar words, and how ya probably do the *Allora Sun's* crossword every day in *ink* and kick anyone's ass at Scrabble. But it's all an act yer pushin', tryin' to fake it 'til even you believe it."

"And you? Are you capable of finishing a sentence, or Hell, a complete *thought* without saying 'fuck'? Have you ever even heard of the letter G, or would that muck up your image as the 'too cool to care' emblem of roguishness? You clearly have the intelligence, but you hide it because you'd rather be underestimated and left alone to…" He's in close too, now. "Read *Wuthering Heights* for the twentieth time while veritably pissing down on anyone who espouses any sort of culture? And you call *me* the *poseur*?"

"You are such a fuckin' asshole." My heart's beatin' so fast.

"And you are an insufferable, incorrigible, *infuriating…*"

We're both breathin' heavy.

I don't know who goes first. I really don't, what I know is that our mouths are locked together, his hands holdin' my head, then mine on his. Sometimes my eyes are closed, sometimes his. I… Fuck, I don't know what's happenin'. I just feel like this is what I gotta do, like… *really* gotta do. I don't know if I'm shuttin' him up or if he couldn't finish his sentence. What I do know is that we're gonna push each other away and then we gotta… Talk about it.

Fuck, I shouldn't be doin' this. What about Thom? Him and I were bangin' holes in the wall with a bedframe a few weeks ago and then I break up and hang up on him and I'm angry-kissin' a Goblin whose blade still got blood on it from the guy he slit not even an hour ago? And both our hands are startin' to go under shirts? No, no. This is adrenaline. I almost fuckin' died, so this is how my body's processin'. He's just here and pissin' me off so it elicited an emotional response. That's all. I just… Won't be anymore bickerin' and bitchin' if we're fuck…

Shadow take me, what the fuck am I doin'?

We both push each other away, break eye contact. Quietly, he puts the car back in gear and goes back to the highway. The next few minutes are silent, too.

"Why'd ya-"

"Why did you kiss me?"

I still can't look at him. All of that gave me an issue to obscure from his view."

"Yer hand was under my… Were ya gonna try to…?"

"I should ask you the same question." It ain't… accusatory. Fuck, were we *both* about to…

No answer on either side. Fuck, is it bein' on a case that gets me revved up or somethin'? Or, yeah, the avalanche of shit I've dealt with in the past two hours. It ain't 'cause he's attractive or anythin' I mean, yeah, he's pretty easy on the eyes for a Goblin and he got a quick wit and ain't no one denying he can't work that tongue, but if there's any sort of romantic lead in my life, it'd be the perfect Disney Phouka Prince who actually wants to marry me, not a stuck-up Goblin poseur divorcee that I only met *an hour ago*.

Thank Shadow ya can't really fuck in a Porsche.

"Wh-why are you looking for sheet music?" Fuck it, I'd wanna change the subject, too.

"I got hired by the parents of the girl he killed. She was lookin' to make it as a composer, and her life's work was a symphony. Ain't no other copies, and it's gone. Human girl, by the way." I'm lookin' out the window, obviously. Don't wanna risk whatever *that* was happenin' again.

"Good thing I got him, then, in case the Ra'keth" (he means the Lightnin' Rod) "comes asking questions. Did you know he was Fae?" I had suspicions, but nothin' concrete. Just a hunch too thin to share, really.

"Nope. Didn't get too good a look at him 'cause-"

"Yes. The knife in his face. He *was* going to kill you. I trusted your reflexes would be good enough to duck in time." No smirk this time. Tiny smile. "I'm pleased I was right." I take a breath, through my nose, and... Fuck.

He don't smell bad. I mean, I can smell the *blood*, but that ain't what- I mean he's- He ain't offensive, okay? I mean we're in a small car and...

And we were seconds away from fuckin' outta nowhere, so the fuckin' car smells of pheromones. Mine and his. Fuckin' Shadow, they mingle well, this is *not* what I need. He's sniffin' the air, too, and gives me a look. Dammit, he smells it too.

This don't mean shit, by the way. It ain't destiny by pheromones. It just fuckin' means our particular scents don't clash, so we won't instinctually hate each other.

So lemme underline it for ya: This is *not* that kinda fuckin' story, okay? Yeah, I see ya shippin' a'ready, so quit it!

"So," Yep. Changin' the subject. "I'm guessin' commoner Sidhe, maybe a Brownie? Dwarf woulda been same height, plus the Germanic name..." Hold on a sec. What'd he say about throwin' a knife at my face?! "Ya weren't sure ya wouldn't hit me?!"

"Dwarf, yes. It's odd though, they aren't the type to murder humans, or steal something like sheet music. My apologies in having a little faith in the great Nick Blackwarren."

"Seriously, though, why ya talk like that? I ain't never met a Goblin that got that kinda diction unless they're bustin' out the white voice. Ya ain't dropped it once and ain't no reason to whiten up yer talkin' for a fellow Goblin." I look at him a few seconds. Nah... Couldn't be. Still... "Ya weren't a human who pissed off an old-world Fae and got transformed into a Goblin, were ya? I mean, I ain't never heard of that happenin' in like, centuries, but legends gotta come from somewhere."

"Is it so odd that I prefer to speak clearly you have to believe that I'm not actually a Goblin? Am I going to have to verify? Cut myself and bleed red?" He grumbles. "Or ratchet mah jab'rin' so I talk righ' proper fer yer narrow feckin' peckerin' gobshite mindin'?"

I blink a few times.

"That was a part of my life I don't like revisiting, and nothing like my accent when I was young. If you think it was, I'll throw you from the car presently." Rhys focuses his attention on the road. "Can't this simply be how I convey my thoughts? Also, if you were suggesting I speak like the character in *Raisin in the Sun*? The *poem* was written by Hughes. The *play* was written by-"

"Lorraine Hansberry. Yeah. Didn't think you'd catch me on that."

The Redcap snerks. "I *did* attend high school here." Another few seconds pass. "What are you planning to do, now that the Dwarf is dead?"

I shrug. "Keep goin'. If someone got him out, they gotta be involved, right? So, all I gotta do is investigate. I gave her mom my word I'd find her daughter's symphony, and I keep my word."

"You would have been killed if I hadn't been there, and you still want to keep going?"

My turn to chuckle. "Clearly ya ain't heard about the triple murder that went down in July. Had the whole damned City after me and still managed to solve it and get a taped confession."

"Nick, you aren't like any Redcap I've ever met."

I grin. "I take that as a compliment, Rhys."

"Good. It was meant as one."

Oh, fer fuck's sake, heart, dontcha go flutterin' at that. This is *not* a fuckin' meet-cute. He just *killed somebody.*

"Rhys, uh, about the uh... You know." No eye contact, nope. "What happened when ya pulled over?"

"I know what you're referring to, yes."

"I uh, don't want ya to get the wrong idea. I'm iffy maybe involved with a guy right now that I broke up with kinda sorta and-"

"Constable Canmore, yes. It's a rather open secret that plays at being gossip. He's rather garrulous while he's taking a bloodstone to a crime scene. He truly does seem to care about you, and I apologize for muddling that, if I did."

Aw fuck, he used garrulous correctly in a sentence. No! No. Focus. Focus.

"Ya think one kiss is gonna fuck that up, really?" We'll just stick to the facts of what actually happened. Not what it felt like we *wanted* to happen.

"Of course not, we Redcaps tend to 'fuck up' such things without any physical assistance." He glances at me, the rain starting to let up the further away we get and the closer home becomes. "You're truly going to continue this investigation of yours?"

"Ya get used to it. Nothin' is ever simple with me, no matter how much I want it to be. But sure as walkin' the Shadow, there's a young woman sittin' in the waitin' room of the great beyond wonderin' if anyone'll remember her, if the world'll know she was here. If I don't try, who will? And if I don't, Bridget O'Hare fades into the unremarkable, and she don't deserve that."

"You'd do this for a human you've never even met, never knew?"

"What's it fuckin' matter I knew her or not? It's what's right to do. Just 'cause I'm a Redcap don't mean I ain't got a godsdamned soul." I quirk at brow at him, his eyes flickin' over to me every few seconds. "What?"

"You really aren't like any Redcap I've ever known or heard of, Nick." He exhales, a slight smile on his face. "Thank you."

"…for what?"

"If you'd like my services… My help. I offer them to aid in your investigation. I feel this woman was robbed of the justice she deserved as well. My blades are yours, if you'll have them."

I chortle, shaking my head. "Might as well, got the feelin' yer gonna be followin' me anyway whether I want ya there or not. First thing we should do? Stop for somethin' to eat and hash out what we both know. After that, we go after answerin' the big question."

"Where the sheet music is."

"Nah, it ain't obvious to ya Rhys? We find the real fuckin' killer. We find *that* fucker, we find the symphony and get a twofer."

"Why do you think Kirschbaum wasn't the murderer?" He sounds intrigued, at least.

"I'll tell ya, soon as ya buy me some fuckin' French toast and hash browns, I'm fuckin' starvin'."

13

The K Street Diner closes around nine at night, and it's pretty dead. Sharon ain't on, nor her sister. It's usually Hannah for the mythics who show up late. For a little extra, the dragon will make what ya want, and since Rhys pulled up in a fuckin' Porsche, he's fuckin' buyin'.

'Least he ain't all hoity toity about the food.

But, of course, Thom's here.

He's leanin' 'gainst the counter, chattin' with the dragon in the kitchen, havin' a good time.

"So, we just get a booth, or eat at the counter," Rhys asks. "I've never been here."

"Let's just grab a booth-"

"Nick?" Fuck. Thom heard me, and now he sees me. He smiles, and waves me over. Can't be pissed at him for how it turned out, really.

"Ah, ya got back okay. We're just gonna grab a booth and get a late dinner. Got business to go over, ya understand, right?" I smile as best I can, not 'cause I'm fakin' it, but 'cause a hound gets a scent too fuckin' easily and-

"I'll join you!" Both me and Rhys give him a look, I ain't got no idea of what Rhys is thinkin', he's just dead silent right now. Fuck, did... Did Thom really not register what happened on that phone call? I mean, I didn't break up with him by text but ya could tell just by *context* that the relationship was on life support and I was lookin' to pull the plug, right? I put that out there, right, buddy?

"Dave? Put theirs on my check, okay? We'll be eating together, whatever the two of them want." I mean, I could charge it but I'm cash light at the moment, so if he wants to pick up the check I ain't gonna say no. Plus, y'know, I don't wanna bring the drama into this place. I ain't gettin' banned, no sir.

He finds a booth for the three of us, Thom and I on the inside, facin' each other, Rhys on the outside. Hannah brings over water, I proceed to run up an order, and when Rhys keeps quiet I order for him too.

"So… who's your friend?" Thom's tryin' to be friendly, but I catch the hint of suspicion, that little hit on the word "friend", seein' this new Goblin who's sittin' right next to me. It's a good thing Rhys and I didn't do the deed in his car or Thom would know about it in one sniff.

"I work with his cousin." He holds up a finger toward Hannah. "May I also have a coffee, please?" The werelioness nods once while the Goblin keeps his hands out of sight. "How do *you* know Nick, if I may ask?"

"I'm his…" Thom looks at me. He wants me to say it, that we're together, probably married someday, but fuck, I ain't gonna say that. Great sex and good romance are not automatically hand-in-hand, y'know? Fuck, why did I look at Rhys? "I'm the one who's going to catch him." He winks at me, and I roll my eyes, but not in a mean way.

"Ya got a better chance seein' me watchin' a baseball game, Krupke. Sober."

"I wouldn't take you to a baseball game. I don't really watch much anymore. I was talking with Dave about the Gryphons. Learn the lingo."

"You. Yer gonna watch football?" Huh, he didn't twitch when I called him Krupke. Well, it's no fun if he don't. Yeah, best I get this back on track. "Ya hear anythin' new about a human woman gettin' slit by a Dwarf?"

The Phouk's eyes go wide. "You're still working the murder, Nick? He was arrested, found guilty, sentenced. You still want to do this?"

I'm not havin' this fuckin' discussion again, Thom.

"No, like I told ya before, asset recovery. But solvin' the murder will probably lead to the asset. Probably. Maybe. I hope." I shrug.

"How it usually goes in books I read. 'Sides, a woman was murdered and findin' out who did it is a nice bonus."

Thom turns his attention to Rhys. "And you're here because..."

"I saved his life, and as a favor to his cousin I'm keeping an eye on him." He smirks at Thom. "No. I'm not fucking him."

I facepalm, Thom sputters, and of course Hannah comes back with drinks.

She looks at the three of us, and subtly takes in the air, her eyes reacting, but that's it, she stays silent. I know what the reaction is, though. We better leave a big fuckin' tip.

"Thom, I am so sorry for him." I'm rubbin' my face, today's been too much for this. I look to Rhys. "Shadow, ya gotta be like that?"

"He suspected from the moment he saw me with you. Besides, I've heard that it's fine to tease Constable Canmore the Keystone Cop." Really had to hit that alliteration, didn't ya, Rhys? He sips his coffee. "Is it true you nearly got him killed in a sting?"

I put my hand on Rhys's, gettin' his attention. "Stop."

He looks to the Phouk, his thumb brushin' my palm. "I apologize. That was out of line."

Thom sniffs the air, but I ain't worried, ya can't smell a kiss, and if he asks I'll own up. Us havin' pheromones just means that we're alive. Don't mean nothin'. Ain't even really cheatin' if ya ain't together. Still to anyone, and obviously Hannah, if ya asked who the couple was at the table...

"Why do you two smell like blood?" Fuck.

"I believe I mentioned saving his life?" Rhys drinks his coffee after that, all matter-of-fact.

"He doesn't like when people die. He gets sick." Thom then looks at me. "Right, Nick?"

"Well, yeah," I answer, "But-"

"You'd rather he'd been slit instead, Constable?" Rhys cuts me off. "I was twenty feet away and I had to make a decision. For what it's worth I'm aware of his reaction to such things and I tried to keep him looking away."

"Yeah, he did," I add, "But I-"

"You *decided* to take a life." Thom's eyes are looking more canine now. "You could have simply warned Nick and he would have found a way for everyone to make it through alive."

"Yeah," I speak up, "I mean I coulda darted him and-"

"You wanted me to leave it to chance he'd react in time? Gamble with his survival? Why?" Rhys asks, showing needle teeth now. "Because that worked out so well for you in July?"

About time to intervene. My hand slips over smooth.

Thom gets up from the table. "Would you like to discuss this further?"

Rhys gets up, he don't notice. "I'll be one step behind you."

Okay. That's it.

I get out from the booth, Rhys's blade "Thelma" in my left hand, the vambrace out, bar raised for the dart launcher. The blade's at Rhys's neck, the dart pointed at Thom's. "A'right. Pissin' match over. Botha ya sit the fuck down and shut the fuck up. This is a nice diner and I ain't gettin' fuckin' banned 'cause you two gotta whip 'em out and measure." I glare at the two of 'em. "Botha ya understand?"

Rhys and Thom nod, scolded.

"You two better fuckin' say 'I understand', got it?"

"I understand." Rhys says quietly.

"I understand." Thom's got a hangdog look on his face.

"Good." I slap the blade on the table (not *into it*, fer fuck's sake), and lower my right arm, the vambrace resetting. "Thom? Rhys and I made out in his car but if he's gonna act like this ya really don't got nothin' to worry about. Rhys? Thom wants to fuckin' marry me and is willin' to fuck up his whole life to do so. Botha ya? I'm seriously not lookin' for a relationship 'cause I'd rather find a dead girl some justice and help her last wish come true. Now are you two gonna help with that or just be fuckin' assholes to each other and by extension me?" I look beyond 'em. "And Hannah? I'm fuckin' sorry. I got it handled so ya can put yer claws back, but that don't excuse this behavior from them, or from me failin' to stop it."

Both of 'em turn to see Hannah's gone full form, well over six feet, tawny fur, solid muscle, amber eyes, big fuckin' teeth. If I were human, or the one she was mad at, I'd be shittin' myself, no lie. Any surprise this place don't get robbed?

I look at the two of 'em. "I'd give her a big tip since she's gotta replace her uniform now."

A silver dragon's head, that of the owner, peeks through the passthrough. "Tommy! Don't make me call your brother! Goblins? First strike. Hannah, get some clothes out of the lost and found, this ain't that kind of place."

I sit back down. "I swear if you two fucked up my chances of ever gettin' his French toast again." I look to the dragon. "We'll just take the check and get outta yer hair, er, scales, sir. My apologies."

Thom looks sheepishly at his feet. "Sorry, Dave."

"Es tut mir sehr leid. Es wird nicht wieder vorkommen." Rhys bows his head. Sounds like apologies, in German.

"Mach dir nicht die Mühe, meinen Arsch zu küssen. Ich weiß, dass Kobolde lügen können," the dragon replies. I don't know what either of 'em were sayin', though some of it sounds like "kiss my ass", but Rhys looks plenty cowed, if I'm usin' that word right.

"Whatever yer sayin', you can get the check. Thom? You can whip out that black card and give Hannah a proper tip. Me? I'm goin' home to sleep in my murder house, thanks so much *again* fer suggestin' it, Thom." I start toward the door. "Any of ya follow me, I'll remind ya I got Captain Blackwarren on speed dial now."

I swear to fuckin' Shadow, buddy, I'm not tryin' to drag myself into a love triangle romance novel. Sure, I *read* 'em, but that don't mean I wanna *live* 'em.

It's an easy train ride home, at least, no mail, no botherin' from neighbors, the walk up the stairs ain't great but at least I got a nicer apartment, even if it was a crime scene not even a month ago.

At least this night'll be fuckin' over. Just gotta put the key in the lock and…

My door's unlocked.

I gently push it open, the blade slippin' outta my vambrace. I whisper a charm to augment my sight, let me see into the black.

The furniture's ripped up, stuffin' and innards and shit all over the floor, but I hear some crunchin' as I walk forward. I try the light switch, no luck.

Phone works though, so does the flashlight. Just gotta shake it a little and…

A grand piano, cover open and propped, but that ain't what's drawin' my attention, buddy. It's playin' by itself, in a minor key, but that ain't what's drawin' my attention, buddy.

A woman, naked, is lashed to it with piano wire, cuttin' into her skin, hair cut sloppily from her skull, bone showin' in places. The wire slicin' her face, her eyes, breasts, blood streamin' in patterns like sheet music. Her mouth opens, her teeth broken, bloody eyes on me, a voice croakin' out.

"Help… me…"

14

I wake up screamin', the sound of my door gettin' kicked open keepin' me awake. I got a cold sweat, but I can still see her, plain as fuckin' day, murdered and dyin' scared and in agony and alone. Just had to fuckin' jinx it, didn't I, with that crack about the murder house.

I expected the landlord, or Thom, but instead it's Rhys, hands on my shoulders. "Breathe. You're awake. This is real. You're safe."

"Did… did ya break down my fuckin' door? I still had to pay a fuckin' security deposit, ya dick!" I rub my head, pushin' his hands away. "Why the fuck ya here, anyway?"

"I promised your cousin I'd keep an eye on you."

"Damon sent ya?" I take a breath, my nerves still pretty shot. "And mind gettin' up so I can get dressed? Make yerself useful and make some coffee."

"You were screaming bloody murder. And I mean you were literally screaming 'bloody' and 'murder.' And you don't have a coffeemaker, one that works, anyway."

"Just… find something that'll take ya outta my bedroom, yeah?"

He leaves, thankfully, and I swing my legs over the side of the mattress, and look down for my clothes and…

No. Nope. None of that outta you, penis. Ya get me in too much fuckin' trouble. Yer gettin' stuffed in my pants and I swear to fuckin' Shadow if ya pitch a tent in front of a Redcap again I'm gonna sit in an ice bath 'til ya fuckin' behave.

Pants first.

"Is tea all right with you?"

"It's all I fuckin' have, get the kettle goin'. Mind tellin' me why the fuck yer over here?" Ruined another pair of socks. I don't know why I keep wearin' 'em, my big toenails don't let 'em last a day.

"I told you I wanted to help you, Nick. And you don't have my number, so you had no means of contacting me." I hear some clatter, sound of a faucet fillin' the kettle.

"And ya, y'know, didn't take a hint from that?" Gotta rub down my feet and spray my shoes. Wearin' Timberlands, or Timbs, in yer bare feet means they're gonna reek and yer gonna get athlete's foot. Another point that we're more human than any other Fae. Ya don't hear about Sidhe bitchin' about bunions or their mani/pedis needin' a hacksaw.

"You'd rather I left? Is this about what happened with your boyfriend?"

"He's…" I take a breath.

"If he were it wouldn't be so difficult for you to say."

I look at my arm, still clad in the joining of Shadow's Edge and the Aeolian Shear. Okay, both of ya, I ain't gettin' a shirt on if I can't fit anything over a fuckin' shoulder pauldron.

"Shut the fuck up, okay? What, ya *want* me to be single? My life ain't that kinda story, okay?" Still freaky to watch it all slowly crawl down my arm in fits and starts and assemble a compound bow, blends of steel and brass, gears always turnin'. Also, my forearm is pocked with ugly scars, like from getting' blood roughly drawn from it, and 'cause I ain't taken this thing off in over three *months*. I spray the damage with disinfectant, muffle the profanity since I got a guest, wrap it with gauze and an ACE bandage, and then grab a shirt. Fuck, I ain't ever seen it this bad. Are magic heroic weapons s'posed to do *that* to ya?

"What's my Shadow-damned relationship status gotta do with your fuckin' life, yeah?" My shirts are all tees, and I'm still goin' off the box of laundry I brought with me from the Benedict, so the only clean one I got left is one from when I was seventeen and still livin' out in California near San Francisco. It's from the time Mom took me to Fisherman's Wharf to pick tourist pockets and buy me a souvenir: a goofy fuckin' t-shirt of the sea lions down on Pier 39.

'Least it still fits.

"I'd rather your relationship status didn't interfere with your investigation, Nick. That's all. What do you have to go with the tea?"

"I don't fuckin' know. My shelves ain't stocked and I ain't paying out the ass for a delivery app." My hoodie's dried out enough, a couple spritzes of fragrance to freshen it up and battle the distinctive scent us Goblins have.

Again, we don't fuckin' reek. Remember, buddy?

"Did you have a plan for how your investigation would begin, at least?" I actually hear him sigh. "Or were you planning to 'wing it', as you've been doing so far?"

Now I'm outta my bedroom and into my kitchen. "Seriously, what the fuck crawled up yer ass?" There's a cup of green tea, at least. Smells okay, and I grab an apple off the mini-tree, already replenished. Bless that little Twin Blood gardener. I ain't got time to savor, though, so I just push the fruit into my mouth, lettin' my teeth do the work. When ya can chomp a cinder block with ease a whole apple's no problem, also when ya pour the hot tea down yer throat.

That bit obviously sets us apart from normal humans. I think it was so the Machinist could just give us whatever and not worry about our care and feedin'. Startin' to put two and two together on why the Redcap's caps originally got so red? Thank Shadow I ain't ever had that cravin'. That, however, don't separate us from humans as much as ya'd think.

"My issue is that you don't seem to be taking this seriously. You have no idea how to begin your search?"

"Okay, first of all, fuck you. Second, I *had* an angle, but you killed him, remember? Can't get answers from a corpse unless ya know a necromancer, and she only works with zombies." No, buddy, I don't know her, but everyone tends to pay attention when a Keth's about.

"So that's all? No further leads?" He's sittin' at my table now, the same one where Bridget's parents sat not two days ago. "Are things too awkward between you and the Phouka to ask for assistance?"

"Shadow, will ya get off that? If yer so fuckin' invested in my relationship, I'm RealGreenGoblin on Insta…"

Wait.

Wait, wait, wait, wait, wait.

"Nick?" Rhys is leanin' across the table toward me, peerin'.

"Hold on a sec." I hold up a hand toward him.

It couldn't be *that* easy, but…

I take out my phone, and load up the app. I post pics of the skyline and motorcycles out in the wild, okay? And occasionally my pics are from high places I shouldn't be takin' pics from. Legally, as it were.

I got forty followers, yeah, I ain't doin' it to be a fuckin' influencer.

But Bridget O'Hare was a white girl in her twenties who was lookin' to make it big as a composer, so she's gotta have an Insta, Soundcloud, probably a Twitter and YouTube, and I'd guess a webpage. Gotta be somethin' that was missed in the scrub that Cenzo was talkin' about.

I swipe over to my phone app and dial the number I received from her mom in a text, holdin' up my hand to Rhys again.

It takes a few rings, but she picks up.

"Who is this?"

"Mrs. O'Hare? Nicholas Arsenne. I'm callin' to give ya an update on the investigation." That "Oh fuck, I can sense he's a monster and inhuman" shit that hampers us face to face vanishes on the phone.

"Oh, yes! Thank you so much for calling, Mr. Arsenne. What can you tell me?" She's hopeful, and I can't give her the information she wants, that she needs.

"Bad news, at least, Dieter Kirschbaum was killed at Kirkland County Men's Prison before I got a chance to talk to him, so that avenue has been closed."

She's silent. I know what's goin' through her mind. She doesn't want to be happy that the man who killed her daughter is also dead, but it's there. It's just… human to want some manner of reciprocity. "I see."

"But I'm not givin' up, Mrs. O'Hare. I just gotta cast a wider net. I've brought on additional help, but don't you worry, he's doin' it *gratis*. I do need something from you, though."

A sigh on the line. "…how much do you need?"

"No, no, nothin' like that. I need the screennames yer daughter was usin' in social media, anythin' ya can find. It'll be a good place to find other leads, anyone else who might've been connected to this. Could you text me what ya know?"

"I… I can do that. Thank you, Mr. Arsenne. I'll send it as soon as I find something."

"Ma'am? I'm gonna find her symphony, don't ya worry none."

She hangs up, and I exhale. If only every conversation with a human could be like that. Rhys has been quiet, at least, watchin' me, listenin' in on both sides 'cause our big fuckin' ears ain't fer show, buddy.

"I'm doing this for free, am I?" He's smirkin', at least. That fuckin' smirk.

"Why not? I am until I can deliver the invoice." I pick another apple and shred it with my teeth. "Seriously, why you helpin' me? And don't gimme any of that 'yer cousin asked me' bullshit. He told ya to gimme a ride home and ya did, ain't nothin' keepin' ya here, so why?" I narrow my eyes at him. "This ain't about the kiss, is it?"

"No. It was good, I'll admit, and your scent is quite pleasant, but nothing so cheap. I'm a Redcap, have been for… a while. I've spent my life around terrible people, and hunting people even worse. I'm sorry if I've been… difficult. I haven't been around a…"

"Thief?" I offer, because if he's a real Redcap, he's talkin' 'bout how he's been killin' people, doin' slits, endin' lives, punchin' tickets, likely all over the world if he's as, well, worldly as he is. Us second-story guys usually want to minimize body count 'cause it fucks everythin' up. Hell, my last "heist" ended up bein' a triple murder that almost got hung on me.

"Someone *good*. I've heard about how you were dipped. You... shouldn't be a Redcap, Nick."

"Don't matter if ya got the blood, Rhys. I'm a Blackwarren. Gettin' dipped was a forgone conclusion fer me, whether I wanted it or not. And yeah, I really didn't want it, but it was him or me." I sag in my chair. I don't like thinkin' about it, y'know buddy? I know you know why. "Thanks fer sayin' it, though. I mean, what was it like when you dipped? Them or you kinda thing, or natural born killer?"

"Nick."

"Sorry, didn't mean to pry, just that ya 'parently know my fuckin' life story so I figure was only fair-"

"I was seven."

So uh, some of the air just went out of the room. "Seven... teen?"

"Seven. My uncle was drunk and..."

I reach across the table, take his hand. "Hey, ya don't gotta tell me, okay? That already sounds like shit ya wouldn't wanna dig up, so we'll just leave it at that, yeah?"

"Thanks."

"Was yer accent slippin' a little, there?" I move my hand back. "I was thinkin' it was a 'dirty British' or somethin' like-"

"Welsh. I was born in Wales, but I've been here since I was eight, when I wasn't on a job. That, at least, wasn't until I came of age and got this cap on my head." He sips his tea. "I'm a Gremlin, if you hadn't noticed."

"I suspected. I even asked, I think. So ya think I'm good, huh?" I chuckle softly. "Thief with a heart of gold or some shit?"

"I'm pretty sure you'll tell me what you are when you know."

"You, uh..." My throat's feelin' tight. "Do you know?"

"Nick?" Damn, his eyes are deep, like the Atlantic at dusk.

I swallow. "Yeah?"

"Your phone's going off?"

And, thank Shadow, that snaps me outta… whatever that was. I really don't wanna feel like that. I mean, I kinda do, and that's what's buggin' me. But at least I got my distraction machine in the palm of my hand.

There's a text from Mrs. O'Hare.

Found her page.

A link's attached, which opens up the app on my phone and takes it to the page with a profile picture of a woman made of a wire frame of piano wire emergin' from an open grand piano. It's enough to make me shudder, buddy, givin' me flashbacks of that nightmare.

Her screen name is across the image at the bottom, artful font.

SettleTheScore

15

I will say this about Bridget O'Hare, the woman can score a film fer damned sure. Well, she would have, if she'd been noticed and snatched up by a studio or media company. No complete movements or pieces, just sixty second "sneak peeks" that vary from synth to rock to full orchestral and blends of all three. Longest she played were on her recorded streams, just her at the piano.

She had a sense of humor, played with lightin' to make it look like she was coming out on stage at the Destry Opera House, or the Palace of Wisdom in Allora, always to cheesy applause tracks, wearin' an LBD (little black dress), and hammin' up the bows and thank-you's to the digital audience 'fore crackin' up. Once she sat on the bench, though, she was all business and nuance.

They're older, recorded streams, but 'parently she'd watch the live chat, talk to the viewers, answer a couple questions, and then open it up to let them decide what genre of film she'd be scorin' that night, even with a basic plot summary, and then just put fingers to keys and go, pulling the music from the aether easy as breathin', buddy.

The music was always good, but buddy, to watch her play was to watch someone in love, in joy, in pain, in grief, whatever the emotion of the music, she felt it, ya could see it on her face.

I mentioned before I love humanity, everythin' they bring to the world when they ain't bein' dicks to each other and us. Fae, we live on dreams, we were created from 'em, Fae other than Goblins, at least. Bridget was a dreamer, an artist, a woman who chased her need to create and was seconds from bein' on the stage fer real. In her music, in her eyes, her face, I saw...

'Cept, ya can't see her face no more. Can't feel that light that would warm up yer heart up when she played, the mirth when she cracked corny music puns like they were high art, ya can't feel it anymore.

'Cause someone snuffed that beautiful light from this earth.

"Nick? You're crying."

I sniffle, wipin' my eyes. "'Cause I got a fuckin' soul, Rhys. Why ain't you?"

"…because I don't often cry to bombastic rock opera played on a synthesizer."

"I'm cryin' 'cause someone murdered her, ya dick!" I've read in a lot of crime books that ya ain't supposed to get too close, make it personal, just see the victim as a pile of facts so ya don't make emotional decisions. I get that. But I ain't a cop or detective or private investigator, buddy.

I'm a thief.

Someone took her life.

Stole her dream.

And I'm gonna steal it back.

"Rhys? Ya still wanna help me with this?"

I feel his hand pattin' my shoulder. "Yes, I do."

I turn in my chair to face him completely. "Then ya gotta promise me somethin', okay? This is non-negotiable." The Goblin waits expectantly. "From here on out? Zero body count. No one dies."

"Nick, what if-"

"No. No what ifs. There's always a way without someone dyin'. I know yer dipped and probably killed more people than I can count-"

"Nineteen." His face has gone hard. "And I don't like taking lives, Nick. I'm *good* at it, but I don't *like* doing it. If you want a job with clean blades, then I'll do it. The Redcaps, we're not that one you slit, Nick. But if your life is in danger, I will choose you over them. Understand? *That* is non-negotiable for me."

I close my eyes. It makes sense that he'd say that, but it don't mean I gotta like it. Just means I gotta avoid situations where he's gotta make that choice. 'Sides, I got a feeling why he's sayin' that.

"Right. Cousin Damon would kill ya if somethin' happened to me on yer watch. Thom would go full hound and rip what's left of ya to shreds." I take a breath. "Okay, but only as a last resort. Got it?"

He nods. "I understand. Are we making this official?"

Meanin', buddy, are we makin' this a bonded oath? Y'see, when yer able to lie, Fae tend to do bindin' or geas or oaths, literal chains of magic to make sure ya follow through on yer promises. Can still break 'em, but you'll get marked as an Oathbreaker, permanently. Like, the oath literally breaks and burns yer skin to leave a bit of Sigil sayin' as much on ya. Even with us Goblins, it's a mark ya wanna avoid. If Damon broke any of his Oaths to the Queen, it'd probably kill him on the spot.

But, askin' a Goblin to swear an Oath is pretty much tellin' 'em yer an untrustworthy fucker who only follows through on their word when there's practically a magical gun to yer head. Ain't that professional, y'know?

"What's yer family name?"

He takes a beat to think on it. "Llewellyn. Rhys Llewellyn." He spits in his palm.

"One more thing. We gotta be honest with each other, hundred percent, yeah?" I'm goin' somewhere with this buddy, trust me.

"Of course." He extends his wet palm.

"Nick Blackwarren." I spit in my mine.

We shake, and yeah, buddy, it's kinda gross, but it's probably the only promise among Goblinkind that ya don't break, 'cause yer showin' a lot of trust. From what I hear the Coyotes do the same thing, but it's to be expected from clans of cutpurses, charlatans, and cutthroats. Ya ain't gotta swear to the gods or any of that shit, ya just have to swear to each other.

And yeah, we fuckin' wash our godsdamned hands after, we're not fuckin' slobs.

"So, Nick, what do we do now?" Rhys hands me a towel to dry my hands, which I do.

"Now? Now, Rhys, ya tell me the fuckin' truth, is what." I roll my shoulders, tense my feet. "'Cause ya know more than yer tellin' me 'bout all this shit, and I ain't a fuckin' idiot." I tic my head at a chair. "Have a seat."

"What in Shadow are you talking about?" He don't sit.

"Fine, buy time. It takes a fuckin' hour to get to Kirkland from the City in good weather, and ya were there in twenty minutes. Ain't no way ya were drivin' a 965 Speedster at over a hundred down State 76 in a fuckin' rainstorm, certainly not in a car ya gave a name to. Damon didn't know I was there 'til I called him, yet there you were with a knife to throw."

"Nick, I *saved your life.*"

"Funny, 'cause while I was pukin' on that dead Dwarf's neck, I didn't see any weapons on him. You seemed to have a fuckin' dossier on me, so ya know I ain't helpless in a hand-to-hand fight. Ya weren't there to save my life or gimme a ride home. Ya were markin' off number nineteen, weren't ya?"

"Nick, you're reading into this too much-"

"Stop fuckin' talkin' like I ain't got eyes, Rhys! I believe Kirschbaum got a backdoor parole, yeah, and I think ya knew it too. Weren't his patron who asked fer the slit, that's a waste of influence to get him out. Someone else wanted it, or..." I look to him, takin' a breath. "You did."

The Redcap closes his eyes for a second and reaches into his coat. The blade slips free of the vambrace as he pulls out two daggers. I ready a stance, the bow extending, taut and stringed, fuck, I didn't want it to turn out like this-

The knives are now on my table, and Rhys is stepping out of reach from them, putting; his hands up, but don't say a fuckin' word.

"Fer fuck's sake, Rhys, just tell me the fuckin' truth! What's goin' on, yeah? Do ya really wanna help find who killed Bridget, or ya just wanna hit a round numb-"

The Goblin lets his jacket drop to the floor, then hands back up. Still quiet.

"What, ya under bindin' or some shit? Yer connected to this, ain't ya? Fuck, Rhys, just tell me!" He looks like he's in pain. I… think he wants to tell me.

"Ya know who it is, don't ya. And yer bound to keep it secret, yeah? How fuckin' bad could it be?"

And now he's standin' shirtless, and yeah, he's cut and lithe. He got his share of scars. 'Specially the gash on his chest, over his heart, ugly and rough, and surroundin' it? A ring of glowin' Sigil. It's an Oathbindin', and that scar ain't from breakin' it. He broke another, a big one, probably to a noble a few steps up in the peerage.

"Rhys? Tell me the truth. Dieter Kirschbaum didn't kill Bridget O'Hare, did he?"

He takes a breath. "No. No, he didn't."

I'm tremblin', now. Fuck. Fuck. *Fuck.*

"Rhys?" My throat's dry. "Did…" I swallow hard.

"Rhys Llewellyn, did you murder Bridget O'Hare?"

16

"Rhys? This is where you tell me no."

He ain't moved, or flinched. No response or nothin'. Fuck.

"C'mon, it ain't that hard. Just tell me ya didn't do it, okay? Tell me ya didn't kill her." My breath is catchin' in my throat. Other than settin' his jaw he don't say shit.

"Fuckin' Shadow, Rhys! Tell me ya didn't kill her! Tell me ya didn't kill Bridget O'Hare! It ain't that fuckin' hard! Say one Shadowdamned syllable or shake yer fuckin' head or gesture with yer hands or fuck, shake yer dick from side to fuckin' side, just fuckin' tell me ya didn't kill her!"

Buddy, I ain't too sure why this is breakin' me up this bad. But other than clenchin' his fists, he don't answer. Fuck, please don't be true.

"'Kay, just… Rhys, ya gotta gimme somethin'. Were ya… Did ya kill her and yer here to stay ahead of me? Make sure I don't find out yer the one who did it? Rhys, I read them fuckin' books before, I know how those stories end! Just… Tell me ya didn't…"

My eyes are hot, now. Wet. Rhys's whole body is clenched, looks like, like he's hurtin'.

"Rhys, just… tell me ya didn't fuckin' use me." I meet his eyes, vision blurry. I can't be used again. Not ever again. "Please, just-"

He looks like he's in agony. Not like he's gonna kill me and hates that it's necessary. Like he's in physical fuckin' pain. I step closer to him, cautious, yeah, but more to get a better look at his chest. Not for that reason, 'course, this really ain't the time or moment to ogle him. 'Stead I'm oglin' that scar, that ring of Sigil.

"Brother Gremlin, lend your sight
Let me see the hidden light
Secrets shown that I will break
Brother, let my blood awake"

Dries the *fuck* outta my eyes, but the Sigil is more pronounced. On the scar is a chain, a broken one, the shards jagged, still protrudin' from his spirit, pulled tense. The ring, on the other hand, ain't a chain, I don't know what the fuck it is, really. Still, there's a reason I did this for more than a closer look. It ain't too hard to figure out someone put this on him, but for whatever reason, I don't know who or why. Up to me to figure it out.

"Rhys? Did ya kill Bridget O'Hare?"

He tenses, trembles, the broken chain diggin' in, fresh blood wellin' from the wound. The ring doesn't spin into his heart. If anything, it flickers, weakens, and his breathin' picks up.

"Rhys? Do you want to tell me no?"

More flickers on the ring.

"Rhys? Am I hurtin' ya right now?"

He nods, quickly.

"Fuck. Ya ain't gotta answer! Ya ain't gotta answer. I'll drop it. I'll uh, just assume ya murdered her and ain't no one else connected to it. At all. Sound good?"

I wanna tell ya, buddy, that he sags in relief and is okay. Instead, he topples over to the floor. And he ain't fuckin' breathin'.

"Fuck!"

I put my ear to his chest. Fuck, no pulse. No fuckin' pulse. Aw, fuck.

No, Blackwarren, ya ain't gonna panic.

Check the airway. 'Kay, it's clear. Uh... how the fuck ya do chest compressions?! Somethin' about the Bee Gees or some shit?! I think I got it. Uh... one. Two. Three. Four.

I place my mouth to his, breathe long into his mouth. Immediately my mouth is coughed into, and I yank my head back. "Fucking Hell, Nick, what are you doing?"

I laugh, for the tension if anythin'. "Aw fuck, yer alive. I thought I was gonna lose ya." I'm so relieved that...

Yeah. I fuckin' kiss him. It's been a bitch of a mornin', 'kay?

The Redcap, at least, pushes me back, but not roughly. "Why were you pushing so hard on my stomach?"

"Yer heart stopped! Ya didn't have a pulse so I was doin' chest compressions and mouth to mouth and-"

A finger's on my mouth now. "Nick. That is not how you do chest compressions, and you didn't have to do mouth to mouth."

"Well, lemme 'least check yer pulse, yeah?" I ain't never been too good at that, so I push my ear against his chest, and he pushes me back, but... "I don't hear a heartbeat, Rhys."

Silent again. Fuckin'...

"That Oath on yer chest, over yer heart, does it stop it when ya try to tell the truth, or go against the Oath?" He looks at me. "Don't answer, don't want ya passin' out again. That's some pretty complex shit, layerin' an Oath to prevent like, *any* answer about what it is or who put it there. But ya got a scar that's still diggin' in when ya try to answer. Yer an Oathbreaker, aren't ya, Rhys?"

He exhales in relief. "Yes. I am a foul, traitorous Oathbreaker such as my nature as a dreg of the Noble Fae. As Fae are concerned, I am naught but a sewer-spawned talking fungus."

Obviously, he's on a fuckin' script for that. If the talk bein' too high falutin' weren't a clue, him rollin' his eyes was the kicker.

I got an answer, at least. "Ya don't gotta answer fer this part, Rhys. Yer an Oathbreaker, meanin' a Noble asked ya to do somethin', and yer a fuckin' Redcap so it's pretty fuckin' obvious what ya were probably s'posed to do: kill someone. Gimme a sec, gotta think on it some more."

I help him to one of my foldin' chairs, put some tea on, and toss him an apple.

"As I was sayin', ya had to swear to a completion for a contract, and ya said ya've killed nineteen before, so it weren't like it was first time jitters or some shit. Yer dipped, and professional, I'm guessin'." He gives me a look that implies that yeah, he's a pro. "So that Oath bein' broken means ya refused to do it. My Pa had to do a job for a Sidhe before and got bound. Soon as the body went cold the chains vanished."

I grab an apple and rip it to pieces with my teeth, because emotional tension's still runnin' hard, buddy.

"But that didn't happen here. It ripped up yer chest and ya shoulda died, let's be honest, but I'm guessin' yer a tough enough fucker that ya managed to either drag yerself to a mystic, or had a stash with alchemical shit to hold ya over. So, no offense, but what makes a fuckin' Redcap change his mind about a slit? I don't factor in this conversation, it was fuckin' self-defense. It was him or me, and ya don't seem that type to end up in that kinda situation, am I right? That ya can answer."

Rhys takes a big bite and shreds a good part of the fruit. Gremlins got scary teeth, yeah, but he ain't a born Redcap, those teeth ain't crushin' concrete. Bone wouldn't be no problem, though. "No, I wouldn't. I was raised in your clan's arts from childhood, and stealth means you never end up in such a situation. And your clan's females excel in both poisons *and* restoratives."

"Exactly." Kettle's ready. I reuse the tea bags from before, 'cause I ain't picked up groceries yet. "I know. My Aunt Cora's a street doc. So many of my cousins would be fuckin' doctors or workin' in pharma if the fuckers in charge weren't always humans. I mean, Sluagh got the best shit, but I'm gettin' off track.

So, there was somethin' about that contract that ya stepped back from even though ya took an Oath to do it. And don't answer, but I'm thinkin' that contract was for Bridget O'Hare, and ya refused because the rule that was a guideline before July is now fuckin' policy fer Redcaps: No. Slittin'. Humans. Plus I think ya got a soul under all them scars, so ya didn't wanna kill an innocent woman who didn't do shit other than maybe not goin' top-tier on her music's SEO."

Search engine optimization, buddy, makin' sure yer stuff is the first that comes up on the internet when ya search. Pretty sure if I'd known about her stuff I woulda slipped her tracks to Cenzo on the DL so she'd get more traffic. Seriously, she was that good, just a matter of gettin' the right people to notice her.

"Nick-"

"I told ya not to answer. Don't want ya bleedin' all over the fuckin' place." I sip my tea, and it's weak as fuck from reusin' a bag, but I don't mind. "Let's use a handy couple words, yeah? Let's say, *hypothetically* and *allegedly*, ya were contracted to murder Bridget O'Hare, and I dunno, ya thought she was a lowborn Sidhe or Brownie or Phouka or Twin Blood or somethin'. Ya ain't thrilled about the job, but them nobles got strings to pull and ya got roped into it."

I roll my shoulders, stretch, put down the bow on the table, 'cause if he was gonna do somethin', he woulda. 'Stead he's listenin', like I'm fumblin' my way through a maze and getting' closer to the exit but he can't tell me nothin' about where to go or if I'm goin' the wrong way, or even if I'm out.

"Ya do yer casin' and stalkin', and find out yer mark's a woman from West Benedict, and then that it's a *human* woman. Ya call yer patron to call it off, they get pissed, ya refuse further, they say yer breakin' an Oath, ya tell 'em to fuck off, and there ya go. Chest ripped to shit, and they get someone else to do the deed, or I'm guessin', do it themselves. Now I ain't got a fuckin' clue what that shit on yer heart is, but I'm guessin' it's a failsafe to make ya take the fall for her murder."

Obviously, he don't say shit, 'cause he can't, lest he fuckin' kill himself givin' me the answer which would defeat the fuckin' point of all this.

"So, now the charmin' roguish Goblin enters the thick of it, swearin' up a blue streak and fuckin' shit up for whoever's behind all this. Her parents hire me on the spot out of sheer fuckin' desperation, and before I can crack that Dwarf to squeeze some truth out... Ya show up and kill him 'cause he's... the one who killed her."

I sit down. "Wait, that don't add up right. I mean, they hired me pretty fast. I don't doubt those were her parents. But they woulda searched the place after she died, gettin' her stuff and everythin'. I think they're tellin' the truth that the symphony was stolen, but I don't think they themselves know why that's so important that they'd hire a sketchy lookin' fuck like me to investigate." I look at him. "Plus, still no explanation why ya were at Kirkland way earlier than ya shoulda been able to get out there."

No answer. I'm sorry fer him and pissed off at him at the same time. It ain't his fault, but this is why ya try not to work for Sidhe, it's always forty levels more complex than just a slit. Plus, they want ya to fuckin' kill someone simply 'cause they said so, and to fuckin' Tartarus with that. Fuck, this is why I try to never use my name around 'em for fear they'll...

"Ya said my name. Ya asked if I was Nick Blackwarren. I thought ya were who my Cousin sent, but ya never corrected me. I don't think he really sent ya, and I know that us Goblins can lie if we wanna. Ya were lookin' for me and Kirschbaum. I'm thinkin' the latter fer yer patron to tie up loose ends, and me…"

I tap the table, reaffirmin' his attention. "Hey. Why were ya lookin' fer me? This probably ain't got nothin' to do with that Oath shit, right?"

"Yes and no." He's lookin' at the table.

"I'll give ya the benefit of the doubt on Kirschbaum. Maybe it was rainin' so hard ya reacted without confirmin' a weapon. I dunno, but did my Cousin send ya?"

"No, he didn't. I did call him, though, and offer to pick you up as I was closer to you. He didn't ask questions, just told me to bring you back to the City as soon as possible." He half-chuckles. "Does your whole family speak as coarsely as you do?"

"Ha-ha, hardy-har, fuck right off. So why me, huh?"

"Viscountess Riverwood, Lord Greenmeadow, Earl Iceheart. All murdered, the killer the subject of a citywide bloodhunt, the Queen's Guard and Left Hand commissioned to tear the kingdom apart to find him, and who brings him to justice? A lowly Goblin thief. Nicholas Arsenne of the Black Warren, Walker of the Shadow's Edge. If you only knew, Nick, how very much *hated* you are by the ruling class for avenging three of their own without their leave or assistance. No credit taken, no favors given. Any leftover glory was reserved for the Left Hand's Fingers and a *scrap* for Prince Thomas. Queen Alana-"

"May Her warmth bless us all," we both say.

"Has been using your victory against her detractors who doubted her raising a Goblin to Left Hand of the Throne." He gets up, lookin' a little better. "If you could do *that*, maybe you could help me with…" He winces again, and I touch his shoulder.

"Ya ain't gotta say nothin', Rhys." I get up, stand before him, respectable distance, though, like what the Catholics do at prom. "'Long as ya understand she's my priority in this, yeah? But I'm guessin' solvin' it will take care of that, too."

"So, you'll help me, Nick?"

I extend my hand, after spittin' in my palm. "If I don't my name ain't Nicholas Arsenne Blackwarren."

He spits in his, "Or my name isn't Rhys Gwydion Llewellyn."

We shake. "So. Gonna guess we're partners."

"It would seem."

"Rhys, uh… We probably shouldn't, uh, get physical, yeah?" I break eye contact. "Y'see, I've been makin' some dumb decisions regardin' guys. Lettin' my heart get dragged into shit that might not be…"

"I understand. You have feelings for Prince Thomas and I'm only complicating matters for you. I will keep things professional, don't worry. My life may very well be on the line, so I'd be comfortable doing so, Nick, whether my hea-" He looks down, wincin' again. "Even if it not connected tangentially, I cannot refer to my…" He gives me a look, implyin' I fill in the blanks.

His heart. Fuck, he mighta caught some feelin's too.

Oh fer fuck's sake, Blackwarren, take yer fuckin' hand off his chest.

"Ya should, uh, put yer shirt back on." Fuckin' Shadow, just take yer fuckin' hand off him so he can do that. It don't matter it feels warm and yer heart aches like fuck when ya feel that scar and ya wanna ease his pain.

"I should." But, uh, Rhys, ya ain't. Stop fuckin' lookin' in my eyes. Those beautiful ocean eyes I feel like fallin' into forever. Yer hand, uh, shouldn't be on my waist.

"We really should stop, Rhys." Stop breathin' so damned fast! It's easy! Hands off. Step back. Go to the bathroom and whack this out so ya can take care of the *much more important problems facin' yer life.* Fuck, his back's like a nest of fuckin' pythons he's so strong and lithe and…

"I don't want you to get hurt, Nick." Both hands on my back, our chests almost touchin'. Fuckin' Shadow I gotta stop this… Yeah?

"Do me a favor and stop fuckin' feelin' so *right*, would ya?" Our lips are brushin' now. I feel warm all over. Fuck, he smells so good. "I feel like we got somethin' and I'm terrified we're gonna fuck it up and if we…"

"It'll change everything. We're supposed to be partners, yes."

"Yeah…" I quickly kiss him, more like gettin' a hit, stavin' it off. "Be my partner." I take a breath. "Fuck, yer wired to confess to a murder ya didn't commit, and yer a Redcap assassin, Rhys. Ya ain't exactly partner material."

We're restin' foreheads to each other now. "I'm not. And you're the one who'd probably catch me, bring me to an ignoble end, likely at the hands of your Phouka Prince." He catches his breath. "But I can't lean away, Nick."

"I should, but I don't wanna." I take a breath. "We start kissin', Rhys, we're gonna end up…"

"I know. We shouldn't." He meets my eyes. "We shouldn't."

"We shouldn't."

"Shadow help me, I want you, Nick." He takes a deep breath. "But I leave the choice to you. I mustn't intrude." Rhys's arms fall from my back. "We should remain partners. Professionally. This isn't the time for matters of… You know what I would say, and Nick, I cannot allow you to-"

"Shut. The fuck. Up." I hold his face in my hands. "Ya don't get to tell me what can and ain't gonna happen with you after ya say it's my fuckin' choice. So, let me choose, yeah? Just answer a question fer me."

"I'll try to." We're still close.

"We both wake up in the same bed, yer up first. Whadduya do?"

"Hm. Given from what I've seen in your apartment?" I nod. "Take whatever book you probably fell asleep reading off your chest and put it on the night table with a bookmark in, then use the bathroom, wash my hands, quick shower to save hot water for you, brush my teeth. This is all given you haven't told me to wake you up at a specific time."

"'Course. Go on."

"Start the coffee brewing, run through my various calls and messages while I prepare breakfast, crack some eggs and mix them with milk, get the bread you probably let go stale, and use it to make French toast, because you've mentioned it *several* times, a few rashers of bacon, knowing the smell will likely do more to wake you up, have it all ready when you come into the kitchen for us to have breakfast and bicker about whatever was in *Jump* that week-"

"I swear to fuckin' Shadow, Rhys, if this is a fuckin' con job on me."

"You're right." He smirks. Fuck him and that damned smirk. "You probably read... *Shojo Beat?*"

"Ya can't tell me that shit and then act like ya don't want somethin' like that! Fuck! Yer too fuckin'... *perfect*, fuck!"

He quirks a brow. We're good at that when we gotta. "For... what?"

"For me, ya fuckin' *mamaluke*." I rub my face. "We only met in the last twelve hours, fuck. This *ain't* how this shit's s'posed to go! We're s'posed to meet, be all awkward and shit, sorta date for a month or somethin' and then one of us says 'boyfriend' outta fuckin' nowhere and we decide that's our label and-"

"Where are you getting these rules from, Nick? I saw a stack of romance novels so I know it wasn't from them."

"I'm sayin' I shouldn't feel a fuckin' connection to ya like I got so somethin' must be goin' on! Fer the Phouk I know I just get fuckin' horny, but I'm fuckin' meltin' here and yer scent's ticklin' me and ya ain't even touched my fuckin' ears!"

At that, he looks hurt. "I would *never* touch your ears, Nick. That's... You're not a... Do you *really* think so little of me that I would..." In his disgust, he looks away. "You're not some broken, fallen Goblin slave, Nick."

"Wait, what?" This is new to me. "Uh, what? I mean, it fuckin' feels good to, right? It's how ya let another Gob know ya wanna fuck."

"It's the leash of the Machinist, Nick. Slave acting up? Grab their ears and let the sexual ecstasy wash away that rebellious spirit. There are still Nobles who do that to us. How else do you think I was coerced into those Oaths? But you *melt* for me?"

"Wait, the ear thing."

"Should've been taught to you by your parents as a warning. You melt for me? Enjoy my scent? I'll admit yours makes me somewhat quivery, but... Are you starting to-"

"Ain't no one outside the Phouka who falls that damned fast. I'm just sayin'... I'm catchin'..."

"Feelings for me? Your scent is rather... salty. I'm telling myself it's only because we met under such harried circumstances, such things fade, but..." Rhys closes the distance between us again. "Truthfully? I cannot fathom why, but I do feel better this close to you. Perhaps it's only lust." He shrugs, but he don't pull away.

"Yeah, kinda sucks bein' the only Fae that can lie, huh? But yeah, so what do we do with tha-"

His chest is to mine, and I wish I could hear or feel his heart beatin', but there's only silence. The kiss ain't like the car, not a storm of emotions and need and clashin' personalities. It's slow, hands explorin' on both sides, needin' to touch and feel and pull us closer together. Fuck, this ain't s'posed to be that kinda story, but with Rhys, it feels like it is. I wanna feel him against me, help him, save his life, walk into whatever this'll be with open eyes and free hearts.

When we join, it ain't like with me and Thom, no raucous passions, grunts or yells. It's slow, smooth, always talkin' to each other, whisperin' what we wanna feel, and for the other to hear. There ain't no shoutin' when we finish, no glorious declaration of hittin' the summit, just a soft word or two, "I'm here."

I get off from atop him, lie on my side next to him. No words for a bit. No need to break the ice or tension, it's just us. I don't feel safe. Not in a bad way, buddy, I gotta make that clear. I don't feel protected. I don't feel like I'm keepin' him safe or protectin' him.

"We're gonna figure this out, Rhys, we're gonna find a way to get you free and unmask the fucker who killed Bridget in front of all of Fae society, and then, we're gonna go to the fuckin' Allora Philharmonic to hear her *magnum opus*. Whatcha say? Huh *Sebas*?"

"You see me as the butler from *Overlord*?"

"Yeah, yer strong, fast, deadly, but ya got a sense of honor and duty that puts 'em all to shame."

"You think I have honor?" He's lookin' away. "I do the thing that you abhor, Nick. I kill. I take lives at the behest of others." He smiles weakly. "I prefer the Little Death I gave you, honorable or no." I turn his head back toward me.

"Sebas, if ya weren't honorable, ya wouldn't be here with them scars and Oaths tellin' ya to keep quiet, and wantin' to defy 'em."

"Very well, Kyo." He smiles to me.

"From *Fruits Basket*." I laugh. "'Course ya'd pick him as me."

"Rough attitude, rough family life, always made to feel less than, like he doesn't belong anywhere, or with anyone, but still endeavors to keep going, do the right thing."

"Sounds good." I kiss him again. "Partner."

"Until the end of the tale," he whispers, kissing me in return. Both of us are, uh, swellin'. Maybe we're gonna go once more. "Partner."

17

For starters, buddy, we don't fuck the day away. Yeah, it was good, and tender, and all that shit that happens in romance novels, but at the end of the day, this ain't that kinda story, got it? A girl is dead and a fuckin' Noble is usin' a Goblin as a disposable patsy, so gotta keep them priorities straight. Spendin' a few hours explorin' each other's bodies would be fun and sweet, but it'd burn fuckin' time that Rhys might not have, know what I'm sayin'?

And that, buddy, is why Rhys and I are in fresh clothes and walkin' the quad at Allora University. It's one of those "Almost Ivy" kinda places, good prestige, high price, plenty of legacy students and money walkin' 'round, tall trees, a place of education sorta cordoned off from actual fuckin' reality. Everythin's gotta be top flight, top tier, A-1 platinum grade.

On a crisp autumn day ya got people walkin' around in branded clothes for the college, leaves on the ground here and there, past peak foilage, the kinda place ya fantasize about goin' to when yer young and poor and don't quite know that the world don't work like that, yet.

And yes, we're gettin' a wide berth from people, even the mythics.

And yes, we both been asked about twenty times if we're holdin' weed or Adderall.

"I have to wonder what college would have been like for me." Rhys is looking around, wearin' some of my clothes that are baggy on me, but fit on him. "If I hadn't had so many choices made for me from one terrible day."

"Yeah, what happened? If yer okay with sayin', that is. Ya said yer uncle was tryin' to kill your brother?"

"It's fine. We still don't know what happened to him. He wasn't the best of people, but I'd never known him to be violent. My only suspicion was he had been poisoned, perhaps, or enchanted to fly into an uncontrolled rage. I was a child, I only wanted him to stop scaring us. There was no malice in my heart when I struck, just fear. I didn't believe he would die, I hardly knew what death was yet. And shortly after, the Black Warren sent someone for me. I… never saw my mother or brother again."

"That must fuck with ya, I'm sorry."

"Yes, it is. I am aware, at least, that my mother and brother are still alive, and faring well enough for themselves, as much as one can in Swansea. I've had my years to come to terms. I send them something for Yule, under a different name, mind you, but I'm certain they know it's from me." He looks to me. "And you? Ever thought about what your life would have been like had you attended university?"

I gotta laugh. "Would ya believe me if I told ya I was gonna go here?"

He stops at one of the unattended benches and takes a seat. Well, it's unattended once we both look like we're gonna sit there. "That will require more explanation, Kyo."

"Hand to the gods, I had a free ride all set up on athletic scholarship for gymnastics. I was hot shit out in California, ya know. I ain't in as good shape, but I try to keep it up on my off days."

"I'm sensing a complication to this."

"You'd be right. Y'see, this is a AAA school, Division 1A for gymnastics. Olympic scouts come here, know what I'm sayin'? So that means, when ya sign a kid from out in California that blew yer scout away, ya gotta go through the standard shit. Includin' a background check." I lean back against the wood slats that make up the back of the bench. "And that was it."

"Checkered past, I see."

"Nope, one Google search and up comes Colton Blackwarren, my Pa, and the guilty verdict of multiple murders and his address at the time bein' the supermax wing at Kirkland. Allora sent a 'we regret to inform' letter, and since it was past June, I didn't have any backups since the word was out on me now. And that was it. I moved from California to here to make a go of it. I mean, what the fuck else ya gonna do when yer one of us?"

I get up. "A'right, enough of that pity party bullshit. We got work to do, partner, let's go."

The target of that "go" would be the music department of Allora University in the Fine Arts buildin', where yer painters and sculptors and artists and musicians tend to gravitate into that protected bubble where ya can just make art all day and not worry yet 'bout how yer gonna pay fer it all.

Most of 'em don't gotta, obviously, this game is rigged for the rich kids with two hundred dollar an hour tutors who can make anybody sound good with enough studio magic. Bridget weren't one of those people, but honest, she weren't no financial need case either. Don't make her talent less than or mean she hadn't earned it. Just means she didn't have those weights.

Sorry, buddy, this is what this place did to my brain, y'know? Put someone like me in a place built on inequality and I'll need a forklift to carry the fuckin' chip on my shoulder.

We kinda stick out, yeah, but we ain't here to blend in as students, and I was fortunate enough to get a pack of somethin' from Cenzo to sell the new business.

"Should we speak with professors? Instructors? Seems like they would be the most likely to remember her."

"Put that on the back burner, I think. Gotta have that CYA in academics, y'know? 'Specially if we start askin' questions 'bout a dead girl. Figure cops had to do their due diligence even if that Dwarf confessed, so they mighta had to answer all these questions before. Try the students first in the rehearsal spaces, then the instructors if we ain't gettin' nowhere. Failing that, we'll check around the art department, the MFA and BFA kids tend to stick together."

"Then let's begin."

Don't know her.

Didn't know her.

Was that the girl that was killed? So sad but didn't know her.

A few more didn't know her much.

She was in another group, kept to herself.

Didn't know her.

This is investigating, by the way. Canvassing, I think they call it. They ain't all gonna to be winners, but that's why you charge a per diem, ya see, and do the work to earn it. If it was simple as asking one person, her parents woulda done it. Also, when the guy who allegedly did it was found in the room standing over the body and confessed directy to the police, let's face it, the cops and DA ain't gonna turn down an easy win. So if Rhys and I gotta accost a few coeds, then that's what we'll do. At least he's good at it, asks some questions that I didn't think of that I can follow-up on.

"Are we keeping to the humans?" Again, it's a good question. Bridget was human, so you have to figure her friends and colleagues would be human too, but if she drew the attention of one of the Fair Folk… He doesn't add to the question, just leaves it out there, open, probably because with all of those of Oaths he can't add anything more than that. He's trusting me to pick up the lead and go with it, that we're thinking on the same throughlines. "And keeping to the music department? I would imagine she had acquaintances in her other courses as well."

"Yeah, let's give that a look after. I see someone over there." I move toward her, but I take pains to do so in a non-aggressive way. If humans see us as the worst of humanity, it ain't too much to guess how young women see us as we're movin' toward 'em. Hands visible, open, relaxed, pitch the voice up a couple steps, like a kid on a high-school tour that got lost. "'Scuse me, miss? Sorry to bother ya, but did ya ever know a girl named Bridget O'Hare? Played piano?"

Sound hopeful, like ya wanna get her autograph or some shit (I actually would, she was pretty fuckin' good). Best to put her at ease so I can ask the questions before she pulls the drawbridge, figuratively.

"Why are you asking?" She's mid-twenties, dressed smart, hair back, stretching her fingers and hands to keep 'em loose. And she's a bit wary.

But she also got eyes like fuckin' fire opals.

"Excuse me." I take out a business card and hold it out to her. "Nick Arsenne, Blackwarren Asset Recovery. This is my associate Mr. Gwyn." Rhys nods. "We were hired by Ms. O'Hare's parents to recover something of hers that hasn't come up since Ms. O'Hare's tragic death."

"You mean her *murder*." A glare, but it's earned.

"And that's what makes it fuckin' tragic, miss. Did you know her well, Miss…?" Rhys, gods bless him, got a notebook out and is scribblin' away.

"Fallingleaf." She folds her arms. "Blackwarren? You're with the Left Hand?"

Yep, definitely a Sidhe, but given that apprehension in her voice? I'm guessin' she's more on the half-side then a full blueblood.

"I ain't… I'm not working for Captain Blackwarren, no. Simply the same last name."

"And your *Redcap* 'associate'?" Now she's glarin' at Rhys, but still tense.

"Miss Fallingleaf, if I had any desire to harm you, I would not do such a thing in a public place." How he can be so matter of fact about that… "We are here for simple information to right a wrong, nothing more. Your name and involvement will be kept out of any record for the Kingdom, and in our records, you will only be acknowledged as Source 11. Would that be acceptable?"

She sighs, looks about to confirm that the room is clear. "What do you want to know about Bridget?"

"Been lookin' up her social media, watchin' her streams up until the last one a month ago."

"The one where she composes a score for a disaster movie that's also a romantic comedy?" She smiles a bit at that, and I nod. "That wasn't from last month. That was from April."

"But… the post date was September." I tilt my head a little while Rhys gets that down.

"Those are the streams that she did for her patrons. Pay twenty a month, get access to the stream, pay fifty, give suggestions for what she'll compose. Should be on her website, I think." She takes out her phone and starts tapping away at it. "Could you try it? I'm not getting it. Think the WiFi dropped on me."

So, I do, and…

"Fuckin' 404? It was workin' earlier." I look at her. "That's… off. Anythin' on her website that might be important, ya think?"

"She was keeping a blog? And the thank you's to her top patrons, of course, but those were all usernames, if I remember right. What was missing that you're trying to find?" Shit, that would be golden fuckin' information. List of suspects fer damned sure. Spilled milk and all that fuckery, might as well keep on.

"Did she ever speak of a symphony she was workin' on?"

Her eyes go wide. *"That's* what's missing? She was putting everything into that. I think she mentioned she'd been working on it since high school."

"Yeah, we know that." Though it makes the symphony all the more precious. Her life's work. "Any idea where she mighta hid it, or put it?"

Rhys follows up, "Or a cubby, or storage especially for students?" Glad I brought him, I wouldna asked that.

She shrugs. "Maybe? I don't know." The Twin Blood looks at my card. "You're really trying to find it? Give it to her parents?"

"Who'll give it to the conservatory, yeah."

"If I can think of anything else, I'll call you, but that's all I have right now."

"Did she have a boyfriend, Miss Fallingleaf?" Rhys asks, and I gotta admit I shoulda asked that question too. It's almost always the boyfriend, y'know? Or girlfriend, or non-binary partner. I'm investigating, yeah, but I don't know her fuckin' life.

"I never saw anyone, but we weren't close friends, just shared rehearsal spaces and talked about music. She was quiet if she wasn't doing it for her fans. Bridget was starting to come out of her shell, I think. Might have been a guy, but I figured you can't do all those livestreams without building some confidence." Somethin' to follow up with her parents on, if she was the type to share that sorta information. "I really do have to go, though, I have a rehearsal in five minutes."

"We won't detain you, Miss Fallingleaf." Rhys steps out of her way, even though she goes to the door behind her. Thought that counts, yeah? "So, now what?"

"Got a few things to follow up. Look for her site on the internet archive, text her mom and ask if she was datin' anyone, maybe look into why the most recent stream is from over five months ago. I'm gettin' the feelin' we're lookin' at a Sidhe noble. I mean *look* at this place. It's a haven for brilliant artists and musicians, that's fuckin' catnip for those pricks."

"Coffee? No offense, but weak tea won't do for me."

I snerk. "Caffeine hound? Yer in the right place. Gotta be at least a dozen little places here to pick up chocolate-covered coffee beans."

Rhys waves his hand, disgusted. "No caffeine snacks, no abhorrent energy drinks, or posh overdesigned, overtweaked, overpriced imitations. I want coffee. Black."

"So yer just a snob." I smirk, and he returns in kind as we stop at a kiosk in the building. Still more to look at. I got the feeling we ain't done in here yet. "City roast for him, Masala chai for me." Then an indulgent look to my partner, to which he grumbles.

"Fine, fine, I've got it." He fishes some bills out of his pocket, passing them to the work-study student behind the counter. "Apple scone for him too. Keep the change."

We all tend to do that, by the way, so they don't think we're going to rob them or swindle. Cash up front, more than the cost, keep the change, friendly as fuck. He just manages it better with the tingles of English and Welsh in his accent. Also, he got me a scone 'cause he noticed me eyeing it, I got him city roast because it's past first crack, but sweet.

Fuckin'… Now we're fuckin' flirtin' by proxy, Shadow take me.

We do leave, though, because a couple Goblins standin' 'round's only gonna invite attention neither of us want. A chat with some of the staff eventually finds us someone who'll tell us that any lockers are cleared out at the end of the semester, and Bridget graduated in May. Pretty sure she was hangin' around and shit, but she eventually had a place, which is now my place. Dead end, buddy, is what I'm sayin'. So, we end up back out on the quad where we ain't gonna draw attention or make trouble.

Though more humans ask us if we're sellin' weed. Or coke. Or speed. Rhys ignores 'em and I just tell 'em to fuck the fuck off.

"I must ask, what is your issue with the Sidhe? It can't be as simple as their station." Rhys is peerin' at me. Guess there's gotta be this sorta talk between partners if yer gonna trust each other when the shit hits the fan.

"Don't know what part of the City ya grew up in, Sebas, but in my neighborhood those prissy fucks never missed an opportunity to piss down on us. Privileged assholes who didn't do shit other than be born and I gotta bend a knee? Gotta keep my mouth shut when they call me sewer rat? Talkin' like they're big shit when they're so fuckin' far behind the rest of the world…"

On fuckin' cue, buddy, one of them hoity toity fucks sneers at me, walkin' by. "Don't ya fuckin' turn yer nose up at me ya shit-"

And now Rhys's hand is on my mouth, the Sidhe and his buddies laughin' as they walk away. "And this is why I call you Kyo. What purpose would it serve, honestly? You're trying to score points in a game he's already won."

"Fuck you, okay?" I look away. "Fuck, I gotta breathe or some shit. This ain't helpin' Bridget." My eyes meet his. "Ya know I'm fuckin' smart, right? This is just how I talk?"

"I watched you deduce an entire investigation while I was unable to give you any concrete answers." He kisses me softly, and then meets my eyes again, warmly. "Yes, Kyo. I know you're smart."

"Good, because it's more than just a simple socio-economic grudge that I bear against the 'Fairer Folk', it's also the rampant abuse of unearned privilege which has no basis other than some obscure titled ancestor from centuries back in the countries and worlds *we all fled from*. Such actions merely make their kith and kin into a nigh-literal personification of stagnation despite the fact that they anoint themselves as children as champions of human ephemera which is chaotic and emotional by nature. Yet, they denounce the one kith that can legitimately claim descendance from the Dreamers they purport to hold in such high fuckin' regard: The Goblins." I look at him. "But I shouldn't gotta talk all high-falutin' to make a fuckin' point, y'know?"

He nods to me. "I know, but it sounded like all that was pent up and you needed to get it out. Our next leg of the investigation?"

"Go with the Art department, like ya said. Just 'cause we whiffed out here with the music majors don't mean Bridget never talked to any of 'em. 'Sides... I'm gettin' a bad sorta feelin'."

We're walkin' again, side by side. It's gettin' later in the day, closer to noon, so the quad is busier. We walk closer together, and to make us seem less threatenin'... Well, Pa and Mom taught me to keep my hands in my pockets, head down, no eye contact, hood up if I could help it, blend into the crowd. But, there's an easier way that I picked up from Cenzo: Do what the humans do.

So, we both walk forward, our phones out, tapping and texting way, or at least pantomiming it on my part. Is it that surprisin' that nothin' says "we're humans like you" better than fuckin' around on a smartphone while walkin' through a crowd? The Arts buildin' is across the quad, named for Frida Kahlo. She didn't go here or anythin', but when it comes to light that the original person the building was named after had a trove of Nazi stolen art, ya try to find someone that'll appease the Lefties ya still got on campus.

It's open to the public, but only the first floor where the student gallery is. My eye's only slightly above "would give a like on Insta", and it don't seem like Rhys is much better, seein' as we just look at the paintings with either simple appreciatives, or "…huh."

"Mind telling me what your bad feeling was?" We're sittin' on a bench, set before a mural that I'm sure is very good. I mean, the colors are nice? "I thought you would follow up on it, but you started doing a sudoku."

"I'm just wonderin' how they met, y'know? Whoever it was behind all this. If they're a Sidhe, why go here lookin' for a musician? They gotta be everywhere here, 'specially over in the theater district, so why approach a college student?"

"Do you want me to answer, or are you working it through?" He's lookin' at me, smilin' a bit. "Seems you have the more deductive mind, perhaps the Socratic method?"

I swing my leg over the bench to straddle it, face him head on. "Sure, could work."

"What would they have to gain by approaching someone that young and unestablished, if they could easily fascinate any number of artists?"

"Well, they don't have any connections, yet. You could dazzle 'em with a pat on the head and promises of fame. Everyone's lookin' fer that big break, ya know?" The Redcap matches my sitting position.

"And the Sidhe do adore the role of Muse." He's wincin'. There's more he wants to tell me, I know, but he's treadin' close to the line for his Oaths. Fuck, it's like readin' a mystery where yer friend already knows who did it and how and why, only in this case givin' spoilers might kill him.

I rub my head. I gotta think this through. Luckily, I got a scone and chai to serve as socially acceptable pauses. Think, Blackwarren, there's all kinds of reason for a Sidhe to find people on a college campus. Why pick her? Maybe they prefer music, and that's why they chose a…

Wait, I'm lookin' at this too, uh, nice? Maybe I don't wanna think about it, but…

"Are we… Fuck…" I take a breath, 'cause buddy, I don't wanna consider this, but we're talkin' the Fair Folk here. "Are we sure there was only Bridget?"

And now I look at Rhys with renewed concern. "Rhys Llewellyn, did you-"

"No. I can't speak to anyone else this could have happened to, but I had no hand in…" He's clutchin' his chest, like he did before he-

"Ya don't gotta answer, ya don't gotta answer!" Both of us breathe relieved. He was tellin' the truth, at least about not killin' anyone else. (Besides the nineteen, that is, but that was Redcap business. Don't make it okay, obvi, but no other humans, at least.) So why would his Oaths start diggin' in? "There were others. Ya don't have to answer."

I get a silent nod in return, more meant as not wanting to answer, but if I choose to take it as "yes, there absolutely were others this happened to", then I can. So I guess this means we're broadenin' the search. I take out my phone and dial the one person who can help me with this.

"Fuck, Nick, yer callin' again? Ya can't even wipe yer ass without me, that it?" Cenzo sounds aggravated, yeah, but that's generally his default, I think. Either that or I'm interruptin' his daily nap. "I see yer at the college, ya still havin' yer Raymond Chandler fantasies?"

"I'm only lettin' ya get away with that because it's an apt fuckin' reference, ya fuckin' *mamaluke*." A sip of my chai while Rhys has his notebook out to probably transcribe the call for reference later. "Just need ya to look up if any other art or music students from the university went missing or died in the last year or so."

"Nick, ya better not have woke me up to fuckin' Google somethin' for ya, or I'm chargin' ya a couple points fer wastin' my time." A soft chuckle. "Yer slippin', Cousin, yer Ma would be pissed if ya had to lean on me this much."

"Ya think I can hack campus security, police records, and some light crackin' of FBI servers with only a general victim profile? Well, shit, Cen, guess I got no need for a man in the chair." Literally what it sounds like, buddy, the one who gives support from afar, usually directin' jobs with intel and up-to-the-minute info. "I mean, fuck, if a *Luddite* could do it, why's anyone need a Grem-"

"Yer a piece of shit, y'know that?" But, he's grumblin', so that's a lock. "What'm I fuckin' lookin' fer, ya prick?"

"Artists with no social media profile, or one that was scrubbed, probably were on scholarship or grants, but no shows or debut on record. Musicians too, like composers, classically trained pianists, singers, all that. Probably nothin' that would interest a Sidhe, so nothin' modern-"

"Got it. No BIPOC. Wonder Bread all the way through." I hear him yawn. Guess he wasn't lyin' about takin' a nap. "Y'know, I could be breakin' into places that could actually affect real social change, Cous."

"Ya hired me to steal fuckin' crypto, Cen. Fake. Money. I do agree with ya that it's something a Coyote probably came up with though." To that I get a laugh. Like, my fuckin' ears are hurtin' now.

"Ya fuckin' think one of those pool hall hustlers could write a-"

He didn't cut me off, buddy. He just busted into a ten minute explanation of how crypto works that I'm not repeatin' fer yer sake because I'm not that asshole that's at every fuckin' party. You're welcome.

"I'll text ya what I find. That was enough of a laugh I'll let this one slide. Fuck, *Coyotes* seein' a computer as somethin' other than a magical porn box, yer fuckin' killin' me, Nick."

With that, he hangs up. But that don't mean this investigation's over, still light left in the day, but still, I sigh.

"I'm gonna have to talk to Thom, because this is somethin' the Guard should know about. Should call Captain Blackwarren, too, keep him in the loop if only for my sake." The UTA station ain't too far. Ain't the Blue line, but ain't too many transfers to get where we gotta go. "Any ideas you got? Angles ya wanna pursue?"

"We've only had watered down tea, coffee, and a scone for you, so I was hoping we could get something to eat. I know a place. It's not the K Street Diner, but it's down in Grunstadt-"

"Is it the ramen place?"

Rhys looks at me incredulously. "In Little Tokyo? Which one?"

"The one a block or so from Ten Oaths?" I shrug. "I gotta light some incense there anyway, drop off a card for the Kitsune there."

Now he's just blinkin' at me. *"...Which. One?"*

"Akimura Shiko-chan?" He breaks eye contact. "What, ya know her?"

"We... travel in similar circles. Must we go to that one?"

I grin. "Well, we gotta *now*."

18

Little Tokyo is one of the three prime neighborhoods of Grunstadt. It was originally German, port city, and eventually the Germans moved to other cities or into the richer parts. Now? It's Little Tokyo, Jamaicatown, and the Irish district, which is so gentrified there hardly ain't any actual Irish there anymore save the Phouka. Also, little neighborhoods here and there for other meaty chunks of the melting pot. There's also Shoreside, but if ya gotta ask about it, ya don't got the money to already know the answers.

Little Tokyo, though, has got shrines, tech firms, restaurants on all tiers, clubs, some very expensive hotels, and Ten Oaths Distribution, a rice distributor that supplies the City and a lot of the state. Out front are torii gates, and statues of foxes at shrines 'cause the whole place is run almost entirely by Kitsune, the fox tricksters who rival the Phouka and the Coyotes.

They're in some sorta Feud and I honestly do not give a fuck about it. Buddy, ya shouldn't either. Ain't nothin' good ever comes from dealin' with a trickster. I learned that all too well in July.

I stop at the shrine, though, take some incense, light it, bow three times, and put the stick with the others still smokin'. I'm pretty sure I ain't doin' it right, but good enough for a *gaijin*, I s'pose. Rhys does the same, but only after he sees me do it, probably 'cause ain't no one gonna think of showin' any kinda attempt at respect to mythics outside the Fae, but we're on their turf, and I sure as fuck ain't gonna piss 'em off.

Even if we're just stoppin' fer ramen. By the way, I ain't talking 'bout the stuff ya get two hundred fer ninety-eight cents kinda ramen, I'm talkin' 'bout the real shit.

"Omakase," is what Rhys says to the server, and I nod to indicate the same. I ain't too good with Japanese, but from what I get, it means "I trust ya" when ya say it to a Japanese chef. I'm pretty sure it's mostly used for sashimi, but I ain't no expert. All I

know is a minute or two later a couple bowls are set down in front of us with chopsticks.

"So, you bring *another* Goblin, Blackwarren-kun?" She hits more on the "warren" part of my name, when yer s'posed to hit the "Black". Still, I ain't gotta turn to know who just sat next to me.

"Uh… *konnichiwa, Akimura-chan*?" I look at her. "Did I get it right?"

I've mentioned this is Kitsune turf, and while they're all trouble if ya make trouble, *this* is the one Fox ya *do not fuck with*. Unlike the other Kitsune who are russet or pumpkin orange, her fur is black, and while she might be dressed like a bored salarywoman receptionist, trust me, she's the fuckin' boss over at Ten Oaths.

"Close enough." She also steals some of my ramen. Because she can. Rhys is focusin' on his own bowl, but she can see him when she leans back a couple inches. *"Anata wa hataraite imasu ka?"*

Rhys don't look up. *"Īe, anata no kangaede wa arimasen."*

Ya got me, buddy. My Japanese extends to *konnichiwa, domo arigato*, and *baka*. I read the translations and watch the fuckin' dubs. Yer free to void my weeb card. Still, how many languages he fuckin' speak?

"I see." The Fox peers at me, then back to him. *"Kore wa anata no atarashī pātonādesu ka?"* Wait, that last bit sounded like "partner."

"Watashi wa kare to issho ni hataraite imasuga, sono gyakude wa arimasen." A'right, this shit is gettin' annoyin'.

"Ā, naruhodo. Anata wa koibito o tsurete ikimashita." She winks, and does that giggle where she delicately covers her mouth with her hand. Okay, I know that was somethin'.

"Guarda! Vedere? Parlo anche altre lingue!" I finally butt in. Oh, 'Look! See? I can speak other languages, too!' 'Cause I ain't an asshole who's gonna leave ya in the dark, buddy.

"We *are* leaving him out, Aki-chan," he adds. I nod in response, so I can keep eating my noodles.

"Fine, fine." I feel her eyes on me again. "Is he at least a competent lover?"

Cue the spit take. The Kitsune busts a fuckin' gut. She ain't coverin' her mouth *this* time.

Damned Foxes.

"That is between us, Aki-chan." He holds up a finger as she starts to reply. *"Don't."* I, meanwhile, am apologizin' profusely to the chef and cleanin' my face.

"Then what brings *two* Redcaps to our territory, hm?" The façade is dropped now.

"Followin' threads, givin' ya an update on what we're doin' so ya don't think we're here for a slit." I reach into my pocket. "Givin' ya my card if ya need my services again."

The Fox takes it, inspectin'. "Blackwarren Asset Recovery. A freelancer outside the Feud can be useful, yes. Following leads on what?"

"Nothin' related to yer Feud. 'Least I don't think. Doin' recovery, and maybe solvin' a murder, possibly a few, freein' someone from a lethal Oath, it's all Fae stuff, 'cept…"

"The murder victim was human." Rhys says, while eatin' fuckin' noodles. "And we'd prefer not to anger the Lightning Rod."

"Are your people *that* afraid of him? As Ra'Keth go, he's one of the weakest and tamest I've seen in my lifetime." She looks curious, but Kitsune are usually older than they look. I was alive for the Recluse and Frozen River before the Lightnin' Rod, but I know there are Fae that remember the Sculptor, and Thom's father, Her Majesty's Riordan, knew… a *lot*. "What sort of things do the Fae whisper about him?"

Rhys and I glance at each other. "Whatcha got fer it?" Yeah, we say it in unison. Cutesy as fuck, yeah, yeah, yeah.

"I know plenty who would give me the information for free." She ain't impressed, but that's why I am who I am.

"Who? Some Sidhe? A Dwarf? Someone who'll drop to their knees at the mention of Queen Alana-"

"May her warmth bless us all." Yeah, yeah. It ain't as cute as ya think, buddy.

"You're defeating your own point, Mr. Blackwarren."

"Yeah? Ya see us on our knees? Huh?"

"You're both seated."

"Not the point," I say, rollin' my eyes. "What I'm sayin' is ya ain't hearin' from the folk who hear all the rumors and shit-talk, even the ones we don't start. The guy killed two Ra'Keth in *one night* for the Throne and then *ended* the world." Relax, buddy, he at least made this new one for everybody and ain't nobody can tell the difference.

The Fox sighs. "I would owe you very, very little."

So I review. I ain't gonna tell all of it 'cause we ain't got that much time, but I do go into the shoe incident, the blizzards he's caused, that the God of the Underworld always seems to be at his beck and call, how he shortcuts through Hell so he don't gotta walk as far, how he forged a weapon that calls down lightnin' that anyone could use, how he burned an entire clan of vampires to final death in the dead of night by openin' a portal to the sunrise, how the dragons of the world and worlds beyond bow their heads to him, how the Knights of St. George have been foiled by him again and again, how he resurrected the Goddess of Spring… Honestly, buddy, I ain't got no idea how he got time to cohabitate with a Dwarf.

"That… Hardly any of that is true, but it served as a worthy distraction from my current ills." The Fox peers at me, a little closer than I'd like. "Are you still a thief, Mr. Blackwarren? Even the Kitsune have heard tell of the Goblin Detective."

I facepalm. Hard. "I'm not a fuckin' detective, fuck. Why ya askin', anyway? Ya got work? Don't know if I'll have time, considerin' my current case lookin' for a noble who murdered a human, and I've gone into why that's top priority."

"I believe you will find reason." She slides my noodles over in front of her, 'cause 'course she does. Rhys turns to me, and shrugs in a way that implies, "why not?"

"Fine. Okay. I'll bite." I rest my chin on my propped-up hand. "Why's yer thing as important as a murdered human artist, hm? What's she gotta do with you?"

"Because she isn't the only one, Mr. Blackwarren." A pit drops in my stomach. Oh, fuck. I didn't wanna be right about that. "I have your attention?"

Rhys and I just stare at her.

"H-how many?" My throat is dry, I feel a little sick. Fuckin' Shadow, please be a low, low number.

"If your artist is among them?" She sips my tea, as well. "Thirteen."

"Why have you done *nothing,* Aki-chan?!" Rhys rightly pissed. I'm kinda hyperventilatin'. Thirteen fuckin' people. Holy fuck. That's...

Holy fuck.

"Because our Accord with the Fae Court permits us to hunt only demons in North Allora. Anything else outside of Grunstadt or St. Benedict must be reported to your Guard. Do not believe, Llew-kun, that I take this lightly. Your own Guard will not investigate, incidents are silenced, likely outside your Queen's immediate influence-"

"Bullshit." I'm glarin' at her now. "Ain't no fuckin' way this would all be happenin' under the nose of the Left Hand. There's a rule: Don't kill humans, and he was as shocked as I was when he found out the girl wasn't Fae."

"But that only applies to Redcaps, Nick." Rhys speaks up, and I feel cold, like all the blood's drainin' from my face. "The other clans follow it out of respect and fear of him, but the rest of the Fae-"

"Aren't subject to it. He... He might not even know." I look to the Fox, Shiko, Demon Hunter of the North Side. "Is this why ya told me this?"

She taps my vambrace. "You bear Shadow's Edge, it is courtesy to share mutually beneficial information. I cannot speak for my own clan, but I will not stand idle as innocents are cut down with impunity. Though I do warn them. Definitively."

I take a deep breath, buddy, this shit just got deeper. "Tell me what ya know."

"He has been tracked." So, it's a guy. Figured. And only one, so not a team or group, sounds like. "Not identified, he vanishes before we are close, so he is vigilant. We have felt... touches, similar to magic when he does so. I would dare say he could almost vanish into shadow on a cloudless day."

That gets my attention.

"Do ya mean shadow, or like, do ya mean *the Shadow*?" Ms. Akimura can see the seriousness in my eyes, catch the touch of dread on the second.

"Shadow is our playground, but you are clearly talking about something else." She taps a finger on the counter. Ya might be wonderin' how we're having this talk at a ramen stand in public, but trust me, the humans think we're talkin' 'bout weeb shit and the mythics know it ain't their fuckin' business.

"I'm talkin' 'bout the Shadow. With a capital S. We can use it to muffle sound, create darkness, shadow-walk between places instantly. It's s'posed to be just a specialty of the Redcaps, or Gobs born pretty unlucky. Ya saw the guy in recon, was he Goblin-sized?"

She shakes her head. "No. From the glimpse I had, I would place him between one hundred ninety and two hundred centimeters."

Uh... Gimme a sec. Divide by, uh... Two and a... Put in the remainder...

"About six feet?" I guess Rhys can do that math on the fly. "Not a Goblin, then. If it's a Fae, then likely a Sidhe or Troll, depends on the musculature. Either kith is capable of such violence, though only the Sidhe would curry the favor and influence necessary to obfuscate their actions."

"Maybe, but movin' through Shadow, if that's what they're doin', a Mystic (Sidhe with a talent that's *like* magic, but ain't) would be outed and likely killed or drafted into the Queen's Guard with that kinda gift. Even for us it's tough as fuck to walk Shadow 'cause it ain't just a charm that's doin' it."

"These… charms, are they only possible for Goblins?" The Fox sounds a little too interested. I'm guessin' in hindsight I'll regret bein' so loose lipped to a fuckin' Trickster, but priorities, y'know?

"There are small charms for each kith and clan," Rhys responds. "The Goblins can do more, generally each clan can do their own specific charms. I cannot do what Nick can do, I was born in a different clan, but the charms of my birth clan do come quite naturally to me. Then there are those born in Darkness, yet in the Light…" He glances to me. "Was there anything odd about…." He looks at the Kitsune. "I believe we will help with your search, as it will likely connect to ours. Was that your intent, Nick?"

I shrug. "Well, ya took all the fun outta sayin' it myself. But yeah, why not, I figure this was gonna be a twofer to find my client's item and solve her murder. If it fingers a killer in more deaths? That's a bonus. If it means Lady Shiko Akimura will be grateful to the Goblins? Well, shit, that's Christmas fuckin' mornin'." I spit in my palm and extend my hand, "We'll take the fuckin' case."

19

"Whatcha smilin' 'bout, huh?" We're on the Blue Line, lunch over, and I just got off the phone with Cousin Damon, who's gonna meet us in an hour at his place in North Beckett. Gives me time to run through stuff in my head, 'cause I got a sinkin' feelin' about what I'm suspectin', buddy.

"That many additional killings, and you didn't miss a beat, seeking answers and justice for the murdered." Rhys is next to me, and we're bein' avoided 'cause we're on the train and I've gone into how humans see us. "I have to ask where all of this comes from?"

I chuckle, shake my head. "I read, it's that simple. Ya can't read as many books as I do without developin' a firm moral foundation, and the life I lead tends to test it as needed. Wish I could be one of those guys who rattles off a dozen books of religion and philosophy and then sips an espresso, but most of it's from literature. I read romance novels, yeah, 'fore ya ask. Since I ain't ever gettin' an HEA I might as well read 'bout other peoples'. How 'bout you?"

"What do I read?"

"If ya want, but I was askin' why yer helpin' me on this. This shit's gonna test those Oaths and I don't want ya dyin' 'cause ya wanted to tag along. Why're ya throwin' in with me lookin' into all these murders... when..." I trail off, I just made it fuckin' awkward, didn't I, buddy? Fuck me.

"When I'm an assassin." He sighs. "A Redcap assassin."

"Fuck, I... I'm sorry, that came out bad."

"I was taken from my family at the age of seven, shipped off to America at eight, and the next twelve years were spent learning your clan's arts. My dipping was a Brownie who had poisoned his master, but instead murdered the master's son. It was different from killing my uncle. That was protection, keeping my brother safe, this... I was nothing more than a knife guided by the hand of the Queen. I..."

I touch his arm, squeeze it gently, "Ya don't gotta say anymore."

"I do. I accepted it as my life, my purpose, to be the blade of Atropos, slit the threads, and I was good at it. Quick, clean, as little awareness and suffering as possible. I thought that granted me some solace, a way to rationalize it. I've been doing this for nine years, and I never thought I could be anything else. But maybe, working with you, I can."

No, buddy, I don't kiss him, though I would have reason. A hug is better in this kinda situation, it's more empathetic, also we're on a fuckin' train that has a computerized voice that keeps repeatin' the same fuckin' advisories to not vandalize the train and that there's transit cops around.

Ya get used to it.

'Sides, I don't give a fuck 'cause he hugs me back. Easy to feel warm 'round him, which yeah, needs some parsin' in my head 'cause I've very anti-killing and he does it for a fuckin' career.

Don't think I forgot about Thom, would never have to wonder if he's gonna off someone 'cause some noble told him do, he is the fuckin' noble and ain't nobody who can tell him to do shit. Also, yes, the sex is more earthshakin' with him, them Phouka got a genetic advantage or somethin'. And I ain't forgot about my feelin's for him either. Can't exactly just brush him off, and I fuckin' know one sniff and he'll know that Rhys and I did the deed, and I ain't got no fuckin' clue how he'll take it. And fuck, even I can smell how well Rhys and I's scents compliment each other.

Scent is big with us Goblins, not in a gross way, and it speaks to our humanity, too. Did ya know that humans can just smell what kinda person they're into just by sniffin' their clothes even if they ain't never met? Same fer us. Mom and Pa didn't fall in love because they had that, but it certainly got their attention. And now, my body's tellin' me to give this Goblin more of my attention. My heart's gettin' on board too, gods damn it.

Y'see, this why I read romance novels instead of tryin' to live 'em, ya know? This shit would be solved with some witty banter and minimal fuckin' stakes. 'Stead I'm dealin' with a Phouka who wants to marry me despite Her Majesty tellin' him to find a spouse who *ain't* a Goblin and me *breakin' up with him,* and a professional killer who could *fuckin'* die if I don't solve this case the right way.

So, I'm gonna try... Focusin' on work. I'm sure there has to be at least one romance where that turns out okay. So, end the hug. After one last inhale of his scent. He does the same. We're both in the same fuckin' boat, buddy.

"Considerin' I just ramped up the workload for this? I gotta check in with Thom, too. He probably still got connections with the police, so I can ask him to look into the deaths in the City that fit the M.O. of the O'Hare killin'." I take a breath. "I thought I ended things with him, 'fore I met him at the diner."

"He didn't accept that?"

"More, I, uh, told him it weren't gonna work out 'tween the two of us and then I... hung up on him." I glance at Rhys, and yeah, that's a disapprovin' look, buddy.

"Kyo..." He shakes his head.

"I know. I know. Can't really see what this is unless I clear the air with him. And make sure he gets the message this time." I take out my phone, run through my list and find him. He ain't in my contacts, more I know his number in the "called by" thrum of numbers. I'm about to tap it, then look at Rhys. "I uh, think I should meet him alone, so he don't think I already replaced, or cheated."

"Probably best. I should check with my own contacts. Should I meet you at your place?" I nod. "I'll get off at the next stop, people probably more comfortable around one Goblin than two."

"Ya know what to do 'round the transit cops, right?"

At that, he smirks, "Yes, Nick, your clan taught me how to speak with the police and Guard at a young age. Hands visible, fingers spread, submissive tone, no direct eye contact. Want my number if you need me to text that I made it there safe?"

It's sad I felt some relief when he asked that. Yet another point against datin' a Goblin 'stead of a privileged white boy from Shoreside. I give him my digits, regardless. We tap them in, and we show each other, elicitin' a little chuckle, 'least. "Sebas" and "Kyo" on opposite screens. He winks at me when his stop comes up, I smirk and wave.

Pretty sure I'm just... Nah, this ain't a crush. We talked, kissed, had sex, and we're talkin' about our lives and families and shit. That ain't... That ain't a crush. Don't really know what this is yet. What I do know?

It's time to rip off the fuckin' bandage and talk to Thom.

It's a few rings before he picks up. "Nick! Everything okay?" Shadow, it's like callin' a fuckin' golden retriever. No, no, don't make him out to be a shit so ya don't feel bad, Blackwarren, yer the shit in this case, and ya gotta come clean.

"Case is takin' some turns, so I wanna compare notes with ya, and I need to talk to ya, too." I take a breath. "K Street Diner okay?"

"Sure, I'll be there in twenty."

Okay, we're both adults. Both mature, intelligent adults. This ain't gonna be as bad as I'm makin' it out to be.

It's a simple sit-down at the diner! That's all. It'll be fine, buddy.

Y'know what I hate in movies and TV shows? Fuckin' smash-cuts.

"What did I do wrong?! Just tell me what I need to do to make things okay again, Nick!" So, uh, yeah, this ain't goin' like I planned.

I walked in, sat down, he ordered a Reuben and fries for me, I waved it off and said I just wanted coffee, he asked if I was doin' okay, I said I'm doin' fine, just caught up in the case. Then he starts askin' 'bout the case, how Rhys is connected to it, and I try to push him away from concentratin' on Rhys so much...

He sniffed the air...

And buddy, that was all she wrote. I also now know that ya secrete different pheromones if yer havin' a more tender, intimate kinda sexual encounter that implies a real connection. Ya also smell happier, 'parently.

"Thom, it ain't that simple, okay? It's ain't like there's a list of stuff to do to turn this around. It… it just ain't gonna work for us." I look at the table. This is in a diner where to the humans around us, the GQ coverboy is gettin' his heart broke by the dirtbag piece of shit that probably reminds them of the worst boy they knew in middle school. My coffee is set in front of me, likely with a healthy shot of spit added at the last minute. "There… really wasn't anythin' between us other than a crush and three times we had sex. I know I'm hurtin' ya, though, Thom, and I'm sorry, okay? Ya deserve better."

"You… We both told each other that we decide what we deserve. Was that a lie?" Fuck, he's cryin'. I feel like shit. I mean, I should, but it don't mean I like how it feels. At least this is goin' better when I broke up with my first boyfriend. He was a Phouk too, and eventually ya get tired of the games no matter how good the sex is (though it was good enough to make me put off dumpin' him for a couple weeks). "Just… Just tell me what I need to do. Please!"

"Thom, focus, okay? I need ya thinkin' with yer head now, not yer heart. *Really* look at what's between us, Thom." I push the coffee away. I can drink practically whatever, but don't mean I wanna. "Really look, and tell me if it looks like a healthy, two-way street kinda relationship."

Fuck, I shoulda gotten the info for the case outta him first, fuck me.

"But you have that with someone you met a couple days ago?" Thanks, Thom, now I'm a cheating fuckbag as well as the big asshole. Pretty sure I ain't gonna be able to eat here again for a while.

"Thom, don't bring him into this. I felt like this before I ever met him, okay?" I grit my teeth, that was a slip.

"You wanted to break up with me, but you wanted to wait until after I helped you chase down a box truck?" I mean I was droppin' hints during the ride, but that don't help me either way.

"Thom? I'm not tellin' ya it's over." I see hope in his eyes. Fuck. "Thom, I'm tellin' ya it never began."

"You said you loved me!" He slams the table, and now we really got everyone's attention. "You told me when you thought I was asleep."

"Thom? That was one of the most stressful times of my life. My Pa died, I was put on the hook fer three murders, the guy who did it put me in the hospital, I got cut up again and dipped my cap savin' yer life for a sting ya set up where I was *bait*." I rub my face. "And we've had this conversation how many times? I'm tired of havin' it, ain't you?"

"I don't want to give up on us, Nick." There's the tears, Blackwarren, you're a certified asshole, now.

"I can't keep talkin' in circles, Thom. It ain't a relationship if one of us don't wanna be in it, okay? All this is doin' is hurtin' you and me to keep draggin' it out. Just, please, Thom, let me go. Move on from me. Find a way for you to be happy that don't center on me, yeah?" I feel dagger eyes on me from the other customers, staff, and the dragon in the kitchen. I'm the villain here, so I gotta accept that.

Like I said, ya get used to it.

20

So… yeah. I ain't really welcome back at the K Street Diner no more. Not surprised, really. To humans, Thom's a super attractive, charismatic, friendly cop. I've gone over how humans see me, and I ain't in the mood to rehash for ya, buddy. Ya understand, right?

No more French toast for me, looks like.

That's right, crack a joke or two. I'm no further on the investigation and I burned a source for personal reasons. I gotta believe I made the right decision, and that it wasn't because of Rhys. It wasn't, it's more he brought shit into focus, got me off the fence, I wanted to finally make a decision, so I did.

Still, shit like that shakes ya, buddy, so I need a minute or three. I could text Rhys, but it seems kinda shitty to interrupt whatever he's doin' with "hey, I broke up with my ex! We're in the clear!" Fuck, I gotta talk to someone, do somethin', or I'll end up dwellin' on it and my day'll get worse and that ain't gonna help Bridget or any of the other people that the fuckbag slit.

I hopped the train from 65th and K out to 90th and V, into the Benedict. Gives me time to give a better look at the armor that's coverin' my whole right arm and shoulder now. I usually get space on the train, but I might as well have my own car right now.

I'll blame it on headin' out to the Benedict before five in the afternoon, not that no one wants to be within fifteen feet of me. Not because I'm some mopey motherfucker or anythin'.

I get off at 90th and V, down the stairs from the station, and out into the not-so-great parts of the Benedict, where I used to live before all of this. My buildin' has its share of signs reading **"CONDEMNED"** and notices from the Board of Health. Now that I ain't been livin' there for a month, let's just say my nose deafness has faded and I hurry on.

East into the industrial slums, where factories are still for sale, most of them picked apart by scavengers, or by companies that own 'em just long enough to dig out whatever machinery's left. People used to believe that it would mean jobs, bring some life back to the Benedict, but the most this homage to the Rust Belt has been are places for shell companies to park cash and launder shit. As a result, "No Trespassing" signs are to be ignored.

Easy enough to duck into the shell of a warehouse, or industrial space, who knows. I know mythics ain't comin' out here because of the burn marks on the concrete and brick, and I don't mean like, fire burnin', I mean like acid burns. There's a rumor, which us Easties know is true, that there's a dragon that's claimed the Benedict as his dominion. A black dragon. The kind that breathe acid 'stead of fire.

He's been 'round long as I remember, but he keeps to himself 'less ya start fuckin' with his territory. Only reason Prince Firemane and the Twin Blood enclave are still around is because how close to Grunstadt they are. Think I mentioned the necromancer earlier? They been seen together all's I know, and it's another reason why I ain't reachin' out to a Keth on my current case.

A'right, 'nuff stallin'.

I extend my right arm. "Okay, uh, Shear? Sheary? I ain't got no fuckin' clue what to call ya, but can ya come out, I guess?"

Nothin'.

"Fuck, has it gotta be Sigil every time? Fuck me… Fine. Extend and string."

SHUNK-SHUNK-SHUNK-SHUNK

…the fuck?

Don't get me wrong, I know my Sigil, but not that quick off the top of my head. The bow is in my hand, and it's practically from my ankle to just over the top of my head. This is clearly not a bow intended for Goblins. Also, I ain't got any experience with archery save a laughable stint in gym class where I snapped the string against my fingers and sent the arrows tumblin' ass over teakettle and bouncin' on the dirt.

Okay, the grip fits best in my right hand, I guess this is how ya hold it.

Now what?

Gimme a sec, buddy, I gotta look up this kinda bow on my phone.

Okay, it's a compound bow. The big gears at the top and bottom are called cams, or uh, "eccentrics"? It uses pulleys, okay, I understand pulleys and levers. Think I'm gettin' in, just uh... Need an arrow.

"Hey, do ya, uh, make yer own arrows? 'Cause I ain't takin' the train to Allora to find a fuckin' sportin' goods sto-"

Fuck! Fuckfuckfuckfuckfuck. "Fuck, can ya do this without suckin' my blood? Fuck!" I grit my teeth, lookin' at it. "Figures ya'd be just like the vambrace. Do all the fuckin' magic weapons need blood to work?"

Oh, right, the vambrace is on the bow now, so my forearm's finally visible and-

Shadow, that's a, uh, lotta puncture wounds. A few in my right palm too.

"Buddy, ya gotta stop doin' that, okay? It hurts, and it's makin' me lightheaded and that ain't what I need right now." I glance at the bow proper. "And ya gotta be just as bad? I did that whole mystical bullshit thing talkin' to some weirdass old ladies tellin' 'em that ya belonged to me and now yer hurtin' me too?"

I drop the bow, shakin' my hand, the wounds on my hand closed, but I can see the marks where it drank from me. "Ya hear that, huh?" I glare at the weapon. *"You do not harm me, Aeo."*

Fuck, again with the unbidden Sigil. Where'm I gettin' these words from?

But there's a reaction. The grip pops, snaps, like the vambrace is comin' loose, but it don't. It's more like it's opened, as if I can stick my hand in there, and I ain't stickin' my hand in there. I hook my fingers into it, try to pull it free, but it don't budge.

"C'mon, buddy, leggo of the bow, yeah?" Nothin'. "Release Aeo, Jerathi!"

Where the *fuck* am I gettin' these names?! Y'see, this is what happens when ya try to extend yerself beyond bein' a thief and tryin' to sneak in some heroics: ya get the attention of the Fates, and they fuck up yer life.

Still, Shadow's Edge pops free from the Aeolian Shear, which is a sentence I feel so fuckin' *chūnibyō* fer thinkin' (quick and dirty? It's when middle schoolers live in their heroic or edgelord fantasies). I pick up the vambrace, which clamps around my forearm again, and it's a little concernin' how weird it felt *not* havin' it on my arm. I pick up the bow and look between the two of them. "'Kay, both of ya are stayin' separate, ya don't play nice together. And you, uh, Aeo, still owe me a fuckin' arrow."

Nothin'. Well, might as well practice holdin' it. Okay, I draw with my left hand, I guess? Fuck this feels awkward, am I doin' it right? I check my phone again: hold it in the off hand, draw with the main hand. Ah! I've got it in the wrong hand!

Okay, it don't feel right in the left hand. Ah, it's a rarity: it's made fer a fuckin' lefty. I ain't one of them. Sidhe don't give a fuck, they're all fuckin' ambi and shit 'cause why give assholes physical limits? Fuck it, I'll try it.

Draw ain't as bad, maybe fifty pounds, and all the dance and parkour and gymnastics gets ya fit enough that it ain't too tall of an order, even with the offhand. All the gears and levers hold the draw easy, the weight on the front keepin' it steady and... My fingers are holdin' a black arrow in place.

It's shockin' enough that I let go, the arrow loosed, I think they call it, and it slams into the far wall, but it don't embed itself, or break, or bounce off the brick. It don't explode or anythin' or have some big sparkly shit. There's just darkness where it hit.

Ohhhhh-kaaaaaaay. Well, in the science books I read, none of it means jack or shit if I can't repeat the same action to get the same results, otherwise it ain't worth studyin'. Still, better to aim at another part of the wall a few feet away.

Look at me, buddy, like I can fuckin' aim this thing that accurate.

Okay, time to train the muscles if I'm gonna keep ya around, uh, Aeo. Take the stance from the video… Huh, there's a little ring lookin' thing snapped into the grip. Vambrace musta been coverin' it. Hmmm, 'cordin' to my phone it's a… hinge release? A'right. Hook it to the string. Draw. Hold it steady. Aim with the sight. Uh, take a breath, exhale, roll the trigger down and-

Huh. Another big blotch of darkness on the wall a few feet away. Well, bein' close to human means yer as stupidly curious as the real thing, so… I place my palm on the darkened patch and…

"Aw, *fuck!*" I tumble into the fuckin' void, oh shit, what's gonna… Where'm I gonna end… It so fuckin' *cold*! Where'm…

Hold up.

Ain't this where I just left?

I turn around, and see the patch of darkness, but not the one I fell into.

Wait. Wait, wait, wait.

I've seen this before. Hell, I've *been* through this before. It was the key to how Lord Greenmeadow and his butler got killed! There was a gate from his basement to a closet in South Allora, which was used by the Redcap who almost fuckin' killed me in July. This… this ain't darkness on this wall, buddy.

It's *Shadow*.

Gotta confirm. Need to be sure this is actually happenin'.

I scan the building, see a platform on the second floor next to the wall. Hope I can hit up there. Okay, draw, steady, aim, steady, exhale, loose!

Yeah, that's a shitty shot. But whadduya expect, I ain't a fuckin' legendary archer or any of that shit. I'm surprised I ain't snapped the string or somethin'.

So, yeah, I didn't hit shit, no new door to Shadow. Also, ain't safe to leave these things, uh, here.

"Okay, ya wanna hear Sigil, so… *Close?*"

The inky black almost gets absorbed into the wall, like water dryin' in the sun, or a sponge suckin' it up. At least I know the things can be temporary. So, I got a bow that makes doors through Shadow. Good to know, always a use fer that without havin' to slit someone for the blood.

"Okay, uh, Aeo? Got any other tricks? Like, against a Goblin without killin' 'em?" You seen what my Pa's side of the family can be like, buddy. Shouldn't be a stretch that I'm curious. "Don't wanna hit nobody, though, so..."

I aim up, like straight up. I'm gonna get out of the damned way after, obviously, I ain't fuckin' stupid. When I aim at the sky, the arrow seems a bit more... silvery? Looks weird, like it's scored, and the arrowhead's a spiral lookin' thing, weird carvin' too. Don't look like it's gonna kill anyone, at least, so, draw, aim, steady, and...

Holy fuckin' fuck that's fuckin' loud holy fuckin' shit!

The uh, arrow's makin' a really high-pitched, really loud fuckin' whistle that is *not* meant for Goblin ears to hear. Fuckin' Shadow, my ears are still fuckin' ringin', are they fuckin' bleedin'?! Shit, I can't hear anythin' right now, just the high-pitched whine of...

Why's the ground shakin'?

Here's what I know: That shakin' came from behind me.

Here's what else I know: The wall separatin' the interior of the ruined factory ain't there no more.

And what I wish I *didn't* know, buddy?

The fuckin' Black Dragon of the Benedict just landed behind me, and he looks fuckin' *pissed*.

And what I *really* wish I didn't know?

What tends to happen after a dragon takes a deep fuckin' breath.

21

Shunk!

Can always count on ya, buddy, to put on the shield when I need it. Granted, I never wanted to test its defensive strength 'gainst a *dragon* breathin' *acid*.

Okay, first strategy.

"I'm really sorry! I didn't know how fuckin' loud that would be! If it's any consolation, Sir, my ears're practically bleedin'." I peek out a little, and then duck behind again as *another* splash of acid splatters the shield. "Hey, ya ain't gotta melt my ass just 'cause ya can't handle loud noises! Everyone thinks yer a fuckin' low flyin' plane that's in a fuckin' holdin' pattern over the Benedict and why none of us can get any sleep!"

Buddy? Why the actual fuck am I admonishin' a *dragon*?! Nerves do weird shit to ya, that's what, and I'm stickin' to that.

The dragon, if yer curious, is about the size of a private jet, inky black scales that seem do devour light. Glowin' golden eyes I'd swear were burnin'.

Time for the second strategy.

"Noble one! I offer sincere apologies for my offense! Might we parley to discuss your recompense?" Sigil might work? I mean, dragons speak Sigil pretty fluently, it's how they talk to Keth and the Ra'keth. Maybe it'll be more respectful?

It could work!

"Gutter rats, all of you!" Dragons are *loud*, and he's right in front of me. I mean, he's talkin' to me, at least, but I got the feelin' this ain't gonna go well. There'll be time to be insulted later for the 'gutter rat' comment. *"Shedding blood for the empty promises of Shadow! Your tainted blood serves as insult to the gods who made you!"*

So, uh, I think I got a sec or two before he kills me, time enough to explain what the fuck he's talkin' about. It also distracts me from the fact that I only got a sec or two before he fuckin' kills me.

"Shedding blood" for the Shadow? Mighta told ya this before, but Shadow's Edge does most of its stuff with blood. Before I got it, it was used to kill people, drain their vitae, and fuel all the wonders that the wielder could think of. Usually, it was scarier weapons. Redcaps usually ain't the type to think of utility. Me? I offer my own blood, and it's changed a bit since then. Grapplin' hook, dart launcher, lockpick, and a blade for emergencies. But it's all fueled by the Shadow, and Shadow and I get along pretty well.

"Tainted blood"? I've mentioned us Goblins were originally human before, we can swap blood and organs, but it's not a perfect match. I can give blood to any human (it's 'cause I'm Type O, not magical), but we're all so close to human, and well, look at us. Ya wouldn't really look at Goblins and call us "clean".

"The gods that made you"? He's talkin' 'bout the fuckin' Ra'keth. Not the current one, but the Ra'keth of old (in the plural sense, one Ra'keth, two Ra'keth, it's like they're sheep that can snap reality if they're bored) that we all rebelled against in the Uprising. They created all the mythics, either through dreams or curses or spells or alchemy or just exposure to all the random magic that was everywhere. And then ya got the Goblins, who were humans that the Machinist altered into Goblins. Why?

What? Fuck, I ain't got no fuckin' idea! But the Machinist was put down with the rest. Still, though, we all got blood relation to her, implyin' that she probably started makin' Goblins with her own fuckin' family.

Fucked up, right? 'Least the Ra'keth we got now keeps either to himself or prefers workin' with gods and dragons. We're just the ants marchin' in his world hopin' we don't ever draw his attention.

And that's two seconds, buddy.

What first happens is pure instinct. I ain't got nothin' to do with it, so I can't explain how I manage to jump into the air when that big set of claws on his foreleg comes swipin' at me. Seriously, buddy, no fuckin' clue.

How I manage to land on that clawed hand and immediately push off with the balls of my feet, backflip, and land with my feet together without bouncin' or stumblin'? Well, I *was* a state champion in fuckin' gymnastics back in California, not to mention parkour, dance, and bein' a fuckin' thief, so bein' light on my feet with good reflexes shouldn't be too much of a stretch, yeah? That shit's all muscle memory, and I'm stickin' to it, thank you.

The bow ready to fire an arrow? I'll put that on it bein' a fuckin' artifact older than its fair share of worlds. My arms are movin' like I done this a hundred times, nockin' a shining bolt, like my want to not kill the dragon flowin' through. I draw, aim, and fire, closin' my eyes.

Ever heard of somethin' called a 'flashbang', buddy?

If it ain't obvious, it's a device that causes a bright flash, and then a loud bang. So, y'know, ain't just a clever moniker. My ears are ringin' like a motherfucker, but I can still hear that howl of pain as "bang" hits those preternaturally sensitive ears, but also when that explosion of light hits as well like starin' directly into a solar eclipse.

This'll give me a few seconds 'fore his eyes recover, I think. Enough time to *attempt* an escape. I got a magic bow that 'parently can form ways through Shadow, connectin' both. Also, this dragon likely is pissed enough to just kill me now, and if I just run away, he'll just follow his nose and wait for my luck to run out.

The arrow that's wrigglin' like a snake outta the fuckin' Void is pulled back, the aim at my best approximation of a forty-five degree angle and loosed. I ain't got no fuckin' clue where it'll strike, but "not fuckin' here" is good enough for me, buddy. My ears are still ringin', so I didn't hear the sound of the arrow flyin', so I'm hopin' he didn't either.

Ever seen a dragon that's decided yer ass needs to die now? Me neither, so I better get the fuck outta here. And that's gonna require me to do somethin' monumentally fuckin' stupid. Like, yer gonna want me committed if I live through this, buddy, that's how fuckin' crazy this is.

I face down the fuckin' Dragon of the Benedict, with a compound bow I just started usin' not even a fuckin' hour ago. I meet those slitted eyes that burn with fury, that mouth that curls with a grin upon seein' my defiance to the very end, a tongue runnin' along dagger teeth. I draw and hold it steady.

"Apologies, m'lord. The fault was mine, entirely." I line up the shot. *"But death awaits me not this day."*

I loose the arrow.

It flies.

His mouth opens, the arrow soaring into his gapin' maw as he inhales.

The acid torrents outward a second later, leaving nothin' of me to remain.

22

…What?

'Course I fuckin' survived, buddy! How the fuck could I be tellin' ya the story if I was just a dissolved puddle of Redcap? But gimme a sec, would ya?

"Close!" I roll hard to my right, avoidin' a splash of acid that comes through, but not on me or anyone else.

Okay, remember the arrow I fired off before he breathed the acid? It hit the ground about two hundred yards away, makin' the door through Shadow. My ill-advised final shot at a dragon preppin' to breathe acid all over me? The one that went straight into his mouth? The other side of that Shadow door.

So, in that second and a half before the acid came out? I jumped *into a dragon's mouth* and through the way I'd made, popped up, landed, rolled away while some of the acid was geyserin', and closed the portal.

Now if you'll excuse me, ya know me by now, ya know what a stressful event like that does to me, 'specially a brush with death. I'm dry heavin', pretty much, but it's that or hyperventilate. I put up a shroudin' charm once I'm into an alley, and in a fuckin' Dumpster. Fuckin' reeks, but it'll cloak my scent so I can hide until the dragon believes that he melted my face off as well as the rest of me.

Gives me time to think shit through, at least.

Like I said, that shit with the dragon was my fault, I ain't tryin' to duck that. I was playin' 'round with a magic bow and blindly shot a screamer arrow into the air which, thinkin' now on physics, would actually make it *louder*, and carry further. I ain't got any excuse. I tried what I could to make sure I didn't hurt him or cause permanent damage, but it ain't never shoulda happened, I want that out there, on the record.

But what he said is still gratin' on me, ya know? Even the fuckin' *dragons* call us sewer rats?!

No. No. I can't focus on that. I gotta think about the rest no matter how it made me feel. I ain't a fuckin' monster, 'kay?

I'm not.

And sheddin' blood? I give my own! Willin', too! Empty promises of Shadow? That don't make no sense, it ain't like I'm truckin' with demons. Redcaps can just do it naturally or learn it if they join the clan. The charms ain't callin' on demons or evil shit, it's callin' on our ancestors, and formerly our goddesses. Shadow ain't ever made me any promises or demands. I ask, I sometimes I receive, simple as that.

Referrin' to me as one of the *tainted blood*? Well, fuck him. Plus, the tainted are usually what the racist fucks call the Twin Bloods, so he ain't even gettin' his fuckin' slurs right. Then again, ya can't expect a bigot to double-check his derogatory shit. And what's so tainted? Other than blendin' of the clans, I'm a purebred Goblin. Only ones who give a fuck… are, uh… The Blackwarrens.

And Mom's a Tinker with plenty of ties to the Gremlins.

So that's kind of a low blow, y'know?

Wait, hold on, I don't care *how* good a dragon's sense of smell is, they

can't tell *that* if I didn't shed any blood, and I didn't. So he couldn't tell… right?

I get my phone on, send out a text to Rhys.

kno anything abt dragons?

A minute later…

Not my forte, no. Why?

Rhys

Huh.

kno peeps who do?

I have an aunt, she's good with arcane subjects. Only thing I can say is that she knows things.

Rhys

Oh fuck, he signs his texts! No. No! Don't laugh, Blackwarren! Yer keepin' hidden, fer fuck's sake, from an angry dragon!

ur pw isnt yer bday is it?

I use a phrase of three to five words that I spell using 1337. For my phone I use biometrics and a twelve-digit PIN. Or do I? >;)
What do you need to know about dragons? I can message her now. I'll have to ask in Gaelic, or I'd just give you her number.
Rhys

Before you ask, I'm using a voice-to-text some of my American cousins let me install cleanly.
Rhys

Fer fuck's sake, that's godsdamned adorable. Despite havin' jumped into a dragon's mouth and crossed through an inscrutable pathway through an abyss that pulls the warmth and light from yer body and spirit... I'm smilin'.

yer such a dork xD ask if dragons can smell if gobs blood is from diff clans

Will ask, may take a while. I want to share information, compare notes, but would rather it were in person. Are you free to meet?
Rhys
P.S. Why am I a dork?

I'll spare ya the rest, buddy, it's just him and I sharin' texts. Fuck, I just ended it with Thom, I shouldn't be feelin' this good about a guy I ain't known all that long, but...

This ain't that kinda story, okay? It just ain't. I don't want ya gettin' the wrong ideas. This is a story where I find out what happened to Bridget O'Hare, and get her some justice, and find her life's work to memorialize her properly, yeah? Ain't no time or space for some romance in the middle of all of that.

Yeah, buddy. Yer right. I'm convincin' myself, not you.

What does askin' about a dragon's olfactory ability got to do with her? Why bother askin' Rhys at all about it?

'Cause what if the dragon weren't talkin' 'bout me? What if he thought I was someone else? Sheddin' blood to offer Shadow fer 'empty promises'? I gone over that, buddy, that ain't Goblins.

Redcaps do it natural, other clans can learn, but ain't none of us actually gotta kill somebody to call on it.

And that's another thing: 'the *gods* who made you.' At first blush, yeah, ya think they mean the gods, but us Goblins only got the Triple Goddesses, who most know as the Fates: Clotho, Lachesis, Atropos.

Clotho, the Spinner of Chaos, that's the patroness of Brother Gremlin, destroy and create whatever comes to mind. Lachesis, that's just Mama Tinker, the Weaver of Order, puttin' the Chaos in structure. Grandmother Atropos, the Abhorred Shear, parent of Father Redcap, and well, there's a reason we call 'em *slits*.

But none of 'em *created* us. We just started followin' 'em after the Uprisin' and did faithfully 'til the Three were forced to become One. *That*, buddy, is why we're fuckin' terrified of the Lightning Rod. He fuckin' ended our *gods*.

And dragons ain't stupid, they would know that, that we weren't made by the Fates. The 'gods' he spoke of are the Ra'keth of old, so he was referrin' to the Machinist, one singular god.

Also, to dragons, the Ra'keth are gods. Ya won't find any bigger cheerleaders or laplogs of the sorcerer kings.

But ya know who was created by those 'gods'? The rest of the Fae. Every one of 'em, 'specially the Sidhe, all their Houses are tied back to a Ra'keth of old.

So, I'll lay down a Benji he thought I was one of 'em. But it's a fuckin' stretch for a dragon to mistake a five-foot fugly Goblin fer a six-foot-four sex-on-toast Sidhe. Okay, Blackwarren, walk this through. Let's call it a given for this scenario that dragons can't smell family differences in Goblins.

From there, ya gotta figure that either the dragon's got a beef with me personal 'cause I fired a screamer (which is still on the table), or maybe just 'cause I fired an arrow in the sky where I almost hit him. Given that's how Sidhe bring a one down durin' a hunt so they can fight it on the ground, he either thought I was a

Sidhe at first huntin' him solo, or that I was ordered to end the dragon's air superiority.

Both plausible, yeah. And would tick a lot of boxes, but… Why bring up tainted blood and truckin' with Shadow? Why bring any of that up if he only thought I was a hunter to floss his teeth with? What if he was goin' off smell, and I was layered in enough scents to confuse him? Nah, that don't hold.

What…

What it weren't me he was smellin'?

I mean, I got Shadow's Edge on one arm and the Aeolian Shear on the other, and *magic's* got its own kinda smell that dragons are *very* good at detectin'. One's the blade of the Redcaps, so it tracks it'd get his attention and make him get all anti-Shadow. But he weren't shot by the vambrace, I fired the bow, which can apparently link points through Shadow for gates.

I facepalm.

"Fuck, Blackwarren, that was a wobbly fuckin' bicycle to get to one fuckin' point, fuck me."

The bow works with Shadow, it's magic, it's old, and I already know its name, and I'm convinced that it's mine. Don't go thinkin' this is destiny one-true-hero bullshit, buddy. Weapons this old tend to have influence of their own, and I'm sure if anybody picked it up they'd be thinkin' themselves the Sacred Archer of Phallisymbolia, too. Don't mean shit, okay?

I gotta focus on one thing. Shadow is the center of this. This would point the finger at Goblins, but I ain't mentioned the creepy fucks.

By which I mean, the Shadow Cultists. Just so ya know, ain't a Goblin among 'em, and we're pretty protective of our trade secrets so it ain't like we're out there teachin' people how to be gifted thieves and assassins. I ain't got a fuckin' clue how long they been around, buddy, but they've either been the butt of jokes or massive pains in the ass ever since…

I know all the clans have choice names for 'em, none of which I'll repeat because all of 'em are racist as fuck. Hey, we ain't a perfect people, never claimed we were saints, but I guess we're tryin' to do better now that we're in America, but let's be honest, if yer people are treated like untouchables and bear the brunt of a lot of shitty attitudes, yer gonna start lookin' fer someone to do the same to, and some fuckin' wannabe Shadow *tourist* is an easy target.

Like I said, buddy, we're the closest to human.

Anyway, they been 'round fer a while. But this ain't the answer I'm lookin' for. The dragon was pissed enough that whoever irked him before has likely done it a few times. And let's not forget that I boosted the Shear from the Prince's treasure wagon haulin' his own shit and stuff for other nobles, looks like. If the dragon recognized the Shear, then someone 'sides me must've fired it somewhere.

But why? 'Less they were huntin' the dragon, why fire a bow that fires portal arrows? Most I could move around was two hundred yards…

I didn't test it any further, though. I could try later, but I wanna check somethin'. I push the lid of the Dumpster up and slip out, pretty sure that all the dragon'll sniff out is old rottin' garbage, not me. Yes, I coulda ate that shit and survived, but no, ain't nobody that hungry.

Step one? Check the skies, see if he's still flyin' round, or if he figured he gobbled the Goblin and called it a day. I ain't seein' anythin' or hearin' him either.

Step two? Fire direct at the brick wall next to the bin, makin' a new portal. I ain't hearin' a rush of wings, so I'm hopin' he didn't notice.

Step three? Run like fuck back toward the more populated areas and tenements. Takes a few blocks to reach 'em, and I get a wider berth from the few people out there considerin' I fuckin' reek without any help from my distinctive odor.

Step four? Fire another arrow into a wall in the alley I just cut into, steppin' 'round the zombies sleepin' the day away. Most see 'em as homeless, and this bein' a big city, most of 'em are flat ignored. Reminds me I gotta set aside cash fer donations and shit. Second portal is made.

Now to see if both are linked despite them bein' made more than few minutes apart and much farther than my previous attempts.

It's a longer time in the Shadow, colder, the waverin' whistle weavin' through my ears, coaxin', beckonin', but I'm out before I'm tempted. But here I am, next to a fuckin' Dumpster. I backtrack, and the Shadowsong still plays, ticklin' my nerves like ivories, and soon I'm back with the zombies.

"Close." Okay, so that's doable. I'm willin' to bet that if I went even farther, I could plant one in Beckettsville and have an express route to my apartment without havin' to draw blood runes all over my walls. Okay, that's somethin' to work with, and about all I'm gettin' outta this.

Now that I'm clear, I get out my phone again and get to textin'.

hey @97H pick me up?

Takes a couple minutes.

In Allora at the moment but I should be there in about- Twll dy din yr hen gont blewog! Can not a one of you drive in this city?!

Rhys

Must be a really good Voice-to-Text app. I think. I don't know what the fuck *that* was.

so how long near slower duckling reed

*need shwer fckin reek fckin autocorrect

I am currently driving my car and cannot return messages presently. Please be patient and I will endeavor to respond as soon as I am safely able.

Rhys

Fates forgive me. I can't resist. I face away from the entrance to the alleyway and do what guys do when they got a smartphone with a good camera.

You are a crassly incorrigible boor of a satyrous Goblin.

Rhys

answered quick tho >;)

I gotta grin at that. Twenty to half an hour to kill if he's comin'
all the way from Allora.

*That's the victory you want to take from something so
disrespectful of me and especially of yourself?*

Rhys

wld bliev u if u not grinnin >;)

*You were just spent Shadow knows how long in a trash bin, and
you're under the impression I'll swoon for the unkempt garbage
knight?*

Rhys

u+me shwer

Yes, buddy, I'm bein' that guy right now. I jumped into the
mouth of a dragon and spent half an hour in a fuckin' Dumpster. Ya
understand that I want somethin' else good to happen today, right?

You're incorrigible, Nick.

Rhys

that no?

No response. Okay, I pushed a little far. I'll keep quiet until he
shows up and then apologize. I don't want to fuck up this partnership
just 'cause I'm kinda horny for him right now.

Turns out a real good way to kill time waitin' on someone is
runnin' through yer to-be-read list that only seems to grow bigger
the longer it's there. That's a boner-killer if there ever was one, but
at least I can plan out what I'm readin' next, somethin' new 'stead of
a reread from my trove of romance novels.

Soon I'm hearin' the honk of the Porsche, and I walk over to the
car. He rolls down both windows and makes a face the closer I
approach. Yep, even if he was in the mood for foolin' 'round or
somethin' I pretty much killed it right there. I get in, buckle up, and
sheepishly mutter thanks as he pulls into traffic. We don't talk too
much. We ain't sayin' anythin', really, so now I know I really
fucked things up.

I shoot a text to Shiko, at least, askin' if she's got names for the thirteen women besides Bridget. They should be more than just a number a tragedy happened to.

Silent elevator ride after we get to my building, the smell probably worse in the cramped space, and I'm probably red as fuck in my face. This is humiliatin', buddy, fuck.

"I'm just gonna, um…" I trail off, head into the bathroom, where I gotta run the bath, since I still ain't got no shower, and get my clothes off. It ain't a luxurious bath, to say the least, more frantic scrubbing and treatin' my washcloth like it's fuckin' steel wool to get the muck and grime and shit off me. Hoppin' through Shadow a couple times probably didn't help either.

I climb out to towel off, admonishin' myself fer bein' so stupid. Sure, we fucked this mornin', and it was good, but it don't mean we got that kinda connection, or if I even want that. First, though, gotta apologize proper.

"Rhys, can I tell ya that I'm…" I've stepped into the main area of my place. I could say somethin' like, 'the real killer's here and he's holdin' Rhys at knifepoint' or 'and just like that, he was gone' or 'he was seated at the table with a we-need-to-talk face'. Any of that could work.

I would not have expected him sittin' backwards in one of the chairs, his naked green body turned toward me, a smile on his face.

Fuck. What was I talkin' 'bout, again?

23

"We do need to compare notes, and no reason we can't discuss while we're with each other, don't you think?" He's got a lopsided smirk, really accents that roguish smile. His eyes aren't mischievous, they can pull off that smolder pretty well, the kind that makes ya shudder, little touches of tingles trackin' all of my body, pairin' with a gentle ache that's growin' in insistence.

"Sebas, are we just playin' 'round, or are we gonna…" I shift my weight from foot to foot, got that towel 'round my waist so my body's approval ain't too obvious, but even I can smell the pheromones I'm startin' to put out there, and these noses ain't fer show, y'know. "Make somethin'."

The Redcap gets to his feet, takin' a step toward me, hands on his thighs to frame his groin, draw my eyes. We're evenly matched in the endowment department, gets the job done, trust me. "What do *you* want, Kyo?"

"I prefer if we could talk without me lookin' at yer dick, Rhys." I end up throwing him the towel, a mistake on my part, because my body's always been kinda eager and now I can point at him without usin' my fuckin' hands. Double standard hypocrisy, thy name is Nick.

He does wrap up, at least. "And I'd prefer you answer my question. Do you want something more than enjoying each other?" I break eye contact, but soon he's in front of me, fingers gently pulling my chin back to meet his eyes. "What I want? I'd like more time with you, but I've mentioned the difficulties of my duty, as well as…"

"Ya don't gotta say it, Sebas." I trail my fingertips over his scars, heart goin' out and achin' fer him. Fuck, he might be dead 'fore I solve this. No. Before *we* solve this. "I, uh, I like you, Rhys."

I'm against him, chests together, mouths turnin' and pushin', tongues glidin' and rubbin', our hands roamin' each other's sides, our readied shafts sandwiched between us, fingers stroking the curves of the other's ass. "I like you as well, Nick. Embrace, or join?"

"Ain't we supposed to compare notes?" How I was able to ask that without kissin' him I'll never know.

He nods softly, kissing me quickly. "You're right. We'll never get any talking done like this." I feel his fingers wrap about me, his free hand placing mine on his. "Blade or sheath, Kyo?"

Yeah, ya can probably get the context, buddy. If not, just uh, just *think about it*, yeah? I ain't gonna spell it out fer ya.

"Sh-sheath, Sebas." Then, well, I turn around until my back is 'gainst his chest. He chuckles, kissing my neck.

"Ah, eagerness noted. However, I'd rather not in your kitchen. You have oil? Condoms?" Another kiss that lingers, suckling and... fuck... Yeah, I'm gonna be marked tomorrow but I don't give a fuck.

"Yeah, yeah, yeah. Uh, should be in one of the boxes near the bed." I catch my breath. "Uh, I'll get 'em, could ya get a towel from the bathroom?"

He nods while I set to findin' the sex stuff I got in my room. Just 'cause we ain't satyrs don't mean we don't get horny. We're still a fair bit human, after all, and ya know how revved up they can get. I know the box, at least, and dig out the bottle of lubricant, the string of condoms, and my uh, 'friend' for lonely nights in case Rhys needs it.

Bridget, if yer out there in the great beyond, I'm sorry, but there's 'bout to be two Goblins fuckin' in yer apartment. Again. Then again ya mighta been into that. The internet is a fucked-up place, is all I'm sayin', yeah?

Rhys don't need instruction, the towel's laid out on the bed fer us, 'cause I don't wanna leave a mess on my sheets, got it? "Preferred position?"

"Right behind me, last time was fun, but I just wanna feel all of ya, Sebas." I chew my lip. "Ya can nibble my ear if ya wanna."

"I most certainly will not, Kyo. I have no need of shortcuts when I can listen what your body yearns to teach me." I shudder as his fingers glide up my side. "Ticklish, or was that a spot?"

"Kinda ticklish. Uh…" I swallow hard. "Could ya, uh, there's a somethin' in the box, should be under the pile of magazines." Off his look. "Yeah, it's fuckin' porn."

A simple shrug, and he bends over to look in, and I get a real look at his fine green ass. Defined, like kidney beans when he flexes it, which I know he's doin' fer my benefit. A few tattoos in Sigil, the translation I ain't sharin', but they imply that one shouldn't chase the fox into his den if one doesn't want to be chased as well. Okay, it's a poetic way of sayin' he's vers.

"Kyo, *these* weren't used with the Constable, were they?"

He's holdin' a set of handcuffs, 'kay?

"I use 'em to practice slippin' 'em, a'right?" And I do! And I ain't tryin' to convince myself. "And no. We ain't never did that."

"Are these for me, or you?" He's checkin' 'em, and yeah, standard police issue. No. Again. They are not from Thom, or from one of the sexual escapades.

I take a deep breath. This is a step fer me, 'kay buddy? I've thought 'bout doin' this with a guy, but I never felt right with anybody. Definitely not Thom, 'cause ya don't do handcuff play with a fuckin' cop.

"Fer, uh… Me." My face is hot, and gee, I wonder fuckin' why. He chortles, shakin' his head, and now I feel like a fuckin' idiot.

"This is a show of trust, Kyo. Are you sure? I'm under Oath to the one who murdered that poor girl, neither of us know what can be done to me, especially if I'm lying with the investigator of the crime." He starts puttin' the cuffs on himself, but I snatch 'em.

"Ya know how to slip these?" I cuff myself, and… I ain't gonna teach ya how to slip handcuffs, buddy. I don't even need a charm. A few seconds later they're off my wrists. "See? Ya try anythin', I can get out."

"Should we use a-"

"Safeword? Probably, yeah. Uh… if I say, uh… 'Evangelion', then stop, 'cause only the most fucked up person would shout that durin' sex." I see him frown, though. "What?"

"It was brilliant, Nick. I'd hold it higher than Akira." I roll my eyes, but he folds his arms. "I'm serious."

"So, what, will I have to tell ya, 'get in my fuckin' ass, Shinji?'" It's everythin' not to bust a gut, buddy. "Are *you* gonna shout out 'God's in his heaven and all's right with the world' when ya finish?"

Fuck, I'm laughin' now, I can't help it, and he still looks sorta pissed. "What?! 'Least I seen it."

'Least I know he's okay with cuffin' me now.

"You can be a nasty little fuck, can't you, Kyo?" Aw fuck, there's a love bite, I… don't know if I like it or not, yet, it's new. "First, for your rudeness."

"Ow, hey, what the fuck?" Hard smack on my ass, yeah, a bloom of heat and pain. "Shit! Ow!" Other cheek. Now my whole ass is warm and tinglin' from the hard, sudden contact. I start slippin' the cuffs. Ain't usin' the safeword, yet. I ain't scared, but I ain't gonna just lie here and let him fuckin' spank me.

No hard contact on my wrists as I slip the cuffs, so no damage, but he has a weight and strength advantage in this position, his chest to my back, takin' my arms out of armbar range, hands pushed through the gaps in the bed's headboard, the cuffs clickin' closer, makin' it a lot harder to slip 'em.

I feel his lips brush 'gainst my right ear, his teeth teasin' close to a nibble, but never hittin' the spots. "Evangelion. Nick, what am I permitted to do with you like this?"

"Take it a little easier, yeah? We're s'posed to be talkin' now."

"Very well, Kyo." Another kiss on the tender spot he's left on my neck, a hand rubbing my still sensitive ass. "I think I'll prepare you for me. You discuss your findings whilst I…" There's a finger rubbin' the entrance. He ain't startin' already, is he?!

"Uh… I uh, got away from the dragon, hid in the Dumpst- ahhhhh!" No pain, buddy, but lubricant gets kinda cold and when ya feel it gettin' massaged into yer asshole it takes a second to get used to, 'kay?

"Yes, you discussed that. And then?" I try to wriggle a little, but handcuffs and some weight on yer ankles keeps ya from movin' too much. "Kyo, if you keep twitching about, this will take longer than it needs to."

"Yeah, uh, I think Shadow's at the center of this." Measured breaths, relax. I feel some pressure, but it's familiar pressure. "Usin' my lil' friend?"

"Not so little." He's goin' slow, at least. "I'd suspected as much, given what Aki-chan had told us. Do you suspect a Redcap, despite the new guidelines? The fallen one you'd killed was hardly the only one who bucked the rules and traditions of the Black Warren."

"I mean…" Another breath. He's turnin' it, listenin' for that little reaction when he hits that special spot inside a guy. "Aw fuck… Yeah, there. Sure yer notin' it fer later."

"Mhm. But please, continue."

"I'm thinkin' a Shadow Cultist, openin' portals through Shadow all the way 'cross the City, like from North Allora out to the Benedict." There's some silence, both of us thinkin' while he's gettin' me relaxed and ready. Ain't like in the books where one guy hops on the other, 'less yer fuckin' a Phouk. "And Shiko said this has been done a few times before, like over ten, all in North Allora."

"Escape to the Benedict would make sense, what with the lycanthropes and the dragon. Were you anywhere near the Benedict Shores?" Prince Firemane's lands. Aw fuck, I'm full mast and twitchin' and leakin', mouth parted, eyes half-closed. No, gotta focus.

"Nah, but that was just me. Killer mighta popped out anywhere out there. I know the dragon was actin' like it weren't the first time he'd sensed someone makin' portals, and fuck knows I didn't start playin' 'round with 'em till today. I doubt it'd be Firemane, though, he's rather progressive, and loves fuckin' humans, at-" I gasp. Ya do that when a dildo's pulled out yer ass.

I feel his hands on my chest now, trailing up and down, findin' where I twitch or inhale sharply, spots 'sides my groin. Rhys is a bit of a biter, ain't drawin' blood, but I hear muffled grunts and moans durin' them love bites. I can feel him pressin' fervent 'gainst my back, along the cleft 'tween the cheeks.

"Need a moment…" He chuckles in my ear. "Don't go anywhere."

I grumble as he gets off the bed behind me, moves around front, and his need is evident, draggin' it along my cheekbone, down my neck, over my chest, his eyes admirin', samplin' my warmth and skin with the throbbin' length of him. "You're beautiful, Kyo."

I look down to watch him stroke himself on my body, down to my groin, meetin' his with mine, hand surroundin' 'em both in one grasp, pumpin' light. "You were saying?"

Oh that sonuva… "So… Fuck, yer a Shadow-damned tease… I'm thinkin' he jumps from North Allora to the Benedict to duck the Kitsune."

"But why?" Fingers on my scrotum, then to the perineum, 'cause he's bein' real sweet and tender so I ain't callin' it my taint. "Why to the Benedict when there are other places in the City to escape from the Foxes? Why not Destry Bay or Beckettsville?"

"Aw shit, Sebas, ya really expect me to figure that out while we're doin' this? Ain't ya s'posed to tell me what ya figured out?" Thing is, I know that he knows who it is, he just can't tell me or his heart might burst outta his chest or whatever that sick fuck did to him. He might not even be able to tell me what he found on his own investigation. "Or, uh, was it at least, uh… Fruitful?"

"I confirmed something, yes." He sounds disappointed, yeah, but not at me, more than he can't tell anyone. Don't know if he was testin' it. "Are you ready for me, Kyo?" When I nod, he kisses me again, long, the kind ya close yer eyes for 'cause ya only wanna feel that. I can feel the warmth of his touch, shudders, the good kind, barest pets on my neck.

"Y'know, I uh, I'm cuffed to the bedframe. Ya could do whatever ya wanted to me right now. So if there's anythin' ya wanted to uh, explore, ya got free rein. Whatever ya need to uh, 'get out'?" If ya ain't picked up on it, I'll explain if he goes for it.

Another nibble on my neck as he moves around back of me.

"Let yer body tell me everythin' ya wanna say, Sebas."

His teeth on my ear, pinched between the sharp points, right on the nerve cluster. That's what the tiny part of my rational brain is focusin' on. The rest of me is cryin' out like Pan just made me feel what the godly goat feels every minute. Rhys stops soon after, no words, my vision comin' back from bein' all cross-eyed, throat hoarse from all the heavy moanin'. If he even looks at my dick I'll spout off, no question.

Okay, Blackwarren. He said he'd never do that with me, but he just did. So, he's a hypocrite? Nah, nah, he came to ya, Nick, 'cause yer smart and ya figure shit out. Why would he make ya feel like that? Machinist designed us Goblins to have that, make us more pliant, more willin' to do shit we don't wanna do. He mentioned the killer got him to agree to the Oaths 'cause of that, and I'll admit, a Goblin knows how to work yer ears better than anyone.

I probably woulda killed fer him if he asked, that's how worked up I was, so he agreed, and managed to resist against *that* to pull back from killin' O'Hare. This is all shit I know, though. Was he made to keep quiet on everythin'… But why is he tellin' me… this…

He was gone. We were separated. He either went to confront the bastard, or to report in. "I, uh… fuck… I think I got it. What next?"

I get a few seconds to breathe, let my head clear. "Can you say anythin' right now, Sebas? Uh, which Goblin would ya wanna fuck in manga or anime?"

"Jugem from *Overlord*, obviously." His tongue along where it bit my neck. "I want to tell you so much, Kyo. Everything."

"Keep goin', Sebas, I trust ya. Yer gonna tell me how ya can without breakin' the Oath." Next is more tender, a kiss to the nape of my neck.

"However this ends, Kyo, I feel lucky to have found you." His arms wrap around me, holdin' me tight to him, breath on my skin. We ain't there, buddy, not for a ways, but if we get him free of this shit, I think that we could make a go of it, y'know?

"Same, Sebas. Now, continue, yeah? Keep goin'." My wrists a little sore, and with some effort I could slip, but he ain't given me a reason yet. "And remember to use the safeword next time ya wanna just talk, 'kay?"

I hear him get off the bed, and for a second I'm thinkin' the message got somethin' to do with him just leavin' me there, but 'fore I can ask, I hear the rippin' of cloth.

Then, the feel of fabric over my face, specifically the eyes, pressure in the back as it's tied off, blindfoldin' me. The scent is of Rhys, likely one of his shirts that he tore up to make it to not wreck one of mine. I don't know if his smell is part of the message, but I could think of worse things to have a nose full of right now. So, bein' blindfolded is part of it.

Am I the one who's blind in this? I don't know what or who I'm lookin' for? Well, yeah, we both know that, so either that's part of what he wants to tell me, or it's part of… of…

"Aw, fuck, Sebas!" He parts me open, the heat of him pushin' in, makin' his presence known, the journey eased by the prep and that we did this earlier today. Knew what he was fuckin' doin', that's fer fuckin' sure. It ain't like in the books, by the way, ya don't get off from feelin' it. It's pressure, some heat, fullness, and a weirdly good feelin' when they hit the right spot.

Which… he ain't hittin'. He's changin' angles, speeds, depths, and while I'm sure it's great fer his dick, it ain't a fun time fer my ass.

"Where are you… where are you…" He's searchin'? The fuck? He found "me" pretty easy this mornin' and I know fer damned sure his memory ain't that bad and aw fuck, I think I got it.

Someone lookin', haphazard, they're in the dark tryin' to find…

Where are you.

They're tryin' to find *me*.

Why? What do I got on my fuckin' left arm right now? On my right? That's as good a reason to hunt me down and kill me as any. The Sidhe wanted Shadow's Edge, I straight up *stole* the Aeolian Shear.

"That the only reason yer tryin' to find me, Rhys?"

No reply, but he holds me closer, movin' into a simple rhythm, the kind that's ingrained into every set of livin' instincts since the dawn of fuckin' time. Okay, gotta be the next bit here. He's fuckin' regular-wise now, picked up breathin', and he's hittin' the right spots. His arms still hold me tight, only his hips pushin' and pullin' him.

Gettin' more difficult to focus, obviously. Okay, is that it? I'm s'posed to be distracted? Then Rhys was sent to be a distraction? But if I'm bein' distracted, and he went to report in today, then why ain't there Guard bustin' down my door to cut me to pieces? Ain't like they'd be bidin' their time. I'm guessin' that Rhys ain't sold me out either, but what is he tryin' to tell me, then?

His hands on my chest, holdin' me tighter, it's startin' to hurt a little, actually. Safeword comin' up in three… two…

Hold up. Wait.

Wait, wait, wait, wait, wait.

He ain't tryin' to hurt me, he's holdin' me tight, my back to his chest.

I put his hand on my heart and leave it there. He don't move it, the squeeze gets lighter. Got it. This is about the Oaths. It's the reason "he" is tryin' to find me. The Oaths… I mean, Rhys came to find me 'cause of 'em, he told me what they're for. First, to make him kill Bridget O'Hare. Then, when he refused, to make him take the fall.

And Rhys had to report in. The bow's a high value target, yeah, but Rhys came to me just after I stole it. I doubt the owner even knew it was gone yet. But what I *was* doin' was...

I was lookin' into the murder. Puttin' together theories, tryin' to find evidence, deduce and shit like some legendary opium addict. If I can solve it, unmask the real murderer of Bridget O'Hare and show receipts, Rhys's confession wouldn't be taken seriously. After all, I'm the guy who cracked the case of three murdered nobles.

I'm a threat to the killer. And 'cause Rhys ain't crackin', he can't find me, or know what I'm doin', or plannin' to do. He offed Kirschbaum before I could question him, yeah, but that's one willin' patsy off the board, and I'm guessin' they don't grow on trees.

"I... I think I got it, Sebas..." I relax back into him, his hand droppin' to my groin, the other runnin' fingers over the spots he's learned on me. My breathin' quickens as he matches his rhythms in front with the one behind. It's gettin' to be a lot, my body feelin' light, senses opened further with the blindfold, the scent of him heavy in my nose, his touch flowin' over and into me. "Ya... Ya close?"

A piston rhythm starts, barrelin' me toward the edge, I can't hold back anymore, and why the fuck would I want to. I can feel it buildin' the sounds I make blendin' into the primal symphony him and I composed in three movements, and I'm about to hit the fuckin' crescendo.

"S-Sebassss..."

A kiss to my neck.

"After you, Detective."

24

It's cold, throat closin' up 'cause yer nuts are lodged in it cold, extremities already courtin' frostbite after three seconds cold. And I can hear that creepy fuckin' atonal shit whistlin' through everythin'. I ain't gotta think too much on it, it's the Shadowsong. So, why the fuck am I hearin' it? I don't remember passin' in or makin' a portal.

I slipped the cuffs after, 'cause I only got my picks to take 'em off proper, and even then not havin' 'em is a good motivator to do it faster and better. When my eyes adjust, I can see the shapes of furniture, walls, my apartment, but not really. At least, if the piano's any indicator.

No woman made of viscera and wires beggin' me for help, and I don't know if I should be relieved or not about that.

"Is anyone here?" Huh. Why'm I talkin' in Sigil? That's new.

Nothin'. A'right, if this is a prophetic dream or somethin' I ain't gettin' the message. Maybe...

"I call upon the one who asked my help." I sound so fuckin' hoity-toity when I'm usin' Sigil. Fuckin' embarrassin', buddy, no lie. *"Your voice is welcome."*

Nothin'. What the fuck?

Since I ain't wakin' up, and can't see a way outta here, might as well look 'round for anythin' to show me why I'm here. Start at the piano, maybe?

It's a grand, no idea how it was able to fit in here. No broken wires, no blood or gore. That's good, but I'm wonderin' why any of it's different. Change is good, yeah, but there's always a reason. Is she gone, maybe? Don't know why else the apartment's lookin' like the Shadow's reflection of it, maybe...

This how it looked *before* the murder?

Time travel's out, that shit don't happen. If it did, I'm guessin' it was cut out more than a few worlds ago by some Ra'keth who might've had the good idea that fuckin' with time could fuck up existence. Or, maybe they were just makin' sure no one else could but them? Ya'd be surprised how much of the mythics were created outta spite.

Other option is I'm either bein' shown this, or the Shadow's showin' me 'cause I'm here and I'm mentioned that the Shadow and I are cool. Dunno why, I try not to think too much on it, Either it's 'cause I was born to a Tinker and Redcap durin' a Shadow-damned eclipse (well, a lunar one) or it just happened and my birth don't mean shit. Or maybe I'm just crazy fer thinkin' the Shadow actually gives a fuck 'bout anythin' and I'm really lucky.

What I'm sayin' is it's a fuckin' Schrodinger kinda thing and I'd rather not end up with a dead cat, y'know?

So, I'm gonna go with, "ya can see what happened before the murder, dumbass, so fuckin' pay attention ya *baciagaloop*" and fuckin' leave it at that.

"Time is a commodity, dally no further with your tale." Ugh, I sound like a douchebag. And tryin' to swear up a blue streak results in… no words bein' said. C'mon, just gimme *somethin'*, it's fuckin' cold!

Three firm knocks at the door. Yeah, I ain't fuckin' openin' it. Three more.

Yeah, fuck you. I ain't into 'em, but I know how a fuckin' horror movie works, pal.

"Coming!" Wait, what? "I was in the tub. Sorry!"

A woman appears out of the doorway to the bathroom, and I seen enough of her on her social media to know who it is: Bridget O'Hare.

She's in a bathrobe, tying her hair back as she walks to the door. Should I say somethin'? I move toward her, behind her, so I can pull her back from that door, I just know that whoever killed her's on the other side. I don't know if I can change the past, but I gotta try.

No, no, put yer knives away. Wait, why do I got knives?

She deserves better. A hand on the mouth, one blade across the back of the neck, sever the cord that will feed her pain, and… And… She's human?

What the actual fuck am I fuckin doin'?! It's like I can't fuckin' control my hands!

Her hand turns the doorknob. No. She's not supposed to be human. No!

The door opens to Shadow. A man made of Shadow. I can't let him get to her. I… I have to… My chest erupts with pain, words etched into my skin burning hot. No. I won't do this anymore! I can feel his gaze on me, heavy, grinding my knees into dust.

"I won't!" The woman turns to see me, and screams, a monster out of nightmares before her, holding sharp blades, in striking distance. I can feel the pressure on my chest, on my arms, hands, pulling me to sink the daggers deep in her chest, extract the…

"No!" The weight of the Oath, the authority of the one before me, this is my purpose, this is what I am *for*. The claws in my fingers dig into my palms, drawing blood, the pain enough to regain some measure of focus, focus on pain that I chose.

The woman backs toward him. I tell her to run, cough up blood as the Oath burns into my chest, the heat setting my lungs ablaze. Her arm is grabbed by the wrist, eyes lit by Fae fire out of the Shadow, on me. The word is a blade through my chest. *"You are Oathbreaker."*

I can't abandon her. I have to stop this. Even as he drags her to the piano, the strings rising and carried on the Shadow like scourges, fangs, sinking into her innocent spirit. The blades dig into the floor, dragging me toward her an inch at a time.

"Help me!" Her life is being pulled into the thing that gave her so much joy, her art, her creative soul. I won't reach her in time. The piano plays in minor keys, the dirge of Shadowsong scraping her soul out of her body, her screams a symphony of blood, agony. And she's still alive.

I only have a breath left before the pain and darkness take me. I raise my hand and throw the knife.

Father Redcap, spare her from suffering. Grandmother Atropos, slit her thread from this unfortunate stitch. Brother Gremlin, forgive me. Let me lay my blades to rest.

I fuckin' wake up screamin', what the fuck did ya think was gonna fuckin' happen, buddy? Fuckin' Shadow that was…

The blade is out on the vambrace. The Shear is on my left arm, a wrist mounted crossbow, a bolt loaded and ready to fire.

"Nick?"

THUNK!

Well, a bolt's stickin' outta the doorframe. Guess I ain't gettin' my deposit back. Ha ha. Yeah, make jokes. Defuse the tension. Ya almost headshot'ed yer maybe boyfriend since yer two magical weapons are always ready to fuckin' slit somebody, looks like. I try to relax my arms, my whole body tensed and mostly clenched.

In, count to three. Out, count to three. Do that a few times like the book on stress and anxiety said. Rhys is keepin' his distance, probably a good idea.

"Rhys?" I take a long, cleansing breath. "I'm gonna ask ya again. One more time. And this time ya tell me the fuckin' truth."

He don't come over, still in the doorframe. It's like he don't know what the right move is here. Don't look like he's thinkin' of runnin', more like he don't wanna be near me when he gives me the answer I got the feelin' he's gonna give me. Y'see, while that fucked up nightmare was goin' on, I was payin' attention.

And I read a lot. A few legal thrillers, and books on actual legal strategy to debunk all the shit ya see in novels and movies and TV. One of the simple rules is this: Don't ask a fuckin' question ya don't already got the dead-to-rights answer to. "Rhys Gwydion Llewellyn, did you end the life of Bridget O'Hare?"

"Yes." He's said it before, but I changed the wordin', catch that?

"Ya were gonna kill her, then ya noticed she was human. Ya saw she was sufferin', in pain, from what the other man was doin', and she was beggin' ya to help her. And the only way ya could was to end it for her." I'm lookin' at him. "Was a mercy, wasn't it?"

"Yes." He's leanin' back against the doorframe, the bolt still stickin' out just above his head. "If I could have traded my life for hers…"

"That's how ya knew where I lived. How ya got in so easily, 'cause ya been here before. Ya already knew how to get in quick-quiet." I swing my legs over the side of the bed, slip down to the floor, get dressed. "What the fuck can ya tell me, Rhys? What the fuck was happenin' to her with the piano?"

"How… do you know about that?" No shock, ain't wonder either, just more of a general "what the fuck" kinda expression. Ya know the kind, with the squinty eyes and parted mouth? "I didn't tell you about that night. I couldn't."

"Well, Fate finds a way, yeah? Shadow flows into some fucked up places, and it's best not to question it. Like, how ya can have a dream then suddenly yer relivin' a murder in… I'm guessin' yer shoes." I walk toward him, rest a hand on his shoulder. "Was it Bridget that made ya decide ya didn't wanna be an assassin no more, or what?"

There's the shock.

"I've never told *anyone* that."

I shrug. "I think I mentioned I was in yer head while the murder was goin' down? At least in the dream. I ain't askin', it's there fer a reason, fer me to figure somethin' out, another piece of the puzzle. I coulda just seen it all from outside yer perspective, like a fucked-up snuff video, but I felt what was goin' on in yer head, the pain ya were in when ya broke the Oath and gave everythin' ya had to end her agony." I chew my lip. "I uh… I don't know how I feel about mercy killin', but I understand why ya did it."

"Nick, I…" He takes a breath. "Let me tell you what I am able to. Upon seeing I was sent to take the life of an innocent human, I broke my oath. I thought I would be stronger, would be able to take action, but if you truly witnessed the event from my perspective as you say…"

"I got no fuckin' clue how yer still alive, Rhys. Don't even have to see what it was when it was intact, it's *still* diggin' in ya, and how it ain't finished ya off-"

"A broken Oath cannot eviscerate the heart if the heart is not there to cut."

"But who put it there?" I step closer to him. "Ya said yer ears were fucked with to make ya do it-"

"The Oath to slit the human was forced on me. The other… was my choice."

I blink, buddy, ya fuckin' bet I do. Who the fuck would *choose* to let that kinda shit be burned into their chests? I mean, I heard 'bout some Oaths that pull bits of yer soul out to keep ya in line, but fuck, a heart? I know us Goblins ain't that trustworthy to Sidhe, but what kinda job would ya risk yer heart for?

"Who the fuck are ya, Rhys?" The Gremlin in the red cap averts eye contact. I'm guessin' he can't say it out loud. He leans against the door frame, his left hand raised a little higher, fingers tappin' like he's tryin' to get my attention without sayin' outright. Ain't nothin' weird 'bout it, so I don't know what… he…

"Brother Gremlin, lend your sight
Let me see the hidden light
Secrets shown that I will break
Brother, let my blood awake"

The Oath's there, in the center, the damaged, jagged remains of the broken Oath overlayin' it slightly, but I seen this before. Rhys's left hand, I guess I never looked at it with the Sight, but I don't get why there would be any point to…

It's a circle, a crest, in red and blue, glowin' in the darkness. A phoenix risin' with fiery wings, clutchin' five and four arrows. Nine. Three times three.

The crest of the Summerswords. The Royal Family.

On the Left Hand of the Throne.

25

"I didn't want to keep you in the dark, Nick. I'm unable to tell you any more, but I want you to know as much as I can give you." Tied up in Oaths to keep him from the truth when it'd be so easy to lie, or just keep quiet, and he's doin' what he can to tell me anyway. Still…

"Damon Blackwarren's the Left Hand of the Queen, Rhys. Not some Welsh-American Gremlin otaku." But I ain't got no clue why the fuck he'd lie about that to the degree where he'd get the heraldry inscribed on his fuckin' hand.

Lemme tell ya about the Summerswords, buddy. It's the royal family, fer starters, and while we got three Princes, there's only two actual Summerswords that are still alive: Queen Alana (may her warmth bless us all), and Prince Hadryn. Prince Firemane is vaguely connected, but elevated by the Queen herself, and Prince Boreas is the Queen's son, but a Winter Prince can't hold the throne of the Summer Court.

Now, don't let the Queen fool ya. She's a classy lady, yeah, the most progressive ruler of the Kingdom of Rainbows since we all came over, but there's a trail of bodies behind her ascent to the throne. Like, three uncles, five older brothers, about a dozen cousins, four husbands. There's always been rumors about her sons, but *they* were takin' a page from their Mom about who'd be the heir apparent.

And yeah, Damon was likely involved in some of the carnage. His body's covered in Oaths a fuck more than Rhys's, and let's be honest, there's been rumors 'round the family he'd slit gods if she asked him to, even if he didn't have those Oaths. Speakin' of Damon…

"How 'bout this, I'll call Damon and give him an update, maybe shoot some info to the Kitsune, too. 'Least with the latter they'd want a tip on how the fucker's been eludin' 'em." I pick up my phone, unlock it.

"Nick, don't." I blink at him incredulously, yeah, 'cause what the fuck.

"Annnnnnnd, why not?" I ain't locked the phone yet. This ain't a trust issue, it's more I don't fuckin' get why I shouldn't be sharin' info. This is okay intel and a decent theory on someone probably connected to Prince Hadryn who's been killin' women and gettin' off clean.

"Are you prepared to explain *that?*" Yeah, yeah, he ain't pointin' at my vambrace, he's pointin' at the Shear that's currently full tactical armor on my fuckin' left arm. "Regardless of whether you believe it yours or not, it is, should your theory prove correct, involved in if not the actual act, but the definite use in the multiple murders of humans."

Ah.

Uh...

Yeah, I got nothin' fer that save the truth.

"Also, you mentioned you stole it from the Prince's mobile vault? Now you're admitting to high crimes, if not outright treason." He puts his hand on my shoulder. "And I know you're more than aware of how Sidhe treat our people when they lack a reason to oppress us. Imagine the consequences when they're given an undeniable one."

I roll my eyes. "Don't get me started, Rhys. Ya don't have to ask me about Sidhe usin' *noblesse oblige* to write off the nastiest..."

Wait a minute. Why his ears prickin' up?

I see his mouth form a word, no sound.

Run.

I wish I could tell ya, buddy, that I followed that instinct, I really do. This is a moment where I'm gonna be askin' myself "what if?" fer a good chunk of my life.

'Cause I don't. I'm confused. I hesitate. I look at Rhys hopin' he'll gimme more to work with. But I don't get no answer, not in time for what happens next.

The front door's kicked in by a troll, followed by another. They're Guard, but the crests on their heraldry say somethin' more.

Royal Guard.

Personal guard and bodyguards to the royal family, the elite, the fuckers ya don't wanna cross paths with. They're trained with everythin': swords, spears, martial weapons, bows, blunt weapons, hand-to-hand, and if need be? Guns.

I feel their eyes on me, both of 'em smirkin' 'cause they know they got me dead to rights. I feel the bow in my hand. I can fire an arrow at the wall, one out the window, make a break fer it through Shadow, drag Rhys with me. We'll figure out why they're here after we escape, just gotta get clear.

One's pickin' up the kicked in door, it's my best chance. I turn to fire behind Rhys, the arrow already nocked. Just have to aim and loose-

"Kneel."

I'm screamin', buddy! My... I think I fuckin' knee's broken! Oh fuckfuckfuckfuckfuckfuckfuckfuckfuckfuck-

"Silence."

Sound's gone, I can't talk, can't yell, can't cry out, can't get up, starin' at the floor, my body tellin' me I ain't *worthy* to look up. I'm grittin' my teeth, the pain even worse now that I can't scream it out or swear up a fuckin' blue streak. I feel the bow collapsin', makin' its way up my arm to cover it. The armor's wet with tears. I wanna look at Rhys, but I can't.

A hard kick to my side, I think a rib or two cracks, rough laughter, somethin' wet on my face, spit, more laughter.

"Lift his head." The voice is almost sibilant, but male, ain't a troll.

Oh fuck.

My chin is taken roughly, yanked up, the muscles in my neck and shoulders resistin', addin' to the pain. My eyes try to look away, but my head is pulled into position, my gaze fallin' on a tall, slender Sidhe with pale skin, cold black eyes, hair black as the depths of Shadow, dressed in royal red attire, a tailored three-piece since he's out among the humans. If ya didn't know who he was, you'd think he was an exec or on the board of some big non-profit or NGO or some shit. His face is comfortin', like he's there to help ya, and has yer best interests at heart.

"Pain?" A fuckin' one-sided smile as he says it, but it comes off like he actually gives a fuck. He glances to the one holdin' my head. "Let him go. Him and I must have a few words. Please wait outside and make certain we're not disturbed."

"Your Highness," Rhys speaks up, voice small. "I believe he's-"

"You were given no leave to speak." I see Rhys in my peripheral vision fall to his knees, clutchin' his chest. "Remember your place."

Fuck, he don't even sound like he's fuckin' scoldin' him, like it's just a fuckin' gentle *reminder* to not talk out of turn. The trolls have a chuckle as they walk outside, doorway still "open" since it ain't got a fuckin' door.

"As for *you*." His gaze is on me. "I will allow you to speak, but you will stifle any shrieks of agony, they are rude and uncouth and not for proper conversation." I'm practically glarin' now. "From what I understand, amongst your kith's countless cabals of criminals, you are spoken to be one of the 'good ones'." I grit my teeth harder. "You'll behave, yes?"

I manage a small nod.

He waves his hand at me like a fuckin' conductor.

"Now address me. *Properly*."

It fuckin' hurts so godsdamned much. Why ain't I goin' into fuckin' shock?!

"Yer Highness-"

"Properly." I feel the pain risin'. Aw fuck, jus' make it fuckin' stop!

"Your... Royal Highness, Prince Hadryn." I take a breath, fightin' the pain with everythin' I got. "Crown Prince of the Fae, True Scion of Her Majesty Queen Alana, may her warmth bless-"

"That's not necessary." Voice is sharper. "Continue."

"I... I bid ya..."

"Finish it. *Properly.*"

"I bid you..." My whole fuckin' leg is pain. "I bid you..."

"Finish. It." I see a smile on his face, cruel like the one Dorian Gray first sees in his portrait.

"I bid... you..." I take a breath, and meet his eyes, "To suck the shit out my green ass, ya kin-killin' motherfucker."

He waves it off, literally. "Vulgarity and insult. I understand that your kith was respectable once, understood the social order, but it seems your manners have grown... lax." He steps toward me, hands behind his back, nobly. "Now, as in the beginning..."

My body is knifepoints on nerves spinnin' like fuckin' dervishes without the holy ecstasy. I'm gaspin', lookin' to anyone fer help. I see Rhys, his muscles strained, tryin' to break free of this fuckin' grasp of authority. Wails escape me, no words, tears streamin', the agony burnin' my body and mind, makin' sure I never forget.

"Pain will remain the only method to insure the simplest of instructions are followed. Will you behave?"

"YES!" I'm... I don't know what...

"Good. It's better when you remember your place, is it not?" I feel my arms lifted. "Interesting. I would normally inquire how you could obtain such artifacts, but your reputation reveals your larcenous tendencies."

"Y-you killed Bridget O'Hare." I manage eye contact, it's the most rebellious I can handle. "And all those other women." I cough, blood spatterin' on the floor. "Yer a monster."

"Am I to be excoriated by the likes of you for loving women? A Goblin known for crowing about his supposed love for humanity?"

He crouches in front of me. "Admiring their technology, their art, their creations, and wanting to bathe one's mind in the seas of their works pulled from the ether of their souls?"

Don't ya fuckin say it, ya fuck.

"Are we truly so different?" Oh, fuck you. He wanders out of my sight. "Novels embracing the romance between two, heavily dogeared. We both admire love and the light it brings, Goblin."

"Noth… Nothin' alike." I cough again. "Yer killin', not lovin' 'em ya sick fuck-"

"Silence." He's in front of me again. "Look at my servant, there." I turn to see Rhys, our eyes meetin'. He's pleadin' with me to stop. "Keep looking, now. Get up, assassin."

Rhys rises, staying in my view.

"Goblin. Your artifacts. Give them to me." My left arm flexes, the bow that makes up my armor quiverin', the vambrace slowly foldin' and openin' and slippin' around my hand, the pain tellin' it what I need. I feel it closin' around my fingers, hardenin' into a gauntlet, Shadow's Edge rememberin' my great-grandfather, claws comin' out the fingers.

I hear the Prince *hmph,* amused. "Defiant to the end. You remind me of the girl, you know. She couldn't simply accept my love, let her art and music be part of my collection, lauded far beyond her own life. It is fitting it be here, Goblin." He speaks to Rhys. "Assassin, you have the opportunity to atone for your insubordination. What is this artifact he wears on his hand?"

"Shadow's Edge, Your Royal Highness, one of the Five. It is the Redcap's blade, a blood-drinker that adapts to the wielders needs." Rhys's face is so apologetic. "It was used in the butchering of the House of Oakdawn and-"

"That will do." The Prince waves him off. Still crouched, the Sidhe looks me in the eyes. "Yes. Bridget O'Hare is dead, killed by my assassin. As are those before her. The painters, the sculptors, the playwrights, the talespinners, all of them poor and human and wretched. All of them ached for my approval, my offer of immortality through their works. They all gave themselves willingly, you know. My hands, Goblin, are bloodless, unlike your own. An instrument of death on your hand? A tool of the Nightmare? Quite seditious."

I'm tryin' to say somethin', but I can't make the words come out.

"Ah, you mean to implicate me. Trap me in some human law regarding conspiracy. You are a Goblin. Who would give your claims any credence? After all, I would suppose you think yourself the hero of your grand Romance." He places his hand to his chest, and looks away slightly, mouth parted. "And you require me to stand against you. Very well."

He beckons over Rhys, snaps his fingers. Rhys is shoutin' curses at him in so many languages, rage fuelin' his lungs, hands strugglin', but still drawin' his blades.

"I will be your *villain*." His fingers motion downward.

It happens so fast.

My body wrests enough control to put me into shock.

Rhys is screamin', tryin' to bring his blades to the Prince. A wave of his hand quiets that, puts the Left Hand of the Prince at ease, obedient, my right hand now in the Prince's grasp, Shadow's Edge still upon it.

"Let him keep the bow. I now have something better." Prince Hadryn beckons, Rhys followin', tryin' to look back at me, hands behind his back. I see his fingers tappin' somethin' before the pain finally takes me. I'm cold, and tired, thinkin' is gettin' harder.

I…

26

"Nick?"

…

"Nicky? Wake up, you gotta wake up, okay?"

…

"Cousin, you have to give me some space. He's lost a lot of blood, and these mixtures are *precise*."

…

"Yeah, yeah. Whadduya need me to do?"

…

"There's a lightning stone in my bag. Get it. He's half-Redcap, half-Tinker?"

…

"Purebred Blackwarren, yeah, on his father's side. Three quarters Tinker and one quarter Italian Gremlin on his mother's."

…

"Fifty ccs should do. Done. Ready the lightning stone."

…

"Ready."

…

"Lightning."

…

"Nothin'. Fuck! It ain't workin', Cora!"

…

"Calm yourself, Damon. Clear your hands from him. And… *Lightning.*"

…wha?

"He ain't breathin'!" Cryin'? "Fuck, do somethin'!"

"Give the mixture some time to work. Panic will not help him." Somethin'… neck? "Start pumping this. Keep the seal on his mouth."

…air?

"Right, right, right, yeah, yeah."

"Steady rhythm. Keep it up." Small pain… arm. "Giving him another twenty ccs."

"Right, got it. I got it. C'mon, Nicky." More air. Too much. Too much!

"Fuck! He's coughin', did I fuck it up?"

"No, that's good, he has to breathe to cough." Pressure on my neck again. "Pulse is weak, but he's got one. Get the clear bags from my kit, they're saline. Any chance you know his bloodtype?"

Another pain on my arm, small. Everythin' is so heavy.

"Fuck. I don't know! I…"

"Relax, Damon. I'm not giving him a blood bag yet. He's back, that's what matters, but we're still in rough territory. I'll take over the breather, you need to prep a gurney and transport. There should be equipment down in the van. Fetch it, please? Thank you."

"Yeah." He sounds relieved. "On it."

Everythin' is blurry.

"Keep still, Nick. You're rather bad off. I'm putting a brace on your neck, okay? You were badly hurt and lost a lot of blood. I'm running saline all the way, but there's a lot I need to work with. Your left knee is shattered, and your right hand has been amputated. I've stopped the bleeding as much as I can, but I need you on a table so I can get ahead of it. Right now, I just need you to stay conscious. Just breathe and keep your eyes open."

"…wh-who…"

"Try not to talk, okay? It's okay if you don't recognize me. I'm your Aunt Cora, on your father's side. Wish we were meeting under better circumstances. Do you know your bloodtype?"

"Uh… Uhhh… Ohhhh… Pah…"

"O positive, thank you."

I'm in and outta consciousness, despite my best efforts. I remember noises, movement, heat, cold, so much cold, more hard jolts to my chest, bright lights, pain in my leg and arm. There's voices too, in varyin' degrees of anxiety, anger, sadness.

When I open my eyes again, I hear a steady beeping from my left. An EKG, no flatlines. Bags are hanging, both red, tubes feedin' 'em into my body. There's also a Gob with big fuckin' ears, a Gremlin…

"Rhy…Rhys…?"

He looks toward me, eyes gettin' bright. "Aw fuck, Nick, ya gave me a fuckin' scare ya fuckin' *baciagaloop*. I mean, woulda been okay if I didn't hafta give ya yer cut."

Not Rhys.

"Cen?" Fuck, everything hurts. "Where'm I?"

"Safehouse in North Allora. Stay awake, yeah?" I hear footsteps movin' away. "Hey Doc! Mrs. Volpe! He's awake!"

"Where's… Rhys?" I don't get no answer.

Hard to keep my eyes open, but I'm doin' it. Tough to look down, somethin' 'round my neck, like a pillow or somethin'. I'm in a room, on a bed like one in a hospital, but I ain't in one. Drapes on the windows. It ain't dark, but it's dim, or my eyes ain't all the way, yet. Breathin' hurts, but it ain't stoppin' me. Just gotta wince through it, is all.

My Mom hurries through a door, I guess, I hear her voice before her steps. Plus her scent. A Goblin never forgets his mom's scent, even if they're taken after bein' born, y'know. "Nicky! Thank the Fates you're okay. We were all offerin' to Lachesis that she'd save ya."

I can tell she's cryin', can't turn my head enough to see her without shootin' pain.

"We offered to Atropos as well, to spare him the shear, Connie." I think I know that voice. My… Aunt? "He's not out of the woods yet, though. Nick is very, *very* lucky. If the armor on his right arm hadn't been secured so tightly, he might've lost more than his hand."

…what? So the vambrace saved me?

I try to raise my arm, so I can at least give ya thanks and…

That's the armor that makes the bow, but it's s'posed to be on my left arm. It hurts, too, bruisin' on the skin.

"…wha… hap… end?"

"You were grievously injured, Nick." I make effort to see her. She's a Goblin, green skin, long ears, eyes with red irises, dressed in red scrubs, bluish-black hair tied back, like Dad's, and mine. "I need to check your vitals, and then I'll leave you with your mother for a few minutes, okay? Could you wait outside, Connie?"

"I'll be right back, Nicky." She kisses my forehead, which she ain't done since she came out to take me back with her to California. I hear a door close shortly after.

"What… happened? Where's Rhys?" My throat is so dry and hoarse.

Aunt Cora takes over, testin' my breathin', checkin' the wounds, the bags, injectin' somethin' into the line. "Whazzat?"

"A serum. It's keeping the pain from overtaking you, stimulating your bone marrow to replace the blood you've lost. There's also a banana bag, blood, plasma, platelets, and you aren't going anywhere until they're all drained." I wince a bit as she tests my neck. "Looks like the swelling has gone down, we can take off the brace in a few hours. Can you wriggle your toes for me?"

I scrunch them, or think I am.

"That's good. Flex and wiggle your left fingers?"

Doesn't seem too hard. I start on the right because that's probably…next…

"Nick?" I hear beeping. "Nick, breathe, stay calm. Your right hand is gone. It's been amputated. Nick, look at me. Breathe, and look at me." I feel fingers on my chin nudging my gaze away.

Hands made me look. Hands made me watch.

I gnash my teeth, bite, try to make sure those hands never touch me again-

"Don't ya fuckin' touch me! Get away from me!" I almost closed my teeth around flesh, a taste of blood on my tongue. I hear a door almost break open.

"Get away from him, Cora! Ya heard him!"

"Connie, I wouldn't-"

"Ya ain't his mother, Cora!" I feel arms around my neck, tension rising until my mother's scent carries into my nose, calmin' me. "It's okay, Nicky, I'm here. Mama's here. Yer safe, I ain't gonna let anyone hurt ya."

Her hands stroke my head, my eyes closin', I just want all this to be a bad dream. This is my fault, ain't it? I mouthed off to the Prince and look what happened, what happened to me.

"Mama?" My voice is so small. "Why can't I feel my hand?"

"Some piece of shit took it from ya, honey. Don't ya worry, though. I'm gonna get to work on a new one for ya. I'm callin' in favors soon as yer asleep, okay? And I'm tellin' that sewer rat Vincenzo he's sourcin' some Faesteel for it. Ain't nobody gonna hurt my *piccola* Lupin ever again."

Get why my middle name's Arsenne, now?

Ya might think my mom's talkin' about hackin' someone's hand off and sewin' it on me like some fuckin' horror movie, but she's a Tinker, not some sicko. I think she means she's gonna fuckin' *build* me a new hand. It ain't unheard of, weird as it sounds, Mama Tinker don't limit herself or her children to just shiny doodads and toys.

Still, it don't mean I'm cool with my fuckin' hand bein' gone. I'm calmed down a little, at least, Mom's helpin' with that a lot. I'm grateful I ain't Cenzo, or Uncle Joey, 'cause she's gonna raise Hell once I'm asleep.

But how did I end up here?

I don't think on the details, but I was in my apartment, and Prince Hadryn was there, and Rhys, and... a lot's gone. Close enough to human that us Goblins block out traumatic shit too, and I think my mind don't want me rememberin' my hand gettin' cleaved off.

I'll skip ahead a bit. It's mostly me restin', bags gettin' swapped, bandages changed, doses of Aunt Cora's serum, which is helpin' the pain a lot. Mom takes measurements of my left leg and right arm, and I see her sketchin' schematics once my neck brace is off.

Vincenzo is now sufficiently scared of Mom, Uncle Joey just knows to stay outta her way. When Damon checks in on me, Mom tells him straight that she ain't goin' nowhere 'til I'm okay.

"Connie, it's complicated, I can't tell ya who did it. I'm locked under Oaths, and the one who ordered it has a fuckin' Blackwarren assassin as his personal guard." He sighs. "Fucker's even better than me. Best thing ya can do fer Nick is get outta play- Fuck! Watch the ear, fuck!"

She was tuggin' him down, grip on the pressure points that, if lighter, woulda made him quiver in ecstasy. Instead, it's really fuckin' painful. "Listen ya Redcap piece of shit, I ain't leavin' him, and I don't care who the fuck I piss off. Yer gonna get me the fuckin' Faesteel I asked for, got it? Yer gonna get off my fuckin' back 'bout Colton. And yer gonna apologize to my son that the shitstain ya work for fucked him up and ya ain't doin' shit about it. *Capisci, pezzo di merda?*"

"Shadow, fuck, I got it, Connie, I got it!"

There are more than a few fights like that between Mom and the various relatives she's pressin' to get materials. When I tell her I'm bored off my ass, Cen gets his ears yanked so he'll lend me his laptop.

"I ain't even do anythin', Cous', fuck," he says, wearing a cold pack on his head. "Be careful with it, yeah? Ya need help with anythin'?"

I'm still groggy, mostly the serums and drugs to help with the pain and nudge my body to replace all the blood I lost. "Did I get any texts?"

My phone was relieved from my person as I was obsessively checkin' for texts from Rhys. It ain't high school bullshit, it's 'just let him be okay' stuff.

"Yeah, ya got a list of names from a rice distributor, so I'm guessin' that's the Foxes. Gimme back the laptop, I'll look 'em up for ya, I can do it faster than you."

"Ain't 'cause I can see ya twitchin' that I got it, huh?"

"Lucy was not meant for Redcap hands, Nick. Seriously. Touch the keys."

I'm expectin' to get shocked, so I'm pleasantly surprised I ain't. Also, my body's been shocked enough literally and figuratively. Instead, the screen flashes alarms, and then friendly messages such as:

Greetings, Redcap. According to Judeo-Christian philosophy, you are going to burn in hell.

Redcaps hate him! Learn to not be a murdering psychopath using this one weird trick!

Nearly all of Redcap murders are committed by heterosexual males, and hardly any males on the LGBT spectrum. Bust those barriers, queen!

"It was one guy, and it was self-defense, Cen. And these seem specifically targeted."

"Says the Gob who wants to do deep dives on a dozen murdered women."

"*Because* it's a dozen, Cen. A number. They got names, they had lives and hopes and dreams and had the misfortune to be talented in the vicinity of a Sidhe. They deserve better, Cousin. They deserve justice and peace." I pull him face to face, my eyes hurting, his eyes wide. "*That* is the work of Father Redcap, Cen. So let me do my fuckin' job, okay?"

He don't look scared, but he's lookin' away when I let him go. "Sorry, Nick. Sorry. I'll lay off, okay? Ya ain't gonna kill anybody else, right? Zero body count?"

I manage a smile. "Zero body count."

"Okay." He squeezes my hand. "Lemme help, then, okay? I'll find more than you could, and faster."

"Let's get to work, then. Hey, thanks Vincenzo, really."

Christine Miller. Neo-impressionist, urban landscapes.

Yolanda Jefferson. Sculpture, marble.

Mika Todoroke. Murals, spray paint.

Hilda Ramirez. Wall sculpture, found material.

Georgia Van. Metalworking, steel.

Kate Quinn-Gray. Pottery, painted.

Lana Reed. Pre-Raphaelite, portraits.

Willa Greene. Woodworking, anamorphics.

Nisha Hill. 3D Printing, mathematical chaos theory.

Xiomara Aguilar. Photography, electron microscopy.

Chae-Yeong "Claire" Park. Pencil, hyper-detail, urban landscapes.

Divya Banerjee. Abstract expressionism, paint splatter.

There's more than that, buddy, they were all more than just their names and the art they did. They had stories, lives, families, dreams, and I read about them all. I ain't sharin' it because I don't want ya to be the wreck that I am for a couple weeks. Ya might ask why somebody would do this to themselves, but every page and article and bio and history I read just begs the question: how the fuck could somebody do this to *them*, y'know?

I lose track of time. Ain't like anybody's lettin' me know how long this recovery is. I do know that when Mom fits the brace and supports on my left leg that it's going to be a while until I can walk without it. Sturdy, at least, light, gears are smooth and quiet. It's a simple brace around my leg, like a cast or somethin'. It's my arm that needs Mom as well as Aunt Cora.

"He's lucky, Connie. It's terrible to say, but the cut was clean, right at the wrist. If the angles were off even a little, I don't know if you'd be able to do this without excising more of his arm." She hands my mother an asked for mini-screwdriver. "You're really good at that."

"Just bein' a Tinker. I did my heists, stole my shinies, but it always comes back to tinkerin'. Never calmer than when I'm puttin' somethin' back together." Mom looks up at Aunt Cora. "Cor... Thank you, fer savin' Nicky's life. I know it was you. I'm sorry I been a..."

"Baciagaloop?" She smirks. "Your Gremlin cousin is chatty."

"Yeah." Mom manages a smile. "I shoulda let ya be a part of his life, too. Yer family, Cor, sorry it took a while to see it. He can't feel nothin', right?"

"Painkiller, paralytic. He's awake, but he won't feel or see what you're doing." A few seconds. "It's beautiful work, Connie."

"Wouldn't be able to do it without your help. Otherwise, it'd be a dead hunk of metal on his arm. I'll admit, I'm basin' it off the armor, I never seen anythin' like it. Hand me the clamp?"

"Here. Old writing inscribed, as well. I don't know if it's Sigil, but the characters look familiar, like Redcap glyphs, but they're not."

"Or Tinker ciphers. I see some Gremlin runes in there as well. Or, they all look like them." A breath. "That should do it. Lemme warm up the shock stick to jump it."

"All right. Opening the line. Grandmother, spare your shear."

I feel some warmth, like my arm is loosenin' up.

"Flow is steady… I have return flow… Circulation. You're up, Connie."

"Mama Tinker, guide the thread." I hear a buzzin', with a low whine risin' in pitch. "It's only gonna hurt a second, Nicky."

Paralytics and painkillers don't do shit when ya press an electrical rod against a conductive contact point in an engineered prosthetic hand that's currently circulatin' yer fuckin' blood through vessels made of a kinda glass that bends and gives and is, as ya might guess, a Tinker specialty. Ya also don't wanna run through every profanity in every language ya know as loud as yer lungs can muster in front of yer Mom.

But buddy?

Sometimes? Shit happens.

27

So, it's been three weeks since that night. Almost November, Halloween's comin' up, and if ya buy the shit they spread around, it'll be the night that the dead and living are closest, either to have a nice day of remembrance if yer Latinx, to pretend yer a monster to score free candy, or if yer into the darker shit, the best day to work with the Shadow.

The Shear is back on my left arm, my right arm recovered as it can be, save the new hand. I don't know how she got this much Faesteel, or how she was able to work it, but ya don't question Tinkers on their work, 'specially if it's yer Mom. It ain't like a normal hand or anythin', anyone who looks at it can tell it's a prosthetic, the gears in the joints and knuckles, the metallic sheen of my fingernails, the ball joint that's replaced my wrist, grip pads on my fingertips.

Spent the last couple weeks just workin' on the fine motor control, writin' my name 'til it don't look like a serial killer's, gettin' better with my left hand, learnin' the strength the new hand's got and controllin' it. It is beautiful work, yeah, as distubin' it is to see gears spinnin' when I do my exercises to get my brain hooked up to the new appendage, make the little edits to correct the differences 'tween the former and the new.

It's kept my mind off Rhys. And that Thom ain't fuckin' called or anythin', but since I got fucked up by Prince Hadryn...

"I told the Dog yer spendin' time with yer mom, so yer off-limits 'cause you ain't seen her in years and ya need the time. He understood, but I'm gettin' tired of givin' him busywork," Damon says, when I finally ask about Thom. I'm gettin' ready to be "discharged", pretty much. "Once yer home, it's up to you. But truth, Cousin? He ain't cut out fer the Royal Guard, he ain't got the ice. Probably gonna move him. Don't give a fuck he's a Prince. His daddy ain't my king."

"Thanks, Cousin." Honestly, I'm glad Thom might have to leave the Guard. I agree he ain't got the ice for it, and I'd rather he not harden enough to be the kind of Guard the Kingdom needs.

Mom's with Joey, and I'm headin' back to my place, though I ain't plannin' on stayin' there long term. I mean, c'mon, buddy, ya ain't gotta read too much Japanese horror to know the best move if yer place is haunted is to get the fuck out. I mean, would *you* wanna live there?

My door's back, at least, sorta fixed. Angry note from the landlord about my security deposit from the damage to the apartment and the floor. Takes me a few tries to actually walk in there. You understand.

It's… one thing to walk into your apartment and smell blood. It's a whole 'nother fuckin' thing to smell yer own. Even though it's been almost a month, it's still there, hangin' like a fuckin' miasma where my knee hit the floor, where my hand was cut off. I'm gettin' lightheaded to be honest, I'm startin' to remember that night, Rhys tellin' me to run, me too stupid to just do it, me tellin' the Prince of the Fae to suck the shit out my ass and payin' fer it with my fuckin' hand.

The gears and joints in my leg brace whir as I kneel down, carefully, where it happened. I take slow, measured breaths, can't panic. I gotta see this, see it's past and done and gone so I can move forward.

Remindin' myself I'm still alive serves some comfort, at least. And the Shear ain't drinkin' my blood like Shadow's Edge did. Small comforts.

The floor ain't been fixed. I came down with enough force to break a board in the hardwood floors. I remember where the Prince squatted, just a foot or two away, knowin' he could do anythin' he wanted like it weren't no fuckin' thing. Rhys followin' him, too, tappin' his fingers behind his back. All I can remember, ya understand why it's blurry.

"Think, Blackwarren, think. Why the fuck would the Prince come over here? Yeah, he confessed to killin' those women, the motive… was… Fuck, I can't remember." Head's hurtin', and bein' here ain't helpin', I guess. Not ready yet, looks like.

I work on gettin' up, my hand pressin' the floor to brace against, and I regret it soon as I do it. It's the broken board. I don't tumble, but I gotta catch myself. It's just a matter of gettin' my bearin' and double checkin' where I'm putting my hand… this… time…

There something under there?

I pull and slide the broken board up, and it's too short for where it is. Empty space underneath, width of four fingers. I really hope I ain't pokin' a rat. Despite the sobriquet 'sewer rat', Goblins and *actual* rats don't get along like a Disney movie, 'less it's one by Bluth. So, to avoid bites, I give the uh, new hand a try.

It's weird as fuck hearin' gears spinnin' in yer hand when ya bend yer "fingers", treatin' the index and middle like a pair of tweezers, the ball joint that replaced yer wrist bendin' at a ninety-degree angle smooth as silk, thumb foldin' perfectly into yer palm. What's fucked up is I kinda feel all of it. Not like before. I feel pressure, some temperature, the pads on the tips having enough give to tell when I'm holdin' somethin'.

I've had a couple weeks to try to get used to it, and I ain't yet, but practicin' with it is the only way I'll get better. I touch the bottom, where wires and such are, work my way up and down until… Takes some work to get a good hold on it, probably more for delicate fingers.

A small cardboard box, like for puttin' a bracelet in, not labeled, not stained or faded like it's been there a long while. I open it, and take out a piece of plastic, painted like piano keys. A tug on the end reveals the USB.

A flash drive, stashed in a slick, painted like a piano. Ya might wonder why it's shoved in such a place, but it's the kinda slick ya only know is there if yer the one who made it. Or if ya break the board hidin' it with yer knee, as well as said knee.

I might've just found the last works of Bridget O'Hare. 'Cording to Miss Greenleaf, Bridget had been workin' on her symphony since high school, meanin' it could be her masterpiece. If that's right, makes sense she'd hide it 'fore she shows it to anybody. If this is what I'm thinkin' it is.

Granted, I gotta load it up first, so I just gotta get to my feet, which takes a couple seconds longer now with the brace, goin' easy to push off my right hand, 'cause even though it's sturdy enough, it's still, y'know, not flesh and bone, so I don't know how much it'll play nice with my radius 'n ulna, y'know? No, don't think about it, focus on the task at hand, not on your body's… new addition.

I'm gonna go to my bedroom, get my laptop, and get outta *this* room fer starters. If anythin', I can at least grab a change of clean…

All my shit's on the floor.

I mean, I been gone for three weeks, and I was out on the floor, dyin', who fuckin' knows when it was done. Ain't hard to guess who, but…

All my shit's on the floor, buddy…

Clothes strewn everywhere. Laptop's gone. Shoes cut up, soles gouged. Mattress is carved and ripped, springs stickin' out, fillin' everywhere. Pillows are torn to pieces, lamp's broke open, my box underneath the bed is dumped on the wreckage of my boxspring, includin', yeah, my "friend", with a few slurs written on it. Handcuffs are gone…

My books.

They fuckin' ripped up all my books.

They fuckin' destroyed all my books.

I figure they were lookin' fer what I'm holdin' in my hand right now, but those are my books. My teachers, mentors, friends, lovers, pathways to wisdom, to other worlds, eyes to see existence through a better educated eye, to see as the humans do, to feel what they do. Read over their poetry, their language of passion, of the soul, see how they make me feel, how I feel the same sometimes, that we ain't so different.

And it's all in a pile, ripped, wrenched, *lacerated* to pieces to find a fuckin' piece of plastic and silicon. I'm on my knees, the pain… not really there. Not in my head, at least. Ya could say they're only books, buddy, but I know ya ain't so shitty as to suggest somethin' like that.

'Specially 'cause of what I see under the torn pages.

The cover needs to have some waste brushed away: pieces of a biology textbook, a Regency romance about a rakish swindler findin' love with rabble-rousin' cobbler, a collection of articles on third wave feminism, a book of Cornish recipes for American cooks, a page from Audre Lorde's *Uses of the Erotic*, all of it reduced to scraps and shreds. Under it, I find a familiar cover, green, gold letterin', faded, scenes in the corners of writin' a letter, ploughin' soil, servin' in badminton, surrounding the words, *Etiquette, and the Language of Flowers*.

From 1883, a first edition I'd read very carefully as to not worsen the foxing that was already present, kept out of direct sunlight. It's honestly the nicest book I ever owned, and the smell, fuck, it could send me to the moon.

And… the cover is here. The pages are tossed, torn, cleaved, all save a few, in order: Xanthium, common almond, evergreen clematis, nutmeg geranium, reeds, dragonwort, night convolvulus, cherry tree, hand flower tree, zinnia, cypress.

Okay. First three are pretty much, "to the impertinent, ill-educated peasant." Fuck you too, Princey.

The geranium, he wants a meeting. Reeds, that's uh… music. He wants Bridget's last works, probably figured I was hidin' it. Dragonwort, night convolvulus, horror and night. Horror night? Fuck. Halloween night. When the Shadow will be strongest.

Hand flower, that's like, stop, or a warnin'. Do it or else.

Zinnia. An absent friend. Rhys. Then cypress.

Death. Do it or Rhys will die.

It's October 30th. I got about a day. I ain't got no phone, no computer, a bow I don't really know how to use yet, and I'd be facin' down a couple elite-tier trolls, a Sidhe Prince trained since birth in martial combat who now has Shadow's Edge, and possibly a Blackwarren-trained Redcap who cleaved my hand off with little effort if the Prince so much as snaps his fingers.

Oh, and I can't get any help, because it's the Crown Prince of the Fae. I wish I could tell ya, buddy, that I'll fight to the last to preserve Bridget's legacy, but I ain't really sold. I don't know if Rhys will be free, but I figure his life rates a little higher than the last symphony of a human girl brutally murdered. If it makes me a shit, I'm a shit.

But I ain't just gonna hand it over. I wanna know *why* all this shit is happenin' for a fuckin' flash drive. Yeah, it's her last works, but... why? I can't parse that shit out. Why hold hostages? Only thing I can think is that maybe there's more than just music on there. Video of those two together? Maybe she was pregnant and he went all Cobalt Order on her? No way to know until I check it, and that fucker made *that* more difficult.

But I ain't panickin', it ain't impossible. I just need to find someone with a computer and a free USB slot. That's easy: Vincenzo. Callin' him will be tough, since I ain't got my phone. Rhys took it, and if it ain't busted too, maybe Cenzo can trace it. Yeah, gotta pull outta this spiral. I'm pissed, yeah, and ripped up emotionally, 'course, but it ain't gonna help gettin' Rhys outta this alive. I can process this shit with buckets of tears *after*.

And, thank the Fates for small favors, the fuckers didn't make off with my UTA pass, so I can at least take the train and bus over to the entry point my cousin's little enclave is. Just gotta measure my breathin', even if I'll end up slowly rockin' in my seats, tend to do it when I'm stressed, when expectations go... badly.

Lucky for me, I been to Cenzo's before, and I've remembered the path well enough after two trips, just have to pick out the little checkpoints I filed away in my head. Shadow charm to see in the dark, since the lights are off, and steppin' easy and light 'cause I ain't steppin' on a fuckin' diaper again. It's harder than ya think, since my left leg is in a brace, and I ain't into a decent gait with it despite all the practice.

I, uh, didn't wanna bring it up, buddy, but uh, it's lookin' like the knee's fucked too. I wasn't up for the "cut the leg at the knee and play with another prosthetic" route, I'd rather keep as much of me as I can. Ya get it, right? Means my thievin' career is probably over 'fore it ever really got started, but maybe I can get a knee replacement, I don't know, it's somethin' to occupy my mind while I follow the map in my head.

"Nick, ya coulda called, fuck." Cenzo's the first to approach me when I come through the door. The others avoid me, look away. No one wants to look at a cautionary tale, y'know?

"Would need a phone for that, Cousin." I smile, best I can manage, I'm mostly just holdin' together. Breakin' down ain't gonna help, it'll just slow shit down, and I'm on the clock. "Could you check and copy a flash drive for me?"

He perks a brow. "Somethin' wrong with-"

"Cenzo." Fuck, Blackwarren, voice shouldn't be quiverin', fuck. "Please."

He steps closer. "What the fuck happened, Nick?" He lifts up my chin. I didn't know I was lookin' down. "Tell me, we're family, we shouldn't be hidin' shit. I set up yer phone and yer laptop, why can't you use..."

I take a breath, the exhale comes out a sigh.

"Aw fuck, they're wrecked? Who the fuck did it? Me and the boys will fuck 'em proper, turn every one of their godsdamned ones into fuckin' zeroes."

"Just... check the drive. Please." Keep breathin'. Don't fuckin' cry, it ain't time fer that, yet.

"A'right, a'right." His tics his head toward his setup. "Over here. Anythin' particular I'm lookin' for?"

Cenzo's rig, as he calls it (he also calls her Irene), got eight monitors, three keyboards, and somethin' he calls a blade(?), but tweaked for his purposes and hacker bullshit that borders on fuckin' magic. The shit they do in movies? He calls it "script kiddie shit", whatever the fuck that means. He got a chair that likely runs people a couple grand, plus a mini fridge for all his energy drinks, one of which he's already cracked and drained half of.

"Sheet music, music files, maybe video files, or photos. It belonged to the girl who was murdered but keep that DL as fuckin' possible. Also, could ya maybe trace my phone? 'Case it ain't busted?"

"Fuck, Nicky, ya coulda done this yerself. This all? Ya got Irene on it, so aim a bit higher. Yer cousin's offerin' to do some work fer ya gratis, gimme a name who ya wanna fuck up." Off my look. "A'right. Yer upset. Offer stands, though, 'kay?"

He plugs the flash drive into a smaller machine, not connected to the larger one. "Gotta quarantine it first, make sure there ain't no surprises." A few taps here and there, I ain't goin' into the details, buddy, 'cause yer guess is as good as mine. "Lookin' clean. I got some files for a program that staffs out music arrangement, seven audio files... First movement, second, third..."

"Her symphony. She finished it, then." Small bit of relief.

"Got some photos, probably off her phone, let's see... who... Oh fuck."

He turns his chair toward me.

"Nick? Why'm I lookin' at pictures of a human girl and..." He drops his voice to a whisper. *"Prince fuckin' Hadryn?"*

I drop my voice as well. "'Cause he killed her, Cen. And a few other women, too. Could ya make a copy onto another drive, without the photos of him? Wanna give it to her parents. S'what they hired me for. Heh, can finally deliver the invoice, 'least." I take a breath, keep centered, focused. "'Stead of fuckin' someone up, could ya gimme a phone? And track my old one?"

"Yeah, yeah, sure, sure. Prolly better, ain't gettin' into this shit if the Royals are involved. Fuck, Nick, why can't ya just be a fuckin' thief? Y'ain't gotta solve every murder ya come across. Yer not-"

"Not human. Yeah. I know." Grittin' my sharp teeth underlines it for me, as well as fer him.

"I was gonna say, y'ain't a detective, or with the Guard, or a sleuth outta yer books, yer a fuckin' thief. Damned good one, too. I figured ya'd be happy doin' get-backer shit, keepin' the heat off ya, lettin' ya use yer skills, make some bank. 'Stead ya ain't more than a season from the last shit, and now yer in it again, and *deeper* 'cause of who yer talkin' 'bout. When ya gonna let some of this shit go, huh?"

Cenzo's my cousin, yeah, and we weren't too close when I was livin' out in California, and it was a slow recovery once I came back. But he was there to help me when I went down after the Prince fucked me up… and…

Wait, how'd he know?

"Cen? How'd anybody know I was in trouble? I vaguely remember Cousin Damon, and my Aunt Cora, but how'd they even know I was bleedin' out with a shattered knee?"

A couple of seconds pass, and his eyes blink once, twice, dartin' back and forth, chewin' his lower lip. "Gotta promise ya won't be mad."

"Heh, well, I ain't dead, so no, I won't be pissed."

"The boys and I, uh, never took off the trace on your phone. Yer with a Blackwarren Assassin, Nick. Fuck, yer fuckin' him-"

"Shadow, say ya ain't got recordin' of that, Cen. Why, huh?" I lean toward him, and he shrinks back. My voice was more edged, gotta walk it back.

"Ya said it yerself. Yer alive, yeah?" He types a bit, one-handed, eyes on me 'cause I've inched closer to "threat" in the last couple minutes. "Ain't like we got somebody watchin' ya twenty-four-seven, we just run a list of keywords at the end of the day, unless the system flags somethin'. Anyway, this is what came in that night."

I look at the screen, the text not coming up like on my phone, but I recognize the texts. Then, a draft at the end, unsent.

I know you're watching his phone. Nick is badly wounded, send help to his apartment imme

"Nick, the fuck? No. Stoppit! Don't hug me ya *mamaluke*! Dammit, Nick, people are lookin'!" He pushes me back, wiping his face with his hands like some of the affection mighta rubbed off on him. Us Goblins ain't too big on showin' affection, 'less we're fuckin', which is why it's easy to pick out who's pumpin' who. I'm an outlier, ya read enough and eventually ya start thinkin' that bein' vulnerable ain't too bad.

"Rhys knew ya were buggin' me and sent ya a message 'cause he knew you'd see it, but wouldn't come up on the text logs. Curious how he beat my biometrics…"

"He's a Gremlin, right? That's fuckin' easy. Ya learn that charm in fuckin' preschool." So, before he killed his uncle, then. "I'll give yer phone a quick ping, but that's all I can do. But uh…"

I gesture to him, hands open. "What?"

"Nick, yer family, yer my cousin, I love ya."

"…and?"

"So, I gotta sit ya down and talk ya down from some shit, okay?" He runs his fingers through his hair, gritting his teeth and grumbling. "Ya talked to the cop at all 'bout this?"

"Thom? Damon's kept him busy, so I don't know. I was laid up in care for a few weeks, Cen, no phone, ya expect me to call him and tell him I got all fucked up by the Prince?" Steely gaze from him. "Fer fuck's sake, Cen, *what*?"

"That the reason? Really? Ya coulda asked anybody to let him know yer okay. And keep him from hasslin' *me* 'bout it."

"What'd ya tell him?"

"I didn't tell him shit, whadduya think? He's a fuckin' cop, ya don't tell 'em anythin'. We practically gotta pack up and find another station since he fuckin' sniffed his way down here lookin' fer answers."

"Fuck, I… I didn't know he was bein' like that. He ain't like… stalkin' ya, is he? Ya feel safe?" Okay, yeah, I thought Thom had taken the hint when I told him that I didn't see things working out between the two of us, but I didn't think I still had to call him after a traumatic event to let him know everythin'. I'm not bein' an asshole, I just really thought he got the message.

"He ain't done nothin', but ya split off right?"

"Yeah, I let him know it weren't gonna work."

"And?" He takes a sip of an energy drink. "Ya really think he'd be almost bustin' down our door if he thought you two broke up?"

"Cen. I told him. I was honest. Fuck, I'm pretty sure the break-up's on fuckin' Instagram. I got banned from the K Street Diner 'cause of it. I don't know what else I gotta tell him. He's a Phouk, they all fall in love real hard, real fast, and it was a little intense fer me. I ain't afraid of him or anythin', he just wanted to go real fast."

"Says the Gob who's gonna take on the Crown Prince of the Fae to save a blooded assassin. An assassin ya've been pokin', at that, who ya known… maybe an actual three or four days together? Maybe you are the one fallin' too fast, Nick."

"Shadow, Cen, I don't love him, or wanna marry him, or move into a duplex condo in Destry and raise a kid from the adoption pool or-"

"Yeah, yer bein' pretty specific, Cousin."

"Cen, I'm just sayin' there *could* be somethin' there, and I want the chance to see, yeah? Let things develop all natural-like? And I'm savin' Rhys 'cause he saved my life, and he's my partner in this, okay? Ya don't fuck over yer partner in crime, yeah?"

Cen smirks. "Sure, Nick. But ya might wanna let the Phouk know that so he can take care of something."

I roll my eyes. "Shadow, Cen, just fuckin' tell me, 'kay? I ain't up fer this kinda shit. Now, ya gonna get Irene to help me out?"

An alarm sound comes from the computer. Cen, taps a few keys. "Yeah, ya don't get to call her that. She don't know yer voice." He turns toward his machine. "Irene, baby? Pull up the audio I flagged in Nick's file, play the section that scored a hit fer ya?"

So… The sounds of me and Thom fuckin'. Again. I flex my metal fingers in his direction. "I will break all your shit, Cen."

"Hold up. Just listen."

"Tha mi a 'gealltainn mi fhìn dhut, a ghràidh, buinidh mi dhuit gu bràth! Tha mi a 'gealltainn mi fhìn dhut, a ghràidh, buinidh mi dhuit gu bràth! Tha mi a 'gealltainn mi fhìn dhut, a ghràidh, buinidh mi dhuit gu bràth!" I'll leave out what his body was doin' at the time.

"Yeah. He was babblin' in Gaelic, I think. So?"

"Irene, my silicon queen? Mind tellin' my ignorant cousin what the Phouka was sayin'?"

It don't talk or anythin', Gremlins ain't there yet, but they're probably gonna figure it out soon enough. It's what's written on the screen.

I promise you, my love, I belong to you forever.

And he said it three times. I told him what it means for a Phouk, or any Fae 'sides a Goblin to swear or promise somethin' three times.

Ironclad promise. Death couldn't break it. The same kind of old magic that weaves Oaths. And he wove one. For me. To me.

That selfish motherfucker.

"Gimme a motherfuckin' phone, Cen. Now." That son of a bitch. That slick, trickster son of a fuckin'…

Cen hands me a phone, at least. I dial the numbers. Don't take too long to get an answer. "Officer-"

"Palace of Wisdom. Thirty minutes. Yer ass better be there, Thom."

I hang up, don't give him a chance to respond. "Cen? Hold onto that file fer me? Just in case I gotta prove it? I gotta go have a chat with my… fiancé."

I'm sure he's got a lot of reasons, but I'm gonna do my last kindness to him, and then that's it for the Goblin and the Phouka Prince.

It's time for his fairy tale to end.

28

The Palace of Wisdom.

It's an Argent City institution, a club that's been in the City since the 60s, when it revived an old movie palace from the 30s, which itself preserved the opera house which served as the center of the artist district when Allora was first founded. It's got history, is what I'm sayin', so says the landmark register. It looks as pristine as the day it opened, the facades and stonework, the murals and carvings, the lifeblood pulse of creation emanating from every heartbeat of rhythm that carries out to the streets.

And unlike a lot of people in line, I at least know it's named for the "Proverbs of Hell" by William Blake. Y'know, "the path of excess leads to the palace of wisdom". Makes for a better club name than "prisons are built with stones of law, brothels with bricks of religion," but the latter's more fun to say.

I'm dressed in my most "human" get-up, which is just my normal clothes, a t-shirt, hoodie, jeans, and my Timberlands, but I could be dressed in Armani and people would still be givin' me a wide berth. I think we've gone over why. The line moves slow, mostly 'cause it's later in the day, and I'm hobblin' along on my bum leg, a glove on my right hand so the fact that it's metal don't get 'round and freak peeps out more.

Also goin' slow when I let people go ahead of me when Fae cut the line, especially Sidhe. I don't want to draw any attention, I ain't here for the investigation, I'm here to…

I'm here to close the door on Thom, buddy.

Now, I don't wanna rehash shit, so I ain't gonna. It'll probably be gone over again when I get a chance to talk to him. Also, this wait's long enough to get in, and there ain't even any guarantee that I will. It ain't that the club's exclusive, it's that the bouncers can tell if yer there to start shit, and ya don't wanna fuck with the two out front, from what I hear.

Nope, never really been in there before. Us Benedict kids don't make it out to Allora too much, 'specially not to drink and dance at the Palace when there's plenty of dives that won't give us too much shit. Hell, Under the Bridge in Beckettsville is ritzier than the places I been to. But there's a reason I chose here to meet up with Thom.

When I reach the head of the line, I'm before two satyrs, both of 'em naked under light cloaks, lookin' like they're twins. I got my hood down, lookin' up at the two of 'em 'cause they're well over six feet tall and I'm barely five. And yeah, I'm very conscious of the fact they're both naked.

"Hello." I smile, best I can. "I'm just meetin' someone here t'night, we gotta have a chat 'bout our relationship. May I go in?"

Folded arms are my response. Gotta think. I don't wanna hold up the line.

"Uhhh, sorry I don't got any reeds to offer ya for the cover charge?" I shrug, my smile more nervous now. "Since they, um… represent music and uh… affability."

The one on the left kneels down, on my level. "Redcap?"

Ya also don't lie to 'em. "Yes, sir. My mom's a Tinker, but uh, I'm…" I exhale. "I'm dipped, yeah. Was self-defense, if that matters. I ain't here workin' or anyth-"

Cue me being pushed out in three… two…

The door is opened, the satyr in front of me ticking his head toward it. "Check the weapon."

Did uh, I just get into the Palace of Wisdom? Made it farther than practically anyone in my family. Well, shit, buddy, I ain't 'bout to question it!

The lobby is a little dimmer, the walls covered in murals, art deco, buttresses, painting on the ceiling and stonework in the corners. It's hard not to fall under this place's "spell", it's a place run by satyrs, rumored to be the domain of the god Pan himself, you just feel inhibitions slidin' away. It's a place to revel in bein' yerself, and, from what I've heard, *the* place to dance fer the sake of dancin'.

Ya might be wonderin' why I'd choose this place to end it with Thom. I'll get to that.

What was formerly the concession stand is now the coat check, and behind the counter is a pale-skinned woman with red eyes who's dressed like she just got back from Goth night at another club. So yeah, vampire. Better to not fuck around.

"Hi, uh, I'm s'posed to check my weapon, do I do that here?" Granted, the "weapon" is the Shear makin' up the platin' on my left arm. She's gotta lean over the counter to see me.

"Haven't seen one of you in years." She sniffs the air. "Funny, only blood I smell is your own, must not be a very good assassin."

"I'm not a…" Deep breath. This is how yer tested, Blackwarren. "I'm here to break up with a guy, that's all. And I figure if it's here, it won't be a scene. He ain't abusive or anythin', just… It's kinda one-sided, y'know?"

"All right, let's see it." She gestures with her hand, and I try to tell the Shear in my head to go full bow so I can check it. Her eyes widen as the gears spin and sprockets whizz, wheels turn, the grip coming into my hand, feelin' awkward 'cause I should be holdin' it on my right. There's resistance when I let go of it on the counter, it not wanting to leave me, I guess, like droppin' off a puppy at the vet. "You make this, Goblin?" I feel a weird weight on my eyes when she looks at me, askin' that question.

"Yeah, I didn't." I meant the second part, where the first came from I got no idea. I take off my glove as well, the Faesteel hand in view. Why'm I talkin' so fast? "Ya need this, too? It's a prosthetic, same with the brace on my left leg. Ya ever read *The Castle of Otranto*? Always felt weird that the cornerstone of Goth pushed the gay-is-evil cliché as a method of homophoic self-loathin', and what kinda fuckin' name is Manfred-"

"Blink a few times," she says, her tone not too threatenin', "Then answer my next question. Does this belong to you?"

"Yes, it is *mine*. No, I stole it from Prince Hadryn Summersword." Why the fuck am I givin' two answers? And *admittin' to grand theft* to fuckin' coat check vampire- Oh, right. They can compel, if the books are anythin' to go by.

"Count yourself lucky, he's banned for life from our club. Are you seeking asylum from him?"

"I am here to end my relationship with the son of Riordan Redmond O'Rourke." Fuck, I sound half asleep! Snap outta this, fuckin' Shadow, just do it! Stop spillin' everything! "I wish to have a clean conscience to explore a relationship with a Blackwarren assassin who makes me feel I never understood love until our eyes met and-"

She waves her hand, and fuck my eyes are dry, but not dry enough to stop me glarin' death at her, though. "What the *fuck* did you do to me?" That was barely my voice. I mean, it was mine, but even my "white voice" ain't that clean-soundin'.

She smirks, "Heh, I just asked you to answer a simple yes or no question, you told me everything else on your own." She takes out a pad and stamps it, then hands it to me, and then puts the bow under the counter. "You can pick it up on your way out. I'd tell ya to have fun, but-"

"What Prince Hadryn was banned for?"

She shrugs. "According to his apology letter from his steward? 'Misinterpreting a worker's intentions toward him, and his deepest apologies if she took offense.'"

"Fuck, he kill her?" Why'm I askin' that? The Prince hasn't killed any women... right? Wait, did he? Shit's been cloudy since I woke up in a safehouse recoverin' from my new hand gettin' implanted. I know Rhys is missin', and the Prince was there when I got hurt. I insulted him, too, so...

"Hm? No, but he assumed that this is a brothel, not a night club, and that while sex happens here, it's all completely consensual. He didn't understand the word 'no', and he faced the consequences." I feel her eyes on me again. "Why are you asking if he killed her?"

"Thirteen women." ...right. *That's* what was cloudy. All the names, their lives, dreams, histories... "Because he confessed to murdering a young human woman, and implied that he's taken many other lives as well. Thirteen artists. The Kitsune are hunting him, but they're unaware that their quarry is Fae royalty. He showed his cruelty when he broke my knee and amputated my hand for simple want of a vambrace he admired. He tempts a lifelong vow of mine to never take a life unless in self-defense, and he holds the one I care for captive under his authority."

A larger satyr is now behind me. I can tell, 'cause he's breathin' cigar smoke down at me. "This Goblin causing trouble, Lady Amelia?" His tone upturns at the end, like it's a private joke between them.

"Far from it, he checked his weapon with no incident, he's here to end a relationship so he can begin another, being true to himself." She says it so fuckin' *casual*, fuck. "Other than not being able to answer simple questions with simple answers, no issues. Though he has a *lot* to say about that Sidhe we banned."

I'm gettin' why Goblins avoid the Palace if we turn into cooperating suspects by a glance from a coat check girl. It's better I leave this situation before I get in any deeper. It says a bit that Hadryn's banned from here though, but the place is run by a god, Pan, god of shepherds and revelry and a bunch of other stuff. Ya gotta fuck up bad to get banned from a place like this. I walked in with a magical bow and I got a check tag to pick it up later with not too much drama, considerin', so this ain't a place that's worried about people like the Prince startin' shit. The Prince apparently tried to... I ain't gonna pretty it up with nice diction. He probably tried to rape someone.

But that ain't why I'm here. But I'll definitely aid in gettin' that fucker off the streets after this.

I slip away, best I can, but I feel her eyes trailin' after me as I make my way to the double doors leadin' into the club, "Watch Your Step" on a sign next to them before I go through.

I'd describe the place to ya, but there's a pretty heavy fog, at least to someone with a big nose like me. Pot, sweat, cigars, cigarettes, perfume, cologne, and quite a variety of musks comin' off the satyrs, weres, Coyotes, couple dragons, Trolls, and all the humans, too. I ain't got a nose like a were or dragon or satyr, I can't filter through 'em all, but I can say this: there's a lot of passion in the air, tonight.

The DJ spinnin' is pretty good, and while I'm tempted to take a lap on the dance floor, I'll have to settle for tappin' to the beat while I make my way to the bar, on the east side of the theatre, lookin' like it should be in some snootyfuck gentleman's club, but instead it's a bar tended by satyrs with a throng of people gettin' in drink orders. There's tables and booths, all of 'em full, stools at the bar, all full too, looks like-

Weave, twist, bend, fuck that hurt, push off the good leg, onto the stool 'fore the other guy takes it and… Oh fuck, that was not a good move for my knee. Hollow burn, like the joint's made of broken glass pressin' into a fuckin' tomato. I made a fist with my right hand, grip the bar with my left, grit my teeth, suck air through the gaps.

"Hey, you gonna live?" I need a second to look up. Very attractive guy, satyr, fuck those eyes feel like home. I ain't fallin' in love, but they can all do that. It ain't magic, just centuries of perfecting that essence of themselves, if the stories my cousins have told me are anythin' to believe.

"Just, uh, messed up my knee pretty bad. Don't worry 'bout it." I'm measurin' my breathin'. Keeps my mind off what's comin' soon.

"Get you something for the pain?"

I don't usually drink. Mostly 'cause I'm poor, but also 'cause me and alcohol make for some bad decisions. Like losin' my virginity to a Phouka, or stealin' said Phouka's Aston Martin after I thought he cheated, and drivin' that ninety-eight-thousand-dollar car into Destry Bay, and then datin' him for another month after I found out the guy he "cheated with" was his brother, and the car actually belonged to who I now know was Riordan Redmond O'Rourke.

So, I don't drink whiskey, is what I'm sayin'.

"Posso avere un caffè corretto, per favore?" Don't worry, I say it right. *"Ci vorrà un minuto, ma sì."* Warm smile from him. I asked for an espresso with a bit of grappa, if yer curious.

"Thanks. Need to dull the pain and get my courage up. Ya seen a Phouka around?" I give him Thom's description. "I told him to meet me here, but I don't know if he got the message."

A tic of his head down the bar, and, well, there's Thom. "Any chance we could get a table? Or a place we can talk alone? Just talk, not for, y'know."

The satyr points to a door at the end of the bar, near the stage, which I'm guessin' at some point led to the stairs to the balconies. "Room twenty-two. The two of you are able to go into Arcadia, so be careful."

"Thanks." I take a minute, workin' up the nerve, and then down my drink soon as it arrives.

It's some effort to get off the stool, and then ease my way through the crowd to get to him. The people seem to move and teem and flow in a way that suggests it'd be impossible to get to him, like there's always someone in the way, exiting and entering. While it don't part like a sea, I flow into the rhythm of the crowd, smooth, glidin' around arms and legs and swingin' hands, makin' sure I'm not impeded any further.

Almost like it's fated.

Thanks a lot, Mama Tinker, I definitely have all this worked out in my head. No problem. Fuck.

This is 'cause I still owe ya a few projects, ain't it, Ma?

Okay, don't lose yer cool, Blackwarren, ya already told him this ain't gonna work between ya, so ya ain't blindsidin' him or anythin'. Fuck, *ya broke up with him in public and sacrificed yer fuckin' French toast.* Just confront him about the Oath he swore, release him from it, and cut this messy thing off.

Don't let that Phouka charm distract ya, don't let him touch yer ears. Remember why yer here, so you can move on and concentrate on more important shit like savin' Rhys and findin' some way to bring down a Prince fer murder-

"Nick?" Did his voice get more Celtic, or is it just me? Eyes are brighter, too, like he's in his element here. Ain't no surprise, it's a paradise here for tricksters, I'd guess, with all the drugs and booze and sex flowin' all hours of the day. Dashin' smile, he's comin' into his Phouka-ness, looks like. "I haven't heard from you for weeks, I missed you."

For anyone else, ghostin' a guy for a few weeks would be the end of things, or at least have him pissed at ya when ya make contact, but here he is, all smiles and ready to pick up where we left off.

He ain't a fuckin' moron, by the way, some insipid lovesick fool who'll roll over for any difficulty, minimize conflict, only want to make me happy. *This* is what a fuckin' Oath can do to somebody. Trust me, before he and I got together, he was interestin'. He went to watch folk punk in Grunstadt, kept a notebook of stats for Allora University's baseball team, particularly pitch counts, a standing "date" every Wednesday to play video games with his friends, a brother he was finally reconnectin' with... And then he met me, and I became, well...

"We gotta talk, Thom. Room twenty-two, follow me." I hobble my way back through the crowd, toward the door the bartender pointed out. I hear him get off the stool behind me, or I think so, it's loud in here for guys with ears like mine.

"Is that a limp? What happened?" I hear the worry. I ignore it for now, we can talk about it once we're in private, and answering the question will start a conversation I don't wanna have in a crowd, y'know what I'm sayin'?

That ain't to say it ain't painful. Not too bad, no permanent damage, but it'll be sore a while. I expect a crowd when I finally make it to the door, a satyr standin' guard. "Room number?"

"Uh, twenty-two. Bartender told me." I turn to point at the satyr who directed me, but I already hear the door openin'.

"We'll check on you in three hours. Any non-consensual acts will result in an immediate lifetime ban. Entrance into Arcadia is permitted, but no cross-enclave travel is allowed. If you need drinks or food, just let us know. Whose tab is this on?" He looks between Thom and I.

Thom steps forward, but I speak up. "I got it. Nick Blackwarren. My stuff's checked out front. Just bill me, don't see myself gettin' in here again."

A curt nod is my reply, and we're shown into a long hallway, rather borin' to be honest. Greens, mostly, the smell of pine, but I think that's on brand for the club's patron.

"This mean I don't have to pick up the check anymore?" I don't see it, but I can tell he smirked. Passin' number five.

"One time thing. Did some work for my cousin, and a job I'm doin' now. Retrieval, ain't stealin' nothin'." I keep walkin' forward, quiet, I can hear reed flutes, drums way off, cracklin' of a larger fire.

"You ever been to Arcadia, Nick?" Notice how he ain't askin' about my leg no more? I didn't give him an answer. He's a fuckin' cop, and is part of the Guard, and he ain't followin' up on it. Because it's me. This is what he believes he has to be to be with me, and the Oath bound him to that. *Forever,* I might mention.

So yeah, like I said, this ain't that kind of story.

"Nope." Four doors away. I can hear some people are doin' what you'd expect people to be doin' in a private room at a nightclub run by satyrs.

"What's on your right hand? Did your vambrace become a gauntlet?" Still observant, at least.

"Yes, but it's not Shadow's Edge." Room twenty-two. It ain't that far from the previous or followin' door, but if there's doors to Arcadia in there, I'm guessin' it's a Hammerspace/TARDIS kinda thing. I open the door, and he holds it open for me as I walk inside.

I know I'm bein' cold, buddy, but there'll be plenty of emotion, count on that. He follows me in, closes the door.

The room itself, honestly, makes me feel like I'm in that old Bradbury story, "The Veldt". Three walls all with deeply detailed, like... Pre-Raphaelite-style paintin' and you can see the woods brimmin' with life if you look long enough. I would guess it's as simple as walkin' into the wall to get to Arcadia. For seatin', there's a stump, couple rocks, a basket with blankets. When I look up, the ceilin' shows a break in the canopy, the stars bright, unmarred by light pollution. The gears in my hand are easier to hear, whirrin' away, optimal efficiency.

Okay, Blackwarren, yer here. Yer the one always yappin' 'bout how Goblins are so close to human ya probably got souls, so act like ya give a fuck 'bout how clean yers is.

"Thom?" I shouldn't sound so nervous.

"Yes, Nick?" That smile again. "Nicholas Arsenne?" My name just tickles all the right places in my ear when he says it. No, this is what ya were preppin' for. Short, succinct, to the fuckin' point.

"Thom, did you swear an Oath to me? Did you promise to love me forever?"

I had to close my eyes for that, or I never coulda got the words out, buddy. However, now that his hand's on my chest, his breath warmin' my ears like he's 'bout to nibble 'em, I'm seein' how that mighta been a bad move.

"I do love you, Nick. I want to be with you. Lay with you. Hold you. Make you feel good, and happy, and warm, and safe, have the life you want with the support you need. You're special, a light in a dark world, an honest heart and a clever mind." His lips brush mine. "The world is better for having you in it, Nicholas Arsenne. May I stand by your side? Be yours in wedded bliss? I offer you all of myself. Mind, heart, body, and soul."

"Thomas Andrew Canmore?" My throat's rough, my body's feelin' like it's gettin' cut and broken all over again.

"Yes, Nick?" Another kiss, it feels like home, like destiny, like my life's been leadin' to here.

"I..."

Gods motherfuckin' damn it all to fuckin' Shadow, fuck, fuck, fuck, fuck, *FUCK!!!*

"I release you from your Oath to me. May you live free of your shackles, and find the heart that returns your love."

And then, as if wakin' from a dream, Thom stands up, and leaves the room without a word. I don't know if Arcadian soil will take a Goblin's tears, but I'm offerin' just the same.

29

Y'know, I always wondered what it'd be like when the only comfort ya get is ya did the right thing. And that while it stung like a bitch, diggin' deep, and twistin' like a fuckin' drill, I wasn't tempted. He walked outta my life, free 'n clear, no Oath, open heart, path wide to find someone who'll give him what he wants.

Yep. Wasn't tempted. Not once.

Not even with the grand Romantic declaration that wouldn't be outta place in the penultimate chapter of any of my books about love and relationships. Nor with words that wove into my ears with a gentle caress to my mind, stirring the faded embers of the crush and interest I had fer him a few months ago.

I'm not a noble. I don't need authority to lock down a relationship.

I'm not a sorcerer. I don't need to weave old magics to command obedience that he'd think was his idea all along.

And with me not takin' advantage of havin' a Phouka Prince sworn to me forever, I ain't even sure how much of a Goblin I am anymore.

But ya get why I did it, right, buddy? Keepin' him tied to his own mistake would be a black mark on my soul, and I already got enough with the red on my cap. At least I can see where things would go with Rhys, now, if I can save him from his own Oath-related problems.

I ain't sayin' I love him or anythin'. We haven't seen each other in almost a month, and we only had a few real days together 'fore all this shit went down, I ain't lookin' to save him in some big Romantic gesture.

I wanna save him because I do consider him a friend, and that's what ya do fer a friend when they're in trouble: ya help 'em out, sexual history or not. Like we told each other: we're partners. And ya don't leave a partner hangin', buddy, not ever.

Also, I now I know what happens when a satyr finds ya cryin' on the border of Arcadia, at least the satyrs connected to the Argent City: They ask if yer okay, and wanna talk about it. I'm sure it coulda turned into sex if I wanted it, but I ain't ever entertainin' that idea. Durin' all this shit the time was still tickin' away, and it's now the 31st.

Halloween. All Saints Eve. All Souls Night. Samhain, which starts at sundown, givin' me 'bout eighteen hours to find a way through all this.

What I wasn't expectin' was Thom outside when I emerged from the Palace of Wisdom at ten past midnight.

"Fer fuck's sake, whadduya want?!" I cannot deal with this shit right now, I swear to fuckin' Shadow. "My partner's held captive, I gotta get him free and make sure there ain't any blowback without killin' anybody. Plus, y'know, solvin' over a dozen murders by the same guy. I ain't got any use or time fer relationships, do ya understand-"

"Nick, shut up. I think I can help you." Huh. Accent's gone. Or it's real faded. No lovey-dovey eyes. "This is about Rhys Lleweylln, right?"

"Yeah...?" I'm a bit wary.

"Then let's talk somewhere else, not in earshot of who knows how many Guard and Sidhe suckups. Nick, please, I'm not going to try anything." His tone's a bit different, too, a little rougher, more... human.

"Yer's still a Phouk, right? Ya didn't tie up yer nature in all those Oaths, or somthin'?" I don't even know if that's possible, but given how fast he was makin' 'em I ain't got no idea.

In response, he pinches the bridge of his nose, lookin' down. "Can we not talk about those? Jesus, it was like I was back in fucking middle school. I know it's supposed to hit me hard, given who my actual father is, but Christ, I'm amazed you didn't file an order against me."

"Yeah. I know." I could be doin' other things than this conversation.

"Listen, I'll take you anywhere you want, just take a few minutes to hear me out, okay? I know you don't have any reason to take me seriously, but I'm asking. Please?" This... ain't charmin' trickster rogue. This is the guy I developed a crush on. I ain't sayin' I'm attracted, I'm sayin' this is closer to what got my attention.

Also, I ain't got no car or bike, and UTA doesn't go the places I probably need to go. "Fine. Grunstadt, take me to Ten Oaths."

At least he's parked close, that kinda Doris Day parkin' ya only see in movies or for lucky people, like Phouka, I guess. I can tell once we pull into traffic that we're headin' in the general direction of where I gotta go.

"Ya wanted to talk, so talk." I ain't makin' eye contact.

"Prince Hadryn is leading the Samhain celebration, marking the new year tonight, but it isn't like anything I've ever seen." He looks to me at a stoplight. "He's presenting a masterpiece, his words, as a gift for the people. I can't put my finger on it, but it feels like something else is going on."

It's fuckin' Halloween in the theater and arts district of the fuckin' City, so ya got parades and marches and lines of people tryin' to get in everywhere, so traffic's at a fuckin' crawl.

"Why should I tell ya anything, Thom? Ya were ordered to run along home and ya did it, without thinkin', like a good little puppy. Fer all I know ya might be deliverin' me to him."

"That's what I wanted to talk about."

"Ya givin' me to the Prince?"

"No, when I was sent away. What was in that truck? Be honest, anything might help here." Few more stoplights and we can at least get to the quicker route leadin' down to Grunstadt.

"It was a storage truck with a bunch of valuables, like the documents on Dieter Kirschbaum which turned out to be a dead end. And the bow, but that's not related. Weird that the Prince was ridin' shotgun, but I guess if it was his stuff it makes sense. Why's that important?"

"You know where it was going?"

"Storage facility, yeah, with a pitstop at the prison to get Kirschbaum out so he could get slit like the loose end he was." Prolly had to combine trips to save on time?

"Storage facility? Nick he was going to the Royal Vault."

Given that the Shear is a fuckin' artifact of a long dead world, it makes sense, buddy. But what don't make sense is why he was takin' it out of the City if it was his tool of choice for duckin' the Kitsune who were probably huntin' him.

I'm puttin' together a theory on that, too. Question is why would the Prince go to North Allora after killin' a woman, and then escape out to the Benedict? Out in North Allora, the Foxes are clear to hunt demons, and they're so good at it that the Fae just leave it to 'em. So if he's doin' Shadow magic, North Allora's a good place to do it, what with the urban malaise goin' on up there, and the darker mythical shit it attracts.

Out to the Benedict so ya not only duck the Foxes, but also only one noble out there, and he's more in South Benedict, so easy to do shit under his nose. Also, easier to pin on said noble, Prince Firemane, the ideological adversary to Hadryn.

And I right fucked it all up when I stole the Shear, 'cept now he got Shadow's Edge, which I know 'cause I ain't got a fuckin' right hand no more, and I don't wanna know what kinda Shadow magic he could pull with the blade of the Redcaps.

"Nick?"

Fuck, spaced out. "The Vault's outside town? That don't make no sense."

"It's not, it's in the City." I give him a few seconds to finish that thought.

He doesn't. "And ya know this how?"

"Rourke took me there, he has a private entrance. Can't remember where it was, but it was definitely inside the City." He looks to me. "I'd tell you if I could, Nick, honest."

So Hadryn was goin' just to tie off the loose end at Kirkland County, and have Rhys do the slit, and be on his way to the Vault before Kirschbaum's body hit the ground.

"Yer givin' me stuff to go off, 'least." I watch traffic go by, brain swimmin' through through the events again and again to see if somethin' shakes loose. Too many missin' pieces. I still need a motive, and "Princey is a privileged fuckin' asshole who don't understand the word 'no'" is a piss-poor motive to nail him on. I mean, it's fuckin' true, but ain't nobody gonna break out the manacles 'cause a royal's actin' like a fuckin' royal.

"I'm sorry, Nick." His eyes are on the road. "I've put you through a lot, haven't I?"

"Not like ya were a fuckin' stalker, Thom. Well... ya kinda were, but I never felt threatened. Anyway, I forgive ya, just... get yer shit together, yeah?"

"Can I ask you something, Nick?" We're at the exit ramp to head into Grunstadt. Little Tokyo ain't too far.

"Sure, go 'head."

"You like baseball? At all?" I perk a brow at him. "Serious."

"I mean, my Pa took me to games when he was gettin' shots fer his job, but I was so bored off my ass. Love football, though. You a Gryphons fan?"

The Phouk can only give a weak shrug. "Football, like in Europe? My younger brother is, I'll go to a game if I'm there with my mom, but otherwise? No."

"The Gryphons aren't a soc-" My tone's raised, yeah, but he's cut me off, hand raised.

"I know. My older brothers are huge fans, season tickets, they do wealth management for the owners of the Gryphons and Stallions, so... No."

"Well shit, whadduya do with yer spare time? Read books at all?"

"I can't remember the last time I read something just to read it." He hears my sigh at that. "My Mom's a lit professor so she pushed all of us to read the classics, so it was also like school. I really like movies though. You know that, you saw my home theater. I like historical dramas, Westerns... What kind do you like?"

"Yeah..." My turn to wince. "I'm more into the serialized stuff. Movies try to do too much in too little time for my taste, but I will watch some. You uh, like anime?"

"The Japanese cartoons?"

"Animation." I'd swear my eyes were burnin' with that glare of death.

At that, he laughs. Actually fuckin' laughs.

"It's not fuckin' funny! It's a legitimate artform and genre!"

"No, no." He waves, dismissively, still laughin'. "Fuck, we wouldn't have lasted a month, would we?"

Well, shit.

"Yeah." I have to chuckle too. "Yeah. Heh, I guess not. S'pose it was a crush fer the both of us, huh?"

"But not with the other Goblin, huh?" I tense up. "Relax, Nick. I get it, we aren't there yet." A couple more seconds. "You got any interest in being friends, at least?"

"Like ya said, we ain't there yet, Thom. Take yer time, figure yer shit out. And uh, keep yer distance, I might end up committin' some form of treason 'fore the day's over and I don't want anythin' to splash back on ya."

Of course, this is where we're pullin' within a short walkin' distance of Ten Oaths. He's smart enough not to cross the border, bein' a Phouka and at least knowin' the Feud now, I'd guess. "Don't get killed, okay? Just promise me you're not going to get hung up on being a Goblin or anything like that. My advice? Be who you are."

I get out, but lean back in. "Wow. That's some deep shit, Phouk. 'Just be yerself.' Ya ever think 'bout puttin' that on a coffee mug?" I see him sniffin'. "What?"

"You've got a snack in your pocket."

"What's it to ya if I do?!"

"Just sayin'. Samhain's a harvest holiday, and you've got leftover harvest in there, and..."

"Oh fer fuck's sake." I take out the 'snack', a half-eaten energy bar, and toss it to him. "There, have at it, fuckin' Shadow, Thom."

He takes a deep breath, and I'd swear his eyes glow a bit. "At the end of the day, you are Nicholas Arsenne. Do not forget that. Embrace it, and a fated defeat will never find you."

Ohhhh kayyyyy...

"Uh. Sure, I'll do that. No prob. And Thom?"

He blinks a few times. "Yeah?"

"I know ya try to be nice, but ya don't gotta take *every* drink they offer ya at the Palace, 'kay?" And then I walk away, toward Ten Oaths Distribution.

If ya figure out what the fuck that was all about, feel free to tell me, okay buddy? 'Cause I'm thinkin' he got some bad molly or some shit.

I stop at the shrine outside of Ten Oaths, the fox statues lookin' at me all judgy, but I still take one of the incense sticks and light it, stick it with the others, and bow properly three times.

On the end of the third, I'm surrounded, three Kitsune all prepared to cleave my head off. I raise my hands, slowly. "I have information fer Akimura-chan, regarding one of her hunts in North Allora."

And then, buddy? A hard jolt of pain to the back of my head, and everythin' goes black.

30

"Would you mind coming around? We got shit to talk about, you know?"

Fuck, my head hurts.

"Well, yeah. You were hit over the head. Head up, open your eyes."

So, I do. And standin' in front of me is... another Goblin? I thought I was knocked out by the Foxes, what the fuck? He's taller than me, about five five, which is a fuckin' giant among Goblins, I can't place the clan, he got scaly skin like the Gremlins, big ears like the Tinkers, and when he flashes a grin, I see them jaws-o-life teeth. Also, he got blue eyes, like sapphire blue. And hair.

"What, ya a cousin? Lost siblin' bullshit?" I try to get up, but I'm tied to the chair. Pretty good, too, complex knots that are outta my reach. Fuck, I need some ice fer my head, godsdamn. Wait a minute...

I didn't say out loud that my head hurts, I didn't prompt that at all.

"Ah fuck, ya tellin' me yer a Goblin mind-reader? Bullshit. I'll lay down a tenner yer a Fox tryin' to fuck with my head. Gonna run through my dossier to prove ya know me? *That* never gets old."

"You done? Can we talk now?" He don't even sound like a Goblin. He got an accent, but I can't place it fer the life of me. "Because the accent is from a world that doesn't exist anymore."

"Fuckin' Shadow, I'm 'round the fuckin' bend, ain't it?" I smirk at him. "'Kay, joke's over. Some notes? Goblins ain't that fuckin' tall. We all got accents. And havin' the same eyes and hair as me's a nice touch, but kinda unoriginal for a Fox trick, y'know?"

"Yes, of course, Nick. But what Foxes don't do? Speak the language of magic." He motions with his hand for me to figure out the rest.

"I don't follow, pal."

He rolls his eyes. "Yes, you do."

"Foxes can speak Sigil, not a lot of it, but anyone can understand it." He waits, expectantly. "I still don't see yer point. What, you're not secretly a Kitsune? Where's your proof? Make yer case, counselor."

"We've been speaking it this entire time." I blink. My throat and tongue do feel a little sore. A "soft k" is a bitch on yer vocal chords. "Now can we talk? You captors are likely on the way back so unless you want them watching you talk to yourself..."

"The fuck ya mean 'talkin' to myself'? Yer right in front of me!" That look again. "Yer in my head? Guess that knock was worse than I thought." I look at my left arm as best I can, the Shear's still wrapped about it as armor. "Weird they didn't take this."

"You know, I can answer the questions you have, if you're done fumbling about with your disbelief. You had no problem doing it with *Gravity's Rainbow*, but *this* has you skeptical?" He squats in front of me. "Nick. We're running out of time."

"Yer givin' me nothin', pal. Who the fuck even are ya?"

"De'vapel, that's the closest approxiamation I can manage in your language. We all had much more complex vocal chords in the older worlds, needed them to speak magic. Call me what you wish, if it gets us talking."

"Ganimard, then."

"Truly? I'm not chasing you or trying to arrest you. Everything you've read, I've read with you, but if you need to, fine."

"A'right, Inspector, then *what* the fuck are ya? Split personality? Ghost? Ancestral spirit? You possessin' the Shear or some shit? Gonna take credit fer all my positive qualities?"

"I was betrayed, twisted, and cast aside. Then, in the Uprising, I was captured, tortured, and ultimately died at the hands of those who were trying to wrench my knowledge from my mind and soul. Then? I'm watching through a window while a Goblin is born, raised, and suffers hardship, and finally, *finally*, I'm able to fucking talk to him and warn him of the danger of the Shadow Prince but he'd rather play Twenty fucking Questions."

"The 'Shadow Prince'? Really? That's what ya came up with fer Hadryn?"

"Don't shame me, it's from your mind. You're essentially arguing with yourself, Nick."

"So yer one of my past lives or somethin'?"

"Can we talk about that *after* we stop the Prince, who is in possession of Shadow's Edge, and seems fare more willing to use its more... creative aspects than you?"

"Fine, I'll bite. So how do we get outta here, then, smart guy?"

"Who *are* you talking to?" That voice was behind me. "And in the future, don't visit past midnight asking to see me. Our working relationship is only known to a selected few."

I feel the bindin' on my wrists loosen, at least. "Akimura-chan? That you?"

"You did ask for me. Though your one-sided conversation in Sigil was entertaining enough." I know that tone. She's trying to imply she understood all of it, but she maybe got the barest gist, and she's hopin' I'll fill in some blanks.

"Yeah, I'm a riot. I know who you and yer hunters are lookin' for in North Allora, the one killin' women?" Now she's in front of me, and I'm rubbing my wrists. Ganimard, conveniently (fer him) ain't there. "It's Prince Hadryn. He was usin' *this*," I say, pointin' at the Shear, "to move through Shadow from North Allroa to a fixed point in the Benedict where nobody'd see him. He's plannin' on doin' somethin' for Samhain when the veil between the worlds is weakest, and it probably ain't too good."

"That's not a dire warning, Mr. Blackwarren." She narrows her eyes, gettin' a read on me. "While I appreciate the information, that you offered freely... strangely enough... you must be aware that we are under treaty to not act upon Fae concerns outside of the Feud, otherwise 'fox hunts' would be the norm."

"He took Rhys, okay? Can ya help me at all?" I let a little
emotion slip, maybe intentionally, I'm just trying to keep rational.
It's been a fucked up couple days, y'know? Shadow, it's been a
fucked up year. "I got somethin' the Prince wants, and he's expectin'
me to hand it over by sundown, or he's gonna kill Rhys, ya get that?
Ya okay with that?"

She fuckin' titters, coverin' her mouth demurely with one hand.
"Mr. Lleweylln and I are colleagues, not friends. We owe each other
very little, and if you are asking help in your rescue, the price would
be higher than you could ever afford. You would be asking for war."

"I don't wanna start a war, I don't want anybody gettin' killed,
or hurt."

She taps my hand, the mechanical one, the brace on my leg.
"More than you already have? You have yourself, a body barely
holding itself together, and a bow. How, I ask you, will you triumph
over the Prince and save someone bound to his authority?"

...what?

I'm thinkin', okay?! Was I expectin' her to gather up her fellow
foxes and hunt his ass down? What endgame am I goin' fer, here?
Confront the Prince in front of an entire assemblage of the nobility?
Fight him? All the while keepin' Rhys alive, who might be ordered
to fight and kill me, or die to protect Hadryn?

Fuck, I don't know how to save him-

"You've already failed, Mr. Blackwarren. You're burning bright
in your mind, chasing answers, plotting plans, and you've still failed.
And until you know why, there is no way to reach the summit."
When the fuck did she get tea? She helps me up, and hands me a
written charm. "Apologies for the injury, Mr. Blackwarren. Place
that against the wound, it should ease the pain. You can see yourself
out, I need to begin my daily work."

Then the Fox just... leaves, the door left open.

"Well, a fat lot of fuckin' good *this* did. Can't expect the
Kitsune to care, though, this ain't any of their biz." I get to my feet,

stretching, my knee aching, but I can walk fine. Running, I don't see much outta me for a while.

It's too early for ramen when I exit Ten Oaths Distribuion, and I'm only thinkin' 'bout food 'cause I'm starvin'. C'mon, Blackwarren, *think,* yer losin' time, here.

"Want to pick apart what she said? She's a trickster, they're never direct, right?" "Ganimard" is walkin' alongside me, people passin' through him to prove he ain't really there. Or real.

"How 'bout *you* suggest somethin', smart guy? 'Cause I'm outta ideas!"

I grit my teeth, now everyone's lookin' at me like I'm crazy.

"Switch to Italian, put your phone to your ear." I blink a couple times.

"That's actually a good..." I pull out my phone, switch to Italian. I need the practice anyway. I'll translate for ya, buddy, I know it ain't one of your stronger languages. *"Gonna hit me with that idea, now?"*

"I don't have the answers, Nick. If I knew, I would tell you. But let's look at what she said. You're going to fail, yeah, because you were planning and plotting, and that's the reason you fail." I don't see him in thought.

"You're a past life, right? You exist independent of me, or what?"

"I'm you. You're me. We're us. I don't remember a lot of my old life, just that I died in the Uprising, and I..." He points to the Shear on my left arm. "Made that. It's mine. It's yours. It's ours. Can we get back to muddling through Fox-talk?"

"Why you in such a hurry?" I'm heading to the UTA station. The train helps me think, and I can slip a turnstile to get a ride. It's free transit, but ya need yer ID, which I don't have.

"Rhys? They're *our* feelings, you know. You're just the one driving. I just... want to *do* things when we're around him. Act, not wait, you know?" Yeah, I feel the same way.

"This how it's gonna be? We gonna end up tradin' the driver's seat for my body?" I'll admit that scares me. Wouldn't you be, buddy?

"No. This is your body, your life. Can we *please*-"

"Fine. Fine. You had to expect I'd have a million questions, right?" Quick tip about bein' a Goblin, bein' on the Green Line out to Victory Station in Allora, lookin' to the normies like a stereotypical criminal, on a cell phone, and talkin' fast, emotional Italian for everyone 'round ya to hear. This is why everyone tends to think we're all "mobbed up". *"So, what do ya think led to her saying I'd fail?"*

"You were thinking when she did, right? What were you thinking about?"

"She ain't a mind reader."

"Facial expressions? Probably good at reading them." Fuck, that's right. I'll work on my poker face later, but I was thinking about how I would confront Hadryn, if I'd have to fight to the death, how I'd confront him in public, probably.

"Confront the Prince, free Rhys, find justice for the murdered women."

He nods.

"And? What's your follow-up, Inspector?"

"I was a tinkerer, a builder." He shrugs. Fuck, that's how I do it. "You're the one who's the detective."

"I'm not a detective. I'm a..."

Holy fuck.

I *would* fail. I'm angling at this like some big damned hero. But I'm not a hero, am I buddy?

I look to Ganimard. "I'm a thief."

Need proof I ain't a hero, buddy? Ganimard was sittin' next to me, on a packed car, where he was on top of someone else. Who I just turned to say that to.

And then got a face full of MACE.

And there ain't no magical Goblin resistance to that shit, by the way. At least I get some space, because that shit spreads *wide* in an enclosed, crowded area.

I don't remember gettin' off the train, but I know I'm in the men's room, splashin' water in my eyes while my nose runs and I cough and run through every profanity I know in Italian. Don't take my calmness here the wrong way, it fuckin' *burns*, and I'm worried I'll have to see if Mom can handle making new *eyes* for me.

"You're not going to go blind, Arsenne. Keep flushing out your eyes." A second passes. "No, I didn't take over. You were fumbling and crying and someone led you in here. I didn't see because you couldn't see."

"Thanks, Inspector," I mutter. When I look at the mirror in the briskly moving facility, my eyes are bloodshot, vision still a little blurry. "This is turnin' into a shit day. Happy fuckin' Halloween, fuck."

"What next, Nick?"

Maybe... 'Can ya hear me like this? Thinkin' it in my head?'

"Yeah, obviously. We share a mind."

'And ya didn't think to suggest it before?' I roll my eyes, and yeah, that stings. 'Okay, I'm a thief. So I gotta think like a thief. A thief doesn't confront someone. If yer doin' it right, they never knew ya were there. First? Set the target."

"Hadryn." Ganimard's heading toward the exit, which I'm doin' too, mostly 'cause I still got no fuckin' idea where we are. "Second?"

'What's the endgame? Clean sweep? Specific loot? First one's out, it's too much for me. So what do I specifically take that will affect the Prince in the way that I need?'

"Blackmail? You're trying to force him to free Rhys. Or maybe take back Shadow's Edge?"

We're into the terminal of Victory Station as the morning rush is coming in, and the vampire graveyarders are leavin'. I'm gettin' a wider berth, more mythics in the crowd.

'Both good ideas. Have to make it that he faces accountability for, y'know, murderin' a over a dozen women. And makin' sure he never does it again. I know he was usin' the Shear to hop around through Shadow, but I'm pretty sure Shadow's Edge can do it easy. And I gotta do all this, takin' from His Royal Highness. Might as well try to rob-'

"The Royal Vault." We reach that at the same time. That *would* be where I'd find everything, of course, and where I can't reach it. Shadow, outside of the Royal Family no one can. I might have a better chance demandin' Prince Hadryn face me in single combat.

'Any chance the bow can magically open doors? Pick locks? Fire grapplin' hooks?' Yeah, I'm kiddin', it's a fuckin' bow. It makes portals by firin' arrows at surfaces, that's it.

"What do you need it to do?"

'I don't know yet. Need to call somebody.'

'Course he put himself number one on my contact list.

A ring later...

"Speak."

"Cen, stop tryin' to be cool, 'kay?" Only a few people can pull that off without pissin' people off. "I need some information. Can you, uh... Do that thing?"

Click.

Then "call me when ya know what ya fucking want". And then a series of not kind emoji. So yeah, I call back. Ganimard just... fades out, I guess.

"Ya got ten seconds."

"Can ya do the thing where nobody can trace or tap the call? I don't know what it's fuckin' called but I figure ya can do it. Am I wrong?" Catch the breath.

"Ya mean give ya a secure line? Ya think I take any calls that ain't on a secure line? Just fuckin' say what ya wanna say, Cous'."

I'm interruptin', I can tell.

"Y'know where the Royal Vault is, how I can get in? I ain't got the runway to case, I'm on the clock, Cenzo." And then... "Cen, stop laughin', yeah?"

"Ya ain't fuckin' serious. That's... Fuck, Nick, I'll give ya credit, ya got me out of a fuckin' borin' conference call, but... Yer aunt give ya painkillers or somethin'? And not tell ya the right dosage?"

"I ain't fuckin' high, Cen. Can ya help me or not?"

"Be an accessory to fuckin' *treason*?"

"Ya can have the cut ya still owe me. All of it. Just fer you."

"Fuck you, Nick. Fuck you fer thinkin' I got a fuckin' price tag. Ya can kiss my scaly fuckin' green-"

"I'll lift what ya want from the vault. Ya know there gotta be old Gremlin tools in there, Cen. That's our heritage, cousin, sittin' in the secure, safe hands of our vaunted oppressors."

Y'see, Vincenzo actually *did* go to college, managed to find a way into Destry Tech, and well, he was *that* college student. Y'know, the one who does petitions to rename a buildin' that's named after a racist, leaks data from administrative servers to let the non-legacies know just how bad they're gettin' fucked by school policies, and singlehandedly DDoS'ed a professor's server into scrap metal for providing fertile soil for techbros who probably have "I DISRUPT" inked on their dicks. And what *really* pisses him off? Cultural theft and appropriation by privileged assholes.

And a *lot* of Goblin culture, Dwarf culture, Brownies, Sluagh, and Troll, too, is kept in the Royal Vaults for "historical study." Queen Alana (may her warmth bless us all) is progressive, yeah, but even the nicest rich white ladies have their blind spots, and this one is a fuckin' Sidhe Queen.

"I know what yer fuckin' doin', Nick. That why yer callin' me from Victory Station? Even if I wanted to-"

"And ya *do* want me to, Cen. Yer clan's seen by the humans as only been 'round fer a hundred years or so, and ya know we're all older than that. And they don't even know 'bout all the schematics and plans and blueprints and diagrams y'all came up with. How much of it is locked away to be doled out to Knockers who kiss the most ass, while the Gremlins get seen as only breakin' shit?"

There's a few seconds of silence. I can hear him breathin', and I can't tell if I've riled him up, or gotten through to him.

"Nick..." Okay, somber? "This guy really worth it?"

"It ain't fer a guy, Cenzo, it's to put away a killer."

"Yer goin' fer the Vault, it ain't hard to see who yer goin' for, and who their bodyguard is. Lleweylln put himself on the line to save ya, ya really wanna spit in his boss's face and get fucked up, again? Nobody wants to see ya like that. Fuck, ya even think 'bout yer Ma?"

"My Mom left when I was a kid, left my Pa-"

"And what, yer fuckin' gettin' back at her by committin' treason?"

I take a breath, my turn. Can't let the anger out on this, it'd go at the wrong person. "My Mom left my Pa 'cause he promised her he'd never take a life, ever, and the moment finances got tight, he took jobs from Damon. She didn't have a pot to piss in, a mark on her back, and not a fuckin' green cent to her name, but she left. And she came fer me the moment I was in trouble. No questions asked. Connie Volpe's got a code, 'kay? And she did her fuckin' best to get me to find my own."

I lean against the wall of the station. People avoid me, obviously, and fer once I'm grateful.

"So, Cen, I'm sayin' I'm honorin' my mother by doin' what's right. Just help me do that, Cousin, please."

Silence. Five seconds. Ten. Fifteen.

"If ya ain't clean on the other side, yer cut. Ya understand, right?"

Cut. As in cut out. And for a couple second generation Sicilans like Cen and I, gettin' cut out yer family, ya'd rather they just killed ya instead. They might spit at the mention of yer name, but they'll at least say it. Not if yer cut.

Fuck.

"Yeah. *Capisco*. So whadduya got?"

"Hold on a sec. Line's gonna seem like it's dead for a few seconds."

And... yeah. It does. Just silence, 'cept some higher pitched nonsense. Added security, I'm guessing.

"Okay, after this, yank the SIM card, break it, and pulverize the phone. Then scatter the parts in different trash cans... Wait. Yer Redcap. Just yank the SIM and eat the damned phone."

"Yeah, understood." It'll taste like shit, but I see where he's goin'. A Knocker could put it back together with time.

"Okay, ya know the thing the lady told ya to do after that one thing?"

Fuck, buddy, are ya lucky I'm hear to translate.

Mom told me to work on my languages after I graduated.

"Yeah, which time? After the first thing or before the last thing?"

Tinkers gotta learn a lot of languages so we can read plans and schematics and warranty information. A Tinker, by the way, does not have a warranty on anything that's still intact.

So I'm askin' Cen which language he's talkin' 'bout. Obviously, it ain't gonna be one of the European languages.

"The one after the first thing."

The first language Mom wanted me to study was Italian, 'cause I wasn't fluent. The second was because Sicily was a stopping point fer a lot of cultures, lot of blendin'. So the next was Egyptian, better known as Arabic. I can't write it worth a damn, which is sad, 'cause it's beautiful when it's done right.

He's askin' which language that ain't known by Fae, that we both know besides Italian. The other one was Korean, which I am *terrible* at. I can order food and ask where the bathroom is, say hello, and apologize. And count to ten.

Obviously, livin' in the country we do, we don't bust out the Arabic unless we're talkin' to native speakers, but this an emergency. I'll spare ya the conversation, buddy. We're both kinda on need to know.

Takes about half an hour. Cops are startin' to walk by me more often, 'cause humans are gonna see an assumed criminal, and now he's in a major transit hub, under a financial center with a stock exchange in the Tower, speaking Arabic. And he's got a funky lookin' thing on one arm, and a shiny glove lookin' thing on the other.

But, I got a plan, a way in. And it's right where I'm standin'. The Royal Vault is on it's own floor of Victory Tower, just a few tricks to get in there.

"Good luck to ya, Cousin. 'Til I hear yer clean, I don't know nothin' or know ya from now on. *Capisco?*

Fuck. Gotta do this, though. I don't kill people, and if I can keep people I know are killers from doin' it to innocent people, I gotta do it. I gotta step up.

"Do me one favor?"

A sigh on the line. "What?"

"Gira per Nona? Per favore?"

Spin a thread for Nona, what we Italians call Clotho, the spinner of fates. It's askin' him to spin a fresh thread for me, and offer it to Her, in case I die.

"Giuro che lo farò, cugino."

Sister Nona, let his hand be steady. Mama Tinker, may my mother's thread be woven away from tragedy. Father Redcap, guide me to threads that do not deserve the slit. Grandmother, if my thread is to cut tonight, I beg you, let your shear be quick.

31

Here's the thing about bein' half Redcap: I got jaw strength for days. My Pa was better, but I can chomp through a two-by-four like it's a slice of cold pizza. Redcaps can also eat damned near anythin', and my stomach's closer to my Pa's than my Mom's. Metal? For a Redcap, it's like tough meat. Damon could eat a fuckin' car if he took the time. For me, it's harder 'cause of my front teeth gettin' capped, but the rest can tear and gnash with the best of 'em.

I'm sayin' this, in case ya were worried, buddy, about my crunchin' through a seven hundred dollar smartphone like I'm double-stackin' an energy bar. It tastes like shit, my tongue's burnin' a bit from the pieces and substances that ain't s'posed to be taken into a digestive system, and it'll feel not too great in a couple weeks when... You get the idea, and I ain't goin' into fuckin' detail.

I'll also translate 'n dub it for ya, 'cause I don't think Arabic is one of your languages. If it is, then yeah, I'm just savin' time.

Cenzo started out with, *"Here's what ya need. Get aluminum foil, a couple sheets. Use your right hand, it don't have any prints. That bow is going to be a problem, it's too big. Break it down, if you can."*

"I won't need picks?"

"There are no picks for this."

The foil ain't too hard to get. It's expensive, since I'm payin' Allora prices, but I get the heavy duty, as recommended. The bow, well...

"What do you need it to do," is what Ganimard asked. And right now, I need it to be stealthy. It ain't so much like with Shadow's Edge, where it drank my blood and gave me what I needed. Instead it's like the buildin' toys my Mom got me when I was young, where you could build it 'cordin' to the instructions, or just put the parts together how ya needed, or wanted.

This is what burns the time, honestly, I have to reach that place where I can just put stuff together without really thinkin' about it, and not be distracted by everything else. Be "in the zone", as it were. It's a beautiful Steampunk-ish compound bow, but it breaks down pretty easy. The hard part is puttin' it back together in a way I can hide it.

Some goes into my leg brace, and the added stability makes it easier to walk. The tension and trigger mechanisms I rework into a wrist crossbow. Range is shit, but it'll work in a room. Hides well enough under my hoodie sleeves. The arms of the bow I put together into shoulder guards that'll make them look a little broader, like I been workin' out a lot, more bulky than wiry, but not suspiscious. Takes a while, but I got it squared away, all under my hoodie jacket.

I practiced a few times putting it all back together. Fastest was a hundred seconds. So not in an instant. Ganimard's been quiet, but I'm grateful. This I understand, at least. Plannin' a heist, puttin' shit together, bein' a thief.

After prep, then I gotta find a way up to the Vault. Cenzo had it ready. I'm curious how he knew all this shit, but he planned the bank job at the start of all this, so I take it this is his Everest, somethin' he's planned in his head fer a couple years, but never planned to actually do it. Until now.

"You're going into the elevators dedicated to the 21st through 40th floors. Take the one that needs an RFID tag. Lift two from people leavin'. If you can't get the tags, it's over 'fore it starts."

Liftin' has never been one of my strong talents. Mom had a jacket with bells sewn into it to practice pickin' pockets without makin' any noise. I didn't suck, but a Tinker Thief should be doin' it clean about... a hundred percent of the time. I managed about eighty percent. Mom joked about disowning me, at least I think she did. The one thing she hammered into my head to get me that high is to use my index and middle fingers like a pair of tweezers if yer goin' fer a pocket. Otherwise, just use a bumper. Distraction's gonna do more for ya than all the practice in the world. Combo's best.

Bump and *tweeze*.

Also, a small charm to make me easy to ignore. Works better than you'd think. Humans, 'specially upwardly mobile finance guys (read: white) generally don't *want* to see people like me (read: whatever POC is pissing them off today). Granted, it don't work for long, but long enough, I'm hopin'.

"Soon as you have the two cards, wrap one in the foil. That's for the ride down. Toss the one ya used as soon as it ya bump the card to the plate and hit for the 35th. The guy has to think he dropped it or it's over."

Easier said than done, buddy, at least with someone who can't move that fast. Buttons are on the right side of elevator, so with my right hand (again, to prevent prints) I tap the card on the ID plate, and scale it like a playin' card out into the lobby, just as the doors are closin'.

The foil on the second card? RFID cards can be tracked by buildin' security. Wrap it in foil, and ya got yerself a crude Faraday cage, blockin' signals. It's the reason tech guys put their phones in the fridge durin' a meetin' so they don't get hacked. I don't just read literature, buddy, I'll read whatever's in reach. And when ya got Gremlin cousins that are on speakin' terms with ya, they're always up fer talkin' shop.

When the doors close, ya'd think I'd breathe a sigh of relief or some shit, but this ain't even close. This is just me gettin' closer to the point of no return. At this point, I'm just guilty of petty theft, possibly some light corporate espionage, but that's human law. I'd get grilled and have to spend some time in jail, but I ain't guilty of anything that would piss off a Sidhe, yet, or someone in the Guard. I can still walk away, is what I'm sayin'.

But ya know I ain't.

In fer a penny, in fer a fuckin' pound, right?

"When you reach the 35th floor, after the doors open, don't leave the car. Start putting in this sequence of buttons, completed before the doors close. If you can't, it's over."

I practiced all the way up, not touchin' the buttons, but buildin' that short-term muscle memory so I'd be ready. It's fifteen total button presses, ended with the emergency stop just as the doors close. If I did it right, onto the next phase. If not, the alarm goes off to signal the emergency, and I'm proper fucked.

I treat it like a waltz, my fingers movin' through the buttons one-two-three, one-two-three to fifteen with the stop button as the big flourish at the end, just as the doors clank closed. I breathe, tense, the second after I finish the sequence feelin' like an eternity.

Like, a real eternity.

What the fuck?

Door's stuck closed, all the pressed buttons are still lit up, a Sigil, drawn in the right order. And Cenzo coulda just told me the word and I coulda done this without gettin' in my own head, but Sigil's my strong suit. I think I'm the only one in the family who's as good with it as I am. I'd correct some nobles on their pronounciation, because they fuckin' mangle it sometimes, but I also like bein' alive, y'know?

Still, bein' stuck in an elevator isn't how I saw this goin'. Do I wait? Need a command word? Is the Sigil a clue or reminder? It just says "summer" so that makes sense for the Vault of the Summerswords, but now what? There's gotta be somethin' that I'm missin'.

Think, Blackwarren. Ya came this far.

"Do you *feel* that?"

"Fuck!" I jump, and on my left is Ganimard. "Don't do that!"

"I didn't mean to scare you." He's dressed like me, clothes even fit him. "But do you feel that?"

'I ain't got no clue," I think, 'cause my jumpin' like a bowl of German cockroaches just poured onto my head ain't helpin' the "stealthy" part of this at all. "What am I s'posed to be feelin'?"

He winces, in thought, like he's diggin' up an old memory that needs every effort. His hand makes a fist, smackin' his thigh a few times, tryin' to jump the thoughts. When he *does* speak, it's a stream of language I don't recognize.

'Ya lost me, Inspector."

Hands open, fingers curled, below his face, tryin' to stitch it together. Other words. I don't know 'em either.

'What language even is that?' I look at him, doin' my best to show my confusion.

I hear about a dozen words all at once, in one breath, and then he punches his thigh again, in frustration. "So many worlds, so much carved away. I don't think anyone is even capable of knowing the old languages, old workings, old magics."

'Ya talkin' 'bout Sigil? That's the language of magic, ya know that.'

"What is... the book about burning the books."

'Fahrenheit 451?'

Ganimard nods several times. "Yes! Condensations and digests and cutting to the snap ending."

'I'm followin', make yer point.'

"Imagine a conversation that would discuss all facets of a subject. You and I talk about the book, but we're also talking about when we first read it, how it changed the more times we read it, how we changed the more times we read it, and a language that would give voice to *all of it* and could be done in five minutes, but it's so much more satisfying and fulfilling that we talk for hours, and connect, and it's just talking about a book we read once. And now... Magic carved, edited, digested, condensed, trimmed to fit buzzwords and simple wants, yoking a great force of creation to make... fireballs and conjure rehashed memories, as if you consigned Pegasus to pull a... a *fucking* apple cart."

'Ganimard? That's somethin' to talk about. When I ain't tryin' to rob the Royal Vault. Still, nice to know that Goblins got to be all wise and learned in the old worlds.' I try a smile at him. 'Got any ideas how to get outta here?'

"I wasn't always a Goblin, Nick." I blink a few times. "And the wall there is another door."

So, uh, all the words kinda left my screen there, a minute, buddy. Enough that I turn around to look at him, half-expectin' him to be a Sidhe or some shit in a past life that was turned into a Goblin. Rare, but it happens. Very, very rare. Involves changin' yer Name, as in True Name that most people don't know, 'less they're a Keth.

But y'know what? That's another fuckin' thing we're talkin' 'bout later.

'Ganimard? Could ya hold off on the *fuckin' bombshells*?' He's still a Goblin, by the way, and there is a door behind him. Not an elevator door, an actual fuckin' door, with the doorknob and fine wood and jamb, all of which look like they came from a world gone by.

'I dunno why ya suddenly felt the need to start talkin' to me, but I gotta focus-'

"I've always been talking with you, Blackwarren, since we were born. But, you're right, I'm pushing a lot on you right now. The door is locked, but there should be a lock in Sigil."

I do see what looks like a keyhole, but... 'I ain't got the Edge anymore, and I don't know if anything I built from the Shear can work as a lockpick, Inspector, so 'less ya got any ideas...'

"I doubt a lockpick would work. Thieves aren't supposed to get in there, after all. I doubt they use actual keys or tumblers or pins. It's likely in a magical language."

Fuck, Knocker work. I done some before, was just a matter of findin' the Sigil inscribed on the interior of the lock, which I did with Shadow's Edge, which I can't do now. This is what fuckin' happens when ya don't have time to case. Everythin' goes wrong.

"Nick. Talk to me. We can figure this out. Didn't Vincenzo tell you something important about security?"

It was, uh... 'There ain't no such thing as a system that's completely secure. There's always a backdoor, a quick way in, or uh, a failsafe in the uh...'

"Administrative privileges."

'How the fuck ya remember that?' I take a breath. 'Not important. 'Sides, this is a lock on a door, not a network to hack into. I don't think they'd leave a backdoor. As fer admin, that'd be the Queen, and I ain't got no idea-'

"Or, someone else. The Vault's here, in this tower. Do they own it? If so, the Sidhe are much wealthier than we imagined."

'What? No, it's Victory Financial, I think it's controlled by a law firm.'

"So, they have control over the property they own?"

'So all I gotta do it convince the lock that I'm the owner?' I chuckle. 'In Sigil, I'm guessin'.'

"You don't *feel* it, Nick? The owner is much, much older than Sigil. Older magic could trump the magic of today, if you're willing to risk it."

"I can't do magic, Inspector. I do a couple charms, that's it."

"Then..." He's thinkin', at least he ain't frustrated. "Try a charm to open a door. Tell me in your mind, how it's put, and I can try to piece it together in..."

Even the name of the language is inscrutable.

Still, I ain't got much choice, y'know? Elevator's stopped, and I'm thinkin' that's gonna get attention sooner rather than later. I tell him the charm, same one Mom taught me when I was a kid.

"You structure it in rhyme and rhythmed meter." Is he smilin'? "That makes this easier. Creation and destruction are like the pulse of life, they have their own endless prose and song. Repeat after me, precisely, and don't just think of the lock opening. You need to have everything in your mind and heart and soul focused. Think about how your mother taught it to you, when you first used it, when you used it for a purpose such as this one, how it connects to your end goal. I know it's hard, but that language needs fulfillment to be satisfied, to know it will be *yours*."

We didn't have the money, or access to get a copy of house key made, so after school she walked me through the rhythm of the "silly song" (I was seven) to open the door. I sang the little song to the teacher's snack cupboard so all the kids who didn't get a cookie could have one too. I sang to the lock in the Greenmeadow's skylight, to slip in and get my father out of trouble. I will break the lock about Rhys's heart and leave no scars.

My throat is burnin' when the words are carried out on my breath, the door shudderin', shakin', then a definite *CLUNK*, the sounds of heavy weights liftin'. I... I cracked the lock.

"Well done, Blackwarren." He points at his throat. "Try not to talk for a minute or two. It's rough on vocal chords that are relying on long faded vestigial fibers."

I cough a few times, and thankfully, ain't no blood on my hand. A bit of mucus, though, so, y'know, kinda gross, but the door seems unlocked. I push it firmly, the wall openin' up into a what looks like a well-lit... subway station?

It's like the one at Victory Station, but it's colder, and I can see water instead of the tracks, longboats instead of subway cars, but it looks just as busy. Plenty of people gettin' in and out, headin' to gates labeled in a multitude of languages.

"Nick. Nick we shouldn't be here." Fuck, Ganimard sounds scared, I turn to look at him and he's damned near hyperventilatin', lookin' around frantic, and I don't need another hint. Startin' to think Cenzo sent me to the wrong place, I don't think on purpose.

What I do see is that the people are... pale? Not like vampire pale, but like a there but not there kinda way. The gates have names, people filin' in, no one comin' out, none of the names are familiar, but...

There are some legible in Sigil.

I start backin' toward the elevator.

Elysium

He's right, we shouldn't be here.

Asphodel

We gotta get outta here. Now.

Tartarus

'Cause I ain't dead.

The doors close before me, and I breathe a sigh of relief. "Thank Shadow we got outta there. Gotta come up with a new..."

This place is much too big to be an elevator. This is an office. A nice office. It's lavish in its wealth, but definite taste, I would have a field day in here and get the score of a lifetime. It ain't just gold everywhere, or precious metals. There's art, sculpture, like seminal works if I recognize anything from the art appreciation textbooks I've read. Two overstuffed chairs facin' each other near the library shelves. The windows are floor to ceilin', corner office, top shelf liquor, old tomes I'd love to get a look at (and yeah, take a hit off sniffin' those spines), and weirdly enough, framed vinyl albums by STYX, autographed.

There's a beautiful view of Destry Bay beyond the ebony desk, top of the line computer system, executive chair that probably costs a few months rent for me. And seated there, a man with pale skin, onyx black hair, pale gray eyes, dressed in a black on black suit. He's lookin' toward me, rather, I think he was waitin' fer me to make eye contact.

He pushes his chair back, gettin' up, puttin' it back, and walks around the desk toward me, hands behind his back in a gentlemanly fashion. "Mr. Blackwarren." He gestures toward the pair of chairs. "Have a seat."

I swallow hard. Ganimard ain't nowhere. I sit down, this ain't the time to be a smartass, y'know?

He sits across from me, and a few seconds pass, him studyin' me, me bein' nervous as fuck. I know that I'm in trouble, that's fer damned sure. I don't know how I backed out of the subway station of the damned into a corner office, but I know when I am outta my fuckin' depth.

"Nicholas Blackwarren." He lets my name hang in the air a moment, watchin' me brace fer it. "You don't prefer to have a dossier on you recited upon meeting, so we'll move forward."

"How..." I'm amazed I'm speakin'. "How'd ya know that?"

"Please, Mr. Blackwarren." He flashes a fuckin' million-dollar smile. "I know everything."

32

Normally when a guy tells ya he knows everythin', he's full of shit. But here's the thing 'bout bein' well-read, ya get to know who the major players in yer city are, temptin' targets, and who the stay the fuck away from. The man sittin' across from me is one of 'em. He's the megarich guy ain't nobody heard of. The managing partner of the firm that owns Victory Financial, the tower, and a bunch of real estate all over the City.

David Aidoneus, Esq.

And if yer well-read like me, ya know that Aidoneus is a name fer someone else. Someone who would have a subway station connectin' to places like Elysium, the Asphodel Fields, and fuckin' Tartarus. The god of the underworld, as well as the god of wealth.

Hades.

I'm sittin' across from a god who caught me breakin' into one of his vaults. Buddy, they ain't even invented a word to describe how absolutely fucked I am, right now.

"Tell me, Mr. Blackwarren, have you any defense to offer for your illegal entry onto my premises and property?" He seems more amused than anythin', but that's usually worse than them bein' pissed. Hades is the cat, I'm the mouse with a broken leg.

And with people like this? Ya fuckin' tell the truth.

"I'm solvin' a murder, Sir." I'm lookin' down, my voice small and meek. Can ya blame me? This is the guy who runs fuckin' Hell. Or at least the version of it reserved fer mythics! "A lot of murders, actually. Murdered human women. Enslavement of a Redcap. And uh..." I take a breath.

"Go on." I ain't got no idea where he got wine. No, wait, I do, he got a liquor cabinet. Use yer head, Blackwarren. "I know there's more."

"Uh... Would help if I knew what ya wanted to know, sir. Otherwise I might waste yer time and I got the feelin' I can't afford yer billables." I grin, sheepishly.

"You can't. You were attempting to break and enter into vault 137, the property of Queen Alana Summersword of the Kingdom of Rainbows. You clearly had inside information to help you, and most interestingly, knowledge of incantations that are *quite* rare, so much so that I haven't heard their like in eons. Murdered women and indentured Goblins do not seem adequate justification for your actions, Mr. Blackwarren."

"There's... uh... historical and cultural-"

"Artifacts and such belonging to your people that you feel should be returned, as they were unlawfully stolen by a privileged over-class?" He sighs, soundin' bored. "Were that the case, you would file with completed paperwork, established provenance, and done through the appropriate channels, not through grand theft, Mr. Blackwarren." He beckons behind me, and before I can turn, I'm lifted in the air by a tall black man, and I don't mean like black, I mean his skin is jet black, no hair on his head. Or the other one. Or the other one. All three are lickin' their lips lookin' at me.

"Mr. Cerberus, I believe it's time for Mr. Blackwarren to leave."

No, no, no... I can't get kicked out! I can't let this happen to Rhys!

"Wait!" I'm still bein' carried off, slung over a broad shoulder, my right leg against the right head of the three-headed security. "The culprit is Prince Hadryn! He's the one who killed those women!"

"A shame, Mr. Blackwarren. But that is a matter for the Fae. Nothing that falls under my purview."

Fuck! Think, Blackwarren! He's god of the underworld, how can I make this mean something to him? "Ya don't mind murders?!"

"I am the ruler of the underworld, Mr. Blackwarren, anyone who has died, no matter their fate, will come through either my office or my partners' to be processed. How they get there is no concern to us." Another sigh. "These are pitiful attempts to gain my interest. I expected better."

Wait.

Wait, wait, wait, wait, wait.

I saw in Rhys's nightmare that he was the one who took Bridget's life, because she was in pain, sufferin', because the Prince was...

The Prince was pressing Bridget against her piano, strings made of shadow diggin' into her, scrapin' out her soul, about to pull it free but...

Rhys killed her, and her soul vanished into the afterlife, out of the Prince's reach, leavin' Rhys to shoulder the conseqences. He took her life, but saved her soul. But what about the other...

"The Prince is targetin' artists! Creative women and he's gougin' their souls outta their bodies, and I think he's keepin' 'em in the vault. Your vault!"

I'm almost through the door.

"Bring him back." Hades sounds more weary than anythin'. I'm roughly planted down in the chair across from him, Cerberus standin' just behind me. "Is that the true reason you broke into my vault?"

"Not... not entirely. But I do wanna free 'em. I ain't got no idea why he's doin' it, but I need to. It's the right thing to do." The god rolls his eyes so well he probably invented doin' it. "And he's taken my partner, and commanded him to cut off my hand, when he clearly didn't want to. Just... gimme a chance to prove it, yeah?"

I'm surpried he ain't gave me shit 'bout how I talk, but when yer harried, it's hard to put together yer "white voice". 'Sides, he'd see right through it. I'm also curious how he knew about the charm that Ganimard walked me through, but if anythin', it gives me a hint just how long ago he was alive.

And I do plan to chat with him about the "wasn't always a Goblin" thing.

"I'm afraid that's not possible. The Summerswords have a contract regarding their vault and its property contained therein. My hands are figuratively tied."

Blackwarren, he was feedin' ya the method to get in there. Think. Remember the words.

I got it.

I dig into my pockets, scroungin', and dig out a not-so-great lookin' ten dollar bill, and offer it to him. "Mr. Aidoneus, I would like to hire your firm in aiding the collected clans of Tinkers, Gremlins, and Redcaps in suing for the return of our cultural and historical artifacts from the private collections of the Royal Family of the Kingdom of Rainbows. If you would supply me with an email address, I can have provenance sent to you immediately." Thank you Vincenzo. "I can then verify which items belong to my people. You may accompany me to detail our complaint fully, and should you find anything that is in violation of established precedent in human or mythic law, you should be able to utilize 'in plain sight' guidelines to establish probable cause for any complaints you yourself wish to file. After all, if souls of the deceased are to be processed by your offices, then finding trapped, unprocessed, and unreported souls would surely be of interest to you."

Ganimard? Was that you? I mean, I know I was sayin' it, and I was thinkin' of all that, but it's rare I can put it together so...

But that don't matter.

'Cause the god of the underworld just took the tenner, and hands me his card, with the firm's number and other contact information.

"Sooner you send the information you promised, the sooner we can inspect said vault. In the meantime, I will have to inform my clients of your intentions. I would say to count yourself fortunate that it's a holiday for your people, but I suspect you already knew that." He looks beyond me. "Send in Sharon, tell her to bring her notepad."

I take the time to get on my burner phone and start quickly textin' to Cenzo to send everythin' he's got. I also tell him he'll probably have to "white hat" those security gaps he exploited for me so he don't end up with a visit from this law firm. I'll save ya the nitty-gritty of it, buddy, but a text of *"sent evryth, few gb's"* arrives shortly after. Ya'd think that'd take a while, but Cenzo's little cabal of hackers is hooked right into the City's trunk line, the backbone of its internet, so as long as this law firm's got a server than can handle the incoming... I dunno, really, that's all the terms I know. Cen explained more but I kinda go glassy eyed when talkin' 'bout computers.

While I'm doin' that, a woman of indeterminate age has come in, takin' dictation from Hades, probably writin' up the suit or somethin', I guess. Or maybe the client agreement? I dunno, honestly, legal thrillers were never my thing.

"Sir?" Another woman, this one with blood red hair, sharp teeth that'd rival any Redcaps, pokes her head into the office. "We've received several gigabytes of documents, images, video, and audio from a non-profit firm calling itself 'The Siracusa Repatriation Project'. Are these expected?"

"Yes, thank you, Kerry. Scrub them for tracking and viruses, worms, and the like. Also, send copies down to Asphodel, we need transcriptions of the audio and video content. Print up the rest, and have it all indexed, cross-referenced with referrals to applicaple precedents, and have secure access links sent to my tablet."

No word of thanks, she just nods once and leaves.

"If you had all of this documentation on hand, Mr. Blackwarren, why not simply file suit?" A sip of his wine, then lights a cigarette for himself.

"'Cause I ain't got that kinda time, sir."

"That's another thing, you spoke so properly when laying out your request, and now you return to lower diction." He takes a puff on his cigarette, exhales a plume of smoke. Heard that shit before, right before they say- "No, I will not remark how 'you speak so well'."

I give him a look. "'Kay, how-"

"I've told you. I know everything. At least you're respectful, unlike the others." The woman with us, this "Sharon" hands the notepad over to him. He signs it, and hands it to me with a pen.

"This is...?"

"New client paperwork. It will be processed, and you'll have to sign more formalized paperwork later on, but for now, this will do."

I look at the pen, and ya'd think that Hades of all people, uh, gods, would use a quill and ink, or one of those fancyfuck fountain pens, but it's a plastic ballpoint with the firm's logo.

"What, ain't gonna make me sign in blood?" I half-chuckle, half-smirk.

"Blood is terrible for signing official documents, especially considering the amount you'll have to sign in a few days." He looks to the contract, and then to me.

I can take a hint. "Full name?"

A nod.

"Full, full name?"

Another.

So, ugh, this is embarassin', but the bitch of havin' some Fae blood is ya got yer "human name", which ya know, but there's extra stuff for the Fae of it all. So, scripty-like, I sign my complete name.

Nicholas Arsenne Volpe Sicarius Venefici Blackwarren.

Most of them ya know. The other stuff? Volpe, my Mom's name, but the rest? Assassin, Poisoner. Yeah. Sucks havin' Redcap blood. To Redcap families though, with middle names like that? I am a fuckin' *catch*.

What I don't feel is an ominous feelin', like swearin' a formal Oath. Probably will happen when I sign the actual paperwork?

"So, I ain't ungrateful, but why'd ya bite? Ten bucks is hardly temptin', and I broke into yer vaults. Was I right about the whole souls thing?"

He raises a brow. "How did you come to that conclusion?"

"I... read a lot? Three to five books a week, more if I'm lyin' low. Whatever I can find, usually, if it's interestin'. 'Lots been written 'bout the Greek gods, y'know, plus all the other gods of the underworld. And us Goblins follow the Fates, and we know what happens when ya fuck with Grandma's threads."

A sigh, slight shake of the head. "That is an answer, I suppose. Shall we get to it, then?"

I nod, 'cause I don't know how else I gotta respond. "We, uh, got the attorney-client privilege?"

"Yes, cone of silence and all that. Ms. Farry will take dictation for my notes, which I will make available to you on request. And as I am now your attorney, Mr. Blackwarren, I believe it is time for you to explain why all of this has a deadline?"

I glance to the woman, and she's lookin' a little more... skeletal-

Fer fuck's sake, Blackwarren, ya ain't that dense. Sharon Farry. Charon the Ferryman, or Ferrywoman in this case.

"At sundown begins Samhain." Yes, I fuckin' pronounce it right, buddy. "The ceremony will be led by Prince Hadryn, and before that, he's demandin' I give him the last symphony of a composer named Bridget O'Hare. She was a gifted musician, beautiful heart, mind, and soul. And he used her, probably kept her dazzled by his Sidhe beauty to inspire her, make her dependent on him. I also got a list of names for thirteen other women, all artists that were murdered, likely by Prince Hadryn, which has been investigated by the Kitsune, led by Shiko Akimura."

I take a breath. Ms. Farry hands me a glass of water. I thank her, and take a sip. Hades waits for me to continue. Probably that thing, uh... deposition?

"Speculation, I know, but I do know how O'Hare's life ended. Prince Hadryn was attemptin' to steal her final works, take her soul at the height of her creativity, upon completin' her magnum opus. He was accompanied by Rhys Llewellyn, a Redcap assassin bound to serve him through coerced Oaths, and physical threat. Both Bridget and Rhys resisted him. Bridget, to hold onto her soul before the Prince could take it, and for Rhys to free her soul to her afterlife before the Prince could prevent it."

"And you know this how?" Not disbelievin', but I'm reminded of Thom, actually, wantin' to shoot down arguments that might arise.

"I was..." How the fuck do I explain this? "I lived the night Mr. Llewellyn experienced, from his perspective, by way of... through the, uh... Shadow."

A few seconds, and he gestures for me to continue. "Go on."

"Uh... Redcaps have an affinity for the Shadow and-"

"I mean after she was killed, and the Prince apparently demanded her symphony. How did *you* find it?"

"I'm currently livin' in the apartment where Miss O'Hare met her death. I didn't know at the time. I found a box under a floorboard with a flash drive that had it. I made a copy for safekeepin', but the Prince outlined a threat that if I didn't give him the flash drive, he would kill Mr. Lleweylln."

"And how did he deliver this message, Mr. Blackwarren?" Ms. Farry starts a new page. "Every detail is important."

I break eye contact. It's kinda silly when ya say it out loud. "Flowers, sir. Uh, he left a message only discerned with knowledge of floriography. Pages were left together, sorted. Xanthium, common almond, evergreen clematis, nutmeg geranium, reeds, dragonwort, night convolvulus, cherry tree, hand flower tree, zinnia, cypress."

'Course I memorized it, I been runnin' through those flowers and that sequence over and over and over tryin' to find a way that it don't mean Rhys might die tonight.

"It does imply that, Lord Hades." Ms. Farry only stops for a second, and immediately resumes her stenography.

"I've no doubt, Ms. Farry. I still have no answer to the urgency of your concern, Mr. Blackwarren. Is this..."

"Rhys Lleweylln, Lord Hades."

"Thank you, Ms. Farry." Attention back on me. "Can you describe the nature of your relationship with him?" Fuckin' knowin' smirk.

"He's my partner. And ya don't leave yer partner swingin' from the fuckin' gallows. Rhys has saved my life, I've saved his. Partnerships come from worse." I ain't in the mood if he got a notion to fuckin' ship. "And if I give the Prince the flash drive, sure he wins, yeah, but there ain't no guarantee he won't do it again and again, and use Rhys to do it. I want him free."

"Will I also have to serve as your defense attorney as well? They're cleverly concealed, but I see you have devices as old as the dialect you were speaking in various places about your body. Should push come to shove, will you make an attempt on the Prince's life to free your… partner?"

"Wouldn't solve anythin'. It'd only make life more difficult for both of us. I want Hadryn's rep put through the shitter, 'kay? I want his title stripped. I wanna make sure that the souls and hearts of the people he's controllin' are liberated. I want all the shit he stole from *my people* to be returned to us." I look him dead in the eyes, my vision burnin', but not hurtin'. "I wanna make sure he can't ever pulverize someone's fuckin' kneecaps by tellin' 'em to *kneel*."

He meets it, his own eyes darkenin', sounds of the damned wailin' in the background, the souls he's sent to Tartarus, I'm guessin'.

"Lord Hades?" The woman with blood red hair from before. It's enough to break our "starin' contest", at least. "The Summerswords are here to discuss the coming suit that is being drawn up? What shall I tell them?"

Hades looks past me. "Tell them we're implementing the Chi-Ethical Wall protocol. As for speaking now, tell them the truth: I'm in a meeting with a client and I'm not at liberty to discuss it with them. They may speak to Minos if they need advice. Loop him in as necessary to maintain the wall."

"Yes, sir." And like that she's gone. Hades gets up from his chair, and Ms. Farry closes up her steno pad.

"It appears we haven't much time. Sharon, come along with us to help with our inventory. Mr. Blackwarren, I am afraid that you will not be able to 'liberate' anything, you are there to validate and authenticate items pertaining to your culture *only*. Is that understood?"

I nod a few times, but let's be honest, buddy, this is more of a job for Vincenzo, he's the one who knows what's good and what's not. This is the Royal Vault, and I'm gettin' a private stroll through it. A Vault full of riches from generations of Fae nobility, carried here from the Old Countries when we all fled. Centuries, fuck, *millennia* of wealth and art and culture and artifacts and plenty of shiny shit that could fit in a pocket.

If only this was the time to steal some shit. Fuck me.

33

It's a good thing my right hand's made of Faesteel, Tinkerglass, and Goblin engineerin', 'cause it's been slapped so many fuckin' times I'd probably have busted fingers too if they were still flesh. Obviously, the entire vault is a siren song to a thief like me, and bein' from a clan of thieves means ya just got a feel for what's worth takin'.

Thing is, *everythin' is worth takin'*.

"Mr. Blackwarren? Mr. Blackwarren!" I shake myself outta it for a second. He's pointin' at a carved piece of statuary, wood, but beautifully carved, detailed, natural flourishes, bloody sap crystallized, human skull encased in amber. "This?"

"Hm?" I look at it longer. "Uh, that ain't Goblin. That's Spriggan. They really hate humans, at least the ones over in Europe did. Don't see many here. The bound plates of metal, though? Those look like schematics, Gremlin runes, so they're pretty old." If I didn't catch that one then Cenzo would make sure I suffered for it.

We been at it for maybe five minutes. A few seconds on each shelf, display, rack, plinth, pedestal, whatever. I ain't s'posed to touch anythin'. We're clearly in a hurry, y'know? We're avoidin' the stuff that's obviously for Sidhe and Trolls and Dwarves and Brownies. Y'know what? I'll just say it, I'm gettin' stopped in front of stuff that looks more... savage? Anythin' that would be closer to "classic" Goblin work has likely been claimed as done by Dwarves, Knockers, maybe Sluagh, and decreed as such by the Sidhe.

Hades will have a better list once Cen's provenance is sorted through (writings, records, art, legendry), that's actual proof it's ours. I'm here to look for shit that's Goblin, but also is connected to stealing human souls and the like. Shadow Cultist stuff, pretty much. I ain't gone too much into them, 'cause there ain't too much to know, but obviously, it's got to do with the Shadow.

Might as well give ya my take on it. Fae are all about bein' made of dreams, I think I said? Dreams are the stuff ya make wonder and beauty and glory and all the parts of the human experience that ya reach for, but can't quite grasp. That's where Fae live, with it all in the palm of their hand.

Imagine goin' to sleep, and yer at a restaurant, and it's servin' the best food, best drink, and ya remember lovin' it so much, and ya wake up and ya can't quite place what the taste was. Fer Fae, 'specially Sidhe, not only do they remember, they don't gotta eat. And, they can take a fuckin' to-go bag with 'em back into the wakin' world to have later.

Goblins... can't do that. We're almost as fucked as humans are if they eat dreamfood, in that they ain't gonna be sated by anythin' else from then on, and then starve to death. Fer Gobs, at least, it just kills our sense of taste fer like... a month.

Now fer every dream, there's its dark mirror, and ya know what they're called: Nightmares. Fear, hate, fear, isolation, fear, pain... Ya get the idea. Fae can "ride" that Nightmare, and that's when they get fuckin' scary. That's when a Troll is the type to grind yer bones to make his bread, a Dwarf forges weapons fer maximum pain, Sluagh summon shit from depths that ain't s'posed to be called, Phouka become the Wild Hunt, and all of it leaves a Fae open to surrenderin' to that power, and becomin', well, a fuckin' demon.

Goblins just get pissed off, or the quiet kinda angry, and lives just turn into cold fuckin' calculus. We don't ride it, we're too human, which can make us more frightenin' if ya think about it.

And between the Dream and the Nightmare? Ya guessed it: The Shadow. Ain't the realm of demons or heroes, sinners or saints, just darkness with the light hidin' behind, where all yer darker impulses live, the part of ya that ya hide from the world, the part that's you and only you. Or, the old chestnut I still subscribe to, "character is what you are in the dark." The Dream gives ya strength ya need, the Nightmare offers strength ya want, and the Shadow just gives what was already there.

I'm familiar with it. For all my proclaimin' I don't kill people, I still impaled a Redcap to save my own ass. But, that's the Shadow.

Redcaps are best with it, but all of us can use it, we just don't wanna. It's connected to darker times, y'know? Still, it's power, and power possessed by the lowest rung of Fae society that the highest echelons *don't* have. Even the Mystics, the Sidhe with little knacks and tricks, can't do the shit we can do. Why? We're Goblins, and what they hate us most for? Bein' closer to human? Means we're closer to doin' magic that they'll never get.

And ya think Fae Royalty likes the idea of an oppressed minority havin' access to power like *that* and not sharin'? So, some of 'em try to figure it out, and fail spectacularly. If Prince Hadryn is one of 'em, there's a good reason why he's able to make it work: Privilege.

I ain't goin' all Social Justice Goblin on ya, it's just the truth. He's rich, with influence, access to resources, and the blood-given impunity to do it all with a fuckin' smile. Add in that he took Shadow's Edge, well, I don't know what the endgame is, but if it needs a steady diet of blood, he's probably got a pool of eager donors.

I been scannin' the room fer it, too. I could point it out and get it back, but I don't... what's the word I'm lookin' for... It don't *feel* like it's here? Have a magical artifact on yer arm fer a few months and yer bound to get a sense of it. 'Specially if it's been leechin' off ya. Y'know, I think I might stick with the Shear.

Still, don't want one of the five magical blades in the City to end up in Sidhe hands. I mean, they already got two of 'em, and one of 'em belongs to the Lightnin' Rod, if staves count. Don't hurt to ask.

"Sir? Y'know if they got a magical artifact? Probably put in here by the Prince, a blade called Shadow's Edge? It's a, uh... metamorphic blade? Changes to what the wielder wants? Feeds on blood? It's a family heirloom, so I'd really like to get it back from him." I hold up my right hand. "It probably ate my old hand after he had it cut off me."

"Can it be used to harvest souls?" Hades asks. Ms. Farry is payin' attention, steno pad at the ready.

"I... don't know. I only used it as a grapplin' hook launcher, shoot tranq darts at people..." I shrug. "Maybe? Don't know how ya'd do it, 'sides killin' someone with it. There's talk 'bout how it holds the souls of everyone who used it, or killed with it? It drinks blood, that's all I know. It's one of the magical blades of the City, too."

"Sir? Minos can't hold them much longer. The Prince is insistent that he fetch something from the Vault for Samhain."

"Did he say what?" Both Hades and I get that out together.

"A tome." She answers him, not me.

"Where is it?" I ask kinda fast, 'cause we're in a hurry, and I got a bad feelin', buddy. I don't know and kinda know. Maybe it clicked somethin' with Ganimard in my head. It's probably urgent. When she don't answer, I look to the god. "C'mon, that might be what yer lookin' for."

"Then we leave. Immediately." I nod quickly, and he walks off, with me followin', Ms. Farry in tow. So, of course, I get a look at the crown jewels as we're goin' by. Just. Fuckin'. Sittin'. There. And they're callin' to me, buddy. I doubt anyone'd notice if I got a little sticky fing-

No. No. No. C'mon, Blackwarren! Focus up!

We're into art, mostly, paintings, sculpture, all probably from older worlds. If ya were ever curious of what the landscapes of the World of Emerald Rivers looked like, looks like the Queen's got four of 'em. A few thick tomes, bound in woods or skins that like the rest of all of this, probably don't exist anymore. I'd guess grimories of Keth, maybe Sluagh, maybe some artifacts of past Sorcerer Kings and Queens.

Upon a plinth, though, I think I see what I had that feelin' about, buddy. It's a tome, but not like any book I ever seen. A book don't have gears, or sprockets, or levers, or dials. It's made of metal, glass, alloys, work so intricate, everythin' workin' together in concert, and fer what I got no idea, but I got the feelin' it ain't fer decoration.

Some wood, too, inlay, filigree, and fuckin' *shutters* blockin' the view of the pages. It's locked up, and I don't quite see a keyhole or anythin' to crack it. If the Prince wants this so bad, how's he plannin' on openin' exact-

Oh, fuck me. Shadow's Edge. It can pop any lock, 'cause I taught it how to do that after givin' it a pint of blood. And now he's got it. And he's plannin' to use this book for... What? What's it gotta do with Bridget's last symphony? Or the souls of artisitic women? Or...

I'm bein' pushed away from it.

"Mr. Summersword, I'm over here." Hades is the one talkin', but Ms. Farry shoots me a look that says "hide". I'll do ya one better, lady.

I run through my cloakin' charm...? Fuck, my throat hurts! Did I speak Ganimard's old-ass language again? Maybe he was helpin' out. I was helpin' me out? Who gives a fuck, I'm pretty sure I just vanished into shadow under a ceilin' of fuckin' LEDs. I know that Hades felt that, but to his credit, he don't miss a beat. "This is the tome you were speaking of?"

"I know where it is, I don't require *your* guidance." The Prince is in formal attire, saber at his side, a deep red cloak with the royal crest upon it, lined with the skin of a white dragon. You can tell because the dragon's head is coverin' his shoulder, but I'm *certain* he killed and skinned it before the ban on dragonhunting. Definitely. The saber's got a hilt that... fuck. Yeah, that's a unicorn's horn. I thought they were hunted to extinction, but fuckin' rich people, I guess. And on his right hand as a gauntlet, Shadow's Edge, same shape it had when it was removed from me forcefully.

"Mr. Summersword-"

"Your *Highness*," he practically hisses back at, again, the god of the underworld, and managing partner of the firm, *and* the owner of the buildin'.

"If you are planning to take this item with you, I need you to sign it out. This is your mother's vault, and her contract stipulates that any items contained therein must catalog any removals, and provide written documentation of her express permission to remove the object in question." Hades stands firm, but I'd be shocked if he knuckled. This draws The Prince closer and...

Rhys is with him.

I ain't seen him since that day, and I gotta say, I'm lookin' better than he is. His shoulders are heavy, eyes weary, but still vigilant. He sniffs the air a few times, his eyes openin' wider a second 'fore he corrects.

He knows I'm here. Even if I'm practically invisible, I've been here a few minutes. I didn't leave a "stink" or anythin', we don't fuckin' reek as I've told ya, buddy, but I still been here. Do I try to free him now? How? Unless I ice the Prince of the Fae, in front of a god and his ferrywoman, I don't see any way to.

"It is *our* vault." He steps closer to Hades, and I see Ms. Farry tense a little, ready to defend. "And might I add the exorbitant expense you demand? That we have fulfilled without fault?"

"And that is appreciated, but it is in *her* name." I gotta learn how to look that unfazed and sound *that* unimpressed. "To simply forgo such express guidelines for your benefit could be taken by an *outside observer* as prologue to *coup d'etat*." I heard him hittin' those words for *my* benefit. "And, Mr. Summersword, you certainly don't want that sort of implication... Do you?"

Then the god of the underworld lights a cigarette, taking a puff, and exhaling the plume of smoke in the Prince's direction, awaiting a response that currently is only growin' frustration. Sorry, but yer authority don't mean shit to a god, ya dick.

It takes a moment to compose himself, but the Prince takes a breath, and says, grandly, "The Samhain ritual requires my attention, so I shall have my mother send your *paperwork*." He looks sternly at Rhys. "Fetch it on my word, and bring it before sundown, or you'll suffer the same fate as your *detective*."

"Yes, sir." The Goblin looks down at the floor, and his chin is yanked up, meeting the Prince's eyes.

"Say it *properly*."

"Is this necessary, Mr. Summersword?" Hades, still unimpressed, but more by the Sidhe's character than anythin' else.

"This is *my* servant and you possess no right or authority to direct me how my property will behave, death god." His attention returns to his "servant". "No more wasting of everyone's time. *Say it*."

Rhys grits his teeth, his hand wantin' to clutch his chest. "As... As you wish and command." A rough pinch of his ears, the Gremlin almost screamin' in agony, and I almost go after him. Rhys looks at the Prince with suppressed rage in his eyes. *"Master."*

When did the bow put itself back together? When did I nock an arrow and draw it? Centered on the Prince's head. No. No, I'm not shootin' him. I don't kill people, though I *really* wanna right now. My eyes are burning, like I'm trying to stare a hole through his face.

No. Calm down, Blackwarren. Ya just got even more reason to free Rhys, and take that fucker down. I blink a few times, but I can tell Rhys clocked me, the two of 'em walkin' out. When the vault door closes behind 'em, I unclench, and the shroudin' fades off. I'm holdin' the Shear, all assembled, and I ain't got no idea how. I at least relax the draw, as Hades is practically stompin' over to me. The bow is already disassembling, takin' the appearance of shoulder armor or pauldrons or whatever they call 'em, on each shoulder.

"What, Mr. Blackwarren, were you expecting to do? Was this your intent? To assassinate a Sidhe prince on *my* property?"

"What? No! He was just really pissin' me off and suddenly the bow was in my hand. I didn't do it, if that means anything. At least we know what book he's lookin' to pick up, right? Any way to slow him down?"

The god takes another puff of smoke, and breathes it at me. "Do not think that we are partners in this matter, Mr. Blackwarren. You are a means to an end that might lead to extended interest. Nothing more. As for your suit, I will direct my staff to direct correspondence regarding the matter to the one you represent...?" He glances to Ms. Farry.

"Vincenzo Giansiracusa, Sir. He's already paid your retainer, but he has to 'liquidate some Thundercoin' for the full fee, which needs to be done before the markets close. He's estimating he'll be able to cover six hundred combined billable hours after the sale." He looks to her. "Yes, Sir. It will be sold for stable currency."

"Excellent." Hades directs his attention to me, finishing his cigarette. "I suggest you get a move on, Mr. Blackwarren. I expect his highness back within the hour, what with sundown only two hours away."

I exhale. I mean, I don't know what I was expectin'. "Wish me luck, at least?"

He thinks a moment. "May fortune lead you to your earned and deserved end." A second passes. "I'll add it to your bill. Good evening, Mr. Blackwarren." And then that fuckin' million dollar smile. Dick.

I gotta go, though, but I got no fuckin' idea what to do now, other than knowin' it's gettin' more urgent. I could just hand over the drive, but I gone over why that ain't the smartest move. I don't drag my feet or anythin', and Ms. Farry is followin' me, watchin' like a hawk to make sure I don't help myself to anythin'.

Fuck, did that fancyfuck asshole litter in here? Wad of paper, like a wrapper on the floor. As much as I wanna just leave it there, I pick it up, 'cause I don't hate Queen Alana (may her warmth bless us all). The Ferrywoman don't stop me, so now I just gotta find a place to recycle it. What kinda candy was the prick eatin', anyway-

I unroll it. Writin', small, but I can read it.

Kyo,

93 s.side ph

Sebas
93 Shoreside Drive. Penthouse.
I got the message, Rhys. I'm comin' to bring ya home.

34

Allora is where the rich people live. Shoreside, down in Grunstadt, on Destry Bay, lookin' out far enough to find the Atlantic, is where the megarich live. Ya might wonder how Fae got that much money, but these are people who came over to America with their own riches already with 'em, and had countless ways to get more. For Fae livin' in Shoreside, it's almost entirely Sidhe nobility, a Dwarf or two, and a Phouka from a one percenter family.

And he lives in one of the *smaller* buildings. In a duplex.

The buildin' I'm lookin' at now? One of a line of six residential buildings ya'd think were five-star hotels. And there is one of those further down the Drive. The tallest is forty-five floors, the residence of the Queen Herself takin' up the top five of 'em. It's built from plans pulled from the dreams of the most inspired architects, followed by Dwarves, appointed with its amenities by Knockers, and staffed by the closest thing there is to highborn amongst the Brownies. The upper echelon of Fae nobility lives in that building.

This one, though, belongs to Prince Hadryn. The penthouse is the top three floors, the level below it kept vacant to keep him isolated from the hoi polloi. It's not as tall as its neighbor, or as impressive. It's like the less attractive parts of the 1980s made a building. It's all flash, corporate art, and any real creations are in the Prince's private galleries, away from anyone who could actually appreciate them.

Always been his thing, really, tryin' to push his way into the art communities by buyin' the most expensive pieces, and his own work, which, I gotta admit, is actually pretty damned good. Always changin' styles, methods, mediums, pushin' the envelope from one piece and payin' the most respectful homage and remix of classical schools. I know this because I paid a guy to walk through with a headcamera that athletes use. Can't beat that UHD, y'know?

I did have to pay his bill at the clinic, though, after security "escorted" him out.

I don't know if Rhys is here, but he wanted me to go. I figure if the Prince has got anythin', it's at the top of this forty floor buildin'. The sun ain't settin', but it's gonna happen, and it'll probably be a good one out here on the Bay. Security fer all of the buildings is out, keepin' an eye on any trick or treaters or would-be pranksters. Or just protesters wantin' to throw shit at super rich people. I'd probably be out here with Vincenzo doin' that if I weren't tryin' to save a life and solve a crime.

Now that I don't gotta worry 'bout someone stayin' my hand... How far am I willin' to go?

Hell, what's the real reason I'm doin' this? I wanna get justice fer Bridget, but I wasn't asked fer that, I was asked to retrieve her symphony for her parents, and I might end up givin' the original drive to the guy who's the reason she's dead. I wanna find peace for the women that Hadryn either killed or had a definite hand in, but they're sight unseen save what I found from researching 'em. I don't know 'em from nothin', they're just women Shiko told me about, and I could just drop a dime on the bastard and let the Kitsune take care of it. But I'm here 'cause I want it to be me.

And why is that? I could act like I don't know, buddy, but we'd both know that's a lie. This is all 'cause of Rhys. We ain't spent the kinda time that would normally inspire a thief who just got out a relationshp to risk his life and standin' in society. It ain't like with Thom, that was lust and a crush past its sell-by date. I never wanted anythin' to do with Redcaps, and now I got cute nicknames with one. I never thought I could trust anyone after Thom, but I'm goin' off a message written on a candy wrapper by a guy who put me in handcuffs and turned out to be the one who killed Bridget O'Hare. And then he cut off my hand on the orders of Prince Hadryn.

And still, my first instinct is to bring him home.

I never felt like this 'bout anyone, is what I'm sayin', I want ya to know that. Despite all the lies and ribbin' and jokes and smartassery, buddy, I want ya to take that to heart. Take it for truth, he's somethin' to me. I don't know if he's a *partner*, or, y'know, a partner, but we ain't ever gonna find out if he ain't free, and I ain't lookin' over my shoulder. 'Sides, he gotta be free if he's gonna make that decision fer himself. Who knows, he might say thanks and then that'll be it fer us, and I'll probably cry for a week or two, but at least I'd know.

What I'm sayin', is that in the *good* romances, both leads walk into it with open eyes and full agency. Anythin' less drags ya into problematic territory. So if I'm gonna commit to chasin' an HEA or HFN, I gotta go in with my whole heart. It's okay, though, buddy. Romances gotta have happy endings, I just gotta make the best one possible fer me and him, right? Simple.

And step one is pullin' the biggest fuckin' heist of my life.

I ain't goin' in alone, though. I ain't stupid.

Cen, need help, gdnce 4 93 s.side, rte 2 PH, plz ++urg

Takes a few minutes, but I see the "..." appear.

no n, got u in2 vault, ur on ur own

cen bggn u plz, got u rep frm A&prtnrs to get history bak frm Ryls

u used me n

ur pyin w/ my $$$ Prnc has clkwrk book

?!

is @93 s.side PH wnt me go stl it?

fk u & call

So it's a matter of poppin' in my Bluetooth, and makin' the call, and tryin' to work out the jitters.

"You are fuckin' crazy, Nick." I'm already hearin' fingers on keys. "Yer askin' me to ask Irene to take on Knocker security. You fuck this up? We gotta pull up stakes and run."

"Thank you, Irene, I know Vincenzo taught you well." I know I'm talkin' to a fuckin' computer and it don't hear me or nothin'. Or maybe it does, I ain't a computer guy. "'Sides, ain't ya the one always tellin' me that Knocker walls ain't shit? And this ain't the *Queen's* buildin'."

"You bring that book back, or ya don't come back at all, ya got me?"

"What the fuck even is it?" I'm creepin', stayin' outta sight, but ready to move once Cen finds me an entrance. Keepin' my voice down, too. "All I saw was a book with the covers made of clockwork, wood, glass, metals and alloys I ain't ever seen before. Couldn't even see what the pages were, they were covered up by shutters."

"Nick, that thing is the reason the Goblins fled to America. All of 'em. We smuggled it over, tried to hide it, and subsequently some fancyfuck Sidhe ordered one of us to hand it over, the fucker. I'm checkin' the doors, runnin' passive scans, findin' a weak spot."

"Ya still ain't said what the damned thing is, Cen." A couple of people walk by where I'm hidin' in the bushes. Funny thing? I could sit out on a bench and humans would see me how I really am, only tonight they'd be okay with it 'cause I probably had a shit ton to spend on my "costume". Yeah, I fuckin' cleaned up trick-or-treating as a kid. Brought home over twenty pounds of candy one year.

Fine, it was fuckin' last year.

"The *Magus Ex Machina Umbra*. The Latin should tell ya how old it is. Everythin' that uses the Shadow? It's in there. Fer Gremlins, Tinkers, and Redcaps. Closest thing we got to a fuckin' spellbook, Nick. It belongs to us, even if it can't be opened up, it's *ours*." That just clicked into place.

"Uh, Cen, would there be shit in there about pullin' souls outta bodies? Or killin' people without a trace?"

"Fuck if I know, Nick. It ain't been opened in centuries and we ain't got no idea how to do it. Dark shit in there is all I know. Yer sure it's in there?" There's some apprehension there, and I get why. This ain't some typical Macguffin bullshit, this is something that could seriously shift balances in the hands of a domineerin' abusive racist fuckface who'd sooner kill somebody than hear 'em say the word "no" to him.

"I saw it in the vault at Victory, he was havin' it sent here for the Samhain ritual. He's still havin' it here, right? Ain't gonna do it in Tolon Park or Elmwood where it'd make more sense?" I mean, I think I *heard* that it's here?

"Looks like, yeah. I guess they can do it anywhere. Ya got wards on ya? Ya know what it'll be like tonight." Wall between worlds is thin, so angry spirits, stuff crawlin' out the darkness, and a bunch of Fae who don't need much encouragement to ride the Nightmare. "I got ya pinged, I can track ya. Sendin' Irene after floor schematics. Gimme a minute, I'm pullin' in some brothers to help soften up the defenses, show those Knocker fucks how slick we slip a firewall."

Gives me time to ward up, at least. This is why it's good to have a team help ya, they got yer back and remind ya of the shit ya were s'posed to do.

"My soul is a fortress never breached, my body forever beyond your reach."

Ow. As in *ow, my fuckin' throat's burnin'*. Also, I... did say that?

'Dammit,' I think as harshly as I can at him. 'Ganimard, warn me 'fore ya do that!'

"Nick! Nick! Nick? Nick, come back. Ya read me? Shit, anybody got him?" Cen sounds a little *too* freaked out to be fakin' it.

"Fuck, stop yellin', I'm trying to stay quiet." I ain't just been sittin' here, ya know. I been watchin' the guards, countin' 'em by haircuts, timin' the patrols. It's a basic snoop n' case, but it's better than nothin'.

"Nick? Ya ain't anywhere on my trackin'. You doin' that Shadow shit?"

"Uh, yeah? 'Course I am..." I push some of the bushes aside to get a better look and... Fuck, my arm's translucent, ghostly, half-invisible. Hand ain't passin' through shit, but *fuck* a shroud's never been this good before.

Breathe, Blackwarren. This ain't the time to panic.

"Ya got a way in fer me? I'm clockin' a gap in the patrol on the northwest corner in about... two minutes, give or take ten seconds, gap for twenty-five conservative, thirty-five generous. Patrols are pairs, 'bout four. Looks like Dwarf and Troll fer three of 'em, last pair's Sidhe, probably the officer-types. What's the wind like tonight?"

"If yer where ya were before? Uh..." Some more quick taps and clicks. "Downwind."

"After the Sidhe, then. Gives me another minute. Whatcha got fer me, Cen?" I take another breath. We're on the clock, yeah, but impatience is what gets us all taken in.

"Northwest corner? Time it right and we can give ya a service entrance. We almost got cameras, good thing I brought everyone in." What's assurin' is how *calm* he sounds. Professional. "Got motion detectors headin' toward it, though. Clocked 'em?"

Takes some maneuverin', but yeah. "Lookin' right at the route, I don't see a way without bustin' 'em and flaggin' alarms."

"It'll take us a while to get those, Nick. Any ideas?"

Think, think, think. Calm down. What tools ya got, Blackwarren? I got the Shear, which I know can make portals, but no idea how that's gonna help me with motion sensors lookin' down at a service lot. If I shoot one, it'd break. I think.

Wait, I shoot one, maybe it's in a portal. If I shoot another portal away from where it's lookin', then *maybe* the sensor's lookin' at another part of the lot and no one's the wiser. Gotta act fast though, that gap's comin' up.

The Shear is already in my right hand. Guess the bow can read my instincts or thoughts or intent or some shit. I ain't complainin'. The grip fits my prosthetic pretty well, my left hand drawin' a shadowy arrow back, the sight in line. Probably good this is a left-handed bow, I guess. I aim at the wall facin' me, and fire.

The portal to darkness is there, waitin', as I draw again, centering the sight on the motion sensor. "Mama Tinker, guide the shot, make it true." I loose. The arrow of darkness whistles softly through the air, just before the two Sidhe reach the corner to move from the north side of the building to the west. No reaction from either.

"Fingers crossed, Nick. Wait. Wait... Go." On Cen's signal I move as quickly as I can, which ain't as fast as it could be since I got a fuckin' bum leg now. I'm countin' in my head to twenty-five, gettin' closer to the limit the closer I get to the service door.

"Tell me it's open, I can't slow down."

"Unlocked in three... two... Get in!" I can see the little red light go to green just as I reach the service entrance marked with "EMPLOYEES ONLY". "There's a supply closet on yer left. Pick it, ya got fifteen seconds."

My picks are already in my hands, the Shear back in its pauldron position. It's more awkward, the prosthetic ain't pickin' up feedback with the tension wrench too well, and I ain't great at doin' it left-handed. Don't worry, though. I'm a fuckin' thief, and Mom made me practice all kinds of lockpickin' scenarios, like this one. (right hand in heavy glove, left hand havin' been in a bucket of ice water for two minutes, and fifteen seconds to pop a lockbox with three Ghiradelli chocolate bars inside.)

That bein' said, I get through that door by the skin of my ass. Door closed softly, carefully. Lock reset. Keep yer breathin' quiet. Count to thirty in yer head. Wait fer Cen to give the all-clear.

where now, I text.

"Checkin' the hallways. We got an idea how to get ya up to the penthouse, but we gotta confirm it first. Ain't no cameras, but we got footage of the Prince headin' up there, and a Goblin carryin' a briefcase about fifteen minutes after him. Money's on the briefcase, but we're keepin' an eye out in case it's a decoy. How 'bout you, Nick? Still feelin' good?"

ok 2 go. rte?

Fuck, I almost believe that, myself.

Shit, 'course the charm faded. It's stronger, but it's takin' more outta me, but at least it ain't takin' blood. Yeah, when I take Shadow's Edge back, I'm handin' it over to Damon, let him stash it somewhere for another Redcap, or leave it in the Shadow until it's actually needed.

"A'right. We got the cameras. Here's the plan: exit to yer left on my signal. Twenty feet down the hall, left at the intersection, there's a ceilin' cam we can loop fer ten seconds, should give ya the gap to get down the hall to ma-"

Static. Did the call drop? Nah, that ain't it, a call just goes dead if it's dropped, wouldn't be no static, but...

I yank the Bluetooth out my ear fast as I can, and just in time, as it starts squealin' at a high pitch that humans can't hear, but Goblins can. My thumb's mufflin' the sound, but I can tell my ears would be shot if I hadn't gotten it out.

"...this...guest...here" Voice comin' out, I hold it close to my ear. "I know you're there. I can hear you breathing." A voice that high-pitched shouldn't sound so damned sinister. Actually, scratch that, I'm rememberin' the nightmare fuel that passed for childrens' entertainment growin' up. "You can't hide from me, sewer rat."

It's feminine, but I know that vocal tone and delivery.

It's a fuckin' Knocker.

Take stock of what ya got, Blackwarren. Janitor's closet, cleanin' implements and tools, floor waxer... Floor map on the wall.

I put the headset back in. "Now that's uncalled for. I ain't called ya wingnut, have I? How ya know I ain't an ambitious twelve-year-old tryin to beg fer candy? I mean, I seen this place. Would be a pretty good haul. You got the bag of 500 Kit-Kats in yer office? Ya do sound like ya got a member card at CostCo." There, then there, then there, then there...

"I've warded the building against Gremlin methods. But, for the new year, I'll let you run along home to your sewer if you come out now." Ya don't gotta be an expert in communication to know she ain't plannin' to do any such thing. She won't hurt me, but the Guard stationed here most certainly will.

"Aw, this mean ya ain't takin' me fer brunch? I mean I wouldn't mind hashin' this out over some mimosas." One part this bottle... two parts that bottle... Yes, they got the tablets I need. The water bucket on wheels is half full of dirty water, but that works out. If this stuff ain't diluted it'll have a much different effect than intended.

What? 'Course I know this shit, I read whatever I get my hands on and I was good in science in high school. Ya think I only got the scholarship offer 'cause I could throw a Kovacs? "Shouldn't I know the name of the lady who's puttin' me in my place?"

"...you first." She ain't apprehensive, buddy. She's typin' and clickin'. Trust me, if my phone wasn't built by my cousin, she'dve had me tossed out a'ready.

"Ven, swear to Bowie." What? It's a shortened form of Venefici. "And you?" Little more water, mix is too dark, it'll pop too much.

"Rose." She *hmphs*, pleased with herself. "You're barely past the front door, aren't you?"

Showtime, I guess. "Listen, I could tell ya somethin' completely unexpected, like the truth, but yer a Knocker, and I'm a Goblin breakin' into yer buildin'. I wouldn't trust a word I said, but here it is anyway: find a new job, another patron, 'cause your boss is a murderer who's killed over a dozen human women. Right now, yer aidin' and abettin' a fuckin' serial killer. Ya didn't know? No beef, ya walk out clean. And if ya *did* know, and ya ain't done *shit* to stop it?"

I open the door, and drop the tablets into the bucket, and push it rollin' down the hall. It don't take long fer the *BANG* and plume of smoke and fumes.

"Then, after I'm done? I'm comin' fer *you*." I know it'll rattle her, but it'll throw her off. If ya think someone's comin' to kill ya, yer gonna go into panic-mode if yer just a chair jockey. I say the

next in Sigil, in the jagged dialect of the Redcaps. *"Because the night is young, my cap is dry, and my blade is hungry."*

Then I turn off the phone and take off into the smoke. I'm blowin' my cover, but I ain't got time for hide and seek if she already knows that I'm here. I ain't gonna hurt her or kill her, or even go lookin' fer her, 'cause I don't kill people, and I ain't gonna kill a Knocker just 'cause she's doin' her job. I'll still scare the piss outta her if it throws a little chaos into the buildin'.

That smokescreen ain't gonna last too long, but it only needs to fer a minute. I checked the map fer a reason, y'know? The stretch of hallway to the first point? I gotta go as fast as I can manage, and I know I ain't got the speed to reach before the sound of approachin' voices reaches me. I can make it to a door, though, and pick it in time to slip into the room before the Guard comes rushin' down the hall.

This room? Shelves and shelves of bottles, empty vases, fresh linens, garment bags, tables in the center kept spotless. Access door to the laundry. Supply room for housekeepin', plenty of workable chemicals, but I ain't here to make bombs. They know a Goblin's in here, and some research on the Net before I started revealed a couple things about the services for residents: free WiFi, and housekeepin' with bespoke scents formulated expressly for the buildin'. It ain't a hotel, not really, more long-term excutive suites (read: visiting dignitaries), but the scent is easy to pick up. Mix of lilac and vanilla and a touch of cinnamon, pleasing and relaxing and a little fun.

It's an aroma that'll cover up my own, and won't be out of place. If they're lookin' for a Goblin, don't smell like a Goblin. Also? This room got a phone.

It's like any other business phone (dial nine to get out), and unsecure as fuck, but if that Knocker can bulldoze her way into Cen's phone call? No chances. I look to the clock on the wall, dial, and when it's picked up, I start countin'. This ain't a trace thing, it's a 'they'll know where ya are' thing.

"I believe you have the wrong number." Yep, that's Vincenzo's "white voice", he based it off some voice actor he admired.

"Y'sure? I'm askin' about the thing."

"What thing?" White voice dropped.

"The *thing*. Ya think I'm talkin' about the other thing? What sorta guy does that?" Things have changed. Old plan's off. I'm blown but I gotta press on.

"What about the thing that guy did that one time?" New plan. High risk, quick and dirty.

I chew my lip, countin' the seconds.

"Talkin' about that time or the other time? 'Cause the other time had the place I don't like." Are you talking about when I broke into the bank vault?

"Yeah, we got lunch afterward." Yes, I am.

"I got sick off that shit." You know I hate doing that.

"Got a new cook." You have to do this without me. "But I heard from that one guy he's pretty good." I know you can do it.

"Maybe I'll try it out." Okay, but I ain't happy. "They got curbside pickup now. Take care of you, Cousin." Outta time. Gotta move, but at least I can get started here.

"Take care of you." And then he hangs up.

I take a deep breath, smellin' the signature scent all over me, and pick the lock to the laundry room. It's loud, a few full carts with dirtied linens, but what I'm lookin' for is just above one that's half-full. The laundry chute. Not a lot of buildings have 'em, 'specially not ones this size, but it'll go up two or three or four floors, and get me away from the floor where everyone's lookin'. Plus, ain't nobody puttin' a camera or alarm in a damned laundry chute.

Now, ya might think it's a tight fit and a dumb idea, and yer half right. It's tight, but when ya freak the fuck outta the Knocker who's advisin' security... Y'know, I should send her a fruit basket or somethin', that was pretty shitty of me.

And there they are: alarms, advisories for residents to stay within their residences and quarters. Ya know what ain't done when a buildin' is goin' on lockdown? Housekeepin', laundry, and the disposal of laundry down chutes. That bein' said, like the bank, I'm stuck in a fuckin' vent again, this time climbin' up with a leg that can't support my weight as I'm climbin', and a prosthetic hand that don't have the traction my left does.

It's also dark as fuck, and I gotta be quiet because too much rattlin' will draw attention. Breathe. Just breathe, Blackwarren, one foot and palm at a time. I gotta think about somethin' other than how it's cramped like a fuckin' coffin. How about... Run through song lyrics in my head? So, of course, my brain first goes with "Work Bitch". Have I mentioned how much I hate fuckin' vents?

35

Skippin' ahead a little 'cause ya don't really wanna hear about the five minutes of me stavin' off a fuckin' panic attack and worryin' I'm developin' claustrophobia. Even *"Disturbia"* didn't help with that.

I reach the third floor, since the second was locked. (Who fuckin's locks a *laundry chute*?!) I have to go by feel, since it's too tight a fit to get my phone out, and my right fingers find the panel that'll slide up. The pads on the tips slow a bit, the hatch dented in, like someone was either pissed off, or tryin' to cram too much down the chute. The damage does me a favor, the latch for the lock ain't aligned, so some effort gets the panel slidin' up.

I ain't gonna just open all the way, I don't know what's out there. I can lift enough to peek, though. Alarm lights are on, emergency red, repeatin' message how everyone's s'posed to stay in their rooms. Don't see or hear or smell anythin' comin' my way. I inch down to get a better look at the ceilin' both ways, and I see 'em. Cameras.

Well, the shroud charm got me through before, why not again? I close my eyes, envision the words in my head, the ones from the old ways, old worlds. I only know it ain't Sigil. Sigil was called Lorus before, and probably somethin' else before that. Names are power, y'know, that's 101, so the older names probably got more power, and stronger magic. I just gotta make any of this make *some* kinda sense, 'kay buddy?

Okay, gotta think of all this at once. Pa taught me the charm, but only after I reached him without him knowin', so I wouldn't treat it like a crutch. The first time I used it... Mom and Pa were fightin' 'bout how he was takin' jobs, and I went through the words so I could hide from how mad they both were. I think of how I need to move like Shadow, vanish into it, border 'tween light and dark, here but ain't. It's like I'm singin' the Shadowsong, but am the Shadowsong, but listenin' to me singin' it to.

Fuck, these charms were the fuckin' shit back durin' the Uprising, seems like.

Just wish it wasn't so rough on my throat.

Weird. Alarms stopped. They give up?

When I push the hatch open and crawl out and then get a bitch of a charley-horse, the emergency red lights are all that's on. Lights are off, fans are off, elevators ain't movin'... My arm's lookin' translucent, but with it this dark I might as well be transparent. The power's out, at least on this floor.

Did I do that? I made the whole lobby of the bank go dark, so it ain't too weird, but it's just darkness. It don't cut the power. Fuck, must be that Knocker, closin' me in. I didn't think she'd know I took the laundry chute, but I gotta tip my cap to her. Rose, right?

So all the doors on this floor? Electronic locks, the keycard kind, 'cause it's a residential floor. I'm penned in pretty good, even the stairs ain't accessible. (Fire hazard! I should write a fuckin' letter.) Elevators... Emergency power, probably to keep 'em in place in case anyone's trapped inside. The doors, though, with the aid of a Faesteel hand, I can open with a lot of effort, which opens into...

Fuck, the damned elevator's actually here. Ain't goin' nowhere, and I don't know when the power's comin' back, and there's a camera in there. Ya know the Knocker is probably runnin' through charms of her own to get everythin' back online. What I gotta do is go up. Wanna know what's a bitch? Wall jumpin' when ya only got one leg that'll do what ya need. Takes a few tries to get high enough to poke the ceilin' hatch open with the bow, and a lot of scrabblin' to pull myself upward.

Which, of course, is when the fuckin' power comes back on. My head's above the car, but I know my wiggly legs are on camera for a couple seconds before I pull 'em up. I get out my phone, and turn it on just to check the clock. I got twenty minutes to sundown-

"Nick Blackwarren." Oh fuck. Bluetooth reconnected.

"Hey, Rose, how's yer night goin'?" I'm assemblin' the bow. A portal won't work here, though. "Gonna let me know how ya know who I am? I know yer dyin' to tell me."

"Oh, you're *famous*, the thief who solved the murders. I have to thank you, Nick, truly." I hear the sound of her drinking somethin'.

"Sweetie, ya can't just leave me hangin' like that." For Shadow's Edge, I just asked it to be a grapplin' hook and then it drilled into my arm. How do I do it with the Shear?

"Well, *honey*, because of your rather human methods of breaking and bypassing our locks, we've all been contracted to design stronger ones. Better materials, better budgets for research and design, and more renown for who can beat the *infamous* Nick Blackwarren. Who is adamant that he doesn't kill people. Also, your website is quite cute."

Yeah, she's trollin'. "I don't even have a website. I'm plannin' to be strictly word-of-mouth, ya know? Though it's nice to hear I got a rep for zero body count."

"Oh, you have one *now*." Fuckin' Knockers...

'Inspector?' I think to myself. 'I need some help here!'

You just have to know what you need. See it in your mind, the words will come.

Okay, an arrow with a line attached, with an auto-ascender in the bow itself, maybe... No, can't be "maybe". Usin' the cams to work the pulleys, line made from, uh... *Gonmut hair*... No idea what the fuck that is, but I'll take Ganimard's word fer it. Good thing I muted for this, 'cause I don't want a Knocker hearin' me rattle off words and thinkin' I'm settin' explosives or somethin'.

"There are better thieves out there than me, y'know, better in the City, even. Gotta be plenty who've pissed off the rulin' class."

"But none that are so hated as you, Nick." I can tell she's smirkin'.

I sigh. "This is about me threatenin' to kill ya, ain't it?"

"Bingo. He's on the third floor, on top of elevator A3. Floor's locked down and that car isn't going anywhere." Another sip of her drink. "I win, Nick."

"Y'know, Rose, I can't help but think that if you and I had met under better circumstances?" I aim the bow up, hearin' boots stompin' closer.

"Tch, we would've been friends?" I pull back, the arrow nocked, a thread running to the center of the bow. Another sip of her drink.

"I still woulda pissed in yer pumpkin spice latte."

Loose.

I hear her spit, curse, yell at security to grab me and pin me down. The arrow races skyward, pullin' the line of dark thread with it, with no idea how long the spool is.

What I do know? It's Autumn, and that fuckin' pumpkin spice is everywhere. Wasn't even a lucky guess. Seriously, how would I know which coffee was hers, how would I get to it, and do it *any of that* without her knowin'?

I couldn't! But? Ya *really* think she was gonna risk it?

I also was smart enough to close the hatch before I fired. I ain't gonna make it easy fer 'em, after all.

The line goes taut, the bow being pulled upward, my hands on the grip, the cams spinnin' to reel me in. It ain't like with Shadow's Edge, which would yank me fast as fuck wherever the spike hit. This is a smoother rise. Not as fast, but still movin' quick, carryin' me up into the darkness of the elevator shaft, at least enough to maintain that shroud that is still active. I hope I don't get stuck like this.

Can't have her tracin' me, can't have her findin' the phone and gettin' Gremlin tech, and don't wanna explain to Cen why I had to bust another one of his toys. Hangin' by one hand ain't fun, but it's easier when ya weigh under a hundred pounds. Lets ya use yer right hand to get yer phone outta yer pocket, use the beautifully constructed, inlayed masterpiece of a Tinker craftsmanship that is yer hand (made by yer *mother*)... to crack and crush it until it is naught but a crumbled creation, cringeworthy and criminal to my core. To my credit, I don't cry, but lament the crossing of the creation into, put crudely, shit.

Alliteration helps me through tough moments sometimes, okay? Ya were expected me to end it different, weren't ya?

Now, I respect Rose, so I know she ain't dumb. If I ain't on top of the elevator car, where the Hell else would I go? 'Specically considerin' I was goin' off 'bout her boss? It ain't like there's only some security in the building and I got time before they reach the floor where the arrow hit. I expect her to have people waitin' fer me the moment I open those doors.

I gotta get up to the penthouse, both 'cause it's where I'm fuckin' goin', and 'cause there ain't no cameras up there. Also have to watch my use of charms. Higher I go, the more anti-Goblin measures are put in, y'know? The elevator goes up to the 30th floor. Any higher, ya need clearance, special cards, and a lot of it is tied to Fae nobility, since this is where the major dignitaries and players live and work for the sake of their Prince. Even money they'd all take his side in a coup.

What all this is preamble to, buddy, is that I gotta do what I don't wanna do. Again. I know I could do a shrouding charm and slip by the Guard, but it's not a certainty, and I'm already pushin' my luck enough seein' as I'm doin' this alone, and not even 'cause of stupid hero pride. I tried to do this with a team and I got cut off. I'm thinkin' I *do* need a partner, not just for the investigatin' and shit, but someone on site with me that I can trust.

I'm hopin' I found that guy, y'know? Just gotta rescue him.

Hate that this is reducin' him to a fuckin' adventure novel girlfriend, he deserves better. We both do. Hell, that whole damned trope does.

So, for him, for us, I'm gonna do what's needed. I hang by one hand, goin' through my tool pack, and pull out the powered screwdriver, and get to work on the grate in front of me, removin' all the screws but one, loosenin' it, pullin' the grate to swing open the gap and just after I release the line on the bow. I'm hangin' off the edge of the passage underneath the thirtieth floor, the bow reelin' in the last of the thread, and then disassemblin' to armor my torso and shoulders.

And then, now with both hands free, I crawl into the fuckin' vent.

I gotta army crawl, find a place where it's safe to come up, and obviously not make too much noise. This ain't climate control, pretty sure it's a crawlspace for maintenance, seein' as it ain't too cramped. Still, though, ain't helpin' my developin' claustrophobia. Upside is this is where wires are run, fixed, and connected. Ain't gonna start yankin' wires, though, that'll just tell Rose my location, 'cause I'm guessin' she'll know screwin' with power and shit can only be done from where I am.

Then again, she might not be this competent, but if she's workin' for fuckin' *royalty* then she's an expert until proven otherwise. And yeah, I get how Cenzo and my cousins get a rise from fuckin' with the Knockers, and likely same for them. They keep testin' each other to push the envelope a bit further.

Speakin' of which...

"Is he here?" There's Rose, but not through my Bluetooth. (I crushed that too.) She's above me, I can hear her through the air vent ahead (so the workers don't suffocate). "The elevators are locked down, but I don't put climbing past him."

"You believe a *sewer rat* can climb thirty floors in minutes?" Yeah... that's a Sidhe. "Return to your station, His Highness is preparing the ritual, and he shan't be delayed."

"Sir, I don't believe it's a Gremlin, I'm certain it's a-"

"Are you hard of hearing?"

"N-no, sir."

"Know who holds your leash, *turnspit*."

I hear the edge in her voice. "Right away, *sir*."

Both of them move outta earshot, so I press forward, hittin' an intersection that goes straight on, and to the left... Where I hear someone who sounds kinda pissed. Sounds like Rose. And if that's her office, she might have access to the upper floors...

I crawl faster, and if I *were* a Gremlin I'd be leavin' little toys hooked into every jack and port I passed along the way. Instead, I'm gettin' closer to the voice, and some light 'sides the workin' lights down here.

"That Redcap is plotting an assassination and I'm *dismissed*?" I hear her sit down, sounds of keys clackin'. "Who even cares about the damned Ritual? It's done at the Palace by the envoys, not the Prince wanting to debut a recording of his latest symphony. New year can come without a blueblood's say-so."

Fuck, we really mighta been friends in another life.

I'm to the grate, no locks. Just a matter of slidin' it back to open it. I hoist myself up, slow, quiet, move up behind her. One quick move, and my hand's over her mouth. "Shhhhhh."

And then a hard pointed force at my hand, which bounces off. I grab... a pair of scissors from her and toss it behind me, holdin' her in place. "Ya realize if that worked ya woulda stabbed yerself, too, yeah? I ain't gonna hurt ya, whether ya believe that or not, but we can do this one of two ways, okay?"

Yeah, that's a death glare.

"I'm goin' up to the roof, ya get me? And I'm either goin' up with yer help, or I'm applyin' pressure to yer carotid artery fer a bit to knock ya the fuck out, and drag ya to the handplate that elevator's got, and dump ya on the roof. Either way, I'm goin' up there, and I'm stoppin' Hadryn from killin' my partner. I'm gonna take my hand off yer mouth now, ya make yer decision."

So, she bites my hand, and likely chips a tooth *'cause it's a Faesteel hand*. Then, well, I ain't gonna share the words she's sayin', none of 'em make me sound good. I mean, I know I got it comin', but nobody wants to *hear* that shit, ya know?

"I ain't got a lot of time, maybe a few minutes. I gotta get up there." Spit in my face. "That was for the pumpkin spice, wasn't it?"

And then two jabs and a right cross. I'm describin' it simply because it *fuckin' hurts*.

Fuck! Gun, gun, gun, gun, gun.

I yank it toward me, stick the barrel into my mouth, and take a hard bite with my back teeth. The metal bends, buckles, tastes like shit, and is torn from her hands by the strength of my jaw as I chomp and tear and gnash, and then spit gunpowder mixed with saliva. I'm gonna need a whole bottle of antacids, shit.

"Fuck! Ya done?! I ain't gonna kill ya. Yer Prince? He murdered the woman who used to live in my apartment. When I found out? Ya see my leg and hand? He did *that* to me as a warnin'. Whatever the fuck he's doin' up there, ya really think it's for Samhain? Why him, huh? Why not have Queen Alana..."

"May her warmth bless us all," we say in unison.

She steps back, leaning against her desk, shocked. "...you're telling the truth."

"*Now* you believe me?" I mean, yay, but I'm confused.

"I received a message from the Captain of the Guard that a loyal subject of Her Majesty would bring me vital intelligence, but nothing about the messenger or what the information was. It's... you."

"That's great, yeah, will ya help me?"

She motions for me to move away from her. I... understand that. I can also probably count on a black eye after all this. "I can clear you to the 37th floor. You'll have to make your way to the roof from there. Take elevator F, down the hall, I'll force it open for an emergency, but you're on your own from there."

I dig into my pack, and take out the flash drive, painted to look like piano keys, and toss it to her.

"What's this?"

I head to the door. "Photo and video of the Prince and the woman he murdered for the symphony on it. *The* symphony. It was composed by Ms. Bridget O'Hare, graduate of the Allora Conservatory, on social media as "Settle the Score", all one word.

Let the world hear her, know her, witness the magnum opus of an artist who was denied countless more. Can ya do that, Rose?"

She chuckles. "Redcap, I'm a Knocker. I'm about to show your cousins how to *really* go viral."

36

The ride up to the 37th floor is uneventful, at least. Just me, the bow, and my anxiety.

"It'll be okay, Nick."

And Ganimard.

"I'm about to go into the penthouse of the Crown Prince of the Fae. I got a fucked leg, and a hand I ain't trained enough with. I got a bow I'm runnin' on beginner's luck, and charms that are taxin' the fuck outta me. I mean, points fer effort, and thanks for the words, but I'm pretty much fucked, y'know?"

He's "standin'" in front of me now. I mean, he ain't really there, so that's why the airquotes. Yes, I'm stallin'.

"Who are you?" It's not with disbelief, closer to a command.

"Ya know who I am, Inspector, I ain't got time fer this."

"Who. Are. You."

I roll my eyes. "Nick Blackwarren," I grumble.

"All of it. I am...?"

"Ya know I hate havin' to say all of that name."

"Your mother and father gave it to you, with love and pride and hope. Who. Are. You."

I exhale. "Nicholas Arsenne Volpe Sicarius Venefici Blackwarren." I shake my head, 'cause I don't see the point of this, really.

"Louder, like you actually fucking *care*, Nick. Or are you ashamed of who you are? I learned to accept that I was a Goblin, and I was *human* before. Is it so difficult? Did you proclaim your bond to your heritage a few months ago?"

"Yeah, so I don't see why I gotta do-"

"Because it was your *heritage* that you were accepting, Nick. Not yourself. Not who you are. Who. Are. You."

"Fuck you! Fuck you fer sayin' I don't accept myself for who I am."

"And that is?"

"You are so fuckin' lucky I can't punch ya in the face."

"Say it."

"I am Nicholas, named for the patron saint of thieves. I am Arsenne, named for the great gentleman thief. I am Volpe, clan of my mother and the sly and clever Foxes of Sicily. I am Sicarius, honoring Grandmother Atropos with my blood and blade. I am Venefici, the blood of sorcerers and the breath of life to the magical world." Fuck, my eyes are burnin'. "And I am of the fuckin' Black Warren, clan of my father, chosen by Father Redcap to follow death's footsteps and bring peace to those who were left behind."

Of course he ain't there when I'm done with all that. But at least I feel a little better. If I am really all of that, then maybe the Prince should be more worried about *me*.

When the elevator doors slide open, the Shear is in my hands. I remember when I first stole it, when Vincenzo started a business for me retrievin' things, returnin' them to who they belong. The Aeolian Shear is *mine*, I didn't steal it, I was returnin' it to its original owner, the long dead human-turned-Goblin who was reborn as me. And the Shear, he don't need blood, he don't need sacrifice from me. He wants to build wonders, and he wants to do it with me. I only need to tell him what I need.

And what do I need?

Crossbow frame, cams and clockwork to pull back the darts, gears and sprockets and cogs to continuously load the projectiles as they're needed, as long as the keyring trigger is pulled, springs in the stock to suppress the recoil, a flipped up scope. And what does that make?

An automatic tranq launchin' crossbow. This ain't about believin' it works, it's followin' my blood, the mind of my mother to see the schematics in my mind, let them guide the Shear in reconstuctin' itself. It's about my Gremlin blood, their ties to Lady

Clotho, to pull from the loom of creation and supply it with the materials it needs. It's about my Redcap blood, the knowledge of poisons and draughts to stun and paralyze, but not kill, not allow long-term damage.

And the rest? Well, uh, the rest is just me usin' techniques from first-person shooters. What? Yeah, I read a lot, but I was in high school with other teenage boys. Ya think I *never* played one of those?

If this were a movie, ya know that the elevator would ding as it opened, the Guard waitin' for me, and me steppin' out with the Shear spoutin' off a one-liner as I flick a spent cigarette away.

Instead, yer gettin' a Goblin shriekin' in terror, openin' up with the crossbow and firin' about forty tranq darts... into a fuckin' paintin'. Wait, that's a paintin' of Duke Tremaine. I *stole* that paintin' and fenced it. Only fer it end up on the wall of the Prince's private gallery. Well, at least I fucked its resale value?

The gallery itself is expansive, takin' up the floor, a few walls set for display, larger art pieces, sculpture, a block of marble chiseled from the ground up, a bit at a time, until it becomes a woman reaching for the sky overhead, her face serene, but her eyes afraid. A paintin' done in cubist style that plays with color not normaly seen in the school. Yes, I'm wonderin' why the fuckin' Guard ain't shown up to bust my ass for bein' up here.

Did he not bring any? This is his home, after all. Where his greatest creative works... are... There's no way he could've done all of this, or if he did, no way he could switch styles so quickly. The marble statue, that can't be his work, can it? I slowly turn in place, seeing it all.

A portrait of a young woman in incredible detail, remimiscent of the Raphaelites. Several lengths of wood impaled on poles, taking the shape of a human figure when viewed from the right angle. A digital photograph of a substance viewed from 25,000 times maginification, almost ephemeral in structure. A cityscape of Shoreside as seen from the bay, the style warm, impressionistic, the city lights lending to the idea of a woman's eye. A twisting structure of orange material branching in countless directions, like a ray of light reflecting until it finds a place to shine free. All of them can, in some way, be seen as portraiture of a woman.

All of 'em would be considered masterpieces, seminal works, breakthrough pieces. If he were the artist, he'd be the most famous one in the world, fer like, all time. Ain't nobody out there who's *this* prolific. Even one of these pieces would be like, the pinnacle of an artist's creative life, the loving embrace of the Muses...

Holy gods, *this* is what he's done to all those women. Artists, creators, minds on the verge of a masterpiece, probably their first, an explosive fount of passion and creativity and dreamin'. And if what happened to Bridget is any clue, this is what happens when they don't die before he's finished. He kills them for their art. The piano strings were pulling Bridget, bloody, in agony, screaming for help, into her piano. Forever.

Was he trying to literally *make* music out of Bridget? Are all these works of art... their artists? Am I surrounded by the trapped souls of dozens of women? The women in the art, the pain isn't just good detail. It's real. They're actually in pain, trapped for his amusement, to claim as his own work, to shred their souls for stolen credit and illusory fame. Over and over and over again.

'Ganimard? You know a way to let 'em out? Free them? Any old worlds magic or charms or methods? I can't just leave them like this.' I'm tryin' to control the anger, buddy, but I'm seein' less of a reason to.

"These works house their souls, wouldn't you say?" He's standin' in front of the marble statue.

'Seems like it, yeah. So how do I get them out? Without hurtin' 'em?'

"*Look at them*. They're already in pain because a Fae excercised his authority over Fate itself, do you agree?"

And... ya don't do that. That's the shit Ra'keth do. Fuck, that's what the *Lightning Rod* did when he just *decided* that the Fates couldn't be three goddesses anymore. But Fate can't end this. She needs an instrument to carry her will.

"Show me the way, Grandmother." I say, the words flowin' easier than I've ever spoke Sigil before. *"Guide me to end their pain."*

I'm holdin' the bow, the arrow large, blunt, resting against the marble. I've already drawn it back as far as I can. I pull the keyring, the trigger releasing all of that power, tension, funneling it into one point, sending the force and vibrations into the magnum opus of sculpture.

The statue explodes, the marble shrapnel scattering, cuttin' my face and arms, slashin' a few paintings, knockin' over smaller works, enough damage and destruction to make an art critic have a stroke. But... I feel it. Energy slippin' free, vanishin' into the aether, souls pulled toward their afterlives. I know Rhys is up on the roof, but I got work to do here, first.

Luckily, the bow firin' darts into the works is efficient, doesn't take long to hit, knock over, or damage the remainder of the gallery. I don't feel gratitude, or happiness, but I ain't expectin' it, these are women who've been imprisoned, *human* women who didn't have the experience with mythics to handle any of this. All they likely know is that the pain is gone and they can run away. And that's all the thanks ya need, buddy.

Now for the fucker who did this to 'em.

When I look up from the last damaged painting, I see the way to the next floor, closer to his residence. So be it. My eyes are burnin', I don't care. He's on the roof. I'm endin' this. End the jailor, end the imprisonment.

"Who are-"

Attendant, Brownie, dressed like housestaff. One dart.

"Guard-"

Butler, Sidhe. One dart.

"REDCAP!"

Houseguard, Troll, dressed in functional armor, wielding axe. Four darts.

"Protect the Pri-"

Houseguard, Sidhe, dressed in lighter armor, wielding saber. Two darts.

Up to the 40th floor, now. Bedrooms, open concept, infinity pool outside, spiral staircase leading up to the roof. Sunset. I can already hear some Sigil coming from upstairs, darker, jagged Sigil. Someone's readin' from the book, opened by Shadow's Edge. A man stands between myself and that staircase. He's dressed in a suit, flame red, tanned skin, pointed ears.

"That's far enough, Goblin." Musical voice.

Six darts.

Which he then brushes off, the darts havin' bent or blunt tips, no sign they penetrated. He gives me an indulgent look, eyes golden, sparklin'.

This one ain't Fae. "Well, shit."

It's a dragon.

He smiles. "My turn."

Flames spew from his mouth bellowin' and spreadin' through the floor, burnin' everythin' they touch. But here's what I learned from the acid-breath dragon out in the Benedict. It's a cone of breath, not an instant wall, so if ya move fast enough, you can slide underneath, only get a little singed, and while that gout of hellfire's eruptin' from his mouth? He can't see under it, or smell anythin' other that the ignited reaction of all the chemicals his body produces.

What I'm sayin', buddy, is that I'm behind him. And the last place ya want a Blackwarren to ever be is right behind ya. Ya might end up with somethin' pressin' into yer neck.

"I am Nicholas Arsenne Blackwarren. Remember the name, 'cause he spared your fuckin' life tonight, but he still might change his mind." I move to Sigil, to underline it. *"Return home, and do not trouble me again. Understand?"*

"Y-yes." Fuck, am I actually scarin' him? This a *dragon*, I shouldn't scare him. Wait, I shouldn't be scarin' him.

"Say that you understand."

"I understand!" Ohhhhhkaaaay. Let's see if this is real?

"Where's the Prince keepin' the hearts? The ones he pulls outta people?"

"In my hoard! They're tied by the workings branded to their chests."

"Bindings?"

"Yes!" I have never known anyone so terrified. But, there's somethin' about dragons that really only Fae know, that and sorcerers. I mean, say yer a dickbag Ra'keth, ya got yer servants, and yer rival binds them to him. Ya gotta break that bindin', right? Go with the sharpest shit ya got.

"Gimme one of your fangs. Just one, don't gotta be a big one."

"And you'll release me?"

"Shadow, fuck, yes. Give me the fang, and uh, then fly far, far away. San Francisco. And uh, take a selfie with the sea lions down on the Wharf so I know you actually went." I let him go, and jump off his shoulders.

So, uh, he jumps over the infinity pool, and over the side. Ya think I'd be worried that he killed himslef, but-

Yep, see? There he is, big red dragon flyin' off into the distance. I know a near death experience can be rattlin', but I didn't think it'd only take that. I didn't even have a blade! It was the torsion wrench from my pick set! Guess the Prince coerced a wuss dragon. Or, more likely, since dragons and Fae don't work well together, seein' as they like to hunt each other, I'm guessin' he saw an out and grabbed it. Freedom for one tooth and let's face it, a magical experience of seein' the sea lions.

A moment later, I see him comin' back and for a second I'm thinkin' a trip to Pier 39 wasn't as attractive as I though, but somethin' drops, bouncin' toward me. A fang, about twelve inches long, sharp point. A dragon's tooth.

The way's clear now for me to run up stairs, to the roof of a building where a book of Goblin methods taken from the Shadow is bein' read aloud. He's standin' in the center, a wooden table there with...

Oh fuck, a bound and gagged human woman. The Prince is there, Shadow's Edge on his forearm, a long, sickly blade extended from the vambrace, and I can feel it from here. It's *hungry*. What the fuck did I have on my arm all that time?

"Stop!" I yell, but I don't just yell it like a dumb fuck and expect him to stop. I shoot at him, too. The darts fly straight and true... and the fuckin' shield pops out, but the blade's retracted, at least. The darts tink rapidly against the metal, fallin' to the ground underneath.

I pull the keyring harder, the Shear tryin' to keep up, the shield bouncing so much of it off, but I move the angles around, I only gotta hit him once and he'll be outta commission. Just fuck up once you overprivileged piece of-

"Kill him!"

No. No, no, no, no, no.

The shadows are gatherin', blurrin', racin' to and fro, nothin' I can keep my eyes on fer long. *This* is a Blackwarren Assassin. One trained since childhood to move in tandem to the flow of the Shadow and the pulse of life and the whisper of death. One whose blades have tasted the final blood, blood that stains his cap.

Rhys Lleweylln emerges from the darkness, mid-flight, his blades out, sharp, and ready, soarin' toward me, comin' to take my head. I hear him whisper, just as he closes the distance.

"Kill me..."

37

The Shear comes between us, the blades, Thelma and Louise he called 'em, tryin' to dig into the metal. I twist them to the side, pushin' him away, gettin' some distance.

"Rhys! Stop it!" I'm blockin' more swings and swipes, clangin' and clunkin' against the Shear. His face is contorted in pain. He's tryin' to stop himself, but he can't. The Oaths won't let him. They won't even let him stop himself.

"Dammit, Nick, he's going to kill her! Just put me down, don't make me live like this, don't make me hurt you! It's my time, just let me end!" Holy shit, he's fuckin' serious. He really don't see a way out, and I can't see a way to free him of the Oaths, return his heart. The Prince still owns him.

"I ain't killin' you, fer fuck's sake! I ain't abandonin' my partner!" I jump back, roll, come up to fire another burst of darts at the Prince, just about to bring his knife down. Again the shield comes out, but the blade ain't.

"Take his leg, servant! This *sewage* has committed *treason*!"

Wait, why was I able to roll that easy? I got a brace on my leg. I look at the Shear, the near endless supply of darts. The brace on my left leg being stripped for material. Fuck. First law of thermodynamics: energy cannot be created nor destroyed, only changin' states. The shear is so versatile because it's changin' states and forms and densities, but it ain't unlimited.

Meanin' the protection fer my bum leg ain't so complete anymore. I move the Shear just in time to block the swing of the Goblin's blades away from my knee. Rhys staggers from the impact, his rhythm thrown, off-kilter. I'm off balance too.

I tumble back, and hold the Shear in my left hand, the dragon's fang in my right. My hand comes up, his blade swingin' at it, skippin' off the Faesteel to carve a gash into my forearm. I shake it off, Shadow's Edge put me through worse. The fang pushes into his chest, through the Sigil encirclin' his heart. He screams, slashin' with his other hand. I'm close enough that I don't gotta aim. I pull the keyring, and a burst of three darts trails up his chest, more than enough to put him down. He slumps, goin' limp. "Thank... you... Kyo."

I kiss his forehead. "You rest, Sebas. I'm gonna take care of this, okay?"

I swing the Shear over my back, feelin' it return to its armor state, and pick up the blades of the Redcap, turnin' toward the Crown Prince of the Fae. "Sunset's long passed, yer Highness. The symphony is playin' 'round the world as we speak, and everyone'll know who really wrote it. That woman there ain't done nothin', she don't deserve a slit, and you ain't the one to give it to her."

I'm hobblin' toward him, yeah, but I got his attention. He's a Prince, a royal, silver spoon asshole, fancyfuck who grew up around yesmen tellin' him how amazin' he was, how he was gonna be King. And I don't doubt he's never been told the word 'no' before. He's got a trail of bodies to prove that.

But tonight? He's hearin' from someone he don't think is above sewage. Someone who's gonna hold his life in their hands.

And most importantly, he's gonna spout off about how I'm wrong and this is his right as prince and blah, blah, blah. His ego won't let him do anythin' else, and while he's puttin' me in my place?

Well, buddy, I'll tell ya after, but I promise, it's gonna be good.

"Why it is that those of weaker bloods, dirty-blooded, tainted bloods..." He motions to me, dismissively, "*Man-blooded* believe that they can address those who are, compared to them, *gods*? This woman, as you put it, laid herself on the table of her own free will, offering her soul and mind and heart to be part of an eternal beauty, *my* eternal beauty. A testament to my talent, my greatness, living on for all I deem worthy to see."

He's movin' out from the table, toward me. I have his full attenion.

"But," he sighs. "As always, the common rabble cannot see the forest for the trees. You fill our rarefied air with your complaints and assorted whining, thinking that *you* have the authority to dictate what a god can and cannot do. That my blood, purer and closer to the Dreaming than any other living being, is to be held to the same standards and laws of *turnspits* and *brutes* and *stonehearts* and *stablemuckers* and..." He points to me. "*Man-blooded* poisoners of the Dreaming."

The Prince looks down at me, smiling. "Oh, no quip? No boorish vulgar argot to spit my way as if it were highest poetry your people could measure? No clever attempt at excoriating your better? Do you find yourself unable to dig yourself some passable jibe from your compost heap of an education? Or you accepted that *I* am your *Prince* and you have finally accepted your place. Silent and obedient. Now *kneel*."

Only I don't. I fuckin' stand there.

"I SAID KNEEL!" I'm pretty sure any Fae in front of him within earshot probably got knees as fucked up as mine now. But I don't heed. *"OBEY YOUR PRINCE, PEASANT!"*

He follows it with a strike from Shadow's Edge, the blade out, slashin' across my face.

And not a single drop of blood hittin' the floor. It's okay, buddy, I can let ya in on it, now.

Y'see, a Thief's got plenty of tricks that we borrowed from the Redcaps. It's a bit of a no-no, but since I'm dipped and I always been BFF with the Shadow anyway, I'm gonna call it in-bounds. Let's say ya need to be seen in one place, while yer in the other? On a dark night, after the sun's down? On fuckin' *Samhain*? Plenty of Shadows to work with, and the Prince? He's about to learn the difference between a Shadow *hobbyist* like him, and a Goblin who was born under the eclipse of the fuckin' Blood Moon to a Tinker Thief and a fuckin' Blackwarren Assassin.

I don't know if yer familiar with Plato's Allegory of the Cave, but the quick and dirty is this: If yer raised in a cave, and ain't never seen the outside world, and yer only field of view is some shadow plays on the wall, that's yer world. The shadows can change shape and position and brightness and darkness, but it's the only thing ya know, so ya think that's reality.

In this fuckin' cave, buddy? I'm the motherfucker who's makin' the shadows, and he's the dumbass watchin' 'em.

So while he's blusterin' like a blowhard full of braggadocio at a shadow play, I'm actually slippin' over to the table to slice the bindings on the woman. She's in her twenties, short black hair, dark eyes, I think I mighta seen her at Allora U when Rhys and I were diggin' for info on Bridget. What I will say is that a Sidhe can get a human woman to agree to be murdered, they are that blindingly attractive and fascinating, and that's just lesser nobles. This is a Prince we're talkin' about.

The point I'm makin' is that even though the bindin' is cut, she ain't movin' or tryin' to escape, 'cause she don't wanna. The Fairy Prince is in her presence, after all, and no Fae can break that, they're somethin' out of your grandest, highest, holiest dreams.

But if all you suddenly see is a face that not only triggers your mind to see humanity, but the darkest, most wretched, corrupted, aggressive, terrifyin' thing outta nightmares? Fight or flight kicks in. *Hard.* And it's the first, then the second in this case. She's kickin' and flailin' to get away from me, even though I ain't makin' any moves to stop her. She punches me, kicks my head, and then my leg, the brace comin' loose, and then she hauls ass to the spiral staircase headin' down, the booming voice of the Prince doin' nothin' to calm her. It's somethin' primal, animal, the need to run away.

Fear and love are the only emotions that can't be supplanted by magic, or royal authority.

However, a screamin' woman is gonna get the attention of the guy who was just about to kill her. He turns to look at the table, sees me, turns back to see the me that he was wastin' all that breath on, which is already fadin' into Shadow.

And while he's realizin' how bad I just fucked him? His attention ain't on a certain mechanical book. Nice thing 'bout a mechanical book when yer a Tinker? Ya got all kinds of ways to attach and secure it to yer right thigh, 'cause the artifact was yer prime target fer the heist so ya thought ahead. All of my weight is on my right foot now, my left leg not recovered, Rhys's blades in my hands, the Shear on my back, ready to go. "It's fuckin' over, yer Highness."

"*You* don't get to say when or what is over." Shadow's edge extends, the vambrace moving down into a full-basket hilt, the black blade like a saber. "You have stopped *nothing.* You have saved *no one.* You are nothing more than a traitor to the Kingdom, and I will perform your execution personally."

"Yeah, about that. Yer gallery's fucked. The souls are free. The dragon has abandoned you. The sacrifice to yer vanity is escaped and once she's outta yer presence she's gonna spill on the guy who tried to kill her. Harald Summer, the sketchy philanthropist who's been usin' his charities as a hunting ground.. The magnum opus you planned to debut to the world as your own has been revealed to be by the woman you murdered. Video and photos of you with the artist ain't gonna help yer credibility with yer Mom, and your bodyguard? I believe he's going to accept a better offer."

Buddy? If ya don't take anything else from this, take this to heart: Never, ever, ever, ever, ever think ya won, and smile all smug at the guy ya think ya just checkmated.

"Is that so?" He sounds too amused for it to be anything good. I turn around, and Rhys is walkin' toward me, his shirt ripped by the dragon fang, and he rips it off. The Sigil around his heart is broken, yes.

But there's a fresh ring of it 'round his neck.

"You see, sewage, I was aware of your paltry efforts to take *my* servant away from me with foolish distractions and feral lechery.

You cannot accept the simple truth. He is my property. His life is for *me*." He looks to Rhys. "Servant? Who is your lord and master?"

The Sigil burns about his neck, he's in so much pain. "Y-you, my liege."

"Good. Dispose of this garbage, return the tome, and bring me another potential for my next masterpiece." The Sidhe still advances toward me, blade in his hand, the regal glint in his eye at the entertainment of kings: subjects killing each other for his amusement.

Rhys comes at me, it's too fast, my leg ain't strong enough to do anything but fall out of the way. His neck is glowing, bleeding as he sweeps past me, his hand scooping up his blade from my hand. He leaps in the air, his dagger high. He's an avengin' angel, the wrath of the gods comin' down on the Prince. Rhys Lleweylln of the Black Warren, offers his blade, and his life, in one final assassinating strike, roaring *"Sic semper tyrannis!"*

And is slapped down hard by Prince Hadryn. *"How dare you!"*

He lifts the Goblin, and holds him over the side of the buildin'. I'm runnin', my left leg explodin' in pain, I'm doin' damage I know I won't heal, but I gotta get to him. Rhys looks upon me, then at the Sidhe holdin' him over... nothin', the Prince's face a mask of true anger, a fire in his eyes that betrays the Nightmare. The Prince looks to me, and I feel the sheer weight of his authority, heavied by the weight of hellish brimstone, fear, terror, the Nightmare's power. *"Slice your nec-"*

A spray of blood. The blade of the Redcap carvin' cleanly into the Prince's neck, slittin' the vocal chords. The end of the Sidhe's words a spatter of crimson, findin' no form. His gaze turns on his betrayer.

The world slows down. The pain is overtaking. Skin is tearing as bone shards cut through skin. Rhys turns his head toward me, the Prince open for the coup d'grace.

"Do it, Kyo."

His mouth opens wide, and closes on the arm of Prince Hadryn.

Rhys falls. The arm of the Prince, clad with Shadow's Edge, falls with him.

One must always pay the price.

I'm dashin', jumpin', adrenaline washin' away the pain fer a second, but it's all I need. The Prince sees me leapin' through the air, the end of his life approachin', inevitible, a long, privileged reign about to be cut short on a Redcap's blade. He protects himself, drawin' the saber with the unicorn's horn from his side, but it can't move fast enough to stop me, to prevent the edge of Atropos' Shear.

His eyes are filled with an emotion I doubt he's ever felt: fear. No matter how noble his blood, how high his station, how safe his home, how protected his body, it can still be finished in an instant by a lowly Goblin with a sharp blade.

But it isn't.

His life don't end.

'Cause I wasn't jumpin' at *him*. I was throwin' myself over the side, in one last effort to save my partner.

My life don't flash before my eyes, no. I just see my hand, stretchin' as far as it can, Rhys meetin' my eyes, reachin' back. My mind is a fury, a tempest, everything I've seen, read, tinkered, broken and built coming together, the thoughts and needs like a river whose dam just broke, floodin' into the Shear on my back.

The bow, the compound limbs flexing and flipping and extending outward six feet, ten feet, twelve feet, sixteen. The last of my leg brace to reinforce the frame. The string knitting it all together, the cables forming the limbs leadin' to points. The fur material used for the extender to weave the fabric and the straps to secure me to it.

I don't have time to check it. I need to believe. I have to *know* that this was built. That it will work. My hand reaches his, our fingers touching, gripping, holding. The street is coming up fast, I have to chance it.

I feel a wrenching, yanking pain as the wings, built from the Shear, secured to my back spread wide as I pull up, Rhys holding onto my Faesteel hand with all his right arm's strength, the arm of Hadryn held in his other, the steel not giving, but secure enough to keep him. I feel the hard yank backward as the wings pull horizontal, the wind from the bay hammering my face and body.

We're aloft, my wings holdin' us in a steady, but fast glide, losin' altitude, maybe twenty feet above the earth, passin' over cars, the parkin' lot in front of the Prince's buildin', out to the beach, the October chill coming off the sea. I see a lifeguard tower, and we're too low, Rhys will hit it.

I reach with my hand to the Faesteel fist, and twist my arm, popping the hand free in a spray of blood, the Goblin droppin' onto the sand, rollin' and tumblin' and stopping before he collides with the wood. I'm feelin' lightheaded, the blood from my leg and arm drainin', the sand comin' up faster and faster and...

I roll, crash, the wings foldin' in as fast as possible, my body startin' to go into shock, the pain too much. I hear panicked voices, people yellin' fer an ambulance, callin' fer help. Y'see? Humanity may hate us, but they're still human, and they got that compassion that supercedes fear when they let it.

The sensation is drainin' from my leg, my arm not bleedin' anymore when the attachment point closes on its own failsafe. I'm on my back, lookin' up at an Autumn sky, at stars that guide and seek the future. Never seen 'em lookin' this bright.

"Nick!"

I guess my eyes were closed? I feel warm pressure on my back, pressure and grasp on my left hand. "Hey... Sebas..."

"What were you thinking, Kyo, that was so foolish. You should've let me fall. The Prince was the greater threat." He ain't angry though. I can tell he's cryin'. "Why did you choose me?"

I reach toward him, and he pulls my hand to his face, I smile a bloody smile, my breath gettin' shallow, vision faded. It's gettin' pretty cold, but I saved him. He gets to have a life now, away from the one who put a leash on him. I didn't have to take a life to prove it. I wasn't there to take any. I was there to save lives, free souls. I manage to hold the smile, feelin' at peace.

"Ze... Zero... bo...dy...count..."

38

Gotta be honest with ya, buddy. I'm fuckin' shocked I ain't dead either. Guess Grandmother ain't done with me yet.

I'm in a bed, a comfy one with an IV stand next to it, a bag of O-positive drippin' in. I'm in a hospital gown, but ain't the scratchy kind. I have a window lookin' out on Destry Bay, so I'm in a hospital, Mercy Hospital. Ya know those hospitals that will move heaven and earth to save yer life and keep ya comfortable so long as ya got good insurance? That's the place this is, and I'm thinkin' I'm gonna be in medical debt until I'm thirty years dead of old age.

My right wrist is bandaged, and my left... stump is elevated. My left leg's been cut off above the knee. It's been cut off. My leg ain't all there. It ain't there. My fuckin' leg ain't all there. My motherfuckin' *leg* has been partially fuckin' amputated. I'm a double fucking amputee.

Okay, Blackwarren. Breathe. Ya got a hand ready to pop back in. Yer mom's a fuckin' genius at this shit and ya got an aunt who's a doctor to make sure it's put on right. It ain't the end of the world. Yer alive. Keep tellin' yerself so ya don't end up hysterical.

A nurse comes in, she seems nice. She's changing a bag.

"Hi?" I chuckle, or try to make it sound like one 'cause this is a place ya don't wanna freak out the humans.

"Ah, Mr. Blackwarren, you're awake!" She's steelin' herself, human instinct tellin' her to be frightened, or hate me, maybe throw the blood bag at me. "I'll go get your doctor!"

Never see anyone move that fast to leave. "Wait! Is Rhys okay?"

She looks back at me. "I don't know who that is."

"Can ya tell me what day it is, at least?"

"Friday, November 11th." Guess I missed my birthday. She's gone anyway.

I been out fer almost two weeks. I mean, I got real fucked up, but... Fuck. I spent too much time in hospitals and in medical care this year. I hear some voices outside my door. I got a private suite. I'm gonna have to empty a jewelry store to pay fer this. Oh. Right. Double amputee. Thievin' is out then. For the rest of my fuckin' life.

"He is wanted for questioning in the matter of treason against the Kingdom, and the maiming of Prince Hadryn Summersword." Firm, authoritative, Troll.

"My client will be doing no such thing until he has been medically cleared by his doctor. Also, I would believe that your Prince should be more concerned with the multiple abduction and murder charges now being levied against him in human courts, and how my client was investigating your Prince for those very crimes when he was *actually* maimed. I've met with my former client, and both of his arms seem fine, almost *brand new*, you could say. The actual and punitive damages we'll be asking will be *quite* attention-grabbing. Mr. Cerberus? Show these men out, please? I need a word with my client."

I blink a couple of times as the door opens, and in walks, flashin' that million-dollar smile, David Aidoneus, also known as Hades. Dressed in black on black, hair trimmed short in that thousand dollar haircut sort of way, gray eyes fixing on me. "I see you've finally awakened, Mr. Blackwarren."

"Is Rhys okay?"

He takes a breath. "Now, I'm here as your attorney, and we need to discuss strategy going forward."

"I'm your client?" Glass of ice chips to my left, good thing, I pour a couple into my mouth, the cold soothin'. A nice lookin' sandwich is on a plate next to it. Shit, that's high-quality meat.

"I felt it necessary, yes. Don't concern yourself with your bills, they're being handled and calculated by the firm for the actual damages in your suit against Prince Hadryn. For punitive... Loss of limb, loss of dominant hand, career focused primarily on ease of movement and agility, physical, emotional, and psychological trauma, a case for it being a hate crime... You won't bankrupt the Kingdom, but as for the Prince I'm going to leave his cupboards bare."

"...holy *fuck*."

He smirks to himself, adjustin' his tie, preenin'.

"Yer tellin' me I ain't gotta pay fer this sandwich?"

That smile cracks, twitches. "Yes. I also told you *other things*."

"So *now* ya gonna tell me if Rhys is okay or not?"

A sigh. "You're clearly useless until you know, so I'll humor you. You were found on Shoreside by several people, who called for an ambulance. A male close to your description was seen at your side until paramedics arrived. After that reports of him drop off. No reports of anyone matching his description in hospitals, morgues, or jail cells. The firm has taken possession of the tome secured to your thigh at the time until the suit is completed where I suspect it will be returned to its historical owners. The files containing the sheet music and previous works of one Bridget O'Hare have been returned to her parents, along with an invoice for your services, and the Allora Conservatory has been informed of the upcoming donation."

"Ya knew I'd ask all that 'cause ya-"

"Know everything." We say in unison.

"May we continue? Once you're medically cleared for outpatient care and physical rehabilitation we'll start depositions. I'll need to know *everything*. Names, dates, places, times, connections. Everything you can both remember and have evidence to support. I'll also need a list of people who can speak to your character and credibility, as the other side will be looking to paint you as nothing more than a thief and confidence man looking to victimize a fine, upstanding citizen in the arts community, and angel investor for multiple arts programs across the City targeted at lower-income citizens. All of this will be gone into further once you're ready for it. Any questions?"

"Is my Mom here?"

A grumble from him. "I'm billing this as a full hour." He turns toward the door and opens it. "He's asking for you."

The god just manages to evade her as she rushes in, cryin', throwin' her arms around me. She says a lot, mostly in Italian, and ya don't need to know exactly what she's sayin'. If ya got a mom, ya know exactly what she's sayin' if ya were in the hospital. And then, a slap, and then a lot more Italian, askin' what I was thinkin', how could I be so stupid, how could I make her worry like that, do I have any fuckin' clue what I've put her and the whole family through, I'm lookin' like a fuckin' stick so why ain't I eatin' anything in this fancyfuck hospital, this is what happens when ya fuck around with Redcaps... And then, just sobbin', both of us, 'cause she almost lost me and she already lost her husband and I almost left her alone. So, tearful apologies in Italian from me, and then she climbs into the bed to hold me close, the only thing her heart will let her do.

"Don't s'pose ya found the hand?" It's a few minutes later, TV is on, Science channel for one of those shows that's just machinery puttin' shit together in a factory.

"Yeah, need to clean it and the jack, but it'll pop right back in."

"Ya get it from Rhys?" I try not to sound too hopeful. A mother knows that voice.

"Yeah, he left it with yer cousin. Got some heat on him. He's dangerous, Nicky." Aw fuck, here it comes. "Yer like me, y'know. Everyone keeps sayin' yer too much like Colton, but I seen the look in yer eyes when ya see somethin' ya want, and ya don't know any better, just like me. I could kill yer father if he weren't already dead, but, Shadow, I still love the insufferable bastard. I know yer sly, Nicky." Gay, just means gay.

"Mom, I told ya that when I was thirteen. Remember? My hand drifted south and I forgot to lock the door and I was lookin' at a poster of that action star doin' a split? Did ya really think I was havin' sleepovers at the Brownie's house 'cause he had video games from two generations before?"

"Nicky."

"I mean, we never even did anythin', neither of us really knew how-"

"Nicky! Focus. I'm sayin' I get why yer drawn to that Redcap."

"Mom. He's a Gremlin, he was just taken in by the 'Caps when he was a kid." I roll my eyes or start to. I stop. Ya don't roll yer eyes at yer mom.

"That cap is dipped, honey. Just know what yer gettin' yerself into."

"Mom, we ain't in love, we're partners for my company."

She smiles, strokin' my hair. "'Course, Nicky. I'm sorry. Want me to start on yer leg for ya?"

I gently nod makin' affirmative noise, eyes closin'. I feel a kiss on my forehead, *Ti amo, figlio.*

The show drones on, it gets harder to pay attention. Easy to drift off when yer in a comfy bed, and yer mom's there to keep you safe and take care of ya. Yeah, I know, typical Goblin, we all love our mothers and are terrified of 'em at the same time. She's also a Thief, which I know 'cause I hear her eatin' my sandwich as I fall back to sleep. I don't blame her, it smelled like a real good sandwich.

It's past sundown when I wake up. Mom is still here, probably told the nurses that family don't leave family alone in the hospital. "Who else showed up while I was asleep?"

She looks over at me. "Joey, Tony, Mikey, Aunt Bella, Grandma's flyin' in..." *Nonna*? She ain't been in America fer years.

"From Sicily?" I sound incredulous, yeah, because she told Mom that I was a fuckin' bastard, and then a lot of Sicilian curses. Mom's socks haven't stayed up in fifteen years.

"'Course she is! Yer in the hospital, Nicky. Yer Aunt Cora dropped by and told yer attending how much of an idiot he is. Vincenzo and some of your Gremlin cousins dropped by, about a dozen of yer Tinker cousins stopped by. Fuckin' *Knocker* sent flowers, you got a big bouquet from a rice distributor? Damon showed up and carved somethin in his forearm 'cause he's a fuckin' Redcap."

I'm still lookin' at her.

"No, Nicky. He didn't drop by."

"Could uh, ya get me somethin' to eat? Ya ate my sandwich, y'know." I try to smile. I'm not gonna let it hurt. "And somethin' to drink. Maybe a book, too? They, uh... they wrecked all my books."

She kisses my forehead. "'Course, honey. I'll be back. I'll tell everyone to give ya some time, but we're all out there, okay?"

I nod. "Thanks, Mom. *Ti amo*."

"Ti amo anch'io, piccola volpe." She leaves shortly after. I turn off the TV, I don't want the noise. I ain't sleepy, just gives me the chance to look out the window, see the bay, the stars, appreciate how fuckin' lucky I am I ain't dead. So Rhys ain't here. He's alive, that's what matters most.

And I can work on that fer tonight.

"Hello, Kyo." It's spoken quietly, to my left. I'm almost afraid to look.

"Sebas? That you?" I feel fingers brush my face, and I turn toward them. He's standin' by the bed, tremblin', like he's worried about touchin' me. "It's alright, I'm okay."

"Look at you. This is my fault. Your hand, now your leg, this is because of me. Shadow's Edge was the treasure of your family and I... I threw it in the bay. I'm responsible for-" I don't let him continue.

You can do that when ya kiss somebody. "Will ya shut up and let me be happy yer here, ya *baciagaloop*?" We kiss a few more times, lips pressed, our warmth minglin'.

"I can't apologize enough for-"

"Sebas, he was forcin' you, I could see that. When it mattered, ya resisted. We stopped him, we saved the girl. And you. As fer Shadow's Edge? Let it stay down there. I'd rather have you than it." I rest my forehead against his own, the closeness more soothin' than anything I've felt before.

"Nick, I don't deserve-"

"Hey. You are not the one to decide that. No one is. Yer my partner. Full stop, remember?" I stroke his face, move his hair out of the way.

"I remember." He manages a smile. "But Nick, I have to leave."

That is not how I saw this going.

"Wh-what? I know my family's a lot but they'll leave ya alone if I tell 'em."

"No, Nick. I have to leave the City." He lets go of me. "I can't do this."

All the air just went out of the room. My chest hurts.

"No. No... No, Rhys, please, no." My eyes are brimmin'. "I *just* found you, Sebas, please don't say that." I feel the streaks down my face. "Don't leave me, Rhys."

"I have to. I'm still bound to the Prince. My heart is free, yes, but his Oath is a noose about my neck. If I'm too close to you, and him, I don't know if I could fight him back." He looks into my eyes. "I will *not* be the reason you suffer more pain."

"But... yer hurtin' me *now*, Sebas." I can't stop the tears, my heart is like an anvil pressin' down on it.

He quirks a brow. "Nick... Why *are* you crying?"

I stare at him, gettin' angry now. "'Cause ya just said yer leavin' me, ya asshole!"

He nods, slowly. "To see a Sluagh in Wales that has worked with my family. She's known for her abilities, one of them rumored to be breaking Oaths. It may be some weeks, perhaps months until it's completely purged from my body. He put a *lot* of them on me, Nick."

I blink. "Ever occur to ya not to bury the fuckin' lede, Sebas?"

"Did you think I was... Breaking ties between us?" His turn to blink. "Kyo, you and I have been through entirely too much since our first meeting to not see this rollercoaster through to the end."

I see his ears twitch. "But I must go now, Kyo, I hear a Guard coming."

"Sebas, just... one question. Do ya see this thing 'tween us turnin' into, y'know, what we talked about that one time?" Meanin', takin' it beyond talkin' about how somethin' would work, or fantasizin', and takin' a shot.

"I don't know, Kyo." He leans in and kisses me, long, the tension drainin' away. "But I pray Mother Lachesis will weave us back together soon to find out."

"Goodbye, Sebas. Have a good trip." I'm smilin', I can't help it.

"I'll text you." And then he's gone in a blur of shadow, just as a Guard comes in to find me alone, and then a bunch of Volpes, a couple Blackwarrens, a lot of Giansiracusas start in on him until he leaves.

Still.

I'll text you? Ya ain't gonna see me for months and *I'll fuckin' text you?!*

That Redcap son of a...

39

This woulda been so much easier, buddy, if I had just stayed in the fuckin' tub and not answered the door. I'd still have my leg, my hand, and a pretty decent apartment, and not havin' drawn the ire of Sidhe royalty. But, sometime's Mama Tinker's got other ideas, even if she ain't all the way there. Sometimes ya answer the door.

Sometimes ya find yerself knockin' on another one.

I'm in East Grunstadt, on crutches, Mom waitin' in a car that probably ain't hers downstairs. It's one of the nicer townhouses, better than the Greenmeadow place. No Fae in the immediate vicinity. It's a sunny November afternoon. I ain't stallin', buddy, honest. I did knock on the door.

When it opens, well, there's a bit of shock, revulsion, standard fer findin' a Goblin on yer doorstep, much less with only half a left leg. "Mr... Mr. Arsenne?"

Mrs. Siobhan O'Hare is standin' in the doorway, lookin' down at me. She's wearing a sweater and a long skirt, red hair done up. Her expression has calmed, at least. "What happened to you? We received your invoice, and the letter from your attorney, is there something wrong?"

"Just uh, checkin' in." I go with a mouth closed smile. Even with the human caps on my teeth, it's still a little unsettlin'. "The flash drive was intact, right? And uh... Don't worry about my leg. Or hand. Nothin' to do with the case. I'm okay, gettin' a prosthetic."

"Um, yes, yes it was fine. Her music was all there, we sent it to the conservatory and they plan to debut it in the spring." She's bein' cordial, best I can hope for, really.

"Could I talk to you about the invoice?" I dig into my pocket to fish out the copy I received from Aidoneus and Partners. "And ya got a pen?"

Now she's wary. Clearly, she's suspecting, I want more money, or I'll bring up the loss of limbs to tack on. The invoice is, uh, steep, to say the least, more than I was expectin'. The number of write-ups for Cen's services, Rhys's assistance, all of it gratis until I found and returned the item. And now the bill's come due. It's a pretty nice payday, is what I'm sayin', buddy. Like, I could head to a Beemer dealership and get myself a bike good.

"I... Could you wait a moment?" I nod, and she heads into the house, closes the door. No invitin' me in. Ya get used to it. But I wait. About five minutes, actually, long enough for people to stare at me while they're walkin' by. When the door opens, she's there, her husband beside her. He still don't like me. She gives me the invoice, and the pen.

"What's this all about?" He asks, more edge in his voice now that he ain't breakin' down. Whatever, pal, we both know who's made of sterner stuff in yer marriage. Don't bother me, none, though.

I review the charges, the per diems, expenses, doin' math in my head. "Yeah... there's a problem with this total."

He looks pissed, but she's lookin' me in the eyes...

When I tear up the fuckin' invoice. "You two paid enough already without any of this shit. Get me tickets to the symphony debut, two of 'em, and we'll call it square."

Fuckin' hell, Blackwarren, ya called out supernatural detectives fer doin' this kinda shit specifically, but fuck. I can't take fuckin' money for this. They lost a daughter, the world lost a gifted artist, dozens of 'em. What kinda fuckbag would charge money fer that? What kinda asshole would say, "Oh yeah, I want hazard pay too", huh? Probably could name a few Goblins that'd do it, but not me. An evil was visited on her family, and I was drawn in, and if this is how Fate has willed it, then so be it. I will be their hero.

After all, I wanna be that guy for Rhys when he comes back. And he *better* come back. I won't bore ya with the goodbye, the thank-yous, all that. I ain't here for reward or recognition, after. A Thief don't wanna be remembered, right?

"I'm both proud of ya, and fuckin' pissed at ya, Nicky," my Mom says as I get back in the car. "Ya did good, but why didn't ya take the money? Ya need it if yer gonna move outta the sewers."

"Mom," I say, leanin' back into the passenger seat. "Let's say I did it fer Mama Tinker and leave it at that. I fixed a lot of shit, so I think her and I are even." My phone starts buzzin', and I take it out as Mom pulls into traffic.

It's a text. From Rhys. He actually fuckin' texted me, fuckin' Shadow.

I open up the messages, and...

Kyo,

Leaving you is the most difficult thing I've ever done, even though I know it's not forever. I sought you in the beginning because I thought you could stop the one who'd taken control of my life, even though I was ordered to surveil you, watch you, find what would slow you down. Instead, I found the one who showed our race that we are more than the Sidhe tell us we are, that we are the waking dream of humanity.

You picked apart my pretenses, my lies, and saw me, saw me, the one I was before, and the one I wish to be. You helped me want to be that person, and despite the obstacles, I succeeded. You put others first, seek justice, closure, peace for those whose lives have been stolen, harmed, and at first, yes, I was ashamed to be near you, to be hobbling your work. But then I found I wanted to help you, not just for this case, but every day after. I'm a better me when I'm with you, and I hope I can one day say that I do the same for you.

You leapt from the tower to save me, unsure if we would perish, but Nick, my beautiful, clever, and funny Kyo, when your hand took mine, I knew I was safe, because I believed in you. I had faith in you, that you would see a way clear, and you did. You sacrificed so much of yourself, and before I thought I'd lost you, you whispered, 'Zero body count'. No lives lost or taken. My hands are bloody, Kyo, but I will follow your example. I will never slit the thin spun life ever again.

And now I return to the land of my birth, shores I have not seen in twenty years, family I haven't seen since that night so long ago, to visit those who can offer cleansing of my chains, slip the leash so that I may reunite with you, and begin our next adventure, whether it's investigations in the halls of power, or puzzling out the ending of your next book as we rebuild your library. I want to be there for all of it.

Because, my Kyo, I stumbled when I was with you, but I can see it clearly now that we are apart. I love you, Kyo. I expect no return of the words, and even if they never come, my life is better, and the world itself is a better place for having you in it. I wish you the best, and a speedy recovery, my Kyo. Know that I will return to your arms, if you will have me, partner.

â'm holl gariad,

Rhys

Well... shit.

Guess that, uh, "I'll text ya" is uh... a, um...

Just gonna uh, save that. Mail it to myself. Couple of times, really, for that redundancy so I don't, uh, y'know, accidentally delete it or anythin'. You, uh, ya know how it goes. He um, he loves me.

He loves *me*.

He loves me.

He *loves* me.

Buddy, I uh, I feel outta my depth, here. I ain't creeped out or anythin', I wanna make that clear, y'know? I mean, I told Thom I loved him once, and he told me, but... Fuck, it wasn't anythin' like *that*. I've read through it a few times and I've been feelin' all fluttery and shit, and warm, and I'm smilin', 'cause he's leavin', but he's comin' back. To *me*.

I know what yer thinkin', buddy. Yer thinkin' "Ha! I knew it! I knew this was that kinda story!"

But buddy? I'm sorry.

Yer wrong. Dead on arrival wrong. This ain't that kinda story.

I, uh...

I think it's somethin' better.

***

Blackwarren Will Return...

About the Author

Writer, Scorpio, and self-professed waffle-addict, Vaughn R. Demont is a graduate of SUNY Oswego and Goddard College, where he studied creative writing and being poor. He is married to a wonderful man and hopes that one day they will finally adopt a cat. He is also the owner of Blackwarren Books, LLC. He hopes to continue expanding The City, and never teach Freshman Composition ever again.

Also by Vaughn R. Demont

The Blackwarren Heists
Redcap, Whitecap, Goblin, Thief
Settle the Score

G&C Ablutions
"Done & Dusted"
Cleaning Hacks (coming 2023)

Broken Mirrors
Coyote's Creed
Lightning Rod
Community Service
Breaking Ties

House of Stone

Acknowledgments

Thanks first and foremost to my husband for his belief both in my ability to write, and his listening to me prattle on about plot points the way he does about comic books. Thanks also to my amazing beta readers, David DeMar, Chris "Mythicfox" Shaffer, and Jamie "Reech" Walker for their invaluable feedback and support. Heartfelt thanks to Ivy Gladstone for her work on the covers that bring Nick to life. Thanks also to Rachel Pollack, who encouraged to me to chase the dream of being a writer when life encouraged me otherwise. And deepest thanks to my mom, who supports my writing even if she doesn't understand the genre. And finally, thank you to all the Damned Coyotes for your support after my time away. There are plenty of stories left in the Argent City, and I look forward to telling all of you as many as I can.